TO KISS OR TO KILL

TO KISS OR TO KILL

SIME~GEN, BOOK ELEVEN

JEAN LORRAH

THE BORGO PRESS

MMXI

TO KISS OR TO KILL

Published by Wildside Press LLC

www.wildsidebooks.com

DEDICATION AND ACKNOWLEDGMENTS

All my work in the Sime~Gen universe must first and foremost be dedicated to Jacqueline Lichtenberg, who many years ago invited me to come and play in the Sime~Gen universe. We have long since become business partners and best friends, and it is sheer delight to have the opportunity to continue these stories at last.

Both of us must acknowledge the fans who kept the dream of Sime~Gen alive after all the books went out of print—I can do no more than sincerely agree with Jacqueline's sentiments below, both about our fans and about Karen MacLeod and Patric Michael. Without their help, we would not have simegen.com, and without simegen.com it is highly doubtful that there would be the opportunity to write new Sime~Gen stories.

Jacqueline and I believe in interaction between writers and readers, and invite comments on our work. Send them to simegen@simegen.com and we will both receive them.

I am grateful for the encouragement my readers have given me over the years, and sincerely hope those of you familiar with my work will enjoy this new adventure. If you've never read anything else I've written, welcome! I hope you'll find something new and exciting in *To Kiss or to Kill*. To old friends, welcome back! I hope you also find something new here, along with whatever has brought you back for more.

Acknowledgments by
Jean Lorrah and Jacqueline Lichtenberg

Firstly and most importantly, we have to acknowledge the extraordinary effort put forth by Karen MacLeod in meeting absurd copyediting deadlines during the final moments of production of this manuscript.

Over the years, Karen has taken skills learned in fanzine editing and honed and then applied them to become a professional copyeditor in the ebook field. With this volume and the October 2003 trade paperback release of *Those of My Blood* by Jacqueline Lichtenberg from BenBella Books, Karen has begun working on "tree-books."

Cherri Munoz enthusiastically volunteered to use her talents as a publicist to line up autographing appearances at various bookstores for us, and has done other publicity work and even proofreading of this manuscript into the wee hours.

Beyond even that, as Cherri and Jacqueline accidentally ended up neighbors in Arizona, she has saved Jacqueline a lot of writing time by helping her pick out a house, teaching her to navigate around town, and pointing out the best places to shop. Cherri even raced around town finding a copy of one of Jean's novels, *Survivors*, when it was suddenly needed for show-and-tell because the producers of *Trekkies Two*, the sequel to the documentary *Trekkies*, (www.trekkies2.com) asked to interview Jacqueline.

Acknowledgments 2011

We thank Robert Reginald at Borgo Press for unrelenting detail work, as well as John Betancourt at Wildside Press for creating an amazing publishing house.

We also thank Karen MacLeod for editing as well as Patric Michael and all the many people who have contributed to simegen.com.

Jean Lorrah & Jacqueline Lichtenberg

CONTENTS

INTRODUCTION

Zeor, Keon, and other Housholdings forced through a treaty to save the world at the end of *Zelerod's Doom*. This is the story of the people expected to keep it. Although To *Kiss or To Kill* is a direct sequel to *Zelerod's Doom*—as a matter of fact begins a few months before that book ends—none of the characters in *Zelerod's Doom* appear here.

This is a book our fans asked for: it's not about Farrises or Householders or the people who run the Tecton. It's about ordinary, everyday Simes and Gens who must rise to heroism and actually do what Risa Tigue, Sergi Ambrov Keon, Klyd Farris, and Hugh Valleroy promised they would. The two main characters are a renSime and a Gen whose Sime parents sell her as a Choice Kill.

It's also a love story, a traditional romance set against a world turned upside down. Love in the time of Unity.

If you are new to Sime~Gen, please don't think you have to read the books in order. As a matter of fact, they were neither written nor published in the chronological order of the universe. Therefore, each Sime~Gen novel is designed as an entry into this science fiction universe.

CHRONOLOGY OF THE SIME~GEN UNIVERSE

The Sime~Gen Universe was originated by Jacqueline Lichtenberg who was then joined by a large number of *Star Trek* fans. Soon, Jean Lorrah, already a professional writer, began writing fanzine stories for one of the Sime~Gen 'zines. But Jean produced a novel about the moment when the first channel discovered he didn't have to kill to live which Jacqueline sold to Doubleday.

The chronology of stories in this fictional universe expanded to cover thousands of years of human history, and fans have been filling in the gaps between professionally published novels. The full official chronology is posted at

http://www.simegen.com/CHRONO1.html

Here is the chronology of the novels by Jacqueline Lichtenberg and Jean Lorrah by the Unity Calendar date in which they are set.

-533—*First Channel*, by Jean Lorrah & Jacqueline Lichtenberg
-518—*Channel's Destiny*, by Jean Lorrah & Jacqueline Lichtenberg
-468—*The Farris Channel*, by Jacqueline Lichtenberg
-20—*Ambrov Keon*, by Jean Lorrah
-15—*House of Zeor*, by Jacqueline Lichtenberg

SIME~GEN:
where a mutation makes the evolutionary
division into male and female
pale by comparison.

CHAPTER ONE

THE DAY THE WORLD CHANGED

JONMAIR FELT VERY MATURE that day, allowed to come along to mind her younger brother and sister while her mother claimed her monthly Gen. Any day now, Jonmair would become Sime, like her parents—strong and graceful and gifted with Sime senses that made it nearly impossible to slip anything past them. She was eager to get on with her future, to start her life's work, her own family—to be an adult, capable of deciding her own destiny.

Jonmair knew what her mother would do with the Gen assigned to her, something her little brother and sister were too young to understand. Her job was to keep them distracted and entertained, so they would not ask awkward questions, as well as to carry packages while Mama coped with the Gen.

As the parcels piled up, Jonmair wished all the more that she were a full-grown Sime, for her fingers were not designed to hold so many objects at once. She envied her mother the graceful tendrils that emerged from her wrists, easily carrying several small packages.

The Pen was the last stop on a long list, and by that time Jonmair's little brother Wawkeen was cranky. Her sister Faleese scampered ahead while the little boy dragged his feet, pulling Jonmair in two directions. Mama, in no mood to cajole children, piled the last of her packages into Jonmair's arms and pressed a coin into her hand. "Buy them a treat," she instructed, "but stay right in this area."

Usually Jonmair babysat at home on Mama's claim day, but this month there were transport problems because boats and wagons had been sent to aid in the war out west, and Norlea's Gen shipments were delayed. So today's task of fitting the three children with shoes had been combined with the Gen pickup. "Why don't I take the kids on home?" Jonmair suggested.

"Do what I tell you!" Mama replied irritably. "I expect to find you right here when I come out." Then she disappeared into the Pen.

Jonmair understood her mother's abruptness: at this time of month, Simes had trouble concentrating on anything other than the Gen that would provide another month of life. Mama would feel better as soon as she had the reassurance of a Gen to assuage her Need.

All Jonmair's younger siblings understood was the promised treat. Jonmair struggled to hang onto the packages as they hurried her toward the vendors. Wawkeen was quickly satisfied with a caramel fruit treat, but while Jonmair was paying for it Faleese skipped on down the street.

"Faleese—come back!" Jonmair shouted as her annoying younger sister disappeared into the crowd. Faleese knew perfectly well that Wawkeen would be impossible to move until he had consumed his sticky treat.

Sparkly objects caught the sunlight at the stand Faleese headed toward. Dragging a protesting Wawkeen, Jonmair came close enough to see that they were toys, small multicolored windmill-like sails, each pinned to a stick so that it spun in the breeze, creating lovely changing effects. No wonder Faleese wanted one—they made Jonmair wish she were not too old for such pretty toys.

"You know you can't have a sweet if you buy one of these," Jonmair warned Faleese.

"This is better than a sweet," her little sister replied. "I'll have it for a long time."

"I want one too." Wawkeen instantly demanded.

"You've already had your treat," Faleese said in exactly the superior tone of voice that would set the little boy off.

"Want one! Want one! Me, too!" Wawkeen wailed, sticky fists rubbing at his face.

Stooping down to try to calm him, Jonmair dropped some of her packages. The little boy grabbed her around the neck, screaming as if he were hurt and rubbing sticky caramel everywhere he touched. Instead of helping, Faleese looked on in satisfaction as Jonmair tried to both calm and clean up Wawkeen, and keep their packages from being trampled by the passing crowds.

And that was how their mother found them when she arrived with a plodding Gen at the end of a white-painted chain. "Jonmair!" she exclaimed, picking parcels out of the dust. "I only asked you to buy your brother and sister a treat. Can't you do even the simplest tasks?"

While Jonmair held her tongue, knowing that her mother would only be more irritated if she responded, Faleese had no such restraint. "Jonmair never bought me my treat!" she complained, stamping her foot.

Jonmair stood, wishing she dared slap her sister, wishing her brother was somebody else's problem as she pushed her hair back and felt caramel goo in it. Wishing above all that she herself would hurry and grow up!

* * * * * * *

ONE STREET AWAY FROM THE HUBBUB in Norlea's square, Baird Axton bolstered his courage by reading the last letter he had received from his sister, then put it away once more under the blotter on his desk. *I only have to make it through today*, he reminded himself. *This could be the day.*

But probably not. It was too early—today would be only his fourth transfer...as opposed to Kill. He would receive selyn—the life force that Gens produced and Simes had to have to live—without having to kill a Gen to get it. In the Householdings, Simes called channels had learned to take selyn from Gens without hurting them, and transfer it to other Simes to provide the life force they needed.

Unfortunately, any Sime who had ever killed was addicted to the sensation of forcefully stripping a Gen's system and reveling in the creature's death agony. No channel in Baird's experience had even come close to reproducing that feeling.

Baird was determined to break his addiction to Killbliss. He tried to tell himself that the reason each transfer from a channel was less satisfactory than the last was that he was about to break that addiction. Next month his crisis might come—if not, most assuredly the following month. Then he would be free of this constant state of depression, anxiety, and chronically unsatisfied Need.

He had been trying to disjunct—to separate himself from the Need to Kill—ever since his changeover into an adult Sime. He reread his sister's encouraging letters each time he was tempted to succumb to his father's disapproval. At Householding Carre, where Simes lived peacefully with Gens who had no fear of being killed, he had made friends with Zhag Paget.

Zhag was undergoing the same process of learning to live without killing. He had been at it longer than Baird—in fact, this would be his sixth month without a Kill—so Zhag now faced what the channels called "disjunction crisis." Zhag's cycle put him a few days behind Baird for transfer, but at this critical time the channels wanted him at Carre well before his Need peaked.

Zhag was a shiltpron player—a brilliant musician who could not command the audience he deserved because he was ill so much of the time. It was a hardship for him to walk across town to Carre, so Baird planned to pick Zhag up in his buggy.

Baird went quietly down the back stairs, but his father was waiting in the hall. "Where are you going, Baird?" Treavor Axton demanded.

"You know where I'm going, Dad. You have no right to stop me." *It's your fault I'm addicted to the Kill and have to go through this,* he wanted to add, but he could not face arguing anymore. Baird's father sincerely believed that a healthy Sime lifestyle included killing Gens "as nature intended." It was hard to argue with a man who honestly grieved that his son had chosen what he perceived as a perverted lifestyle.

"Baird—look at the condition you're in," his father pleaded.

"I'm in Need!" Baird snapped. "I'll be fine as soon as I take transfer."

"Son, you won't be fine. You're getting sicker and sicker—"

"Once I disjunct I won't be sick anymore. Please don't make me force my way past you, Dad."

Sadly shaking his head, Treavor Axton stood aside, and Baird went out to the buggy their groom had waiting for him.

Now running late, Baird set his spirited mare trotting. He preferred to ride her, and would have gladly let Zhag borrow a horse, but his friend was too weak to handle a mount even for the ride across town to Carre.

Although Zhag's house was not far away in distance, it was worlds away from the affluence that the Axtons lived in. Near the docks, Baird drove past Milily's Shiltpron Parlor, a shabby dive where Zhag played for the couple of hours he could manage each evening.

The street leading to Zhag's place was a rutted dirt track lined with homes that had never been built well in the first place, and now were run down rental property. Zhag's house—shack, rather—had an untended front yard sporting a woodpile, a front gate that hung by a single hinge, and an excellent crop of weeds. The back of the house was so overgrown with kudzu that Baird suspected the stuff actually held the structure up.

Zhag himself sat on the rickety front steps, shiltpron on his lap. Sweet, sad music greeted Baird, not only touching him through his sense of hearing, but echoing on the nageric level, affecting the fields of life energy in the whole area—but especially within Simes themselves.

It was Zhag's special talent to transform the world through music. But as soon as Baird drew his buggy to a halt at the gate, the music stopped.

"Hi, Baird." Zhag called, pushing himself up with one hand as if he were an old man instead of only five years older than Baird. "Thanks for the ride," he added as he placed his instrument carefully in the buggy first, and then climbed up onto the seat beside Baird.

It was not very encouraging to see the condition Zhag was in. All Simes were slender, but Zhag was practically skin and bone. He was so pale, even his eyes seemed drained of color—not that you could see them with his perpetual squint. His hair hung lusterless in a way no barber could correct, even if Zhag could afford a good cut.

Zhag insisted that his condition was temporary: that he was nearing the point at which he would reject the Kill once and for all, and thereafter live without the temptation that tortured both young men each month.

Zhag must have zlinned Baird's Need depression, for although Baird was healthier, he was closer to using up his month's supply of selyn. As they drove, Zhag tried to cheer him up with tales of goings on at the shiltpron parlor. Baird barely listened, trying to bolster his determination by taking the most direct route to the Householding. That was a mistake: it took them through the center of Norlea at midday. The steady stream of wagons, buggies, riders, and pedestrians slowed progress more than taking a longer route would have.

The occasional pedestrian led a monthly Kill home: a vapid Pen Gen, unaware of its fate, following at the end of the white-painted chain attached to its collar. It was an ordinary enough sight, for the city's main Pen was just off the square. Baird paid no heed to such creatures, for their fields of life energy were too dull to impact the busy ambient nager—the total impression of all life energy in the vicinity.

From the direction of the river, a wagon loaded with Gens fresh off the boat plodded its way toward the Pen. It was too far behind Baird's vehicle to make much impression, but he was aware of those brimming lives, and the free-floating anxiety the creatures felt at being moved through strange surroundings.

Traffic slowed even more, vehicles coming to a dead stop while pedestrians and those on horseback filtered between them. Word came back along the street that a wagon had overturned.

Vendors added to the congestion, hawking their wares from wagons at the sides of the street. When a police officer on horseback told them to move, a fruit seller argued, "I got the right to this spot for the whole day."

"Come back after the congestion clears," the officer told her. "Right now we have to move traffic through this lane."

"I'll follow those wagons off the square," Baird told Zhag. "It'll be faster to go around the accident."

The light buggy was more maneuverable than the lumbering wagons, and Baird knew his spirited mare, so he was able to get into the curbside lane when the vendors began reluctantly to vacate. In the lane he had left, traffic filled in the gaps, bringing the wagonload of fresh Gens close enough to be an irritant to both Baird and Zhag. The fruit seller shouted at the vendor in front of her, who was securing breakable ceramic utensils before trying to move. The tinker yelled back, and traffic once more came to a halt.

Zhag picked up his shiltpron, and strummed a soothing tune. Baird tried to let its nageric resonations wash away his jangled nervousness. He knew he had plenty of time, that he would not run out of selyn before he got to Carre—but his Sime instincts insisted his life was draining away pulse by pulse, and if he did not renew it soon, he would die in agony.

In the crowded street, Zhag's playing could not affect the ambient as strongly as it did within the confines of a shiltpron parlor. The instrument also picked up and amplified Baird's Need, the anger of the shouting vendors, and the anxiety of the wagonload of Pen Gens now drawn up close behind them. Baird was about to suggest that his friend was only making things worse when they began to get better—the music was, indeed, soothing the vendors, the Gens, and Baird.

Able to think again, Baird realized that their buggy was going nowhere until the way was cleared. He dropped the reins on the seat and went to help the tinker secure the last crate of tea glasses. "Thanks." the man told him, and flipped a rude signal at the impatient fruit seller behind him before he jumped up into the seat.

* * * * * * *

JONMAIR, IN DISGRACE THROUGH NO FAULT OF HER OWN, paced ahead of her mother and siblings through the stalled traffic. At least she was relieved of trying to take care of Wawkeen and Faleese. Along with the slow-footed Gen, they would keep Mama from catching up to her and scolding her some more. At least until they got home.

But Mama would kill her Gen tomorrow, and be her normal, rational self again. Then Jonmair could explain what had happened with the kids—there was no use trying to talk to her until then.

This area of Norlea, around the Pens, was especially crowded today because of the delay in Gen shipments. They had passed two wagonloads of the creatures, and down the street she could see another caught in the traffic, green pennant flapping limply in what breeze penetrated from the waterfront to the center of the city.

Jonmair's eye was caught, though, by a buggy moving toward her from the center of the street into the lane the police were clearing. It was the kind of vehicle she dreamed of having someday, shiny and smart and drawn by a beautiful prancing gray horse.

There were two men in the buggy—master and servant, Jonmair guessed, for one was nondescript and dressed rather shabbily, while the other—

Jonmair's heart gave a lurch as she looked closely at the driver of the buggy. He was young, with thick black hair cut collar length in the latest fashion, and his skin had a shining copper tone. Despite the whipcord slenderness typical of Simes, his shoulders were broad, making him look as if he could take on the world. His clothes were exquisitely tailored—everything about him signaled "wealth" and "power."

But as she drew closer, it was the man's eyes that held Jonmair's attention. They were very large, gray, and fringed with thick black lashes. Somehow she knew those eyes were capable of dancing with merriment or flashing with anger...but what she saw in them now was Need.

He was in the same state as Jonmair's mother, yet he was not irritable and annoyed at every little thing. When the other man in the buggy began to play music, the handsome man Jonmair was watching got down from his seat and went to help one of the vendors move his wagon.

Jonmair was amazed to see a man who was not only self-controlled in Need, but able to think about other people. She watched admiringly as he started back toward his buggy, but then she caught sight of her mother approaching, and slipped between the vehicles to get out of her sight.

Once on the other side of the street, though, she could not help but turn to look again at the handsome, wealthy man—just in time to see her foolish little sister, running ahead of their mother, skip right out into the traffic that was ready to start moving again.

* * * * * * *

BAIRD TURNED AWAY FROM THE TINKER'S WAGON and began making his way back toward his buggy.

A woman with two small children and a Pen Gen in tow looked for a path through the stalled traffic. She kept her little boy close by one handling tentacle. The girl had a pinwheel on a stick, waving it in the air to make it spin. She darted between wagons, her mother calling to her to wait.

The child danced to Zhag's music, oblivious of her mother's concerns. She moved toward Zhag, laughing and waving her pinwheel—

Right under the nose of Baird's skittish mare.

No one was holding the reins.

The sparkling object spooked the horse, who reared, backing against the traces and nearly upsetting the buggy.

The music stopped abruptly as Zhag held the seat with one hand, his shiltpron with the other—until he saw the child under the flailing hoofs of the horse. Her mother tried to run to the little girl's rescue, but she was hampered by her frightened son and the shuffling Gen she dragged.

* * * * * * *

JONMAIR SCREAMED AND TRIED TO RUN, but she had no Sime strength or agility. It felt as if her feet were moored in molasses—she could never reach the scene in time.

Shoving his instrument aside, the musician grabbed up the reins, pulling the horse into a rear.

With speed only adult Simes could muster, the man Jonmair had been watching leaped in to scoop the child out from under the horse before the hoofs came down. Fighting the unfamiliar driver, the mare bucked and kicked, but Jonmair's eyes were only for the safety of her little sister, and the heroism of the man who had just saved her life.

* * * * * * *

BAIRD DEPOSITED THE LITTLE GIRL in her mother's arms and turned to rescue his friend and his horse. When he jumped up on the buggy Zhag yielded him the reins, but the mare seemed intent on kicking her way out of the traces.

A heave sent Zhag's precious instrument flying off the buggy to certain destruction. Occupied with the horse, Baird could only zlin the effort it took his frail friend to rescue the shilt-pron with a diving catch—but he made it. Baird sighed with relief. That shiltpron was not merely Zhag's means of earning a living—his music gave meaning to his life.

But Zhag was too ill to get away with the agile moves that

healthy Simes took for granted. Clutching his instrument to his chest, he stumbled in a most unSimelike way, and sank to the ground. He radiated Need—he had expended extra selyn both to hold the bucking horse and to rescue his shiltpron—and with his precarious health he had no control left.

Zhag's Need grated on everyone's nerves, Baird's most of all—he, too, had expended extra energy, bringing him deeper into Need and closer to the moment when he would have to receive selyn or die. Looking down into his friend's emaciated features, he felt as if he looked into the face of death.

Although he did not work as one, Zhag was a channel, his field stronger than that of an ordinary Sime like Baird. With his musician's training, most of the time he was able to keep from broadcasting his personal feelings to all and sundry. But now his fields were in chaos, setting all Simes in the vicinity on edge.

Baird knew what he had to do—lift Zhag back up into the buggy, and get both of them to Carre as fast as possible.

But his Need screamed for satisfaction. The world dissolved into selyn fields as he went into Sime hunting mode, fixing on the bright Gen fields in the wagon now close behind the buggy.

There was no thought now—only instinct. Pure predator, he shoved aside people who would have hindered him as he stalked that source of satisfaction. Some lives there understood enough of what was happening to flare fear.

It was all Baird needed. He leaped—

—and was caught and tossed backwards by the wagon-master's whip.

Raging with both pain and Need, he landed on his feet next to the woman with the two children...and the Gen she was leading home.

The dull Gen field erupted with startlement, its nearness overwhelming the more tempting fields now at a distance. Baird whirled, he grasped, he connected with the nerve points—and sweet fear laved his anguished nerves as he tore life from his prey as Simes were meant to do—as *he* was meant to do! Pure energy filled him, soothed his jangled nerves, gave him strength, warmth, joy—

* * * * * * *

JONMAIR STOOD WIDE-EYED, HEART POUNDING with unfamiliar emotion. She had never actually seen a Sime kill a Gen before. It was what Simes were meant to do. They were designed as perfect predators...but she could see that the heroic man she had just watched fulfill his destiny was upset at what he had done.

As the creature's corpse dropped from the man's hands and tentacles, his look of feral satisfaction changed to one of mortification.

Of course it was highly improper to kill in a public street, even worse to steal someone else's Gen—

Jonmair ran to her mother's side and took charge of Wawkeen and Faleese, both sobbing in shock and horror. She turned the children to her, letting them bury their faces in her skirt to shut out the sight of the dead Gen. They were too young to understand.

Mama was too angry to think—her lateral tentacles, the small organs which actually drew selyn from a Gen, licked out of their sheaths as she clenched her teeth in fury at being deprived of her rightful property. For a moment Jonmair thought she would leap for the man's throat.

The man immediately pulled out his wallet, and said soothingly, "Ma'am, I am so sorry. It was all my fault. Please, please— here. Take this." He pressed coins into her hand. "I never meant to deprive you," he pleaded. "Buy a Choice Kill. I'm so sorry," he repeated.

And Jonmair, despite not having the Sime ability to zlin emotions, knew that he truly was. Apparently her mother did, too, for she gained control of herself, although she was still shaking. She counted the astonishing amount of money the man had given her, and managed to say, "Yes. I'll do that."

Released, the man turned to help the obviously ill musician into the buggy, and drove away through the passage that had finally cleared.

Jonmair stared after him, aware that he had committed a social gaffe that he might never live down—but after all, he had driven himself to the limit saving her undeserving little sister. Jonmair could not help but admire him.

She heard her mother draw a sharp breath through her teeth, and wondered if, especially sensitive right now, she had read her daughter's sympathy for someone who had stolen her Gen. Jonmair braced herself for another scolding, but, "Take the children home," was all her mother told her, before turning back toward the Pen.

All that evening, Jonmair's thoughts turned toward the handsome, brave young man in the square. The more she thought about it, the more certain she became that he could not be blamed for stealing her mother's Gen. The other man, the musician, was obviously very sick to collapse like that over nothing. Her hero must have been taking him for help—perhaps to the Pen for a good Kill. Maybe a Choice Kill that the shabby musician clearly could not afford.

So he was a good, kind man, trying to help a friend or servant when he himself was deep into Need. He had saved Faleese's life when the girl's own willfulness had put her in danger, and to do so had used up the last of his selyn reserves. That was what she told her little brother and sister as the task fell to her to explain the Kill they had seen. Wawkeen didn't really understand, and was soon distracted with his toys. Faleese, though, was pale, fighting down sickness.

"It's what Mariah told me happened to the Gens our parents bring home," she explained. Mariah was Faleese's best friend. "I didn't believe it."

"It's what Gens are for," Jonmair told her. "They don't understand what's happening anyway. We'll all have to kill when we grow up and change over, Faleese—the Kill is a natural part of life. You'll see how much better Mama feels after she has her Kill tomorrow. Nature designed it that way—Gens are just creatures who produce the selyn Simes Need. They don't have any other function."

The words came straight from the changeover classes Jonmair had just completed. And until somebody—probably Mariah—told Faleese that there were perverted Simes who actually refused to kill Gens, and somehow got their selyn from other Simes, she was certainly not going to confuse the little girl with such unnecessary information. There had never been any perverts in her family, and it was best not to put such notions into a susceptible child's head.

Mama was certainly pleased with the Choice Kill she had bought, which she placed in the family Killroom as soon as she got home. She even had some money left over, which pleased Dad. "Still," he commented, "it's not enough for me to have a Choice Kill too."

Mama put a hand over his. "Wait and see," she said. "There might be a surprise for you."

In all the excitement, Jonmair was glad to be forgotten. She made supper for the children, knowing her mother hated to cook just before a Kill, and then heated water in the big kettle so she could wash out the caramel Wawkeen had smeared into her hair. Afterward, though, her mother took the comb from her and gently worked the tangles out.

At times like these, Jonmair was not so eager to grow up. It felt good to have her mother comb her hair, and braid it so that when she brushed it out in the morning it would have waves in it. She leaned into the massage of her mother's tentacles, glad to be back in her good graces. But she could feel her mother's Need and nervous tension in the way her moist lateral tentacles grazed the back of Jonmair's neck.

"Go to bed," her mother said. "It's been a hard day." There was something odd, ragged, about her voice, but Jonmair put it down to Need, and anticipation of an exceptional Kill.

In the morning, she got up and dressed, then got Faleese and Wawkeen up and gave them breakfast. Her mother came in just as Jonmair was telling her younger siblings to go get their clothes on.

"Yes," said Mama, "run along and get dressed, and go over to Miz Hetson's."

Usually Jonmair was assigned to take the kids somewhere while her parents took their monthly Kills. But this morning Mama said, "Come here," and when the girl did, she closed her eyes and nodded. "Go put on your work clothes."

Work clothes? What work would Mama want her to do this morning? Surely she didn't want her daughter around when—

"Go on!" Mama said irritably, her laterals fluttering in and out of the orifices on either side of her wrists.

It must be the anticipation of a Choice Kill that was making her especially nervous. Best to humor her now. After a good Kill, Simes were affable and in excellent humor.

Jonmair went upstairs and changed into an old shirt with paint on it and a pair of ragged denims that she had nearly outgrown. She didn't bother to unbraid her hair, but went back downstairs just as she heard the sound of a heavy wagon pulling up outside.

Mama opened the door before anyone knocked. Two men were coming up the walk, Jonmair's father and a man wearing the green-and-white uniform of a Gendealer.

No!

Jonmair's father would not meet her eyes.

She looked past him at the wagon parked at the curb—the wagon with a cage big enough to carry twenty or thirty Gens, although at the moment it was empty.

Jonmair's mother moved behind the girl, blocking her way to the kitchen and the back door.

The Gendealer moved toward Jonmair, eyes unfocused, laterals extended, zlinning her. "Caught 'er early," he said, "but yer right. Not much selyn production yet, but a few days and it'll be ripe and soaring. Choice Kill fer sure."

"Mama!" Jonmair gasped, as the Gendealer brought out a collar and reached for her. "Dad-dy!"

"Shut up, Gen." said the dealer, clasping the collar about her neck. "You got no family no more. Don't make no trouble, you don't git hurt. Make trouble—" he laughed, "—well, the spirited uns jes bring a higher price."

CHAPTER TWO
REASON TO LIVE

JONMAIR SAT ON THE THIN MAT that lined her wooden bed, wishing she had a book, some sewing, even cleaning supplies to scrub the already-clean floor of her narrow holding cell. Something to do, so she wouldn't have to think.

It was three months since her parents had handed her over to the Gendealer and collected the bounty. Jonmair's first terror was long past—she would not be killed at once. But all she had to do most of the time was think.

It had finally sunk in: she was Gen, and her remaining lifespan was numbered in weeks, perhaps days.

There was no one to blame. A third of all children of Sime parents established as Gens, and no one could predict which ones they would be. It was a mere whim of fate that she was in that one-third, and not in the two-thirds who at maturity changed over into Simes. All she was good for now was to provide a Sime with the life energy to survive for another month. All the years it took a Gen to mature, just to keep one Sime alive for as long as it took the moon to go through its phases.

Some Simes believed that it was not a good system—Jonmair had heard the Householders' claims that it was economic and ecological folly to use a Gen only once. Out West whole territories were collapsing because, despite Gens being bred to Gens on vast Genfarms, there were not enough to go around. But that couldn't happen here in Gulf Territory, with its healthy climate and wealth of resources.

But then, she would not live to see if it did.

Jonmair stared at her naked arms. They would always be so. She would never have the convenient, efficient tentacles that graced Sime wrists, never have Sime senses, speed, strength, or balance.

Who would want to live as a Gen? She would not fight her fate. When she was chosen, she would go with her head high, proud to provide life to a Sime in Need.

Nevertheless, when the lock of her cell door turned, her stomach gave a lurch of fear. *See?* she told herself. *That is what it means to be Gen.* But she forced the fear away. *If this is my time, I will not be dragged kicking and screaming. I will go with outer dignity, no matter what Simes may be able to read in my nager.*

"All right—come on now," the penkeeper told her. "Got customers lookin' fer somethin' special today."

He hooked a lightweight chain to the collar around her neck, but Jonmair did not resist.

At least she would not die like the pitiful Pen Gens. Jonmair was a Choice Kill, a self-aware Gen who would provide an extra thrill to whoever chose her. Her price would be high, far beyond the tax assessment that permitted each citizen to claim an ordinary Pen Gen each month. She would go to someone with wealth and prestige.

Two other female Gens were brought out and herded toward the display chamber. One of them was a Wild Gen, an illegal rarity. The Choice Kills were not permitted to talk to one another, so Jonmair had not been able to find out even if the Wild Gen knew enough Simelan to tell them her story.

Jonmair's parents had always prevented her from staring at Householding Gens. She had never had a good look at a mature Gen before. This one was not old—not as old as Jonmair's mother, she was sure—but she appeared to be older than Jonmair. She had the fabled Gen physique, rounded flesh on arms, legs, hips. Her breasts—obvious, like those of a pregnant Sime woman, although she was not pregnant—seemed almost obscene. *If I lived, would I develop into something like that?* Jonmair wondered.

Partially healed whip cuts showed that the Wild Gen had fought her captors, perhaps tried to escape. Now, though, she was pale and empty-eyed, plodding in the direction she was prodded without protest or even care.

The other Gen was young, like Jonmair, but she had succumbed to her Genness. Tears streaked her face, and she snuffled loudly as she stumbled through the corridor to the display room. She shied away from Old Chance, the penkeeper, and toward the other Gens. Jonmair whispered, "You're going to be killed no matter what—so act like a human being!"

Chance shoved his whip between them. "Shut up!" he said to Jonmair, threatening to hit her but not doing so when she looked calmly back at him and did not answer. The frightened Gen scrambled away from both Jonmair and Chance. As they entered the display room she cowered as far from the customers as her chain allowed.

Jonmair stood tall. While the keeper prodded the other Gens into place, she mounted the platform and looked at the two customers.

Both were Sime, of course. They were male, one old, one young. Only female Choice Kills had been brought out. Were these jaded Simes who bought their Kills a month early, used them as sexual playthings, and then killed them at the end of the month? Her stomach clenched again—she had been counting on a quick, clean death.

At least one of these Simes, the younger one, was in hard Need of selyn. He would have no interest in a woman until after he had killed. And the older man did not even look at the Gens as they entered—his attention was all on the younger Sime.

So was Jonmair's—she had seen him somewhere before, and yet she did not know his name.

"Dad, this scheme won't work!" the younger man said wretchedly.

"We won't know until we've tried, will we?" his father

replied. "Baird, nothing else has helped. I won't let you give up. I want you to be happy—and I want grandchildren."

"It's an old wive's tale!" Baird protested. When he turned away from his father, it brought him to face the three female Gens. Incidentally, the move placed him under the skylight, where the light emphasized his strong features.

Something stirred in Jonmair's breast, choking her heart for a moment with the sheer beauty of the man in contrast to the pain he was feeling. Now she knew him: he was the man who had saved her little sister the day before Jonmair's life changed forever. The one who had stolen her mother's Gen.

So it was exactly three months. Not only was he in Need again, a state every Sime suffered every month, but an emotional weight lay on his shoulders that Jonmair could not fathom, but recognized—she could not for the life of her have said how.

Baird was taller than his father, but his clothes hung a bit too loose, and she could see in his corded forearms that he lacked some of the flesh even a Sime should carry. She remembered the haunted look in his eyes that day in Norlea's square. Whatever had troubled him then had worsened in the past three months. Both Need and stress caused Simes to virtually stop eating. Living on selyn alone was possible for a considerable time—but it was not a healthy option.

What Jonmair saw in Baird's eyes now was the dull overcast of chronic pain. Emotional pain, she guessed, for other than weight loss he showed no sign of physical illness.

"I can't do this," he protested to his father again.

"You won't be able to help yourself. Old Chance has heard the same wisdom I have, Son—we're both sure this will work for you. Now...pick one of the Gens."

Stiffly, Baird studied the three females. Jonmair could see that even on the ragged edge of Need, he was only looking, not using the Sime senses that would tell him so much more. Gray eyes moved from the Wild Gen to the cringing frightened girl, and then came to rest on Jonmair.

"Zlin them!" Baird's father said in annoyance.

Both Jonmair and the frightened girl had grown up among Simes—both should have been equally accustomed to Sime tentacles. It was only the tiny moist laterals that Baird allowed to slip out of their sheaths on either side of his wrists—the delicate sensing organs that allowed Simes to read a Sime's or a Gen's field of life energy, and any emotions carried in that nager.

In the same order as his gaze had moved over them, Baird extended those vulnerable organs toward the Wild Gen, then the crying girl, who cringed as if they had touched her. But when they turned toward Jonmair, she...felt something.

No, she couldn't feel anything except her own emotions. She was Gen, blind to the shifting ambient nager. She would never have the senses that Simes relied on to know the world.

Yet...it was as if she sensed his Need, his frustration, his despair—and her heart went out to him.

Baird gasped, and withdrew his laterals.

But his father had been zlinning, too. "That one!" he said to the keeper, pointing to Jonmair.

"Good choice," agreed Old Chance.

"No," Baird whispered, but there was no conviction in his protest.

"Yes," said his father, smiling in satisfaction. "It'll set you up, Son." Then to the keeper, "You understand the agreement?"

"Yes, Tuib Axton!" the penkeeper replied confidently. "If it don't work, you pay only for the Kill."

As father and son left, Old Chance came over to Jonmair. A strange sense of unreality settled over her. *This, then, is the day that I die. At least I feel Baird Axton will do something worthy with the life I give him.*

Attendants led the other Choice Kills out of the display room. Chance looked Jonmair up and down, not zlinning, and nodded. "Listen, Gen—you got a chance don't come t'most. You do right by me, and by that young man, an' you kin stay alive fer months, mebbe years. You understand me?"

Jonmair didn't, but the only way she dared respond was, "Yes, Tuib Chance." What could he mean, stay alive? Baird

Axton was going to kill her, and that would be the end of it.

Chance took Jonmair's chain and led her from the display room through a different door, into an area of the pen she had never been in before. "You ever seen a Kill?" he asked.

"Yes, Tuib Chance." She dared not elaborate, explain that she had seen this very man kill before.

"Good, good—'cause yer gonna watch Tuib Baird take his Kill today. An' yer not gonna get all upset and scream and cry and ruin it all—you understand?"

He gave a tug on the chain that almost pulled her over, but Jonmair managed once more to gasp, "Yes, Tuib Chance."

But she didn't understand, not at all.

The section of the pen Chance took her into now was completely different from the utilitarian holding cells. Instead of plain painted wood, the walls were white plaster with stenciled green borders. Soft green curtains hung at the window at the end of the corridor. He steered her into a bathroom tiled in green and white, with big white fluffy towels hanging on a lacquered wooden rack.

Chance unclipped the chain from Jonmair's collar. "Git in there and shower," he told her. "Wash yer hair—I want you smellin' real good when thet boy is post—understand?"

Suddenly Jonmair did. It was not her life that Baird Axton was to take today. It was her virginity.

No! something inside her protested. *I don't want to live on for a few weeks or months, offering perverted pleasure to men who get some kind of kick out of sex with Gens!*

Chance, of course, zlinned her change of mood. He leaned close to her, saying, "Listen, Gen—you give me no trouble so far, so I been treatin' you good. You don't cooperate today, don't expect to be handed over fer a nice clean Kill. You spoil this, an' I'll sell you straight into Shandy's place. You know what goes on there?"

Cowardice was indeed inevitable in a Gen. Much as she wished to defy him, Jonmair felt a bolt of fear strike through her at the idea of Shandy's place. She didn't know the whole of what went on there...but she did know it was frequented by the most jaded of Simes. They never took simple Kills, but tortured Gens into quivering objects of pain and terror, making death a welcome release.

Whatever she might have to do with Baird Axton, it would not involve torture. Nevertheless, she swallowed down bitter shame as she responded, "Yes, Tuib Chance. If you please, Tuib...what am I supposed to do?"

"Good girl," Chance told her, as if she were a skittish horse. "I'll tell ya—but scrub down first."

It was the first hot shower Jonmair had had since being taken from her home. When she closed her eyes, the feel of the water, the smell of the soap, brought back unwelcome memories of the life she had once known, the future she had once thought was hers.

My parents didn't trust me not to try to join the perverts in the Householdings, Jonmair thought sadly. And for the thousandth time she wondered, had someone informed her that she had begun to produce selyn...would she have run for Householding Carre and pled for sanctuary?

Maybe I would have run for the border, came the thought that had cycled through her mind ever since her parents had handed her over to Old Chance. But she knew the futility of that idea. Here in Norlea, the nearest boundary with Gen Territory was the Mizipi River—how could she possibly have gotten across?

Ever since the founding of Householding Carre, Gens who found out that they had established selyn production had made the coward's choice of trying to reach the Householding, even if it meant a life of perversion. Little wonder her parents had not risked such shame to their family.

Still...they could have told me it had happened. Maybe it wouldn't have seemed so bad, coming from Mama or Dad. *At least they would have acknowledged that I was still their daughter, that I was still...human.*

The shower spray hid her tears at the thought, but Old Chance would not let her linger once the soap was washed away. As he prepared her for her destiny, he told her a story she had never expected to hear: Baird Axton, that outward example of the perfection of Sime manhood, had almost become a Householding pervert himself!

Baird, it seemed, had fallen very ill as a boy. In last-ditch desperation, his father had taken him to Carre, for the one thing that made people tolerate the Householders was their healing ability...although some people feared their powers might be due to the forbidden magic of the Ancients.

The channels had indeed healed Baird, but at the cost of instilling their propaganda. The boy had told his father that he wanted to live without killing. Tuib Axton was too smart to make an issue of it with a child—but when Baird went into changeover, the process of becoming a Sime, his father refused to take him to the Householding or call one of their perverted channels to his home. When the boy's tentacles broke free and he was presented with a Gen, he did what a Sime was supposed to: he killed it, draining it of life force so that he could be strong and graceful and free.

But instead of being proud to be Sime, Baird was ashamed of having killed. Once he had changed over, he was an adult under the law, and his father could not prevent him from going to Householding Carre the next month, to get his supply of selyn from a channel instead of killing a Gen.

"He learnt," Old Chance chuckled as he roughly toweled Jonmair's thick burgundy-colored hair, "oh, yeah—he learnt what them perverts do. He had selyn to live for another month, but he had no spark, no vigor. Ya gotta kill to feel really alive."

That was what Jonmair's parents always said. If nature had not intended Simes to kill Gens, then Gens would not have that inborn fear that attracted the Sime in Need and capped off the Kill in a way that put the Sime in perfect health and spirits for another month.

Baird Axton, torn between his belief that the Householders were right and the demands of his Sime nature for the Kill, tried to find in Householding methods the satisfaction the channels told him would come if he persevered. Every month he went to Carre for what the channels called "transfer," and returned home replete with selyn, but lacking in life.

As Simes put it, Baird did not experience post-syndrome, the heady sense of health and well-being that a Sime was supposed to get from a Kill. And without post-syndrome...he had no sex drive.

The Axtons ran one of the finest entertainment establishments in Norlea, called, in fact, The Post. People came to dine, to dance, to gamble, and to sample the variety of delights a Sime could experience at the monthly peak of good feeling. While his experiments with channel's transfer continued, not only was Baird Axton's presence a blight on the customers' enjoyment, but the day came when his experiment in Householding perversion ended in a public scandal.

Jonmair did not have to listen to Old Chance's version of what had happened three months ago: she had been there when the son and heir of one of Norlea's most prominent families disgraced himself in the public square.

* * * * * * *

"WHAT IF SHE KNOWS?" BAIRD AXTON ASKED HIS FATHER. "She seemed to recognize me. If that girl is from Norlea, she'll know who I am and what I did."

"Girl?" said Treavor Axton. "It's not a girl—it's a Gen. Stop that shenned Householding thinking! Baird, you'll never be normal till you stop thinking of Gens as people."

"Then why do you want me to have sex with one?" Baird demanded.

"It's the only way I know!" his father admitted wretchedly. "Son—you're my only heir since your sister died fighting the Freebanders." Baird zlinned his father's sorrow, exacerbated by the fact that Elendra had died with Gulf's army, far away, and they had not been able to bury her in the family mausoleum. To make matters worse, she had been dead for over two months, her grave somewhere in the foothills of the Western Mountains, before they had received the news.

It had come just after Baird's changeover, and made him even more determined to live without the Kill, as his sister had reported many soldiers were learning to do. In the letters she sent to her father, she said they had to do it to conserve selyn... but in her letters to her little brother she had encouraged him in his intention to live nonjunct.

I am learning to know Gens, little Bear, she had written in her last letter, not knowing her pet name for him was no longer appropriate since he had already reached their father's height. *The leaders of this combined army are both Sime and Gen— and the Gens are as human as you or me. You already knew that, Baird, but I could not let myself know it until I fought side by side with them against the Raiders. You've made the right decision, and now I've made it, too. I've talked to the channels. I will not kill again.*

She hadn't...because as it turned out, Elendra died in battle less than a week after she wrote that last letter, leaving Baird the only surviving Axton of his generation.

"You will carry on the family business," his father was saying, "and you must carry on the family as well. This," he shrugged, gesturing at the trappings of the Choice Pen about them, "is private, and will be forgotten. The Gen you picked will go to someone else as a Choice Kill, and I'll see to it Old Chance keeps his mouth shut. Heh! I could report that Wild Gen he showed us, and set him up for shedoni."

Deep into Need, Baird barely controlled a shudder at the mention of the worst of all punishments under Sime law: to be caged as a public spectacle for all to zlin, while dying of attrition—the denial of selyn, of life itself.

But no one would report Old Chance. He was too useful and, Baird suspected, knew too many equally damning things about all his customers for them ever to risk his being questioned by the authorities.

If this insane scheme actually worked, there would be no

scandal concerning Baird Axton bedding a Gen. Nothing to add to the scandal he himself had caused.

The shameful scene in Norlea's square was as vivid in Baird's mind as if it were happening today. Even three months later and deep into Need, he felt guilt at what he had done that day—not only taking a Kill in a public street, but stealing that Kill from another citizen....

The moment he had come out of it, post-syndrome manifesting as burning shame, he had done everything he could to make amends. He had given the woman three times what her Pen Gen was worth, and then he had bundled Zhag Paget into the buggy and out to Carre—where he had handed him over at the gates of the Householding and left as fast as he could, never going near the place again.

Baird's father was delighted to have his son and heir abandon Householding notions, but Baird was guilt-ridden at killing, no matter how right it felt at the moment it happened. The Gens he had met at the Householding were people.

It had not helped his frame of mind, either, when a week after that fateful day his conscience had sent him to see whether Zhag had survived...and he had found the musician in greatly improved health, playing an entire evening's set at Milily's Shiltpron Parlor. Zhag had not killed, he informed Baird proudly, and was certain that he never would again. He tried to talk Baird into going back to Carre—but Baird, satisfied that he was not responsible for a Sime's death as well, had walked away from his friend and never gone back.

And so he had lived for the past three months, a proper killer Sime once again, trying to bask in his father's approval...when he completely lacked any joy in life.

It's all the fault of the Householders, he told himself. *Their perversion has tainted me.* He wanted to tell his father, *It's your fault, too! If you hadn't taken me to the channels when I was a child—*

—I would almost certainly be dead, he had to admit.

His father had made a calculated decision then, just as he had today. This one was intended to preserve the family. The one when Baird was ten years old had been meant to save the boy's life. The channels had cured him of pneumonia, but a week at Carre had trapped him between two worlds, neither content to be junct, nor capable of disjunction.

His father didn't understand. Baird had broken the most sacred vow he had ever made in his life. It didn't matter that his father was pleased, nor that Norlea's most influential citizens believed that he had returned to the right and proper way of life.

I betrayed myself, Baird recognized. *If I cannot trust myself, how can anyone else ever trust me?*

* * * * * * *

DRESSED IN A WHITE SILK GARMENT THAT CLUNG to her form like running water, Jonmair entered the killroom. This one was much fancier than the ones in people's homes. Here, too, the green-and-white color scheme prevailed, green stencils on the white plaster, the doors painted green, even green and white ribbons braided into Jonmair's long, thick hair.

Baird Axton's Kill waited, a male Gen with the vacant look of one raised in the Pens. Not a Choice Kill. But then, given the man's flirtation with perversion, he probably preferred a Gen that was more like an animal.

I don't feel like an animal, Jonmair thought—an idea that had come to her over and over since the day she had been taken from her home, no longer considered human. *Why do I feel so much like myself?*

Because I didn't turn Sime, she reminded herself. *I never became fully human. I only think I feel like a person because I don't know what it feels like to really be one. To be a Sime. To zlin. I still feel like myself, all right—like a child who can never grow up.*

Nevertheless, she was better off than the Gen that waited, unsuspecting, to be killed. It was a healthy male, dull-eyed only with witlessness, for any drugs would have been allowed to wear off. It must experience its death fully for the Sime who killed it to obtain satisfaction.

The Gen looked up as Jonmair entered. It was dressed in the white cotton yawal of the killroom, a poncho-like garment that left its arms and legs bare. Like Jonmair, it wore a collar, but unlike hers, its was attached to a chain hooked to the wall high enough that it could not reach to loosen it. Not that it was trying.

But Jonmair was grateful for the chain when the Gen gave her a loose-lipped smile and tried to move toward her. Its eyes showed some interest now—in the form of lust. She realized it was a breeder that had outlived its purpose—male breeders were seldom used for more than a few months.

The chain brought the Gen up short. It tugged futilely with clumsy hands, then beckoned her, "C'mon, c'mon." Probably one of the commands it was used to obeying on the Genfarm where it was raised.

Sickened, Jonmair backed against the door where she had come in, just as the other door opened and Baird Axton entered.

His face was even more ravaged with Need, and he was hyperconscious—his unfocused eyes and extended laterals indicated that he was sensing the world only as shifting selyn fields. Once again Jonmair's heart went out to him—he so desperately needed to be warmed and filled with life.

"Stop that, Girl!" Baird said sharply. "You're not my Kill."

Jonmair was surprised, for she was not afraid.

Maybe she just didn't know she was.

But she had also learned in the three months she had waited to be sold into death, that if she imagined a selyn-shielded curtain surrounding her, not allowing her feelings to get out, her field did not impinge on nearby Simes and she dared to think and feel in the privacy of her own mind.

When she drew that imaginary curtain around her today, though, Baird Axton was the one surprised—so much so that his eyes focused on her as if to verify that she was still there. "Are you a Companion?" he asked.

Companions were Gens who lived with Simes in the

Householdings, giving them their selyn without being killed.

"No, Tuib," Jonmair told him. "I've never been inside a Householding. But I do know how to keep from interfering with your Kill."

He was too strung out with Need to question her further. With her field no longer distracting him, he turned toward the Pen Gen. The creature stared dumbly from Baird to Jonmair, only puzzlement to be seen on its face.

For the first time today, Jonmair saw Baird's handling tentacles—Simes normally used them nearly all the time. There were four on each hand, graceful tendrils that emerged from wrist openings over the back and the palm. Sime tentacles were beautiful. Not limited like fingers, they could move and twine in any direction, making Simes the most dexterous creatures in the world.

Jonmair had been touched with handling tentacles all her life—her parents' had caressed her, held her, braided her hair. Those tentacles were warm, dry, strong, often comforting. And, most important to Jonmair since she had learned she would never have them, they were the outward mark of Simeness.

She wanted to be touched by gentle tentacles again, not efficiently and impersonally, as the pen workers did, but tenderly, as her parents had once touched her...before she had proved less than human.

The Pen Gen made no protest when Baird Axton grasped its arms, then wrapped his handling tentacles so that the two were aligned forearm to forearm in an unbreakable grip. Only when that grip was secure did Baird touch the Gen with his delicate lateral tentacles, wet with selyn conducting fluid. When they were securely seated on the nerve points in the Gen's forearms, Baird pulled the Gen toward him.

For the first time, the Gen resisted, turning its face away as Baird sought to press his lips to the Gen's. It was not a kiss—it was simply the most convenient fifth contact point, a grounding to allow the flow of life energy through the nerve-rich lateral tentacles.

With incredible patience for a Sime deep into Need, Baird allowed the Gen to turn its head away. Jonmair marveled, drawn to him even more, wanting to see him satisfied and healed, made whole and happy as a Sime ought to be.

Baird made the connection when the Gen automatically turned back again. It struggled, trying to step back, but Baird easily maintained contact. Jonmair hoped the struggle indicated it was feeling the fear Baird needed to make the Kill work for him.

The creature stiffened, and, that fast, it was over!

The Gen crumpled to the floor as Baird retracted his tentacles and let go. His eyes were closed, and he drew a deep breath as a peaceful expression replaced the pinched look of Need on his face. Now he was even more handsome.

And Jonmair realized that sometime during the process she had let go of the shield about her emotions, so that if he cared to, he could zlin her every feeling.

Baird opened his eyes, looked straight at Jonmair, and smiled. Ignoring the body at his feet, he held out his hands to her. She took them, her heart surging when warm handling tentacles caressed her fingers.

"Let's get out of here," said Baird, and led her through the door by which he had entered. They had to step over the corpse of the Pen Gen. Its empty eyes stared at the ceiling, face frozen in a rictus of fear. It had served its purpose.

And now Jonmair's purpose was to give Baird a satisfactory post-syndrome. She wanted to wipe away the last vestiges of his pain. She smiled into his eyes and followed him to the nearby pleasure chamber.

Here, too, they found the green and white color scheme, but Jonmair would not have cared if the place were decorated in orange, purple, and chartreuse. Her eyes were only for Baird Axton.

There was food elegantly laid out on a table covered with a fine white linen cloth. There was the same fresh fruit Gens were fed each day, but instead of the plain gruel and bread that Jonmair was thoroughly tired of, there were light biscuits, cheese, nut butter, and honey cakes. Jonmair would have liked to eat something, talk—get to know this man.

Baird, though, was only interested in Jonmair. When she would have moved toward the table, he picked her up and laid her in the nest of soft green and white pillows spread on the clean white sheets of a wide, comfortable bed. Having her there when he killed seemed to have worked: he began stripping off his clothes without taking his eyes off her.

But Jonmair had never done this before. She felt drawn to him, but not ready to plunge directly into sex.

As Baird fumbled with shirt buttons, Jonmair realized, *He's never done this before, either! I'm his first...and he is mine.*

"Tuib Baird," she ventured. "Zlin me—please." He would have to make a special effort to do so this soon after his Kill.

He gasped when she called him by name, but she saw his laterals lick tentatively out of their sheaths. It was safe enough to let him zlin her apprehension now, at least as far as her life was concerned. As to the success of their encounter, though... had she spoiled it?

Baird smiled, baring strong white teeth, and drew a long, deep breath. He dropped his shirt onto a chair, but did not shed his trousers despite the evidence of arousal that Jonmair could see outlined there. He held out a hand to her. "We don't have to rush," he said.

"Thank you," she told him, letting her genuine gratitude well up as he pulled her to her feet. She could see him relax a little, and her own breathing became more normal.

Baird ran fingers and handling tentacles through her hair—the tender touch she had so yearned for—and in response she put her hands on his broad shoulders, taking strength from him as she laid her face against his chest.

He was warm, and hard in a way that made her feel protected. She slid a hand down his chest, between his dark copper nipples. His arms came automatically around her, and she put her face up, expecting to be kissed.

But Baird's lips did not seek hers. He cupped her face with one hand, while its dorsal tentacles untied the bow holding her garment at the shoulder. In a moment he had untied the other bow, and the dress slithered to the floor. Baird stood back and looked at her—just looked. "Beautiful," he said.

Jonmair had been raised without body consciousness—what use was it in a world of people who could zlin?—but nonetheless she felt exposed and once again apprehensive. When Baird moved to pick her up, she twisted and pushed him down onto the bed instead.

He let her, amusement in his beautiful gray eyes. As long as she was doing something, perhaps he would allow her to set the pace.

If she didn't try to delay too long.

She pulled off his low-cut boots, and then his socks, revealing high-arched well-formed feet. Finally, she unbuckled his belt and unbuttoned his fly. He rested on his elbows, watching her, but she saw the tiny laterals peeking out of their sheaths and knew he zlinned her every feeling.

This may be my only chance to make love, she reminded herself. *At least it's with someone attractive and gentle.* "Lift your hips," she told him, and stripped his trousers off as if he were her little brother. It left him in nothing but expensive silk underdrawers, tented still with the desire he seemed satisfied to delay assuaging.

For the moment.

Jonmair knew she could not delay long—she was awash in gratitude that he had allowed her this much. But much as she wanted this man, what she wanted was to be held in his arms, to feel even a temporary illusion of safety, for the first time since she had been taken from her home.

She knew, in theory, what the sex act was—but she felt no desire to perform what sounded merely...uncomfortable.

Baird sat up and took Jonmair's hand. "Lie down," he said. "I won't hurt you."

"I know," she replied, letting him guide her to stretch out

next to him. Then his arms were about her again, and he gave her her desire, as if he could read her mind and not merely her selyn field.

She reveled in the comfort of his warm, strong Sime body. But after a moment he rolled her on top of him, hands and tentacles stroking down her back, over her buttocks, caressing her thighs. It felt good, his laterals leaving little tingly trails wherever they grazed. Without thinking, she sought his lips with hers, but again he turned his head away, this time saying, "Don't."

Wanting to please him, but not knowing how, she kissed his cheek. That he did not seem to mind, so she trailed kisses down his neck until her face met his hand, which had just stroked up her arm.

Again Baird cupped her face, sliding dorsal tentacles into her hair. But then he pushed her over onto her back again, stripped off his drawers, and drew their naked bodies together. His warm skin the full length of her body made Jonmair more bold. She put her arms about him again, writhing upward, feeling his hot manhood between them. It felt huge, demanding!

He inserted a hand between them. Handling tentacles slithered into places she could not remember anyone ever touching her before. Jonmair gasped in a combination of pleasure and fear. Her heart pounded and her skin prickled.

She wanted to be kissed, but Baird remained stubbornly uncooperative, although the fingers and tentacles of his other hand continued to caress her cheek and hair. Yearning for some more intimate connection, she turned her face and licked at one of his laterals.

He gasped audibly, but did not withdraw the vulnerable appendage. She sucked it into her mouth, lolling it gently, feeling little tingly sparks resonate through her tongue and down into her nerves. Baird trembled. Jonmair marveled in her power at that moment...and his utter trust.

Both of them were covered with a sheen of perspiration, their bodies sliding slickly—and finally, uniting.

Jonmair let Baird's lateral slip from her lips as discomfort interrupted her pleasure. Why did he have to—? Owww—he was too big!

Then something inside her yielded, her pain faded to a tolerable level, and she rode out his thrusting until he stiffened in her arms and cried out. When he began to breathe again, panting, he fell heavily on her.

But, zlinning that she could not breathe, Baird quickly moved off her, and cradled her gently. "It will be better next time," he promised.

"It was your first time, too," she said, stroking his shoulder soothingly.

His eyes flew open. "How did you—?"

"You and your dad were talking about it, remember? When you chose me." She let all her sincerity flow to him on her field, unable to find words to tell him how happy she was that she had been able to free him from what the Householders had done to him.

He looked into her eyes. "You're different from other Gens," he said.

"I'm not a Pen Gen."

"I...know other Gens who are not," he admitted.

Perverts, Jonmair thought, but did not say it. Could Gens be perverts? She had assumed they could only be used by the Simes at the Householdings, doing whatever the Simes wanted out of fear for their lives.

Is that what I'm doing? Am I fooling myself into thinking I feel something for this man? Chance had threatened her. Did her Gen nature twist cowardice into false desire?

* * * * * * *

SILENCE HUNG HEAVILY between Baird and the Gen woman as he realized he had said too much. She was sweet, lovely to look at and to zlin...and now very confused.

"We should eat something," he said to change the subject.

As soon as he said it, though, he realized that he was actually hungry. He could zlin the girl's hunger, too, as they approached the table. Chance kept his Gens healthy, but it was clear from the way she dug in that she had not had such tasty dishes for some time.

When he reached for a honey cake, the Gen put out a hand to stop him. "Fruit and cheese first," she said authoritatively. Immediately, she blushed and dropped her eyes. "I'm sorry," she said. "My mom and dad would always remind each other: you have to get those vitamins and proteins first, not waste your appetite on sweets."

"You're right," said Baird, selecting some melon slices and a piece of cheese. He didn't want to hurt this girl, or even spoil her mood. He wanted her again. Pleasant as it had been, their first encounter had lacked something.

At the end, she had stopped feeling pleasure. He had felt her desire to please him, but her own satisfaction in the encounter had disappeared.

He wanted to bring it back. They had all night. He could try again to zlin what felt good to her—and not get carried away with his own desires this time. Without her participation, he had gotten little more from the final moments of their encounter than he did from his own hand.

No wonder she had known it was his first time.

Replete with selyn, he was able to look at the girl as well as zlin her. She was a lovely creature with a porcelain complexion and a youthful blush across her cheeks. She was not tall, coming only to his shoulder, but she filled his arms nicely.

Even though she was young as a Gen, she had more curves than a Sime woman—lovely soft flesh it felt good to touch. She liked to be touched, and her pleasure resonated in him.

Would it be like that with a Sime woman?

He didn't have to think about Sime women today. He could feast his senses on this Gen, without remorse. She had beautiful hair, soft and thick, falling in waves over her shoulders, over his skin when he held her. It was an unusual color, like fine wine, and her eyes held wine-colored glints in their depths.

Because he liked touching her, he reached across the table and took her hands. Caressing her fingers with his, he used his dorsal tentacles to feed her bits of fruit and honey cake. She licked juice and crumbs from them, and he had a sudden memory of her sucking his lateral—and the amazing jolt of pleasure that had shot through him at that unexpected intimacy! He suspected that if she had kept it up, she could have brought him to climax doing nothing more.

Where could an inexperienced girl get such an idea? She had been virgin—of that he had no doubt. She was such a perplexing combination of innocence and sensuality!

The Gen might have eaten herself into lethargy if Baird had let her, but he didn't. When the edge was off her hunger, he took her back to the bed and began to caress her again. She snuggled against him, soft and clean-smelling, her hands stroking over him as he zlinned that she liked touching him, too.

He refused to lose contact with her feelings this time, holding himself back as he sought ways to arouse her desire. Her pleasure provoked his, perfect reciprocity, so whenever she felt apprehension he backed off to find a new approach. It was harder this time—the memory of her pain the first time haunted her, and he had to experiment, suckling her softly rounded breasts, tickling her navel with his tongue, delving gently into the mystery of her womanhood to locate the secret nerve center that, he had been told, brought women to higher peaks of sexual pleasure than men could know.

Unless men zlinned what women were experiencing.

To his amazed delight, he was able to send her into spasms that proved the stories true—but who cared whose nerves experienced the pleasure when he could share? Laughing with sheer release, he held her close again, enjoyed the way she clung to him, the incredulous joy in her nager.

* * * * * * *

JONMAIR COULD NOT BELIEVE the things Baird Axton did to her. It was obvious he was experimenting, and clear that her pleasure triggered his. If this was how it felt when she could not share his feelings, what must it be like for two Simes to share every nuance?

Well, she would never know, would she?

When her mood shifted, Baird gathered her into his arms again, stroking her—he had quickly learned how much she liked to be caressed. To her surprise, she felt lassitude in his limbs—he was relaxed and sleepy, not eager to proceed to his own satisfaction.

In fact...he appeared to have shared her own experience completely. Happily, she settled into his arms and fell asleep.

He woke her a few hours later, and made love to her again with even more new-found skill. Simes required far less sleep than Gens—how long had he lain awake, plotting how to bring her whole body alive with pleasure? Jonmair almost thought she might not survive the blissful celebration of life.

And then the dawn broke, rosy light filtering down through the skylights. Baird rose and stretched, gorgeous to look at, young and healthy and full of potential—

But he did not look at her. Instead, he disappeared into the bathroom. When she heard the shower running, Jonmair realized that it was over. He would leave her now, and she would be returned to her holding cell to await her death.

* * * * * * *

WHEN BAIRD CLOSED THE BATHROOM DOOR, he was cut off from the Gen woman's amazing nager. The lavatory facilities were selyn shielded because the pleasure rooms were most often used by Sime couples. There were, after all, some things one wanted to keep private—especially during romantic moments.

And last night had provided the most romantic moments of Baird's life. He had never even thought in such terms before!

This Gen woman made him feel good—better than he had felt since his changeover, when his father had refused to honor Baird's desire to be taken to the channels at Carre, or to bring one of those channels to their home. A brand-new Sime, driven to the depths of Need by the spasms that broke his tentacles free, had no ability to control his actions. Baird had helplessly killed the Gen his father presented him with—and then sunk into profound guilt and despair.

He had suffered the same emotions when he failed his disjunction attempt so spectacularly in the square in Norlea, and again the last two months when he took what his father and everyone else except Householders deemed a "proper" Kill, privately in the family killroom.

But yesterday— Yesterday he had felt what a Sime was supposed to feel after a Kill: elation, fulfillment, and sexual desire. For the first time, he had not given a single thought to the drained corpse that only moments before been a living, feeling—

A chill of infinite horror raised gooseflesh all over Baird's body, although the water washing over him was warm. He *knew* Gens were people! He had made friends among the Gens at Householding Carre during the four months he had tried to disjunct.

And yesterday it was as if none of that mattered—as if he were as thoroughly junct, joined to the Kill, as his father was. It was what his father wanted—but not what Baird did!

Baird knew, as every thinking Sime must certainly know in the privacy of his heart, what his sister had seen with her own eyes and written to him about in the last days of her life: the Kill could not go on forever. As Simes lived longer, healthier lives, it was simply not possible for each Sime to kill twelve Gens each year and not have the world run out of Gens.

But it was more than just an ecological necessity that Simes stop killing. Gens were people, with as much right to live as Simes had. How could Simes, who would not mistreat a horse or a dog, convince themselves that Gens were animals who each existed only so that a Sime could have one more month of life?

And...how could a Gen, that creature that had spent the night casting her spell upon him, her nager affecting him even as she slept—how could she so betray her larity, making him see the Gen he had killed yesterday as no more than...a melon? Consume the ripe inside, discard the empty rind.

What was she, this temptress who had so controlled his mind, his feelings, all night long? Certainly not what she appeared—not some local girl with the misfortune to be the one in three who turned out wrong. Even Choice Kills had no such powers over Simes.

The Companions in the Householdings—the special Gens who cared for and gave their selyn to the channels—they had some such powers, but none of them would ever use them to cause a Sime to take a guiltless Kill! So what was that creature he had spent the night with?

* * * * * * *

WHEN BAIRD EMERGED FROM THE SHOWER, damp and beautiful, Jonmair had to grasp hold of her shattered emotions to keep from throwing herself at his feet and begging him to stay—if only for another hour!

No. She might be Gen, but she would not be a whore. She drew the imaginary selyn-shielded curtain around her again, determined to maintain her dignity.

When she did so, Baird gasped, staring. "You are a Wer-Gen!" he exclaimed. "Did my father—? Can you—?"

He came to the bed and grasped her hand, pulling her to her feet. "Go on," he said. "The sun's up. Turn back."

She would have laughed, except that he was so obviously serious. And...frightened? Of her?

It was the most absurd superstition, a story for children. How could this well-educated man possibly believe there were such things as Wer-Gens, Simes who could turn themselves into Gens—or were turned by the wizards in the Householdings—so as to provide selyn for other Simes without being killed? She had heard the self-assured Gen Companions of the Householdings referred to that way, but only in jest. No one over six natal years actually believed such nonsense!

Before she could stop herself, before she remembered her place, she asked scornfully, "Do you think if I could turn into a Sime I would be in this Pen, waiting to die?"

"A witch, then," said Baird. "You cast a spell on me last night. I still want you!" He began dressing, quickly, as if his clothes were a protective barrier to ward off her spell. "I can't feel this way! No matter what you are, it's wrong!"

What way? What did he feel? "I was happy to be able to help you," she began—

"I won't have your Gen pity, either!"

In shirt and trousers, shoes and jacket in hand, Baird Axton moved toward the door. "Stay away from me, Gen! I won't have any more of your dark magic. I hope you are really what you say—because then you'll be dead soon!"

When he was gone, the door vibrating from his slamming it, Jonmair sank back down on the bed, wondering what could have gone so wrong. Baird Axton believed the old superstitions, it seemed. Well, many people fell back on such nonsense when things went badly.

But things had not gone badly last night! Why was he so upset? What had she done?

And what was she to do now?

Other than die.

At that thought, Jonmair realized that during the night something had changed. Yesterday she had been resigned to her death, merely hoping that she would go quickly in a clean Kill.

But after what she had experienced last night with Baird Axton...she now desperately wanted to live!

CHAPTER THREE
UNITY

THE DEFINING MOMENT OF BAIRD AXTON'S genera-
tion would always be summed up in the question, "Where were
you when you heard the Unity Proclamation?"

It was an early summer morning, already hinting at the stick-
iness of Norlea's summer heat. Baird, in shirt sleeves, listened
and zlinned as another shiltpron player auditioned. Only because
it was cool in the parlor did Baird not stop the audition. The
musician had some skill on the audial level, but his control of
the nageric ambience was tentative at best. It grated on Baird's
Need-strained nerves. He was due to collect this month's Kill
later this morning.

The Gen shortage had grown so bad now that there was
only a five-hour leeway. Of course his father would gladly have
bought him a Choice Kill, but even this close to hard Need,
Baird could not consider killing...a person. Last month's liaison
with the beautiful Gen woman might have awakened his sex
drive, but it had only increased his conflict at having to kill to
live. He knew what he felt was Need anxiety, and that he would
succumb to his Sime nature when confronted with a high-field
Pen Gen. But it became harder and harder to silence that little
voice that told him they were all human beings, even the mindless ones raised strictly for the Kill.

Turning his attention back to the music, once again Baird
wished that Zhag Paget were in good enough health to play
for a full evening—he would hire him at once, never mind his

father's objections to the man's lifestyle. However, even though he had supposedly passed his disjunction crisis, Zhag's health had not improved beyond what that one good transfer had done for him. He still had little appetite, tired easily, and moved like an old man.

Zhag played a set at Milily's every evening, but he didn't have the strength to play for hours, as working at The Post would require. Still, Baird realized he hadn't seen his friend in over a week, and Zhag would have taken transfer in the meantime. Maybe it was a good transfer. Maybe Zhag was getting stronger.

He couldn't take any more of this fellow's aimless noodling! "All right—that's enough," he told the shiltpron player. "I have a couple more to audition, and then I'll let you know. Be sure to leave your address with Charl."

It was a polite lie; there were no other applicants after him, but this young man really should be looking for some other employment. Baird decided to wile away the time before his Kill by going to visit Zhag.

Baird took his cloak from the back of the chair, but hung it on the rack by the door—at nearly noon it was already far too warm. Then, considering the part of town he was headed for, he went upstairs to change into plain shirt, denims, and the old boots he wore when he rode out into the country.

He was taking off his ring when his father came up the stairs and paused at Baird's open door. "Where are you going, dressed like that?" Treavor Axton demanded.

"To try to find us a decent shiltpron player," Baird told him.

"Not that pervert friend of yours! Last time I saw him, he looked like a day-old Kill. You've left that sick lifestyle behind, Baird. Leave him behind as well."

"He's the best shiltpron player in Norlea," said Baird. "That should be all that matters."

"It would be if he weren't likely to drop dead in front of my customers. Come on—Sellie's got some new dancers. Let's see if they're any good."

"What will they dance to if we don't have musicians?" Baird

asked.

"Charl can play the piano. We'll break out those casks of Gen wine I bought—it's fine stuff. Did you try it?"

Baird had, and found it excellent. The wine was surely contraband, a bonus picked up on an illegal raid out-Territory and sold on the black market. Probably another of his father's deals with Old Chance, the penkeeper. Idly, he wondered who had ended up with the Wild Gen he had seen that night his father had set him up with the lovely—

He pulled his thoughts from the Gen woman who had so bewitched him. Something about her had made him react like a normal Sime...but left him torn between his broken vow to his sister's memory and the reactions his father wanted from him. If only Elendra could have lived to come home, if the two of them could have stood up to Treavor Axton together.

Deliberately, Baird focused on what his father was planning. The wine was more expensive than porstan—but without shiltpron music to enhance the potency of the more common Sime drink, a few special evenings with wine and dancing girls would preserve the reputation of The Post as the best establishment in Norlea. Simes liked wine because it gave them a quick high, but no hangover. They would have until the wine ran out to find a decent shiltpron player.

Leave it to Treavor Axton to make a virtue of necessity! Baird didn't like his father's dealings with Old Chance. One of these days the penkeeper would go too far, and then how many of Norlea's wealthy and powerful citizens would he take down with him? But despite last month's normal post-reaction, Treavor Axton still didn't accept his son as an equal—and Baird had no idea what it would take to convince him that he should have more to say about how the business was run than auditioning mediocre shiltpron players.

The two men were walking across Norlea's square—a place that made Baird shiver to this day with the shame of his all-too-public Genjacking—when an official crier entered, ringing his bell. "Gather round, gather round all!" he shouted. "Official proclamation from the legislature!"

"Another Gen shortfall, bet on it!" said Baird's father as they joined the crowd of jittery Simes to listen to the latest news. "Shen that war out west! Why is Gulf involved in it anyway?" And Baird knew he was thinking of the apparently senseless loss of Elendra.

The crier had a large document scrolled up, and was followed by a man and a woman, each with several scrolls. Those would be copies of the same document. After the official reading they would be posted in all the public areas of Norlea.

The crier unrolled the top portion of the scroll and, with a flourish, turned it so the gathered crowd could see the large black headline as he declaimed the best news they had heard in months: "The war is over!"

The cheers greeting that statement drowned anything the official reader might have tried to say for several minutes. Baird turned to hug his father who, for once, accepted the gesture. But in a moment he felt his father tense, zlinned the tension building within the crowd as they quieted and turned to the crier again.

"Who won?" someone shouted.

"We did! The Freeband Raiders have been defeated!" the crier replied, and another cheer went up as he turned the scroll so that he could read the lengthy proclamation.

A hush fell over the crowd as they listened, knowing that until the official reading was completed the copies would not be posted for those who could read to absorb perhaps more quickly, perhaps with greater belief.

The Sime and Gen armies that Elendra had written about had survived a terrible winter in the mountains—and as the war resumed in the spring the Raiders cut their supply lines. The Gens ran out of food. The Simes ran out of Pen Gens. As Elendra had told Baird, many Simes and Gens had gotten to know one another, had fought side by side, had saved each other's lives. Many Sime soldiers found it hard to face killing even mindless Pen Gens—but now even those were unavailable.

There was no way to prevent the army of Simes from killing

the army of Gens—their allies against the common enemy of the Freeband Raiders—except to separate them. But that would leave the Simes to die of attrition, and the Gens under the tentacles of the Raiders.

But then the Householders—those perverted channels and their wer-Gen Companions tolerated by both armies because of their healing powers—had suggested a solution: if the Simes gave the Gens all the food in their supplies, and—through the channels—the Gens donated their selyn to keep the Sime army alive, they could stand together against the Freebanders.

Despite his state of Need, tears caught in Baird's throat. *Oh, Elendra, if only you could have lived to be part of that!* And then he realized, *You were there in spirit—you believed Simes and Gens could survive without killing, and two whole armies proved you right!*

Beside him, Baird's father whispered irreverent words in a reverent tone: "Bloody shen!"

"We won," Baird murmured. "The war is over—it's all over."

"We? Some kind of perverted witchcraft—"

But as the murmurs of amazement dwindled, the crier held up his scroll again, ready to read on. "Furthermore, a peaceful accommodation having been achieved between the armies of all Sime and Gen Territories east of the Great Mountains, the leaders of those territories have entered into a Unity Treaty together to maintain that peaceful accord. In exchange for trade across the territories, and an end to border raids from either side, the governments of the Gen Territories known as Ningland, Heartland, New Washington, Mizzoo—" the list continued through names Baird knew and others he had not known existed, exotic Gen names that even the professional crier's tongue tripped over "—have agreed to allow tested and licensed channels to be stationed within their territories to collect selyn to provide for the continued welfare of the citizens of the Sime Territories."

A gasp went up from the crowd. This could not be real! Wild Gens agreeing to give their selyn to Simes? In return for what?

Sime Territories didn't grow enough food to support the huge population of Gens—the Gen population had to outnumber the Sime population many times over, or else—

—or else the Simes would kill all the Gens, and die in the agony of attrition. Those Freeband Raiders who had caused such havoc were the result of NorWest Sime Territory running out of Gens, and desperate Simes banding together to raid across neighboring territories. The largest band of Raiders ever known had caused the war that had taken Elendra's life.

Baird looked around. Did anyone else in this crowd understand that? Had anyone else's brother or sister, son or daughter, written home about their experiences?

Again the crowd fell expectantly silent. The crier proceeded to the next section of the proclamation.

"In return, the governments of the Sime Territories known as Gulf, Lakeland, East Nivet, West Nivet—" again a long list as the crowd waited impatiently to hear what new taxes they would have to pay for peace with their Gen neighbors—and for the reassurance that Gulf Territory would never experience a selyn shortfall such as had destroyed NorWest. Even someone as set in his ways as Treavor Axton, Baird was sure, would accept occasional transfer of selyn from a channel if that were the only way to live for another month.

And then came the unbelievable words that would become the most famous in the proclamation: "these Sime Territories, joining as one entity under Tecton law, agree to disjunct all Simes and put an end to the Kill."

Even Baird, who had wanted so desperately to end the Kill in his own life, could not believe what the crier read. Put an end to the Kill? For all Simes? It wasn't possible!

There was stunned silence. Then a woman said, "You mean when my son changes over, I have to take him to the perverts? That he won't be allowed to kill, like a normal Sime?"

Of course, Baird realized. That had to be it: all new Simes would be given First Transfer, as he had wanted, not a First Kill. In one generation, there would be no more killing.

The crier, though, cringed as he looked down at the document he held, the whole top section now rolled up, already read—only one brief section to go. Baird could zlin his fear as he looked around, sweating in the heat and humidity.

Only then did Baird notice the platoon of Home Guard soldiers that had quietly drawn up around the crowd while they listened to the proclamation. *They think there's going to be a riot!* he realized. What could the proclamation say? It couldn't possibly—

The crier swallowed hard, and plowed into the final sentences of the proclamation. "In compliance with the terms of the Unity Treaty, the Legislature of Gulf Sime Territory hereby declares that twenty-eight days from today shall be the day of the Last Kill. During this month's transition period the Pen system shall be replaced by a new selyn distribution system whereby every adult Sime shall receive a month's selyn ration from a channel, the distribution of selyn being managed under the supervision of the Tecton. In order to achieve a smooth transition and maintain distribution of selyn in a safe and timely manner, the Tecton is now a branch of the Gulf Territory government, under the supervision and protection of the Office of Selyn Management."

There were a few more sentences of legal complications, but no one was paying attention. The blow had fallen: the entire population of Gulf Territory were, by government decree, to be turned into what almost every Sime in the territory considered the worst of perverts!

* * * * * * *

JONMAIR NOTICED A BUSTLE IN THE PENS, but could not find out the cause. She and the other Choice Kills were brought out more often, and the Simes who looked them over had a nervy anxiety that could not be accounted for by mere Need. In fact, many of them were not in Need at all, purchasing early for future use. Not wanting to be used sexually, or possibly tortured before she was killed, Jonmair only allowed her field to show when the customer was in hard Need. Then she knew she would get a quick and clean death. Otherwise she drew her imaginary curtain of privacy, and was ignored.

Finally, Chance told her, "All right, Gen—you want to be saved for the Final Auction? You got it. But if I have to beat you to heighten your field and bring the price I need, I ain't gonna hesitate *that* day!" And he locked her back in her cell to ponder his words.

Final Auction? She had never heard of a Choice Auction called the Final Auction. And Chance had used the term "Need" for money instead of selyn. Using the term associated with the very biologic energy of life in some other context indicated utter desperation. Why would Old Chance be desperate for money? Everybody thought he had tons of it, considering all the bribes he had taken over the years. But then, who knew how many bribes he had had to pay?

Each day as usual Jonmair was taken into the exercise yard with the other Choice Kills—and as the days passed, their numbers dwindled. Almost no new Gens replaced those sold. How could fewer children in Norlea suddenly be establishing as Gens? Where were the new Choice Kills going?

The Pen smelled of newly sawn wood, fresh paint, and antiseptic. Sometimes Jonmair heard hammering. Repairs and remodeling—but Chance was not supervising. He avoided the areas where the work was taking place. Had he sold the Pen? That must be it. Old Chance must be retiring—that was why he wanted to make every bit of money out of his final sales.

Then one morning at exercise time, Jonmair was led past open doors of what had been other holding cells. The area had been remodeled into rooms each the size of two cells, lined with new cabinets. In one of the rooms two women were putting vials and bottles in the cabinets, laughing and talking as they worked. But—one of the women was Sime and one was Gen!

Ignoring the Sime holding her chain, Jonmair stopped in her tracks and gawked. "You're Householders!" she exclaimed.

The two women turned, and their bright mood fell away,

replaced by looks of pity. "What are you doing here?" Jonmair demanded, setting her feet as the young Sime leading her tried to drag her toward the exercise yard. "Has Old Chance sold the Pen to Carre?"

The Gen woman put an arm protectively around the Sime woman's shoulders, saying in a choked voice, "It's not fair—but what can we do?"

"Nothing," the Sime woman said grimly. "Nothing but wait. Just another week, Janine, and it will be over."

"What will be over?" Jonmair tried to ask, but the Sime leading her set his own feet and yanked. The collar cut into her neck, and she had to follow him out into the hot sun.

The exercise area was surrounded by Pen buildings so that Simes on the surrounding streets would not be irritated or tempted by Gen nager. Jonmair could not see or hear what was going on in Norlea outside the Pen...yet she had a feeling, somehow, of a pall over the city, a desperation she could sense, although she could not explain how.

There were four other Gens in the exercise area. They were forbidden to talk to one another, but today Jonmair didn't care if she was beaten, or if she was locked in her cell or even drugged—she had to find out what they knew.

As soon as the chain was unclipped from her collar, she ran to the two men and two women, exclaiming, "What have you heard? What's happening? Why are there Householders here, remodeling the Pens?"

"Hey—you—shut up!" demanded the young Sime guarding them. He put a threatening hand on his whip, but the five Gens ignored him.

"I don't know," said one of the males. He was already taller than most Simes, broad of shoulder, with powerful thighs. "I was moved out of my area into another."

"Me, too," said the other male. "They tore down that whole row of cells. They're turning the Pen into something else."

"But where will the Pen be?" asked a short female with curly black hair. "There has to be one near the center of town, and

Norlea's all built up."

Suddenly the other female, a pale girl with pimply skin, spoke angrily. "Won't be no more Pens!"

"Shut up you!" their guard yelled, but it was too late. None of them would obey after what the girl had said. She was the newest addition to the Choice Kills.

As the other four Gens urged her to tell what she knew, their guard ran off to get help.

"We're the Last Kills," the girl said. "I dint hafta be kilt—my ma an' pa coulda give me to the Householders, all legal—but they wanted the money for their own Last Kills!"

"What are you talking about?" asked the shorter male.

"The war!" the girl told them. "We won—but only because the Sime and Gen armies joined together against the Freebanders. The Gens traded selyn for the Simes' food, so they could all keep fighting. And afterward they made a treaty to keep the peace. Out-Territory Gens—they agreed to keep giving us their selyn!"

"What?" asked the other woman. "I don't believe it! Let themselves be killed?"

"No," the girl replied. "Like the Householders. The channels will take selyn from the Gens, and give it to Simes. No Kills. No more Kills after the end of this month."

"That's not possible," Jonmair whispered, although the hope vying with fear in her heart almost overwhelmed her.

"Don't make no difference to us," the girl said. "We'll be sold at the Final Auction, and die in the Last Kill."

That was all Jonmair could find out, because the penkeepers arrived to herd the Gens back to their cells. They were not allowed out again, nor were they fed anything but gruel that day—but Old Chance dared not weaken them too much: the Final Auction was approaching, and he had to keep his stock in top condition.

The news was simply too much to grasp. Simes and Gens were going to live together without killing. How could it be? Everyone hated the perverted Householders! How could people bring themselves to rely on the detested channels for life itself?

Now she understood the two Householder women she had seen—the Sime must be one of those channels, the Gen a wer-Gen Companion. They had looked healthy, and were obviously friends.

Was it possible? Could Simes and Gens really live together the way the Householders claimed to do?

All her life, Jonmair had been taught that the only way for Simes to be healthy was to kill, that the Householders were sick and perverted.

And yet...people went to the Householders for healing. How could they heal other people if they were sick themselves?

The glimpse of those two healthy women, obviously friends, yet Sime and Gen, played over and over in her mind. Then, when she was so exhausted that she slept despite her excitement, other images took its place.

Instead of the two Householder women in that cabinet-lined room, another Sime/Gen pair worked together side by side: Jonmair and Baird Axton. In the way of dreams, she could not tell exactly what they were doing, but it was together. Their hands touched. Their bodies touched. They looked into each other's eyes.

Then they were in the Post-Kill Suite again, and Baird laid Jonmair down on the soft, clean bed. He held her close, and she snuggled against his warm strength, knowing that now they would never have to part. The world had changed, and they could be together.

The dream shifted again. Baird and Jonmair walked together down the corridor in the Pen, past the open doors of cells remodeled into rooms where lives would be saved instead of taken. She saw the two Householder women again, laughing as they worked until they turned and looked at her—a look of pity.

Why pity? She was all right. The world was all right. The Kill was over! She and Baird could be together now, Sime and Gen—

She looked to Baird, and it wasn't Baird. Old Chance held

the white-painted chain attached to the collar around Jonmair's neck. She was being taken to auction, to the Final Auction!

She woke with a start, tears streaming down her face. The barren holding cell was her reality. There would be no Unity for her, nor for any Choice Kill in Old Chance's Pen.

That brave new world would begin just one day after Jonmair's death.

* * * * * * *

AS THE DAY OF THE LAST KILL APPROACHED, Baird Axton tried to decide what to do. After the reading of the proclamation last month, he had allowed his father to take him to the Pen, where, his Need exacerbated by the threat of attrition—for that was how Simes felt what their government had done to them—he still refused to allow his father to buy him a Choice Kill, and instead took one of the mindless Pen Gens.

It had not gone well. He had had to go nearly into attrition—physical, not merely emotional—before his body's survival reflexes had kicked in and he had killed it. He had emerged, not post, but in a state of such guilt and anxiety that he wanted more than anything to get out of his own skin!

Sime emotions other than fear of dying were suppressed in hard Need, so Baird had felt only that fear while first trying to absorb what the government in Lanta had done to Gulf Territory. After his system received enough selyn to live for another month—even without true satisfaction—he began to feel hope. *Now I have to disjunct. There won't be any chance to Genjack someone's Kill, because there will be no more Kills, no more Pen Gens led through the streets.*

It was terrifying, but it was what he had wanted ever since he had spent that week of his childhood inside Householding Carre, cared for by the Simes and Gens who had saved his life. Gens who were people. Gens like that female—woman—who had finally awakened his sexual desire. Was she still alive, or had she long since been sold as a Choice Kill?

He watched the Householders try to prove that transfer could be as satisfactory as the Kill, holding open demonstrations to which no one came until they offered tax rebates. Then many people were ready to try the channels, planning to use the extra money to buy a final Choice Kill.

Many Simes were surprised to find channel's transfer as satisfying as the Kill, and ended up indisputably post. The information passed in whispers, and over the first two weeks of the month—while there was plenty of time to augment into Need again for the Last Kill—increasing numbers of Simes availed themselves of free selyn.

Baird recalled his own First Transfer. Yes, it had been good—as satisfying as his First Kill, and his post reaction unsullied by the guilt he had felt after his changeover Kill. But he had been only one month old as a Sime then, too young to have a sexual reaction or notice the lack. And each succeeding transfer had been less satisfying until his third transfer, which should have brought about the normal sexual awakening of Fourth Kill, failed to do so.

So when Baird heard people talking more and more openly about their transfers, saying it wouldn't be so bad to do that every month, he had to hold his tongue and remember that if the vast majority of Simes were not convinced it was the best way, if they broke the Treaty and returned to the Kill, then in a very few years first Nivet and then Gulf would face the same devastation that had destroyed NorWest Territory.

The Numbers of Zelerod were discussed everywhere now. Newspapers carried a full explanation, and for those who could not read there were free lectures with the inexorable truth spelled out in the simplest of terms: if the current generation of Simes continued to kill twelve or thirteen Gens each year, their children would change over into a world of war and deprivation…and their children's children would not survive to change over at all.

So Baird suppressed his personal knowledge of how hard it was to disjunct, and just how sick these Simes currently enjoying transfer were going to get. Even if they successfully disjuncted, as Baird's friend Zhag claimed he had, many would be as weak as the shiltpron player for the rest of their short lives.

Unless they were supported by a Gen presence.

Baird was determined to rescue the lovely Gen woman who had given him a single night of normalcy. Something told him that with her by his side he could survive enforced disjunction and come out healthy.

Deliberately, Baird put on an uncaring air before his father. He waited a full two weeks, to be sure that Treavor Axton was no longer watching him like a hawk, before he went to the Pen and asked after the girl. She was still alive, he learned, and tagged to be sold at the Final Auction. No, Chance would not sell her to Baird early—he was running out of Choice Kills since it had become legal for families to turn their newly established children over to the Householders instead of selling them into the Pens. For this one month it was still possible to do either one, but after the Last Kill it would no longer be legal to sell Gens, period.

Or to kill them.

Chance was predicting disaster, the collapse of the government in a revolution that would re-establish the old system—but in the meantime he was being put out of business, and was not about to go without making enough money to last the rest of his life. "The Final Auction should be quite an event," he predicted. "Definitely not enough Choice Kills to go around, so be sure to bring plenty of money!"

Baird had little cash of his own—he would inherit The Post one day, but that was far from a liquid asset. He never even considered asking his father, for he knew what the response would be: Treavor Axton would gladly buy his son a Choice Kill, but the one he would never buy him was the only one Baird wanted.

And not to kill.

Unfortunately, Baird's father knew his son could not kill a Gen he had even talked with, let alone touched intimately.

Furthermore, everyone was liquidating assets to buy the best Final Kill they could afford. People who had never had a Choice Kill before would be bidding for one final opportunity to experience the best life had to offer. Treavor Axton purchased a Choice Kill—one that Chance was willing to part with at an inflated price—and caged it in The Post's gambling hall. He made more than he had paid for it the first day they sold raffle tickets.

Like Old Chance, The Post would first profit from the Last Kill, and then, as people no longer got post from the fake Kills of the channels, suffer a decline as months passed. Baird's father, too, was making his money while he could.

Eventually, of course, there would be more and more Simes who had never experienced the Kill—people perfectly satisfied with channel's transfer. The Post would adapt to whatever happened—Baird shared a certain pragmatism with his father—but in the meantime, times would be hard. And for Baird, if he did not fulfill what had become a virtual obsession of saving that Gen who intruded on his every thought, life would be nearly impossible.

Even by selling his two fine race horses, Baird was not certain he could afford the only Gen he wanted. His best chance was to attempt to be Most in Need at the auction—and bribe Chance to put the Gen he wanted up early.

But then, everyone else was also bent upon being Most in Need.

At the Choice Auctions the first few Gens went to those Simes who were in hardest Need, closest to attrition. Simes who could afford to bid had been augmenting—doing extra work in order to use up selyn as rapidly as possible—all month long. Some had already taken either a Kill or a free transfer, and were wasting selyn in order to take a second at the last possible moment. There were, of course, plenty of Pen Gens to go around, as none had to be saved for next month. Anyone who missed out on a Choice Kill would not be deprived of a Last Kill of some kind.

Baird gauged his selyn consumption very carefully, beginning to augment only the day before the Last Kill lest some emergency cause him to use up his supply before the Final Auction began. Anyone not in Need at the Final Auction would be obviously intent on saving any Gen he bid on—not acceptable when it deprived someone of a Final Choice Kill. Householders had been firmly barred—a last snub before they were given the power of life and death over everyone else.

Baird's plan was difficult. He would augment into hard Need, tell Chance that he had become addicted to the nager of that particular Gen, and wanted her for his Last Kill. Then he would bribe the Penkeeper to put her up early in the auction. Despite his Need he would take his purchase to Carre—for if they headed into the part of the Pen already set up as a Tecton selyn dispensary, everyone would know he intended to save the girl rather than kill her.

Somehow, he was determined, he would get the girl to the Householding, where he would turn her over to be trained not to provoke his Need. He would get his transfer of selyn from the channels there—and after the girl was trained, he would bring her home, no matter what his father might say. She would be Baird's responsibility. Treavor Axton would have no say in it.

Something told him that Gen could keep him sane and healthy while he completed his disjunction—and he was certain that once his father discovered how soothing it was to have a trained Gen on the premises, he would come to accept her to ease his own disjunction as well.

Baird's plan went well enough until the day of the Final Auction. Bidding would start at noon, and end an hour before midnight, giving even the final bidders time to take their Kills before killing became illegal. Employees of The Post were scheduled to take their Last Kills in shifts, as the establishment would be crowded with people celebrating what might be their last post reaction ever.

In hard Need but still under control, Baird went to the Pen just before noon. Chance knew which Gen he wanted, but,

"She's gone, Baird. I sold her this morning."

"What?! But you wouldn't sell her to me a few days ago! You said she had to go into the Final Auction."

"Now, Son, you know money talks. You just don't have enough to pay for that kind of favor. The auction starts soon. Come and bid on another Choice Kill—you should have one in your lifetime."

But Baird felt sick at the very idea.

On unsteady feet, he left Chance's office and saw Simes streaming into the big room where the auction was about to begin. He had no desire to join them—and no desire, either, for the selyn he knew he needed.

It was the oddest feeling, his life force draining away heartbeat by heartbeat...and he just didn't care. He thought about collecting a Pen Gen, and grimaced in distaste. He thought about going to the channels for a transfer, and was equally repelled.

Maybe he should just go home and die.

Through the open doorway of the Auction Chamber, the ambient nager hit him like a storm. Sime Need lashed his nerves, while the fearful nager of the first Gens on display punctuated the general stress with flashes of terror.

The nager of the Gen he yearned for was not there. He had no concern he would not recognize it again—after the night they had spent together her signature seemed burned into his soul.

Shen! Why hadn't he asked Chance who had bought her? He couldn't think straight in his state of Need and disappointment. His father had taught him that there were things money couldn't buy—and that equally, there were things to be had for something other than money. The sum in his pocket might not be enough to buy the Gen woman from her new owner, but perhaps that money plus some kind of favor would do it.

He could not just give up! This was his last chance—in a few hours the Gen would be dead...if she wasn't already.

No—the kind of person who would pay a high enough premium to buy a Choice Kill rather than let it go to auction would not just take his or her prey into a Killroom and have the whole process over in seconds. He was sure the Gen was still alive—but she wouldn't be for very long.

Baird turned back, and braved the driving ambient to seek out Old Chance once again.

"No!" the penkeeper told him. "It was a confidential deal with one of my best customers. Buy yourself something at the auction before you use up your last reserves. You're definitely Most in Need right now, Baird—go find yourself a bargain!"

"I don't want a bargain!" Baird insisted. "I want that Gen and no other!"

Chance stared at him. "Your father was afraid of this—but if you want to kill that Gen—"

"Yes!" Baird lied desperately. "I want to kill her!"

"Your dad will be proud of you," said Chance. "Come on, then—that Gen and its owner are in one of the Killsuites."

Chance led Baird through the corridors of the huge pen complex, to the suites where Baird had spent the night that had changed him forever. Here the Tecton had not yet penetrated—the green-and-white decorations were still in place, for these rooms had seen much service in the past month, and would get even more tonight.

To Baird's surprise, when they reached the door to the Pomegranate Suite Chance didn't signal, but threw the door open, announcing, "Good news! Here's Baird, in Need and ripe for that Gen you bought."

Baird heard and saw no more, for the nager of the Gen he was fixated on assaulted his nerves like lightning laced with honey. He gasped and reached for her, ignoring the bright, recently-renewed field of his father as it flared relief. Then Treavor Axton left, and all was right with the world.

The Gen woman's field laved Baird with promise. She did not shrink from him, but instead ran into his arms, hands seeking his forearms, face turned up to his, her field a brilliant wash of desire—

—desire—

He had never, ever, zlinned anything like this Gen's..."Need" was the only term that came anything close to what he sensed. A "Need to Give." Selyur nager—he had heard the term at Carre when he had studied there, trying to disjunct—the sign of a Companion, a Gen who could be trained to give selyn to a Sime without being killed.

Baird's thoughts were all jumbled, but one thing he knew was that this girl was not a Companion. She didn't know what she was offering—and if he tried to take it, he would kill her!

She had to be trained first. He didn't know how he could let her go, but he had to get to Carre, to the channels—had to save this woman who was trying to give him her life! Couldn't she understand? He didn't want a Kill—he wanted a future!

* * * * * * *

JONMAIR LOOKED INTO BAIRD'S EYES and saw desperate Need. Her last wish was granted: she would die providing life to this fine, strong man.

Overwhelming attraction pulled her to him. She grasped his arms, felt his handling tentacles lash warm and firm about her forearms, binding them together.

But his laterals did not emerge. He could not draw the life he needed.

She tried to press her mouth to his, but he shied away just as he had when she had tried to kiss him on their night together. Then, to her astonishment, she saw his eyes focus on her. "No," he whispered. "I won't kill you!"

"Then let me give to you!" she pleaded, her heart telling her that she could, and that it would be wonderful.

But he shook his head. "You can't. I don't want you to die!"

"I won't," she insisted, not knowing where her certainty came from.

But Baird was not listening. "We have to get to Carre!" he said.

"There are channels here," Jonmair told him. "I've seen them—they must have bought the Pen."

"The Pen is being turned into a Selyn Dispensary." She saw urgency penetrate his Need. "Tonight is the Last Kill. Tomorrow you'll be free—if you can survive till then."

"What?"

"It's the law. No more killing after midnight. Come on!"

Somehow he managed to let go of one of her hands to open the door, although he still held tightly to the other with fingers and tentacles. Jonmair followed in his wake, wild emotions chasing one another. Free? If she could just survive until midnight, she would be free?

Treavor Axton stood in the corridor, barring their way. "Get back in there!" he exclaimed. "No son of mine is going to be a pervert by choice!"

"Out of my way, Dad!" Baird replied. "This Gen is mine, and I will do with her whatever I please!"

"You'll kill it, like a proper Sime!" insisted his father. "This is your Last Kill, Baird. I won't have you—"

Treavor Axton's words were cut off with a grunt, as his son's free hand connected with his jaw.

Baird dragged Jonmair over his fallen father and demanded, "Where?"

She ran with him through the corridors to where she had seen the row of cubicles and the two women from Carre. Yes! Two doors in the row stood open, light spilling into the hallway.

There was the Sime woman Jonmair had seen before! This time the Gen with her was a man, but that didn't matter. They would help Baird.

As he pushed Jonmair into the cubicle, the Sime woman—the channel—gasped, and reached out a hand. "Baird!"

"Please, Hajene Thea," he gasped. "I don't want to kill. Help me save this girl."

Thea, the channel, turned large brown eyes on Jonmair, then looked down to where her hand clasped Baird's, his handling tentacles still desperately clutching her. Then her eyes unfocused, and Jonmair knew she was zlinning.

"Ronmat, close the door," said Thea, and the male Gen

followed her instructions. Then he moved back to her side, watching carefully as the channel held out her hands, cupped, and waited for Baird to lay his and Jonmair's clasped hands across them. "Baird," she said, "can you hear me?"

"Yes, Thea."

"All right then. This will be very difficult, but you can do it." She paused, looking now at Jonmair. "What is your name, Dear?"

"Jonmair."

"Jonmair," Baird whispered reverently.

Thea smiled. "Yes, Baird—you must release Jonmair so that she won't be hurt. You don't want to hurt her, do you?"

"No."

"That's good. Jonmair, don't move until I tell you to. Baird, dismantle your grip on Jonmair. She's not going to desert you. You don't have to squeeze her hand so hard."

It seemed to take forever before Baird's grip slackened. As Thea had instructed her, Jonmair did not move. When she remained holding his hand, he finally withdrew his tentacles. "Very good," said Thea. "Now, when I ask Jonmair to let go of you, relax and rest on my field. It's all right. Jonmair is not deserting you—but she can't give you transfer. You have to turn to me for transfer, Baird."

Slowly, Baird nodded.

Thea spoke to Jonmair then, as if Baird couldn't hear. Perhaps he couldn't—he might be hyperconscious, reading the ambient with only Sime senses. "He's fixed on you. I'm going to have to entice him from you, and then I want you to leave the room and close the door. It won't be easy—but we cannot risk his killing you. Do you understand, Jonmair?"

"I don't care if he kills me, as long as he survives," she told the channel.

"He wouldn't survive killing you by more than a few months," Thea told her. "I'll explain later—can you accept that, much as I wish you were, right now you are not capable of providing what he needs?"

Jonmair swallowed hard. "All right. What do you want me to do?"

"Ronmat," Thea said softly, and her Companion moved to stand side by side with Jonmair.

* * * * * * *

TO BAIRD, WHEN THE HIGH-FIELD COMPANION MOVED so that his nager competed with Jonmair's it was as if his sun was obscured by a thundercloud. "No!" he gasped, trying to zlin his only hope of life.

"She's still there," said Thea.

"I'm here," Jonmair's voice echoed. He zlinned her field trying to escape from the Companion's shadow as she began, "Let me—"

"No, Jonmair—you'll hurt Baird," said Ronmat. "Don't compete with me—it will just make it harder for Thea to give him transfer."

Baird wanted to cry, but could not in his state of Need, as Jonmair withdrew, first her field, then her hand. The murmur of Thea's voice grew dim as his hope dwindled. He was going to die.

When all trace of the luminescent field he wanted disappeared from the ambient, he felt himself collapsing. Vaguely, he was aware of Thea and Ronmat maneuvering him onto a couch. As he drifted, disconnected from life, Thea tried to coax his tentacles out of their sheaths to entwine with hers.

He didn't fight, but he had no interest in drawing selyn. Thea tried to imitate Jonmair's sweet field, but he knew the difference, and rejected it. In desperation, she grasped the fields entirely, and drove unwanted selyn into his parched nerves, while he lay passive, uncaring.

Finally, though, Baird realized that once again he was going to live. He had a supply of selyn—not the sweet, bright life he craved, but energy to keep him breathing, to keep his heart beating for another month.

Thea stood beside the couch, her plain heart-shaped face showing both weariness and concern as she leaned on Ronmat, breathing hard. Baird blinked at her, and whispered, "I'm all right."

She smiled and straightened. "You will be. That girl—Jonmair—will be able to make life much easier for you. But she has to learn not to be a danger to you or herself."

"I'll leave her with you, or else take her to Carre right now," said Baird. "I want her to have that training."

"Good," said Thea. "I'll take her field down, and then you can take her to Carre. I can't leave here right now."

Baird sat up, still feeling hollow. However, his legs seemed to support him, so he stood, and found that he could move—just as if he were well and whole. He could wait, he decided. Jonmair was on the other side of that door, and in a month, perhaps two, she would have the training to be safe around Simes. And once he had her by his side, something told him that he would not feel like such a hollow sham anymore.

So Baird opened the door—to find his father holding a white-painted chain that he had clipped to Jonmair's collar. "Well," said Treavor Axton, "you won't be needing this anymore. I'll just put it back in the auction."

"No!" gasped Baird. "She's mine! You bought her for me!"

"You're right on one thing, Baird: I bought the Gen. So I am the one to decide what to do with it."

"Mr. Axton," said Thea, "if you want your son to live for more than a few more months, I suggest you think twice about letting anyone kill that Gen."

"Pervert!" Treavor Axton spat. "Your kind made him into a spineless weakling!"

"No," the channel replied, "he is actually very brave to go against all that he grew up with in order to disjunct. And he will succeed. Will you have the strength your son has?"

Baird's father stared at the channel for a moment, then at Baird. "All right," he said. "You're the only child I've got left—maybe you'll give me grandchildren with some spunk to them.

I won't sell the Gen. But I'm not handing it over to the perverts, either."

Baird sighed. "I'll just have to wait until after midnight to take her to Carre."

"You haven't been paying attention, Baird. This Gen is not yours to take anywhere. According to the new laws, any Gen still alive and in the possession of a Sime at midnight tonight becomes the ward of that Sime. This Gen becomes my ward, not yours. *I'll* decide what to do with it."

CHAPTER FOUR
LAST KILL

BEFORE THEY COULD LEAVE THE PEN, Thea, the channel from Carre, said, "I don't advise taking a high-field Gen through the streets tonight of all nights."

"I'm not leaving it with you, Pervert!" snapped Treavor Axton.

"What I'm suggesting is that you leave her selyn with me. The Tecton will pay you for it."

Baird's father stared at the channel for a moment as if he were going to refuse. But then he said, "All right. It won't hurt it, from what I've heard." He handed Jonmair's white-painted chain to Thea. "Go ahead—but don't take too long!"

Thea took Jonmair back into the cubicle and shut the door. "Jonmair," she said, "be as cooperative as you can with Mr. Axton. Let Baird persuade him to bring you to Carre for training. You trust Baird, don't you?"

"Yes, ma'am," Jonmair replied. "I know I can give my selyn to him if he'll let me."

Thea smiled at her. "I know it, too—and you may be the only person who can get him through disjunction crisis."

"What do you mean?" Jonmair asked.

"I don't have time now to tell you everything, but try to work with Baird. He has never wanted to kill—so he has the will to survive, with your help. After what he did tonight, you know how strong his determination is, even in Need."

Never trust a Sime in Need. It was a commonplace. Yet Thea was right: Baird had gone against his own instincts and his father's goading to keep himself from killing Jonmair.

"Now," Thea continued, "I am going to take selyn from you, so you can safely be around Simes."

"But what will happen when Tuib Baird needs my selyn?" Jonmair asked.

"By the time he's in Need again, you'll have plenty," Ronmat, the Companion, told her. "Simes and Gens were meant to be together, not divided into separate territories, and not killing and murdering one another. Every Gen produces enough selyn every month to support a Sime for a month."

"Then why the Kill?" Jonmair asked.

"Because of fear," Thea told her. "You don't have far to go, Jonmair, especially with Baird. If you don't fear, you will be able to give him transfer."

"Then I could have done it just now!" she protested. "Why didn't you let me?"

"We couldn't take that chance," said Ronmat. "But it won't be long before you can."

Jonmair's donation, though, was a major letdown. Thea gently took her arms, wrapped handling tentacles about them, and then allowed warm, tingly laterals to touch her skin. The channel leaned forward and touched lips for a moment. When she leaned back, Jonmair asked, "Why didn't you do it?"

"I did," Thea said with a smile. It was a lovely smile, Jonmair noticed—in her loose-fitting coveralls, with her hair pulled back in a long braid, she seemed very plain until she smiled.

"That's all?" Jonmair asked. "But—why would anybody be afraid of that?"

Ronmat laughed. "No—that's not all in a real transfer. Believe me, transfer is...one of life's major pleasures. What you just experienced is called donation. Gens are often startled the first time they feel selyn movement. Even just that little fear causes resistance, so the channels make sure Gens don't feel anything in donation. That way there is nothing to be afraid of."

Treavor Axton knocked at the door just then, demanding,

"What's taking so shenned long?" and Jonmair had to leave, her burning curiosity unsatisfied.

She didn't mind the stares, nor feel exposed in the blue garment that barely covered her nakedness—it was heavenly just to be outside the Pen. As they walked along, Treavor Axton demanded, "Do you understand your situation, Gen?"

"Her name is Jonmair, Dad," said Baird, and Jonmair wanted desperately to hug him for his kindness.

"It's got no name till it earns one, and then I'll give it a name," said Baird's father. "For tonight it's my property, and from tomorrow it's my ward." He paused. "Shen. It'll have to have a name to register it. Jenni. That's your name now. You understand? Jenni the Gen."

Knowing that being low-field did not protect her from being murdered, and not knowing what rights she would have tomorrow except a right to life that she did not have tonight, Jonmair decided to be very cautious now and weigh options when she had more information. "Yes, Tuib Axton," she replied.

"You know what will happen to you if you try to run away?"

"No, Tuib Axton," she replied honestly.

"You're a Gen in a city full of Simes. How far do you think you would get?"

She curbed her tongue and her field—it was better for him not to know she could draw a curtain of privacy around her field and become virtually invisible to zlinning Simes. Besides, she had no intention of running away from Treavor Axton... although only because it would mean running away from Baird.

"I won't run away," she said, letting the truth of her statement show in her field.

"Good. We'll find a way for you to earn your keep—understand that even if I can't kill you after tonight, I can still lock you up, I can beat you—anything I have to do to make you obey. You're my ward, like all Gens except those Companion lorshes in the Householdings. They get to be Free Gens tomorrow—but you don't, Jenni, and don't you even think about it."

"No, Tuib Axton," she replied, eyes downcast, absorbing the

knowledge that she had no hope of freedom. Only the perverted Householders allowed their Gens that.

But...she was alive and would stay that way. And she was with Baird. For now, that was enough—a thousand times better than when she woke up this morning.

Treavor Axton must have zlinned her gratitude, for he said, "Good. Now go with Baird. If you can get a post reaction out of him, I'll give you a special treat tomorrow."

They were in the entertainment district now, jostled by crowds of desperately celebrating Simes. Music of various kinds competed for the attention of passers-by, and barkers on the pavement tried to entice them into already-overflowing clubs and parlors.

At the entry to The Post, Treavor Axton handed over the white-painted chain to his son, and disappeared into the gambling parlor to the left of the entry hall. Jonmair had never been in one of the expensive entertainment establishments that Norlea was famous for, although one time she and her little sister had been left with a neighbor while her parents spent a night at The Post, celebrating some extra money her father had made that month. Nine months later, her little brother Wawkeen had been born.

The Post was crowded and noisy. Everybody was high-field, and most seemed to be drunk. Cigar smoke mingling with the smell of wine and porstan made her cough as Baird led her between the two big parlors off the front entry, and toward the carved oak staircase. Piano music and off-key singing filled the air, while shouts of gamblers echoed from a room full of brightly-colored tables crowded with players.

As they approached the stairs, a Sime woman came out of a room behind the staircase. It was strange to see a Sime dressed very much like a Gen for a Choice Auction. She wore a short tomato-red dress, low-cut to reveal her chest and back, shoes with heels so high it was a wonder even a Sime could balance on them, and red feathers in her black hair.

The woman stopped, zlinned Jonmair, and then said, "As I

live and zlin, Baird, yer gonna be as good a businessman as yer father. Shenned clever buyin' a Gen bitch afore they can't be sold no more!" And she lurched forward as if to take Jonmair's chain out of Baird's hand.

He snatched it back. "She's not to be one of your girls, Emlu!"

"Well, don't tell me you finally got a post reaction!" the woman said with a drunken laugh. "Never figured Treavor Axton's boy fer a Gen-lover—but hey—whatever extends yer laterals!"

Emlu sidled past them, into the parlor with the music. The last glimpse Jonmair had of her, she was putting her arm around a handsome man at the near end of the bar and whispering in his ear.

The second story of The Post contained post reaction suites, Jonmair surmised from the closed doors, as well as some open rooms with food laid out. As good smells assailed her nostrils, she remembered that she had had nothing to eat since that morning's gruel. Baird turned to her with an audible gasp. "Oh, my! You are hungry, aren't you? Come on—let's get something to eat."

First, though, he unclipped the chain from Jonmair's collar. Then he opened the collar, took it off her neck, and snapped it in two. Removing and pocketing the tags that hung from it, Baird dropped the broken pieces and the chain into a trash receptacle as Jonmair fought back tears of gratitude.

The room he led her into had two people in Post livery, and a handful of Simes sampling delicacies laid out on a buffet table. This food was far more elegant than what had been served to them that night at the Pen. Jonmair stared, not even knowing what some of it was.

A couple of Simes, male and female, bristled at the approach of a Gen—but then Jonmair saw the woman look at Baird and murmur something to the man. He chuckled, and spoke softly, but she heard his words, "Apparently it's true then. Poor Treavor."

"Poor us!" responded the woman. "That's what they want all

of us to be: Gen lovers!"

That couple rather pointedly left the room, but the others just gawked as Baird led Jonmair to the table and helped her choose from the array. "These casseroles are delicious, but I don't know which mushrooms they're made with. I'll get a list from Carre of which ones Gens can eat. Here—this cheese is good, and the bread and fruit—"

Jonmair was too hungry to worry about anything else just then. The food was so good! Tender young asparagus shoots. Citrus compote. Crusty bread with nut butter. She ate like a Gen, for that moment not caring what even Baird thought of her unladylike appetite.

He also ate, a bite of this, a mouthful of that—but it was good that he was eating at all. Even as she thought that, Baird laughed. "I already know one job you can do around here," and he surreptitiously pointed a handling tentacle at the other Simes restocking their plates.

When Jonmair had eaten her fill, Baird took her up two more flights of steps. "These are the staff quarters," he told her. "The rooms are shielded. You can have one of them until...we determine exactly what you can and cannot do."

He stopped before one of the doors, and after a few moments an elderly Sime man opened it. "Mister Baird!" he exclaimed. "Is anything wrong? Someone not doing his job?"

"No, no, Cord, everything is fine. All the guests I saw are having a good time. But we have a new resident."

Cord stared at Jonmair with bleary eyes, and then his laterals emerged from withered sheaths to zlin her. "A Gen? What are you doing, Mister Baird? Does your father know?"

"Jonmair is Dad's ward. She'll require a room and some proper clothes, and then we'll have to see how she can earn her keep."

Cord frowned, but led them to a room at the end of the hall. It was clean but tiny, one wall the slant of the roof, with a small window. There was nothing in the room but a shelf bed, a comfortable-looking chair covered with worn chintz, and an empty chest of drawers with an old, faded mirror over it—but to Jonmair it was heaven. A room of her own, with the lock on the inside. She was a servant, a ward—but those were terms that applied to people, not animals. She had hope now. She had the possibility of a future.

Cord showed Jonmair where there were clean sheets and towels, and the bathroom she would share with the other servants. Everything was a bit shabby but sparkling clean—the staff apparently got furnishings that had once been used down-stairs, still good, but too worn for the paying customers.

It was easy enough to find a soft cotton nightgown in the wardrobe, but daytime clothes presented a problem. The livery of servants at The Post was form-fitting, black trousers or skirts, white tailored shirts, and vests in a variety of colors and patterns. And all of it made for Simes, cut wrong for Jonmair's increasing Gen curves.

Embarrassment burned her cheeks as skirt after skirt refused to go over her hips, or to close at the waist if she put it on over her head. The trousers were even worse. The shirts gaped open over her breasts. She began to feel clumsy and ugly, like a dairy cow.

To make matters worse, Baird said, "Wait here," and disap-peared down the stairs, leaving her alone with the old butler, Cord.

"I can sew," Jonmair told Cord. She found a vest that fit at the waist, and turned the lining inside out. There was enough material in the seams of both the fabric and the lining to allow her to let it out to fit. "Do you have a sewing kit?"

Instead he led her into another room, where there were two sewing machines, spools of thread of many colors on the wall, pins, needles, patterns, scissors, tape measures, irons. Jonmair smiled in delight as she found all the tools to allow her to sew again. How she had missed it!

But although she had found a vest she could alter to fit, she had nothing to wear with it.

Baird solved that problem, coming up the stairs with a pair of lightweight black trousers and a white shirt of the finest lawn. As she held them against her, she realized that they were his.

The shirt fit well enough, the soft fabric accommodating to Jonmair's breasts rather than Baird's broad shoulders, and the trousers had enough seam to be let out at the hips. Then all she would have to do was shorten them.

"Thank you, Tuib Baird," she said. Then, to both men, "I can demonstrate my skills as a seamstress with these clothes. That's one way I can earn my keep. If you have a room like this, there must be a great deal of sewing to be done."

"Good," said Baird. Then he hesitated. "I suppose it's best not to give Dad a reason to be upset with you in the morning. It's still early. You fix those clothes to fit, and I will come up and see you in an hour or so."

* * * * * * *

BAIRD FOUND HIMSELF WONDERING, as he returned to the frenetic party below, why he had promised to go back to see Jonmair. He didn't need her now—he had enough selyn for another month of life. And he certainly didn't feel post.

But there was something about just being in the same room with that Gen. She made him feel good...complete.

Baird knew more than most Simes did about what would happen in the next few months. They expected to suffer physically—but they had no idea what the mental anguish would be like once they got to know Gens as people.

Baird moved through the crowd, trying to control his nager so as not to disturb the ambient. His job was to see that everyone had a good time, that no one was without a drink, food, entertainment, or congenial company. Wandering through the rooms, he found everything running like a well-oiled machine, The Post living up to its reputation.

The lack of a shiltpron player didn't seem to matter—people were content with the dancers, the piano music, and the rare wine for those who could afford it. But they would probably run out of the wine before morning. They really had to get a new shiltpron player soon!

Directing Chef to replenish the table that Jonmair had nearly decimated, Baird made a foray into Emlu's territory, where the ambient told him a good time was being had by all. So he brushed off girls with hopes to gain points by pleasuring the owner's son, and made his way to the gambling salon.

He couldn't look at the Gen caged at one end of the huge gambling salon, a boy who had grown up here in Norlea no doubt, expecting to change over and have a life. Now his despair tainted the ambient with the knowledge that he would be dead before midnight.

Two hours before midnight the winning number would be drawn, allowing the losers time to claim a Gen before the Pen closed forever. There were black pockets of Need scattered throughout the room—people who could never afford a Choice Kill, hoping for a peak experience just once in their lives.

Baird could zlin far fewer Simes in Need than had purchased lottery tickets. The Post had made much more money than the Gen had cost—but most of those who had bought tickets had already killed today, regular customers who either always took Choice Kills or who certainly would not risk their last chance to do so. If one of them won, the Gen would be auctioned right here. Baird didn't want to be around for that eventuality.

The Simes in Need added to the free-floating anxiety that tinged the lust and laughter of high-field Simes partying madly, trying to forget that they had just had their last Kills ever. The sensation triggered unwanted memories, not of Baird's most recent Kills, but of the one he had so badly not wanted that day in the square. Only at his changeover had he ever been so help-less against Need.

How was he to prevent it from happening again? And if he, who wanted never to kill again, could fail so badly, what was to prevent these juncts who resented what their government had decided for them from failing with far less provocation? What would happen to them when they did? There had so far been no announcements of punishments for breaking the new laws. It was almost as if the government expected no one to rebel.

Almost.

There were soldiers in the crowd at The Post, veterans recently returned from the war in the West. How many of them had killed today...and how many had gone to the channels as they had had to do in that final battle against the Freebanders?

As he walked through the crowd, Baird deliberately zlinned the soldiers. Tears burned behind his eyes as he zlinned the first one—barely post, probably only a day or two from turnover. She had not killed today. Nor had the man sitting with his back to the bar, nursing a porstan and zlinning the crowd. He was about a week from hard Need.

"Baird!" His name and a nageric call made him turn back to the first soldier he had zlinned. Now he recognized her.

"Conta! Welcome home!" he said, holding out his arms and allowing the Sime in greater Need to decide whether or not she wanted a hug. She did, coming into his arms and giving him a fierce squeeze.

She looked up at him, then, and exclaimed, "Oh, my—you have grown up! You were just a boy when we left."

Two years ago—yes, he had been a gangly child when Conta and his sister Elendra, best friends all their lives, had gone off with the Gulf army to fight Freeband Raiders half a continent away.

He couldn't help asking, "Were you with Elendra when...?"

Her face and nager saddened. "We were in the same unit, but...I wasn't close enough to save her, Baird. We were all strung out along a rock ledge."

"You don't have to apologize, Conta. It was war. But...can you come and talk with me in private?"

She glanced around, then said, "For a few minutes."

"You're on duty," he deduced as he led her into his father's office.

"It's just a precaution," she said. "I'm sure lots of people realize why we're here."

"That the army is mingling with the populace in case of rioting, yes. But do most people realize that the veterans of the Western Campaign are the ones on duty tonight?"

"Probably not," she said with a smile.

"You didn't kill today," said Baird, trying to keep his curiosity from being too embarrassingly obvious.

"Not for seven months," Conta replied.

"Then you've disjuncted!" he said.

A brief shadow passed through her field, but she nodded, and he could feel the truth in her words as she said, "I will never kill again, Baird. But I'm one of the fortunate ones. I made a friend among the Gens—well, he's much more than a friend, now. As soon as the border opens I'll meet him at the crossing up near Keon. We're going to live in Laveen—"

"You're planning to live with a Gen?" Baird asked.

"It's harder for him than it is for me," she replied. "He has to come in-Territory—but he'll be safe in Laveen. Have you ever been there, Baird? The city is like an extension of Householding Keon. A good two-thirds of the Simes are nonjunct or disjunct. Families live together, Sime and Gen."

"There are a good number of families living that way in Norlea," Baird pointed out, "under the protection of Carre."

"Yes—there are lots of role models here, too. The real problems in Gulf are going to come in Lanta and Nashul."

Those were the two largest cities in the territory, and neither had a Householding. Conta was right—those cities would be very hard to bring under Tecton control. Baird was glad he lived in Norlea.

But something else Conta had said made him ask, "You and Elendra both made friends among the Gen soldiers?"

"Practically everyone did, except for a few unrelenting juncts. Shen it, Baird, those Gens were just as smart, just as determined, and just as fierce fighters as we were. But...I don't know if you've gone through with your determination to disjunct...."

"I'm...in the process," he replied. "I took transfer from a channel today."

"Good for you!" she told him. "I...uh...heard about what happened to you...."

"My Genjacking, you mean," he said flatly. "I don't suppose I'll ever live that down."

"Oh, Baird—don't feel that way!" Conta told him. "There will be worse than that, believe me. We're in for a rough year in Gulf—in all the Sime Territories." She shook her head. "Not all Simes are going to be as lucky as I am. Robert is willing to come in-Territory for me."

Something in the way she said the strange Gen name made Baird realize, "You love him. A Gen." He knew it was possible—there were Sime/Gen couples in the Householdings, and even among a few families living in Norlea under Carre's protection, but it was still strange for him to think of the possibility of treating a Gen as—

—as fully human, it came to him.

But Gens *were* fully human. Wild Gens—

Again he examined his thinking. Not Wild Gens, like wild animals. That was his father's voice. Everyone knew, but no one ever faced the fact that Gens had their own civilization: farms, cities, government, art. Everyone knew, if they would only admit it, that Gens were just as human as Simes.

And so, they refused to think about it.

"You and this...Robert," said Baird, realizing as he said it that it was the Gen variant of the common name Robair. "Are you planning to...get married?"

Conta flashed him a smile as warm happiness permeated her field. "We're already married," she said. "The Sectuib in Keon officiated at our pledge ceremony. It shouldn't be long before Tecton laws are adopted for everyone, and we will be able to officially register our marriage."

Laws, perhaps, Baird thought, but customs? Acceptance? Perhaps up there in the north around Keon, where the Householding had reached into the Sime community a generation ago and enticed local Simes into their lifestyle with the carrot rather than the stick. "I hope everything works out for you," he said, wondering how she could trust that a Gen would risk his life to come into Sime Territory.

Conta must have zlinned the doubt in his field, for she flashed him another grin, this one brimming with confidence. "You've never had transfer with a Gen, have you?"

"No."

"Well, when you do, you will know why a Gen who once gives transfer can't just stop. The sensation is as addictive for them as it is for us, Baird."

Now there was an incredible idea—and one brimming with hope. Conta was clearly not talking about the bland, unsatisfying transfer of selyn that a Sime got from channel's transfer. If the transfer were direct instead of through an intermediary....

"I have to get back out there, Baird," Conta told him. "We all have to be in position before the lottery begins." Still, she looked into his eyes and added, "If you can find someone to do for you what Robert does for me—believe me, you will never miss the Kill."

Perhaps I already have someone, Baird thought as he returned to making his round of The Post. The desperation beneath the revelry was still there—but now he thought perhaps people were anxious over nothing. Well, not really nothing. He spotted his father, playing cards with several wealthy customers, and wondered where a Gen willing to provide transfer for Treavor Axton would come from. And all these other Simes.

Conta's Robert was willing to come in-Territory specifically for her. There might be others who had bonded with Simes during that winter campaign in the far Western Mountains. But other Gens would not come into Gulf—they would have no incentive. The channels would buy their selyn, and bring it in for their insipid transfers. Life, perhaps, but at what cost?

Riots? Revolt? How many Sime deaths to make up for the Gen deaths that had gone before? Life at the cost of placing armed soldiers in places of entertainment, just in case....

Three other soldiers Baird zlinned amidst the crowd were high-field, but he had no way of telling whether it was from the

Kill or channel's transfer. In the gambling hall he zlinned two more who had obviously not taken a Last Kill today.

The troops had not yet been demobilized. Conta was not free to travel north to meet her Gen lover, because they might have to keep the peace in Gulf. Baird wondered if his father knew. Of course he did—Treavor Axton knew everything that happened in Norlea. Would he and his cronies actually attempt the rebellion they muttered about? Would they incite riots against the Tecton? How could he persuade his father not to get involved?

It was no use asking Conta to speak to Treavor Axton—he would just see falling in love with a Gen as perverted. Perhaps, though, if Baird shared Elendra's private letters....

Baird loved his father, and knew his father loved him in spite of the disappointment he had turned out. Treavor Axton was a mix of idealism and pragmatism, a combination which had built The Post into the most successful entertainment establishment in Norlea. He treated his employees well—and they were loyal because they could not get better places anywhere else. He would break some laws, such as those concerning contraband, for he always knew which tentacles to grease—but he had never done anything to Baird's knowledge that could result in anything worse than paying a fine.

Sometimes Baird wondered if his father regretted taking his son to the channels to save his life. Of course, if he had not done so, and Baird had died, he would never have known the emotional impact being nursed back to life by Gens would have on the boy. So he certainly would have regretted it had he not made that pragmatic decision.

Would his attitude change now that Baird was no longer a special case? Now that all new Simes had to start their adult lives on channel's transfer, as Baird had wanted to do? Perhaps under these new laws, Treavor Axton might take the pragmatic stance again, and see his son as better off than most Simes because he *wanted* to disjunct.

He could only hope.

Treavor Axton folded his cards and got up from the table.

Baird didn't want to stay and watch the lottery, zlin the fear of the Gen boy as he was handed over to his death. But as he started to leave the room one of the waiters stopped him. "Mr. Axton says to come and draw the winning ticket, Mr. Baird."

Shen!

He turned to find his father approaching. "I won't do it, Dad," he said. "The Kill is over for me."

"It's not over for two more hours," his father replied. "This has nothing to do with any differences you and I have about the Kill. This is about your responsibility as proprietor of The Post."

"You're the proprietor," Baird told him. "I'm just your son."

"And heir. This lottery is the biggest event we've had at The Post in months. You've been full of good ideas about how to keep business going after tonight. Everything changes at midnight—let people enjoy themselves until then. Come and draw the winning ticket. The winner will take the Gen away— it's not as if there's going to be a public Kill."

That stung.

Trust Treavor Axton to know how to use both carrot and stick: Baird wanted desperately to be his father's partner—and now that the Kill was ending, it was possible. If people could only forget Baird's worst embarrassment.

He squared his shoulders and walked with his father to where the Choice Kill was caged. People crowded into the hall, brandishing lottery tickets.

A hush fell over the room, and the boy's anxiety level rose, to the delight of the room full of juncts. Hardened gamblers deserted dice and cards to watch the show, as the pack of Simes in Need edged closer to the cage, clutching their ticket stubs.

Baird looked at and zlinned the men and women in Need, each hoping to get that one Choice Kill to remember for the rest of their lives. Almost all of them were people who could not afford to buy such a Kill, especially tonight. All but one of them would flee from here to the Pen, to claim the empty-eyed Pen Gen paid for by their taxes.

Baird found himself wanting one of these people to win—not one of the wealthy patrons who had already killed today and would simply sell the Gen to the highest bidder. And yet he didn't want the boy to die!

The Gen was the child of Simes, like Jonmair. It was even possible that his parents were in the crowd at The Post, spending the windfall they had gotten for him. *We are insane*, Baird realized as those contradictory thoughts rose in his mind. *But in only two hours we will have sanity imposed on us. I will survive for two more hours—but this boy won't.*

Still, as his father instructed, Baird went to the locked barrel that contained the lottery tickets. It was an honest lottery—there was never a reason to cheat, as ticket purchases always totaled more than the price of whatever they gave away. The Post had never held a lottery for a Choice Kill before, and Baird was very grateful they never could again.

Baird spun the barrel. It was heavy, clogged with tickets. Then he and his father each probed the lock with a combination of tentacles.

Baird opened the little door in the barrel, reached in, and stirred the tickets some more as his father announced, "My son will pull three tickets. The first one will be for the Choice Kill. The other two will each be for a free night for two at The Post, including a room, all food and drinks, entertainment, and a stake for the gambling tables."

"Just get on with it!" somebody yelled.

"Yeah—who gets the Choice Kill?" responded another voice.

Baird was desperately glad that he was both replete with selyn and not truly post. He stopped zlinning, then pulled the first ticket, and handed it to his father.

"This one is the winner of the Choice Kill," said Treavor Axton, holding it up for all to see—but no one was close enough to read the numbers. He held out his hand to his son.

Baird handed him another ticket.

"This one is for a night at The Post," he said, and everyone groaned. Axton read off the numbers, and one of the women in Need screamed in a combination of joy at winning something and frustration that it was not the prize she wanted. Axton handed her the ticket, saying, "Go claim your Kill, and then come back and enjoy yourself."

People applauded, and cleared a path for her as she bolted for the Pen.

Baird chose the final ticket. When his father read the number, Weln Varrier, the owner of the bank and a regular patron responded, "That one's mine!"

There was laughter, and good-natured shouts. "You've already got all the money in Norlea—what will you do that you don't do already?"

But then a hush fell as Treavor Axton held up the first ticket Baird had drawn. "And the lucky winning number is—"

As Treavor Axton read the numbers the crowd remained hushed, the Simes in Need crowded near the cage struggling to use their eyes to read their tickets. Raw disappointment rose from them as Grennij Prebolt, another of The Posts's regular customers, searched through a handful of tickets and held one up. "The Gen is mine!" he announced.

But Prebolt was not in Need. He strode forward and said to the Simes in Need, "Don't go yet—one of you can still have this Choice Kill, at a price even you can afford. It's no good to anyone after midnight. So let's have our own little Choice Auction right here!"

Baird felt sick at the expectation rising from the crowd, the satisfaction he saw on his father's face. It couldn't have worked out better for The Post, of course: their customers were getting far more entertainment than if one of those in Need had simply won, and dragged the Gen away to a private Killroom.

Prebolt came up front as Treavor Axton made a great show out of opening the cage and clipping the white-painted chain to the boy's collar. When he resisted, Axton dragged him from the cage and shoved him toward Grennij Prebolt.

The boy fell to his knees at his new owner's feet. "Please," he begged. "You're not in Need. Let me live. I'll work for you—I'll do anything you want—just don't kill me!"

The crowd roared approval at the unfolding drama.

Grennij Prebolt jerked the boy to his feet. "You got just one thing to do tonight, Gen. Die!"

Laughter echoed through the gambling salon. Prebolt laughed, too. The only Simes not laughing were Baird and those in Need, pitted now against one another.

Prebolt strutted back and forth, mimicking an auctioneer. "Zlin that field, folks—ripe and full and aware! The best Kill you'll ever have! What am I bid?"

The bidding began—absurdly low, but all these people could afford. It rose, and two men turned and dashed out, obviously unable to compete and now desperate for a Kill—any Kill. As the price rose, one after another dropped out and ran for the Pen—a show Baird knew their audience found supremely entertaining, while he could hardly control his gorge at the display of junctness, feeding on the suffering of others.

Finally the bidding was down to two women, glaring at one another as they upped their bids by the tiny increments that were all they could afford. One of the women had obviously had a hard life. Her hair was thin, her face deeply tanned and lined, her clothes often-mended denims. The other woman was young, probably changed over within only a year or two, dressed in a plain but new dress. She would be pretty, Baird realized, if her face were not pinched with Need. Her close-cropped black hair was thick and curly, her dark eyes enormous. She desperately counted the coins in her hand and when her opponent made one final bid, she shook her head in frustration. "No! I've got to have that Gen. I've never had a Choice Kill!"

"Unless you got more money, you ain't gittin' one tonight!" gloated the other woman.

"I don't have any more money—but I'll share my post-syndrome with you!" the young woman appealed to Grennij Prebolt.

The crowd cheered with wild delight.

"No fair, you bitch!" screamed the older woman, leaping at

the younger one. "I won fair and square!"

The two women were at one another's throats, the gathered Simes egging them on. They fought with teeth and nails, tearing one another's hair and clothes while the audience roared its approval and the Gen cowered away from their flailing tentacles.

Then the younger woman had the older one pinned, and began to bash her head against the floor.

Treavor Axton signaled, and several of the staff converged to pull the two women apart before either was seriously hurt. The crowd yelled "Awwww" in disappointment, but it was not a serious protest. This was, after all The Post, not one of the dives along the waterfront.

The two women were set on their feet, and the one who had won pulled out a worn leather pouch and began counting coins.

As she did so, the young loser shook herself free from the waiter holding her, saying, "Let me go! I have to get to the Pen!"

But instead of dashing for the door like all the previous losers—she turned and snatched up the Choice Kill!

Both Baird and his father were too far from her to stop it, Grennij Prebolt was busy accepting payment from the winner, and the waiter was taken completely off guard.

The Gen screamed as the woman grabbed him, but with the speed of an attacking Sime she wrapped her tentacles about his arms, jerked him forward, and when he tried to turn his face away took her fifth contact point on his cheek.

The Gen was still screaming—and looking straight at Baird—as fear turned to agony. His eyes widened, his mouth spread into the square of horror as his voice choked off—and then the life went out of him and he dropped, limp, from the woman's tentacles.

Baird wanted to turn and run—but he could not. The same burning shame that had overwhelmed him when he had committed Genjacking threatened to freeze him—but he had been raised always to do the right thing. And the right thing at this moment was to placate the customer who had had her rightful Kill taken from her.

Quickly, he moved to scoop the coins she had counted out of Grennij Prebolt's hand and back into hers. Then he pulled out his own purse and added to her sum more than enough to buy one of the last Choice Kills at the auction that now had less than an hour to go. "Buy the best," he told her. "Go now!"

The crowd cheered her out, then turned to booing the young woman who had stolen her Kill. But she refused to be embarrassed. "I'm glad I did it!" she declared. "At least once in my life I had a Choice Kill!" She stepped over the body of the Gen and approached Grennij Prebolt. "My offer still holds," she said—and the audience howled with laughter.

Prebolt laughed too, and put his arm around her. "Why not?" he asked of the world at large. The young woman, now replete with selyn, was pretty enough, and both of them were seriously post.

"Be sure you make her pay you, Grennij!" someone taunted as Prebolt escorted her off the stage.

Baird took the opportunity to make his escape, his emotions a jumble. His was no longer the last or most public Genjacking in Norlea—people would be talking about what had happened tonight for years.

But on the other hand the taunting, the laughter, the pleasure in pain that he had witnessed—that was the nature of junct society—and juncts had little desire to change. What would happen four weeks from now, as all these people who had forced themselves into Need today came into Need again...and were not allowed to kill? Would there be riots then? Would juncts attack any Gens they could reach—including the Householding Companions, the so-called wer-Gens who had the capability of killing Simes?

And what of those who were not Companions? There were thousands of Pen Gens—supplies intended for the months to come—all somewhere in the selyn distribution system. There was a Genfarm not many miles from Norlea. What would happen to those Gens, raised as animals? Who was going to take care of them now, keep them from being targets of juncts who saw them as their rightful prey?

As he reached the top of the stairs, though, Baird knew even before he saw her that there was only one Gen he cared about. What would happen to this frighteningly enticing Gen woman who was now a member of their household?

Jonmair had finished her sewing, and dressed herself as an employee of The Post. It gave Baird an oddly pleasurable twinge to see her in his clothes. She was lovely...but he felt no such sexual stirring as he had that night two months ago. Still, he wanted to be with her—he couldn't have said exactly why.

She looked up at him expectantly, waiting for a cue as to what he wanted of her. She might be his father's ward, but she acted as if she belonged to Baird. And that was how he felt, too—fated, somehow. She had given him his manhood. He realized as he took her hand and she stepped willingly into the circle of his arms, he now hoped she would give him freedom from the Kill.

Jonmair's narrow bed would not be very comfortable for two, so he took her down one flight of stairs to family and guest quarters. "You don't have anything," he said, stopping at the linen closet. He found a comb and hairbrush for her, a toothbrush, and some shampoo. "These will see you until you can buy the kind you prefer."

"Yes, Tuib Baird," she replied. "Thank you."

"Just call me Baird," he told her. "After midnight you're no one's property anymore, even though my father will still have rights over you. No one knows what will happen to the Gens who survived the Last Kill. We still need your selyn—the legislature has already declared that you can't leave Gulf Territory."

"I wouldn't want to leave," she said as he sat down on the bed and indicated she should sit beside him. "I don't know anything about Gen Territory. At least here I speak the language."

"Can you read?" he asked, piling cushions against the headboard and settling the two of them with his arm around her. He could zlin her body producing selyn, pulse by pulse, just as his body was using it. It felt good, reassuring. He imagined what it would be like to have that steady pulse-pulse-pulse beside him when he descended into Need.

Then he realized, it didn't have to be imagination. He could have Jonmair at his side when the bleak cold of Need threatened, her field a promise that there would be warmth and fulfillment again. The very thought was bliss—and he had to pull himself deliberately back to reality.

"Oh, yes. I went to school," Jonmair answered his question, oblivious to the effect she had on him.

That would be the basic schooling most children in Norlea got: reading, writing, figuring, some history, some geography. By the natal age of twelve, they were equipped with enough skills to help out their families until they either changed over into Simes or established selyn production as Gens.

During the First Year after changeover, new Simes were able to learn very, very quickly. So it was only after changeover that Simes received the specific education or training to prepare them for their future. Baird himself was still technically in First Year, although it was almost over—in that time, despite his problems, he had learned the business side of running The Post: accounting, purchasing, marketing, personnel management. What had seemed impossible—and boring—adult mysteries only months before became not only easy, but fun in First Year.

At Carre, until he failed his disjunction and stopped going there, Baird had added lessons in the Gen language—or at least the Gen language spoken in the neighboring Gen territories—to his list of accomplishments. Now he asked Jonmair, "Would you like to learn the Gen language?"

She looked up at him, those mysterious wine-colored eyes puzzled. "How can I do that?"

"You'll be going to Carre for lessons in how to live around Simes without provoking a Kill. They can teach you English."

"Ing-leash?"

"That's what the Gens call their language—the ones nearby anyway. My sister met some Gens in the army who had different languages. Espanyol, Fronsay. They were all learning each other's languages so they could fight together."

"What...are you talking about?" Jonmair asked, her eyes wide with astonishment. "Fight together? Our soldiers and Wild Gens in the same units, actually fighting side by side?"

"Yes, against the Freebanders," he explained. "You must have heard."

"No—we weren't allowed any news in the Pen. Only a few days ago did a new Gen dare to tell us we would be the Last Kills. The guards broke it up before we found out very much. Your sister was in the army?"

"Yes. She wrote to me about getting to know Gens as people. She had stopped killing—but then she died in battle, before Faith Day."

"What happened on Faith Day?" Jonmair asked, and curled against him like a child as he told her about the Sime army running out of Gens, the Gen army running out of food, and the Gens donating their selyn to the Simes in exchange for food so that they could all fight that one last battle.

She frowned, eyelids growing heavy. "I was told they traded selyn for food—like business."

"Does it matter?" Baird asked, and quoted one of his father's sayings, "Good business makes good friendships." He continued with what he had heard about that final battle—and its aftermath with all the Simes and Gens around the camp-fires, together, singing. He didn't quite believe that one himself, but two different soldiers he had met had sworn that they were there...and he could not help picturing Elendra with them. She just had to know that it had all been worth the sacrifice!

By the time he finished his story, Jonmair was asleep. It didn't matter; her sweet field still laved him with promise despite how little selyn she carried. It was just exactly enough, he realized, to equal the amount he had used up in the brief time since his transfer.

Was this what had happened to the Sime soldiers when they became allies with Gens? This feeling of...security...so foreign to the junct state? Having Jonmair close to him made it possible to believe the impossible stories he had just told her...and to believe that the insane scheme to disjunct the Sime Territories might, by some miracle, actually work.

He eased some of the cushions out of the way so that they could both lie down, and Jonmair half awoke as he moved her. "What?" she whispered.

"It's midnight," he told her. "The Kill is over. You are completely safe now."

She accepted the news with a sleepy smile, then once again snuggled against him. Although it was long since dark, it was too warm for any kind of covering. She was not seeking warmth. What did she seek? He knew perfectly well what he got from having her there—but what did this lovely Gen feel? Gens couldn't zlin. They couldn't feel anything other than fear and pain, he had always been taught.

But he knew that wasn't true. Brushing his lips against her soft hair, he let his own mind surrender to sleep.

CHAPTER FIVE

RIOT

JONMAIR WOKE ALONE IN A STRANGE BED in a strange room.

She wasn't in the Pen!

The moment she realized that, it all came back. She had a life to live! Her nightmare of the past four months was over—she was no longer an animal to be bought and sold and finally killed. She might be Treavor Axton's ward, but she was nobody's property.

She left Baird Axton's bed and his room, picked up the toiletries he had given her, and scurried upstairs. No one was about, and she remembered that the rooms were selyn-shielded. She wouldn't attract notice if the other servants were asleep. Simes required less sleep than Gens, but everyone else at The Post had surely been on duty until dawn.

She quickly showered, braided her hair, and dressed in the clothes she had altered last night. Then she ventured downstairs, hoping to find Baird—and some breakfast, for she was once again "as hungry as a Gen."

The only food smell was kafi, so she followed that to the kitchen. It was huge, with the soap smell and damp, humid feel of recently completed cleanup. Obviously no one had been allowed to rest until it was finished. Everything was spotless, not a dish out of place.

A huge kafi urn kept warm over a small flame. It was not what Jonmair wanted, but there was no food to be seen, and she feared to incur the wrath of Treavor Axton or his chef if she did not obtain permission before rummaging in the cabinets and storage bins.

There was another door on the other side of the kitchen. Jonmair pushed it open and found a dining hall with a table that would seat more than a dozen people. However, there was only one person at the table right now: Treavor Axton, drinking kafi and reading the morning newspaper.

He looked up the moment she entered. "Good morning, Mr. Axton," she said.

"That's Tuib Axton to you, Gen," he told her.

"No offense, Sir, but I am no longer your property. I heard the other staff members address you as Mr. Axton, so I believe that is the proper term of respect."

"So you're going to start making trouble already," he said, folding the paper.

"No, Sir," she replied. "I am greatly in your debt for rescuing me. I'm willing to work—but you will have to tell me what I should do."

"What can you do?" he countered.

"I'm a fine seamstress," she replied. "I can design costumes for your performers."

He gave a sharp burst of laughter. "You are some uppity Gen! Cord will give you the linens to mend—after last night, there's plenty." He eyed her, and added, "At least you're willing to work."

"Of course I am," she replied. "I've worked since I was old enough to thread a needle. One of the terrible things about being in the Pen, waiting to die, was having absolutely nothing to do."

He stared at her in annoyance. "I wanted my son to kill you," he said flatly. "Now I'm stuck with you until the shenned legislature figures out how people can trade the Gens they got stuck with. I'd ship you up to Laveen today if I knew how to do that legally." Laveen was in the far north end of Gulf Territory, several days' journey away.

Just as his father was saying that, Baird Axton entered the

dining room. "There you are," he said to Jonmair with a smile. Then, "Dad, you won't want to send her away when you realize what a boon she will be to this place. Zlin her!"

"So?"

"What do you want most right now?"

"Nothing from her," the older man replied. "I think I'll see if there are any cheese rolls left."

"Exactly!" said Baird.

"Exactly what?" asked his father.

"Her hunger makes you hungry. I've been thinking—what are most Simes going to be concentrating on for the next few months?"

"Not post-syndrome, that's for sure!"

"Fewer each month," Baird agreed. "Everyone will be focused on disjunction. Soon they'll feel sick—and when Simes feel sick, they stop eating. Which really only makes them sicker."

"So?" his father repeated.

"So," said Baird triumphantly, "we make Simes better. We keep offering good food—but we have hungry Gens, like Jonmair, circulate among the guests. I saw it last night: when she ate, all the Simes in the Gold Room ate too. So did I—when I had no appetite at all."

"You can't seriously think we're going to recoup the losses we'll have because of no one being post—" Treavor Axton began.

"No—for the time being we'll shift our primary emphasis to gambling, like we talked about. But if we get Simes to eat while they're gambling or listening to music here, they are going to feel better. And if they feel better at The Post than anywhere else, then they're going to come back to The Post."

"And if we starve this Gen to death making our customers hungry?" suggested Baird's father.

"Very funny, Dad. Jonmair, he's teasing now—you'll learn to understand that. It means he agrees with me."

"Her name is Jenni," said Treavor Axton.

"No it isn't. You'll be registering her today—and if you don't want her confused with a hundred other Jenni's, you'd better register her under a more original name."

"Shen!" muttered the older man. "All right, Jonni, then. Girl—go get us all something to eat!"

It was the beginning of Jonmair's new life—and not too bad a beginning, considering the alternative.

Treavor Axton, she knew, had a bite—but if she followed Baird's lead, she was able to figure out when his bark was worse. It was, in fact, harder to interact with the rest of the staff, who resented a Gen on apparently equal footing with them, than the owners of The Post. She tried to be friendly, but no one would talk to her except to order her around. She tried not to feel lonely, reminding herself how much better off she was than in the Pen, but although she now had work, her mind was still free to wander as she carefully mended torn sheets and reattached lace to pillow cases.

At the end of the first week, Axton's employees were paid. His ward was not. Jonmair was once again reminded of her uncertain status as she watched the others put on civilian clothes, collect their pay, and go off to spend the morning elsewhere.

Baird, though, said, "Dad, Jonmair should have an allowance."

"I'm already clothing that Gen and giving it a place to live," replied his father. "And what it eats—it's worse than a plague of rats in the pantry!"

"You'll get that back and more for her selyn at the end of the month," said Baird. "And look—" he pointed to the ledger, "my scheme is working. We're selling more food than we did before Jonmair came to work here."

Treavor Axton frowned, but could not argue with the figures. "We've still had a drop in revenue," he said.

"Compared to last week, sure," said Baird. "That was a windfall. But compared to a year ago we're holding our own in spite of the drop-off after everyone's postsyndrome wore off. Until cycles drift apart again, we can continue to expect one good week each month."

Then Baird added, "The mending is all done—Cord says Jonmair has done a good job. Why don't you give her an allowance and let her buy something for herself at the market? I've scheduled her to start lessons at Carre."

"You've scheduled her? What do you have to do with the Gen? Other than sleeping with it?" Treavor Axton demanded. "I don't want it learning wer-Gen tricks. Neither would you, if you weren't thinking with your laterals!"

"Dad, until she learns some Companion's techniques it won't be safe for her to leave the premises alone. Shen, a week from now it won't be safe for her to be on the premises when more than half the Simes in Norlea hit turnover!"

"Well, we can expect a certain number of accidental Kills, can't we? The shenned Tecton should know better than to make a promise to the Wild Gens that we can't keep."

"We can keep it and we will," said Baird firmly. "The Gens are donating selyn so we won't have to kill. You saw it in the paper, Dad—they don't really trust us, but they're willing to try. Are we going to prove less honorable than out-Territory Gens?" Jonmair admired the way Baird pinned his father with his own beliefs. "Besides," he added, "if you let someone kill Jonmair before the end of the month, even if it's ruled an accident, you won't get paid for her selyn."

It was one of the protections in the new law for Gen wards of Simes: a guardian received no compensation if his ward was killed—but the killer would have to prove it was an accidental death or forfeit his own life. That new law had been as much of a shock to Jonmair as to the Simes. Gen life was now as valuable as Sime life, and the penalty for killing a Gen was the same as for murdering a Sime: death by attrition.

Of course. The law was not intended for unusual cases like Jonmair's. Pen owners and Genfarmers were now guardians to huge numbers of Gens—without that threat to anyone who tried to purchase a Gen for the Kill, business would simply go on as usual. Still, the law protected her too.

Treavor Axton stared from his son to Jonmair. Then, "All

right—take her to the shenned channels. But no more than one day a week."

"After this week," Baird countered. "She has to be ready not to provoke anyone on their turnover day."

Eager to learn other things, Jonmair did not tell either Sime that she already knew how to shield so that Simes did not notice her if she didn't want them to. She had done it with both of them and the other Simes any number of times, and none of them had ever commented. She was quickly learning that despite their special senses, Simes almost never noticed when a Gen did what they didn't think a Gen could do.

So preventing her field from provoking Simes was not a problem. What Jonmair wanted to learn was how to give transfer.

A day out with Baird was a great treat. She had found in the rag bin some light blue cotton sheets that had been badly wine stained. After cutting away the stained portions, she had pieced together enough for a dress that fit her properly. It felt good to get out of the livery she had worn all week, washing the shirt and ironing it dry every day. She put on her new dress, and combed out her hair to lie in loose waves on her shoulders. Shoes were a problem: she had a pair of ill-fitting black pumps, the only thing Cord had been able to find that even came close to her size. She kept them shined, but took them off the moment she left her duties, for they rubbed blisters on her toes.

"My you look pretty!" Baird said when she met him in the foyer. "Your class starts at noon, so we have time to stop by the market on the way to Carre."

"I still don't have any money," she pointed out.

"I'll keep working on Dad. I keep the books, so I will figure out exactly what it costs to keep you compared to what Dad gets for your donations. You should have the difference as an allowance." He smiled, and Jonmair thought he looked even more handsome than he had a week ago. He certainly looked healthier and happier—and she hoped that it was because he slept well with her in his bed. From Treavor Axton's words, she gathered that he did not know that all his son did with her was sleep—but then, Baird had had a very difficult transfer the day of the Last Kill. Perhaps, if she studied very hard, she would be able to give him his transfer at the end of the month...and then he would want to make love again.

At the market, Baird encouraged her to choose some sprigged dimity for another dress—and then he found some wine-colored ribbons. "Look!" he said, holding them up. "These match your hair and eyes."

People were staring, for Jonmair was the only Gen in the crowded marketplace. Following close after Baird as he moved to pay for her purchases, she drew her imaginary curtain of privacy about her as they squeezed between other Sime customers.

Baird turned, gasping, laterals out.

Then his eyes fixed on her. "How do you do that?" he demanded. "You disappeared from the ambient!"

"I didn't mean to startle you," she replied, releasing the image of the protective curtain from her mind.

He zlinned her from head to toe—and winced. "Your feet hurt," he said.

"These shoes don't fit me very well," she explained.

"You can't walk around in pain," he said. "It's a safety hazard. You've been hiding it, haven't you—the way you just hid your whole self?"

"Simes are provoked by Gen pain," she explained.

"Which is why you should have told me before. Or Cord. He should have taken care of it."

"Oh, he tried," she explained, for indeed, the butler had been uniformly polite to her, if as cold and distant as all the other staff. "These were the best fit he could find."

"We'll have proper shoes made for you," said Baird. "In the meantime, let's find something for you to wear today."

They found soft felt slippers in a shade that nearly matched her dress, and also in black to go with her uniform. Then Baird took her to a shoemaker's shop and had her feet measured. "Are you sure?" Jonmair asked. "I'm still growing in other ways. My feet could grow as well."

"Then we'll have more shoes made!" he replied, and instructed the shoemaker to make her two pairs of sandals, a pair of oxfords, and some riding boots.

"Special boots just for riding?" she asked. She had rarely ever ridden a horse at all, and couldn't imagine her duties at The Post calling for her to do so.

"I'll teach you to ride properly," Baird told her.

She watched the shoemaker watching and zlinning them, obviously curious about their relationship.

What *was* their relationship? Most of the time Jonmair tried to put it out of her mind, for every time she was tempted to think about the future she was forced to face facts: there was no place for her in Sime society. Not the society Baird Axton lived in. She could sleep with him. She could make love with him. But unless they both pledged to a Householding—which she could not imagine Treavor Axton allowing his son to do—she could not marry him.

Perhaps eventually things would change. And in the meantime, she would live from day to day and simply be glad that, thanks to Baird's refusal to take her as his Last Kill, she had those days. She was alive. She had a future. Now all she had to do was figure out how to spend it with Baird.

* * * * * * *

THERE WERE MANY SIMES IN NORLEA WHO CLAIMED to have been in Milily's Shiltpron Parlor on the historic night when Zhag Paget met Tonyo Logan. Baird Axton was one of the few who told the truth when he said it.

Despite the shift in emphasis to gambling, patronage at The Post fell off drastically as the first month after the Last Kill approached its end. Emlu gave her girls a week off.

Jonmair was a blessing, making it possible for Baird to sleep without Need nightmares, even at this time of month. He was thus more stable than most people were now—but oddly glad that the channels at Carre had warned him not to attempt transfer with the lovely Gen this month. She felt frustrated, he knew—but every time he thought of the possibility, he saw her dead beneath his tentacles. And the more he got to know her, the more he wanted her alive.

Business didn't improve much after Norlea's juncts had their first enforced transfers from the channels. Baird's went as well as could be expected—the channel he had this time might not be as skilled as Thea, but because he was a junct pressed into service to handle the sudden huge load, he was able to produce something closer to the satisfaction of the Kill than the Householding channels could. Talk began to circulate about the hastily-trained new channels. Everyone agreed that the junct ones were better than the Householders—a new twist on old prejudices.

Some people got good post reactions, but Emlu's girls still had few customers. Baird found Jonmair's presence pleasant, comforting, but not sexually enticing—and he was certainly not attracted to anyone else.

He had still not succeeded in hiring a shiltpron player for The Post. A really good player could affect Simes as much as the trained Companions in the Householdings—and music did not produce the resentment juncts felt at a Gen's "manipulation."

The ideal solution would be to hire Baird's friend Zhag, who was indisputably the best shiltpron player in Norlea—which meant he was the best in the entire territory. But Zhag was dying, each transfer worse than the last. He never complained, but it was obvious to anyone who saw or zlinned him. He could play for perhaps an hour at most, and then he had to rest. Baird doubted he would live through his next attempt at transfer.

However, Baird had heard good things about another young shiltpron player Milily had found. So, one evening soon after his transfer, when The Post was almost empty, he decided to go and listen.

Milily's was the kind of place you didn't want to see in

daylight if you planned to go there at night. When Baird arrived, the new player had already begun a set. He was good: excellent fingering technique, fine nageric control, hammers in his handling tentacles producing tones of the proper resonance and intensity. He was a consummate technician.

But he didn't have heart.

Zhag had everything that this young man did, plus the ability to make his audience weep, to make them laugh, to lift their spirits even on the brink of attrition. Zhag was what The Post needed—yes, needed—but Zhag was not able to take the job.

So this young man would have to do.

Baird had just decided to talk to him between sets when he zlinned something—a Gen—approach the swinging doors. Not even a Householding Companion would dare this neighborhood alone, and this Gen's nager was not the calm, reassuring presence of a Companion.

It was a male Gen, walking through the doors as if drawn by some irresistible force. He moved with the adolescent awkwardness of someone in the midst of a growth spurt—and indeed, his well-worn denim trousers bared his bony ankles. His clothes were faded and wrinkled and—Baird realized with a shock—of out-Territory design.

A Wild Gen? Here? Was he insane?

The Gen zlinned wary, but not frightened. His field was high—Companion high, Baird realized, carrying far more selyn than an average Gen did—but not replete. At a guess, not knowing how this Gen zlinned at high field, he felt somewhere in mid-cycle. A donor, then.

Baird wondered if this could possibly be Conta's Robert come looking for her, for the troops had not yet been demobilized. But no, this boy was too young to have served in the war, and he certainly had no military bearing.

He came in as if it were perfectly normal for an unescorted Gen to enter a Sime saloon, went to an empty table near the door, set down a small satchel and a battered guitar case, then eased himself into a chair. His nager was intriguing—instead of pulling that odd disappearing trick that Jonmair could do, he sent out a soothing reassurance that it was all right for him to be there.

Then...his field began to do something Baird had never witnessed before. It resonated with the shiltpron music, first picking up the nageric tones and amplifying them, then harmonizing, and finally playing variations around them.

Laterals slipped from their sheaths all over the room, as Simes drank in the amazing performance. Baird shook himself out of it long enough to signal Milily's son. Still a child, he was the only person unaffected. Baird pressed a coin into the child's hand, and whispered, "Go get Zhag. Wake him if he's asleep—tell him to get over here right now. It's really important. Do you understand?"

"Yes, Tuib Baird," the boy replied, and ran out the door.

The shiltpron player came to the end of his set. The young Gen took a deep breath—this was what he was nervous about, not being in a roomful of junct Simes—and went up to the small platform that served as a stage.

"Excuse me," the Gen said to the shiltpron player. "I wonder if you would allow me to sing with you?"

He spoke Simelan fluently, but with an accent. Baird realized that while some of it was in his pronunciation, the Gen's speech reminded him of the way Jonmair spoke—everything in words and voice, without the nageric inflections of Sime speech.

The musician stared at the Gen. "Of course you can't sing with me!" he said. "What do you think this is—a Householding?"

The Gen's shoulders sagged for a moment. Then he squared them and went over to the bar to ask Milily, "Ma'am, is this your establishment?"

"What's it to you, Gen?"

He held out some coins. "This is all the money I have left, and I'm hungry. I'll perform for a meal."

Milily gave a snort. "You think this is a charity? Go on over to Carre. And mind yerself walkin' the streets, or you'll get kilt fore you ever git there." She let her laterals display menacingly.

The Gen only smiled at that. "I'm not afraid, Ma'am. You could use a Gen to make you and your customers feel better."

"Listen, you," said Milily, "buy a drink or get out!"

The Gen sighed and walked back toward his table.

Baird went to the bar, bought a porstan, and carried it to the Gen's table along with a bowl of nuts—all that passed for food in this place. "Here," he said. "I've sent for a friend who plays shiltpron. He'll let you sing with him."

The young Gen's incredible nager washed him in gratitude as he said, "Thank you! You don't know what it means to me! I came to Norlea for the music—it's all I've ever wanted to do."

Then he stuck his hand out, and Baird realized he was offering to shake hands, Gen fashion. At least he waited for Baird to decide whether to touch him. He took the large Gen hand—a calloused hand, he noticed, realizing that the boy had been working his way toward his extremely odd dream.

"I'm Tony Logan," the Gen said.

"Baird Axton. How did you get here?"

"Mostly I walked, but sometimes people gave me rides." He shrugged. "Simes are just like Gens. Be nice to people, and they'll be nice to you."

Baird laughed. "You are the strangest Gen I've ever met!"

"How many do you know?" the boy responded.

"More than most Simes, especially the ones that come to a place like this."

"Ah, but this is where the music is," the boy said, as if that were the only consideration.

Just then two young women entered the shiltpron parlor. They were high-field, Baird zlinned, apparently having had transfer within the past few hours and fared well on what the channels had to offer. Both were nicely post, feeling well and whole. Now they sought shiltpron and porstan to celebrate.

They zlinned the out-Territory Gen curiously as they passed, but at that moment the Gen was more focused on his empty stomach than on pretty girls.

"You're a very good performer," said Baird.

The Gen had just put a handful of nuts into his mouth, so he had to chew and swallow before he could reply, his field for once inflecting his speech with surprise, "But you haven't heard me yet!"

"I've zlinned you. What you were doing was astonishing."

"...what?"

"With your nager."

The Gen stared from huge blue eyes that dominated his still-immature face. Then he said thoughtfully, "Yeah...of course. My field reflected the music in my head."

Baird procured a second bowl of nuts, which the young Gen devoured before Zhag finally arrived. Baird's friend looked and zlinned as if he might fall over at any moment. He came up short practically every month, and by now was a good two weeks off from Baird's schedule. It was depressing to see his old friend so very ill, especially knowing that the cause was his determination to disjunct.

But Zhag was a channel, Baird reminded himself. He had to have direct Gen transfer—no other channel could support a channel—but the channels at Carre had not been able to find a proper match for Zhag. There were lots of matches for renSimes like Baird. Matches like Jonmair.

When Baird introduced them, Zhag zlinned the young Gen and said, "You want to sing?"

"Yes, Sir," the boy replied politely.

Zhag managed a wry laugh. "Call me Zhag."

"I'm Tony," the Gen said.

"Tone-nee?" Zhag stumbled over the Gen name.

"It's short for Antoine," the Gen explained.

"Oh," said Zhag. "Tonyo."

"No," the boy corrected, "Tony."

"Well, Tonyo," Zhag continued as if he hadn't heard him, "let's find out what you can do."

Tonyo drank the rest of his porstan while Zhag set up his shiltpron. His was simpler than the other musician's instrument—just the most basic components—but he didn't require all the extras to create his signature blend of sound and nageric performance.

Then the young Gen joined him on the stage, and Zhag began an old tune everybody knew. Tonyo launched enthusiastically into song—in Simelan, with slightly different lyrics from the ones Baird knew.

The words didn't matter. Tonyo's nager enthralled, twining about the notes like golden vines. Baird zlinned Zhag's amazement. It lasted only a few moments, though, and then the shiltpron player began to test this incredible find.

Tonyo was equal to the test, following Zhag's variations with both voice and field. Everyone in Milily's was riveted. By the second song people were coming in off the street—for besides being pure, sweet, and enticing, Tonyo's voice and nager were also the loudest Baird had ever experienced.

Porstan flowed, Simes let themselves flow with the music, and Baird zlinned post-reaction on every side. He wished that he had brought Jonmair with him.

The two young Sime women moved up near the platform, flirting shamelessly with Tonyo—who flirted shamelessly back. Young the boy might be, but from the evidence tightening his already too-tight denims, he was definitely sexually mature.

Customers bought porstan for both Zhag and Tonyo, and when Zhag had to take a break after nearly two hours, Tonyo took out his guitar and continued alone. He did little more than chord to accompany his singing, but his voice and nager were so dazzling that it didn't matter.

Baird thought about hiring Tonyo on the spot, until after resting only through two songs, Zhag rejoined him on the platform. He said something softly to the boy, Tonyo asked a question in return, and soon they began another number. This time it was something known as the Freeband Raiders Song, although Baird doubted that Raiders ever sang.

"Through the moonless night we ride,
Speed and death our only pride.
Gens can run, but they can't hide.

Life is short and life is hard.
Burn it up and play the cards.
Death is swift—live on guard."

At first Tonyo's nager merely echoed the music, which was a quasi-military marching rhythm. Then he tried to get into the feeling of the words—and failed abysmally.

This young Gen had no idea what it would feel like to burn oneself out, augmenting constantly, raiding for Gens, stealing, killing—and dying in a few weeks or months of system failure or a bullet from the Gen Border Patrol. Tonyo was too innocent for that song.

So Zhag began a song about frustrated desire—and suddenly Tonyo was a virtuoso performer again. Baird listened and zlinned, amused, as Tonyo turned a song about Need into a song of unrequited love—or perhaps just adolescent lust. Zhag let the Gen take it in the direction he understood, and soon everyone in Milily's was feeling post again.

Including Baird. Happy to see his friend inspired by the young Gen, he decided not to try to hire Tonyo away from him. The boy clearly had a great deal to learn—who better to teach him than Zhag Paget? They would be good for one another...and when Zhag's decline reached its inevitable end, Baird could hire Tonyo with a clear conscience.

Zhag launched into a raunchy song about post-syndrome. Tonyo didn't know the words, but he obviously understood what it was about—and in a moment he was singing snatches of words from other songs, half of them in English, again flirting with the two women who were so fascinated by him. The music and the entwining fields lifted Baird's spirits...and, he realized, something else as well. For the first time since that night he had spent with Jonmair in Old Chance's Pleasure Suite, he felt arousal!

But it was Jonmair he wanted, not any of the women at Milily's. So he slipped out into the night, humming to himself as he hurried home.

* * * * * * *

JONMAIR'S DUTIES WERE OVER FOR THE DAY. She was in the sewing room, making a new skirt for her uniform, when Baird came in. He took the cloth from her hands, saying, "That can wait until tomorrow." Then he drew her into his arms.

She had gotten used to the fact that he would not kiss her, so she laid her head on his shoulder and just enjoyed being held. Then he led the way down the stairs. With The Post so empty, they encountered no one—not that the entire staff didn't know she slept in Baird's bed every night. What they didn't know was that nothing ever happened except sleep.

Until tonight.

Jonmair abandoned herself to Baird's desire, boldly stripping him even as his fingers and tentacles undid her buttons. What she had learned he liked in their one night of lovemaking quickly came back, and she gently sucked one of his lateral tentacles, making him gasp with pleasure.

He was as generous a lover as he had been the first time, seeing to her pleasure as much as his own. Afterward, she snuggled against him despite the warmth of the night—it felt so good to have someone not find her a useless nuisance.

"What?" Baird asked, and she realized he had picked up her feelings from her nager.

"It's just...nice to be appreciated," she said, not wanting to spoil the mood.

"Something is bothering you," he insisted. "What is it?"

"One of the customers yelled at me today, and your Dad got mad at me for provoking her."

"Did you?"

"Not intentionally. I could tell she wasn't feeling well, and I guess it showed in my field when I brought her wine. She said she didn't want pity from a Gen."

"Ah." He threaded fingers and tentacles through her hair, just the way she liked. "She could have mistaken sympathy for pity. Or...."

"Or, I might have felt pity?" Jonmair thought about it. "Why would I feel pity for a Sime? You have everything. I'm not even considered a person."

"I consider you a person," said Baird. "So do the Simes and Gens at Carre. You've been spending a good deal of time there. What have they taught you about disjunction?"

"That it won't be easy. Baird, I know some Simes don't like channel's transfer—that it doesn't make them post." The Householders were concerned that the dissatisfied Simes, although a minority, were influential people either by virtue of age or because they were wealthy and accustomed to Choice Kills. "What happened to you tonight, by the way? Or don't you want to tell me?"

"I'll show you," he told her, "but you'll have to wait till tomorrow. Don't change the subject. Should I recommend that Dad keep you behind the scenes till you learn to deal with Sime mood swings?"

"Then how will I learn?" she asked. "Baird, tell me why a Gen would pity Simes."

"Because any Gen who can control her field can wrap a Sime around her little finger," he replied.

"How?"

He gave a chuckle that reverberated in his chest as she rested her head there. "Look at what you just did to me."

"You came home post," she reminded him.

"True—but if my Dad knew I came to you—"

She dared not reply to that, and concentrated on not allowing her hope to show. The uncertainty of her future kept her solidly rooted in the present—she would simply enjoy the fact that Baird wanted her tonight.

In the morning, Baird was gone as usual before Jonmair woke up. But that afternoon he found her back at her sewing, for only the gambling hall had customers at this time of day. "There's someone I want you to meet," he told her.

They took his buggy, with the fine gray mare, and drove away from the center of town toward the dock area, then off on an unpaved side road lined with tumble-down shacks. Baird pulled up at a gate that was off its hinges, resting against the fence, while a young man worked at reconnecting those loose hinges with a rusty screwdriver.

The young man was Gen!

"Hello, Tonyo!" Baird greeted him.

"It's Tony, Mr. Axton," the Gen replied, "though I can't seem to get Zhag to pronounce it right. I'd invite you in, but Zhag's still asleep." He spoke with a peculiar accent.

"Jonmair, this is, uh, Tony Logan," Baird told her. "The Gen I wanted you to meet. Tony, this is Jonmair."

Tony smiled at her, and offered a hand to help her down from the buggy. He was cute, in a coltish way, with curly blond hair and big blue eyes that were his best feature. His hands were calloused, his fair skin tanned from the harsh Gulf sun that had bleached the top layer of his hair to a tow color. He was dressed in shabby, ill-mended denims and a faded shirt that had been high quality when new, and his sandals were of fine out-Territory leathercraft, made for endurance and support.

At a second glance, she realized that the design of his clothing was also out-Territory. A Wild Gen.

"Did someone save you from the Choice Auction, too?" she asked.

"Choice Auction?" He looked blank for a moment, and then said, "Oh! Is that what happened to you?" He looked beyond her to Baird with a big grin. "I'm glad for you. But no, I came into Gulf Territory when the border opened."

Tony led them to a faded wooden table under a tree outside the house. It felt good to get into the shade. The table was warped, the benches uneven, but they had obviously just been swept clean of oak leaves and other debris. "I didn't have any place to go last night, so Zhag took me in. I'm trying to repay him by fixing the place up a little."

"Why did you come in-Territory?" Jonmair asked in wonder.

"I'm a singer," Tony replied. "Mr. Axton, I can't thank you enough for introducing me to Zhag. I suppose I'm no judge, as

I never heard anyone play shiltpron before, but Zhag's really the best, isn't he?"

"Yes, he is—but what you do is equally amazing."

The boy grinned again. "I didn't know I was doing anything but singing till last night!"

"Maybe not while you were performing, but you had to know what you were doing with your field the rest of the time. You said you came all the way from Keon alone."

Jonmair was amazed. "Why would you do that?" she asked.

"My mom came from Norlea," Tony explained. "She established and escaped.... Well, actually, her parents helped get her across the border."

Jonmair's throat tightened. Parents who loved their daughter so much they broke the law and helped her to escape instead of selling her into the Pens for the price of a Choice Kill.

When Baird looked sharply at her, Jonmair realized her dismay had shown in her field, and returned her focus to what Tony was saying. "My mom sings the songs she heard in Norlea—I grew up hearing them and loving them. It's such different music from what you hear in Heartland—and it seemed to draw me here. For a while, I thought it was a sign that I was going to change over. I guess Mom thought so, too, because she made sure I knew Simelan, even if Dad was angry that she taught me."

"Tony," Baird interrupted, "Jonmair has been going to Carre for lessons in conduct around Simes. Where did you learn?"

"Some of it I learned at Keon," he replied, "but they wanted me to stay and be a Companion. I wanted to come to Norlea and be a musician, so I just went out and mingled with Simes. Of course it was safer to do that in Laveen than here, because most of the Simes there are not junct."

He smiled at Jonmair. "But juncts aren't really that different, Jonmair. I mean, look at what they're doing—disjuncting to keep the Unity Treaty."

"Most people aren't doing it for themselves," Baird said. "They're doing it for their children. The collapse of Norwest Territory highlighted the weaknesses in our own selyn delivery system."

Tony nodded. "I know. Even Gulf Territory was less than a week's supply of Gens away from Zelerod's Doom, and Gulf was better off than Nivet. In the Gen Territories we didn't know how bad things were—luckily, or the war would have been right here instead of out west."

Jonmair, protected as a child and then kept ignorant as a Gen, had not known how bad it was, other than grumblings about delayed Gen shipments and late pickups. "By the time of the Unity Treaty," she realized, "it was too late for anything but mass disjunction. Still, I don't know how you have the courage to come here, Tony, when no one knows whether it's going to work."

"It will work," said Baird, "because it has to. I suppose some people won't believe that, hence the strict laws and harsh punishments. But if the vast majority of Simes are not convinced that disjunction is the only right path to take, no punishments will be harsh enough to stop the Kill."

Tony looked from Baird to Jonmair. "I guess you and I can't really understand what Simes are going through, but you really have to admire them, don't you? And help them."

"One on one, you mean?" Jonmair asked, renewing her determination to learn to give transfer to Baird.

"Yes, but also a Gen can make things easier for any Sime, at any time. I suppose you've gotten beyond the lessons I took at Keon, because after my second donation I left for Norlea."

"Mostly they've tried to teach me how to control my field if I get frightened or startled, so I won't provoke anyone, or if I'm angry or sad, so I won't make Simes feel the same feelings."

"Well, yes," said Tony, "but that's all just protection. Haven't they taught you how to make Simes feel good?"

"I think only the Companions are supposed to learn those techniques," said Jonmair.

"Why?" asked Tony.

"Because," Baird answered him, "Simes don't care to be manipulated by Gens."

"Is it manipulation to make somebody feel good?" Tony asked. "Zhag and I made a lot of Simes feel good with our music last night."

So that was what happened to Baird, Jonmair realized.

"Look—" Tony continued, "if your dog dies, you should feel sad. It would be wrong for a Gen to try to stop you."

He's so young, thought Jonmair, *that having his dog die is the worst thing that's ever happened to him*. But still, Baird had brought her here to learn something from this Gen. "I don't think a Gen could stop a Sime from feeling something like that," she said.

"Yes," he said solemnly, "you could. Except maybe for a channel, but then you and I don't have anything to do with channels, do we?"

"Zhag is a channel," said Baird.

Tony blinked. "He is? He didn't tell me."

"I don't suppose you had much time for talking last night."

Tony blushed. "Uh...no, we didn't. I've never drunk that much porstan before—Zhag says he didn't know porstan and shiltpron music could make a Gen as drunk as a Sime. I've never had a hangover like the one I woke up with this morning. Good thing Zhag keeps fosebine on hand."

That was medicine for Simes. "I didn't know fosebine worked on Gens, either," said Jonmair.

"Most awful-tasting stuff," said Tony, screwing up his face, "but I went back to sleep for a couple of hours and woke up feeling fine. Except for being hungry again. I ate the last of Zhag's bread and fruit, and that's when I decided I should do something to earn my keep."

"You'll soon be earning it by performing," said Baird.

"But you were telling me about making Simes feel good," Jonmair began, just as Zhag made his appearance from inside the shack, blinking at the sunshine. Jonmair recognized him: the shiltpron player who had been with Baird on that day in the town square, when Baird had Genjacked her mother's Gen! How long ago that seemed now.

Zhag was about as opposite in appearance to Tony as it was possible to be—not merely Sime to the boy's Gen, but with dark hair, squinting eyes, and the pale skin of someone who only went out at night. He was also still obviously ill, unSimelike in the way he moved. "Tonyo makes me feel good just by being around," said Zhag, although Jonmair had to wonder if anyone who looked as sick as Zhag was capable of feeling "good" under any circumstances.

"Tony," the Gen corrected.

Zhag ignored it. "Hello," he said to Jonmair. Then to Baird, "Is this the woman you told me about?"

"Yes, this is Jonmair."

"Well, if you can do for Baird what Tonyo has already done for me, he will be a lucky man."

"But what do you do?" Jonmair asked Tony.

"It's the other half of what they've already taught you," Tony explained, moving off the bench and onto the table to allow Zhag to have the place where he had been sitting. The Sime sat cautiously, as if every move hurt—little wonder, as he seemed to have hardly any flesh on his bones. Jonmair shifted closer to Baird.

Zhag chuckled. "Oh, you'll do fine," he said.

"What do you mean?" Jonmair asked, puzzled.

"You don't know what you did just then?" asked Zhag.

"You moved to balance the fields," said Tony. "I didn't know I was doing it either, until the channels at Keon pointed it out to me."

"What? I didn't do anything."

"Yes, you did," said Tony, pulling his legs up to sit tailor-fashion on the table. "It's instinctive among Gens who live with Simes. We move so that our fields blend most comfortably for the Simes. There are two Simes and two Gens here, so we can achieve a perfect balance. Last night, I wanted to drift all over the saloon, trying to balance it all alone."

"Just don't think about it," said Zhag, "unless you're also planning to be a performer?"

"No—but I know what you mean, Tony," said Jonmair, realizing now what had happened with the woman yesterday. "When I'm serving, I feel as if every Sime is somehow calling to me, and I should try to do something for all of them."

"Well, until enough Gens mingle with the Sime population in Gulf, it's going to be that way for all of us," said Tony. "In some situations it's best to try not to be noticed."

"That one I figured out for myself while I was in the Pen," said Jonmair.

Tony shuddered. "It's amazing that you can be so comfortable with Simes after that experience."

"I grew up among Simes," Jonmair explained. "All the adults were Sime, except for the occasional Pen Gen in the street." She remembered the feel of her mother's tentacles braiding her hair—then shielded her emotions as the sense of betrayal overwhelmed her once again.

"Jonmair," Zhag said gently, "you don't have to shield to that extent. In fact, both of you could use more nageric inflection in your speech. You sound like children."

"Nageric inflection?" asked Tony.

"You do it when you sing, Tonyo. Just do the same thing when you talk—don't hide the feelings that go with your words. Simes aren't as delicate as you think we are!"

"After all," said Baird, "we zlin one another's feelings all the time. The only feelings likely to get a Gen into trouble are pain or fear. You don't have to shield anything else."

"It makes me feel good to zlin Tonyo's simple good health," added Zhag. "Go ahead and be yourself, Jonmair. It's quite a lovely self, as I'm sure Baird will agree."

* * * * * * *

JONMAIR TOOK THE LESSONS TO HEART, and found them increasingly useful. Still, on the day that would mean turnover for most Simes in Norlea, Baird insisted on taking Jonmair away from The Post and the city in general, on the pretext of visiting the local porstan brewery. There was no real reason for Baird to take Jonmair on such an errand, except that he wanted her with him. That made her feel good.

Along the way, he corrected her riding, as well as pointing out landmarks by which a Gen could follow the road back to Norlea, eastward to Lanta, or northward to Nashul and Laveen. "Dad took Elendra or me on all his trips when we were kids," said Baird. "He used to make us choose the road at each cross-roads, and figure out the direction by the sun."

Tears choked Jonmair's throat and blurred her vision. "What's wrong?" Baird asked.

"Nothing's wrong," Jonmair managed to get out. "Your dad loved his children, that's all."

"What?"

"If you had established, and had to run for the border, he prepared you as much as he possibly could. My parents never taught me anything like that—they never even took us kids outside of town if they could help it."

Baird shook his head in puzzlement. "I never realized it...but you're right."

"He couldn't tell you what he was doing, Baird," Jonmair told him. "Kids talk. If parents explained what those lessons were for, children might say something in school, and get their parents into trouble. But you don't know how lucky you are. Your dad may be hard to please, but he loves you."

"I just wish I weren't such a disappointment to him," said Baird, and Jonmair rode beside him in silence, wishing there were more she could do.

Baird reached turnover—the point at which he used up half the selyn in his system and began the long descent toward Need—sometime during that morning, but he showed no reaction other than that same worry about disappointing his father that he had on every other day. When they finished at the brewery, they rode back by a road where Baird knew of a blackberry patch perfectly ripe at this time of year. They gathered a basket full, scratching their hands and purpling their fingers with the luscious fruit. Then they found a spot to spread a blanket while the horses cropped the soft grass.

Jonmair spread out the berries, bread, apples, and cheese, but Baird had no appetite. Unbothered, he smiled at her. "You made me forget all about turnover. Thank you."

"I didn't do anything," said Jonmair, letting her own hunger show so that she could get him to consume a thin slice of cheese and two berries.

"I'm beginning to think the Companions are right," said Baird. "Simes ought to have Gens with them all the time."

But it wasn't that simple, as they found when they returned to town. The direct route to The Post would have taken them through the busy weekly market, but Baird knew better than to take Jonmair through a crowd of junct Simes today. They detoured onto a narrow side street where people had left horses and wagons awaiting their owners. Baird rode ahead of Jonmair, charting their way around the obstacles.

It was early afternoon, the peak of market day just over, although the stands would be open for another hour. The occasional shopper came out to their street with packages, and rode away. A family with two young children began loading a wagon, the children tired and whining in a way that reminded Jonmair painfully of her own younger brother and sister. The parents, irritable with turnover, snapped at them, causing the younger child, a girl, to start to wail.

Over the child's screaming, though, Jonmair heard something else: shouts, the cracking of whips—

Baird's gray mare suddenly reared, backing against Jonmair's bay gelding. Although well exercised, her horse had enough spirit to nip at the gray's hindquarters.

Jonmair pulled on the reins and her mount's head came up, but he danced sideways in the narrow street. As she was trying to bring him around to move forward again, the noise in the marketplace increased—screams, more angry shouting, and crashing sounds of tables and tents being overturned.

Baird shouted, "Hurry! We have to get away—there's been

a Kill!"

Even as he spoke, Simes poured out of the alleys between the buildings, fleeing the riot in the marketplace. The narrow street was soon choked with horses, wagons, and people on foot trying to get away—followed by those who wanted nothing more than a good fight!

Jonmair struggled to control her horse and her fear as people came between her and Baird.Children screamed as their parents dragged them away.

People attacked one another at random, and folks who a moment before had wanted nothing but to get away turned and fought back. Untended horses reared and kicked.

Somehow, Jonmair found that curtain she could draw around herself—thank goodness for the months of practice!

But when she did so, Baird cried out in panic, "Jonmair!" and redoubled his efforts to reach her.

"Go ahead!" she shouted. "I'll follow you!"

But he wasn't listening! In an emergency, he was zlinning—and that left him vulnerable to everything in the ambient nager! Jonmair kicked out of her stirrups, slipped off her horse, and wormed through the crowd on foot.

"Gen!" somebody shouted.

"Where?" someone else asked in confusion. Her shield was working—the problem was, while she shielded herself, she could not shield Baird. Where had he gone?

Jonmair struggled toward where she had last seen him—when suddenly a hand grasped her arm and tentacles wrapped about her wrist. "Mine!" exclaimed her Sime captor—a conservatively-dressed woman who on any other day might have been teaching school or keeping accounts for a business.

It took Jonmair only a moment to realize that her shield would not get her away, although it might prevent the woman from trying to kill her. The woman was not in Need, any more than Baird was—her laterals were out, ronaplin smearing them with desire, but it was a false desire. The glands were not swollen. She had a good two weeks of selyn left.

What had Zhag and Tony said? She should be able to use her field to calm this woman down if only she didn't let the wrong emotion show. No fear. And no pity. Just....

She let go of her shield and said, "It's all right. I won't deny you—but you don't really need me right now, do you?"

The woman gasped, and her grip tightened bruisingly.

Gritting her teeth, Jonmair tried to ignore the pain as from the woman's unfocused eyes she realized her captor was hyper-conscious—only zlinning, not using her other senses. She was reacting to Jonmair's field, not hearing her words.

How to get her to hear, so she could reason with her?

Even as she thought it, though, the woman's eyes focused on her, widened—and then the woman dropped Jonmair's wrist as if it had burned her! "Wer-Gen!" she gasped.

That was what the juncts called the Companions in the Householdings—the Gens who could not be killed.

But they could be murdered!

The woman lunged for Jonmair's throat.

But just then a strong arm came around her, and she was lifted safely up before Baird on his gray mare. "You belong to me!" he said through gritted teeth—and fought his way through the packed street, using his horse as a weapon. Jonmair clung to him, horrified to see two people go down under the flying hoofs—but Baird guided the horse through, bursting out of the narrow street into Norlea's square, where he recklessly blud-geoned his way through the traffic with the beautiful animal.

It was only a short distance to The Post, however, and although the groom tsk-tsked when he took the mare after Baird slid down, still holding Jonmair, he dared not say anything.

The bells of police wagons rang in the square as Treavor Axton came out into the courtyard. "What's going on?" he demanded.

Baird continued to hold onto Jonmair as he replied, "There's a riot on Third Street—it started in the market."

"We got caught in it by accident," Jonmair added. "A Sime woman tried to capture me, but Baird rescued me."

"Where's the horse you were riding?" Baird's father asked.

"Don't send anyone into that fighting!" Baird said, finally starting to sound like himself again. "We had to leave Diamond behind. If he doesn't find his way home I'll go get him later."

Within an hour the city was abuzz with news: the inevitable had happened, less than two months into the grand attempt to disjunct the Sime population. A public Kill in the Norlea marketplace, followed by a riot. Over fifty people had been arrested before it was over, and while most would only pay a fine for destruction of property, one man was in jail, awaiting trial over an illegal Kill.

Treavor Axton grilled Baird and Jonmair as to why she had required rescuing. "Why did you go into the middle of a riot?"

"The riot came to us," Jonmair explained. "We were just riding down Third Street and were caught when people started pouring out of the market. Baird zlinned the Kill, and helped me get away."

Baird's father both zlinned her and looked her over, noting the bruises on her right arm where the woman's tentacles had held her. "How did you manage not to get killed?"

"The woman wasn't in Need. It was just turnover, and then the riot. I was able to calm her down—but then," she admitted, "she wanted to murder me for being able to do that. That's when Baird rescued me."

Treavor Axton shook his head. "You are a dangerous little bitch, aren't you? If we lose a perfectly good horse over you, I'll take it out of your hide."

But they didn't lose Diamond—in fact, a police detective named Kerrk recognized the animal and the logo of The Post carved into his saddle, and brought him back that evening.

Another Sime of Treavor Axton's generation, Jonmair recalled seeing Kerrk once or twice at the poker table with Baird's father. He must have been handsome in his youth, for his worn face was still attractive. Deep lines surrounded his mouth and haunted eyes as large and blue as Tony's. He questioned Baird, all the while zlinning Jonmair curiously.

Kerrk was clearly suffering from a bad turnover, and when he zlinned her Jonmair had to strongly resist trying to soothe his jangled nerves. His presence was so strong—

"You're a channel," she said. "You can zlin that Baird is telling you the truth."

Hooded blue eyes bored into her and his laterals moved restlessly in her direction as he suddenly focused all his senses on the Gen who had dared speak to him. "I am not a Householder," he said.

"You're at the same stage of your cycle as Baird," Jonmair explained, "but I feel your discomfort more than his. The only cause I know for that is that you are a channel. You should have a Companion."

"Is that what you are?" he asked suspiciously.

"Not yet," she admitted, not daring to speak publicly her plan to become Baird's transfer mate.

Kerrk shook his head. "My partner has been telling me for years that the Householders could make my life easier. But I don't want a Gen in my way."

Jonmair promptly shut her nager off from the ambient, even though it made Baird wince.

"Yes, I see," said Kerrk, "a little wer-Gen in training." Only a man taller than Baird, Jonmair thought, would call her "little."

But the detective could not read the amusement in her field while she was damping it, so he continued, "Don't stop protecting Baird. You're right: I am a channel, although I don't use my secondary selyn system to—" a slight shudder, "—give transfer. The Tecton lorshes decided I'm too old to be dragooned into doling out fake Kills."

Jonmair recognized another conflicted Sime, this one entrusted with enforcing the law, even when the law suddenly changed. She carefully suppressed her sympathy while he completed questioning Baird. Then she allowed her field to support Baird once more.

Kerrk turned to her. "Tell me about the attack on you."

"I wasn't hurt," she said. "Baird rescued me from a woman

who was angry that she couldn't kill me."

Those hooded blue eyes tried to stare into her soul again. "A woman," Kerrk said. "You don't say a junct, or even a Sime."

"Obviously she was both," said Jonmair, "but it wasn't her fault. There was a Kill, and then a riot. Emotions got out of control, and just then she encountered me, right in her path. Inspector, I don't know who she was, and I don't think it would be right for you to arrest her."

Kerrk rubbed his eyes and then ran fingers and tentacles through his hair, which was thick and curly with just enough color left in the white strands to show that he had been blond. "It's unnatural," he said. "You don't even know that woman, she would have killed you if she could, and here you are protecting her. All I want to do is question her. If you won't press charges, I can't arrest her."

"I won't press charges," Jonmair assured him. "What happened was as much my fault as hers. By next month I'll have enough training not to provoke a Sime that way. Deal with the Kill that did happen, not the ones that didn't."

Kerrk had also investigated the Kill, but gossip quickly outran any official report of the incident. By the next morning it seemed everyone knew the story, with only some differences in interpretation. The local Genfarm owner had brought a worker Gen to help sell the farm's produce on Market Day. Something had spooked the untrained Gen, resulting in the Kill—and the Kill had started the riot.

Of course at The Post everyone said the Kill was an accidental death—that the Sime had been provoked—but this would be the first test of the new laws in Norlea. Word was, in Lanta the Kill still occurred regularly—that Gen corpses were often found, faces frozen in the rictus of fear, but no one ever found out who was responsible.

Norlea was surely more civilized than Lanta!

"How could a Genfarmer, of all people, be stupid enough to take a Gen into the marketplace yesterday?" asked Baird, cutting to the heart of the matter. "That was criminal negligence."

Jonmair looked at him in admiration, although Treavor Axton scowled. They were seated at the breakfast table, drinking kafi while Jonmair ate.

"Make up your mind, Boy," said Baird's father. "Do you want Gens living with Simes or not?"

"Living with us, of course," said Baird easily, refusing to respond to the older man's irritation. Jonmair had soothed him through the night, and this morning he was himself again. "But they have to be given time to learn. And there have to be more of them, not fewer."

"Baird is right," said Jonmair. "If there had been Companion Gens all over the marketplace, they could have controlled the ambient and prevented a riot."

Treavor Axton shuddered and spoke pointedly to his son. "You're letting that Gen take over your life."

"And feeling all the better for it," Baird countered. "Zlin me, Dad. You're tense and jumpy, while I'm as stable as I was pre-turnover. If you had a Gen like Jonmair—"

"I do have Jonny. It's my ward, and I plan to get rid of it as soon as the legislature provides the procedure."

"My name is Jonmair," she reminded him, pleased that he was as frustrated at the legislature's delay as she was. She wondered if his trying to rename her was as hopeless as Tony Logan trying to get Zhag to use his right name. It was more important to her than to the Wild Gen, for Tony could go back where he came from and be a free citizen with all rights, any time he wanted to. All Jonmair possessed was her name, and so it had become a contest of wills with Baird's father.

Treavor Axton glared at her. He was in far worse shape than his son, the lines in his face carved deep by the stress of an unsatisfactory transfer followed yesterday by what she could only surmise was a bad turnover.

Suddenly Jonmair was sorry for her annoyance. It wasn't Treavor Axton's fault that he had grown up junct. The older the Sime, the harder it was to disjunct—and she really didn't want him to suffer. She remembered what she had learned yesterday, how he had secretly prepared his children with the knowledge to escape to Gen Territory had they established.

"Stop that!" he snapped at her, and she saw his laterals retract tightly. "I won't have Gens pushing me around with their nager!" He got up and stalked out.

"You're not afraid at all," said Baird.

"Of your dad? He's not a bad man, Baird. The same pragmatism that made him take you to Carre to save your life will make him accept Gens when he sees what they can do for Simes."

Baird nodded. "But what about most people? I'm worried, Jonmair. When the rioting was in Lanta, I thought we'd be safe here. But now it's come to Norlea—and yesterday was only the beginning."

CHAPTER SIX
ZHAG AND TONYO

BAIRD WENT TO SEE ZHAG PAGET AGAIN two days later, after the shiltpron player's next scheduled transfer...to see if he had survived. He had been to another performance at Milily's a few days before, and almost not gotten in, the place was so crowded. Zhag and Tonyo were the talk of Norlea—but Zhag could hardly manage to play a full set despite the nageric support of his Gen. Fearing to find out that Zhag was dead, Baird did not take Jonmair with him that afternoon when he rode over to the shack his friend called home.

His heart sank at what he saw: the yard was cleaned up, all the brush was cleared away, and a patch of mismatched shingles now covered the hole in the roof. The gate was back on its hinges, straight and oiled, and the old warped table and benches under the tree had been scrubbed down. His first thought was that the landlord was preparing for a new tenant.

But then he heard music drifting from inside the house—a guitar chord, a shiltpron tone, a delicate harmony that drifted into jangled discord. A burst of laughter erupted into the ambient. Laughter from two men.

But it was...disembodied, as if there were no people in the house—at least no people he could zlin as he walked up to the front steps, leaving his horse tethered to the fence.

In the heat, all the doors and windows were open. "Hi, Baird! Come on in!" Zhag called. Suddenly the two men in the house "appeared" on the ambient as they turned their attention to their visitor. It was something Baird had only witnessed when a channel and Companion were focused on one another.

Baird could hardly believe the evidence of his laterals. Gone was the sick, feeble man he had feared to find dead. In his place was Zhag Paget as Baird had first known him—healthy and brimming with energy.

And Tonyo—

The young Gen glowed with well-being. He was low-field now, although the power in his nager still outshone any Pen Gen Baird had ever encountered. He grinned and said, "Yes—we did it! I'm Zhag's Companion now."

"That's...just great," Baird said inadequately.

Zhag got up and poured Baird a cool glass of tea laced with fruit juice. He laughed again, saying, "I've never felt this good in my life—not even after my First—" He broke off in embarrassment.

But "First Kill," said Tonyo. "It's all right, Zhag. You're disjunct now. It doesn't bother me that you used to kill." He looked up at Baird very seriously. "Zhag almost died shenning himself to keep from hurting me."

"And then this young fool risked his life to save mine," said Zhag. "So I suppose we're even."

"What happened?" Baird asked.

"We were in the marketplace when that Kill happened the other day," said Tonyo. "I guess I had bought the party line: the Kill is outlawed, so it's over. I'd never seen it happen, certainly wasn't expecting it in the market in broad daylight, and I... reacted."

"You took Tonyo into the marketplace on that day?" Baird knew how fond Zhag was of the Gen boy—why had he taken him into danger?

Zhag shook his head. "I was an idiot. I'm so far off from the Last Kill schedule that I never gave it a thought. And I forget that Tonyo's been in-Territory only two months. Most of the time he zlins as if he'd been born in a Householding."

"It all worked out for the best," said Tonyo. "Zhag needed a good transfer, I'm his match—it was inevitable. But if I hadn't gotten scared when I witnessed the Kill, I wouldn't have gained the trust in Zhag that I needed to be able to give him transfer."

Only his vocal accent now gave away Tonyo's out-Territory origins—he had taken Zhag's advice to allow his field to underscore his speech. He spoke like a Companion now, distinctively Gen, but pleasantly so. Thus Baird recognized that he was not misusing the word "Need." He meant that he had needed to trust Zhag as much as Zhag had needed selyn.

Baird looked at Zhag. "You attacked Tonyo?"

Tonyo's field flared defensively. Zhag lifted a tentacle to forestall his outburst and said, "Yes. That reflex doesn't disappear with disjunction."

"Just the Kill reflex," said Tonyo. "Mr. Axton, I was no help. First I saw the Kill, and then Zhag grabbed me—I was sheer, pants-wetting terrified. I forgot everything I know about handling myself around Simes. It was Zhag who shenned out of the Kill." He shook his head. "If he weren't disjunct, I'd be dead."

Baird could zlin several emotions in the Gen's field: regret, embarrassment, residual fear at what had almost happened, but most of all a warm combination of pride and trust in Zhag. *Will anyone ever feel that way about me?* Baird wondered. *Can I ever deserve such trust?*

Tonyo continued, "Zhag collapsed—and I forgot to be afraid. Thank goodness there were some nice folks in the market who helped me get him away from the fighting, and then when it was all over they helped me take him to Carre. The channels explained about us being matchmates. They didn't want me to try to give Zhag transfer till next month, but I was afraid—" He looked for a word that didn't exist, to differentiate types of fear. "Not afraid of being killed. I was afraid Zhag would die. He was so weak."

"I know," said Baird. "I hesitated to come here today, for fear he hadn't survived another bad transfer."

Tonyo grinned. "You don't ever have to worry about that

again!" He got up and refilled their tea glasses, then began puttering in the cupboard. "I hope you don't mind if I put out some lunch—I am *so hungry* today!"

Zhag joked, "So what makes it different from any other day?" Then, as Tonyo was distracted, he said softly to Baird, "Zlin him."

"I have," said Baird, and added in a combination of amazement and amusement, "He's as post as any Sime."

Zhag chuckled. "You should have been at Milily's last night. At least half the crowd was at turnover, and Tonyo had them post." Controlling his nager, he added, "Some of the channels and Companions from Carre decided to come to the performance. It got...pretty raunchy."

Tonyo returned to the table with bread, nut butter, and an orange. He sectioned the fruit and put it in the center of the table. Even Baird, riding on Tonyo's hunger, ate a segment of the orange, while Zhag ate three pieces and half a slice of bread that Tonyo spread with the nut butter before handing it to him. "Thea enjoyed the performance," Tonyo said teasingly to Zhag. "But I think she enjoyed your performance after the show even more."

Baird recalled that the channel, Thea ambrov Carre, had become good friends with Zhag. From Zhag's blush and the way he sharply controlled his field, he gathered that last night their relationship had gone beyond friendship.

Tonyo piled as much filling into his own sandwich as the bread would hold. "What are you embarrassed about?" he asked. "Thea's really nice—and don't try to tell me you don't like her as much as she likes you." He took a bite.

"Forget it, Tonyo," Zhag warned. "Thea and I are from different worlds."

The Gen answered that with a derisive flick of his nager as he paused to swallow the sticky nut butter before answering, "And you and I are not? It's a whole new world, Zhag. All the old rules are over."

As they talked, the Gen consumed the rest of the fruit, his

sandwich, and the other half of the slice of bread he had prepared for Zhag. Tonyo made no apologies about "eating like a Gen," as Jonmair sometimes did. Come to think of it, it made sense for Gens to eat far more than Simes if they were to convert nutrients into enough selyn for two people every month.

Simes used nutrients from food only for growth and repair of tissues—they drew energy for living from selyn alone. Zhag was thin almost to emaciation—Tonyo was right to get as much food into him as he could to restore the same health to his body that now shone in his field.

It didn't seem to bother Zhag to let Tonyo control him. When the Gen got up to put the food away, Baird asked Zhag, "Aren't you worried about being dependent on Tonyo?"

"Simes have always been dependent on Gens for survival," said Zhag.

"Yes, but we controlled them. What if Tonyo decides he doesn't want to give you transfer?"

"How could I ever decide such a thing?" Tonyo asked.

Baird blinked. "What do you mean?"

"You've never given a Gen a good transfer, have you Mr. Axton?"

"Given—?" The syntax was possible in Simelan, but unthinkable. Gens gave, or were taken from. Simes received.

"It's completely addictive," Tonyo explained, coming to stand behind Zhag with his hands on the Sime's shoulders. "I can't imagine going without what Zhag shared with me yesterday." His field underscored the truth of his words.

"Ask the Companions," Zhag told Baird. "They all say the same thing. So no, I'm not afraid Tonyo will refuse me transfer. I'm afraid of something happening to him, as he is such a daredevil, but I'm not afraid he won't want transfer next month."

Baird looked up at the young Gen, then at his friend Zhag, and zlinned the interaction between them. They had been together less than a month—but their bond zlinned as if it had been building for a lifetime.

"Let's play Mr. Axton the song we've been practicing,"

suggested Tonyo.

"I'd like to hear it," said Baird. "And then I'd like to talk to you about coming to work for me."

* * * * * * *

JONMAIR WAS PLEASED TO HEAR that Zhag and Tony were coming to perform at The Post, especially when Baird told her they had become transfer mates. She liked both of them, was delighted to see how much better Zhag was, and wanted that example before Baird every day. She wanted to do for him what Tony did for Zhag. And more.

When Tony complained about not being able to find clothes to fit him, Jonmair said, "Me, too. The Householdings are the only places where they make clothes that will fit Gens— but you require costumes for performing, not work clothes or Householding cloaks. I'd be happy to make them for you."

"That would be great!" said Tony. "Can you make something for both of us? Zhag's clothes aren't really up to the standards of this place, either," he said, making a sweeping gesture that included the stage, the crystal chandelier, and the elegant tables and chairs of the main salon where they were rehearsing.

Zhag didn't seem to mind Tony speaking for him, Jonmair noticed. He was a quiet man most of the time, surprisingly so for someone who earned a living by public performance.

"Whatever you make for Zhag, though," added Tony, "be sure to allow room to let it out. I intend to get him to eat more."

"More!" exclaimed Zhag. "I'm already eating enough for three people."

"Three Simes, maybe," said Tony. "Gens are people— remember?"

"If I forget, you'll remind me," Zhag told him, and went back to noodling on his shiltpron.

Zhag never had the outbursts of anger that the Axtons, father and son, both exhibited—or that caused fights to break out all over town. Jonmair hoped that Zhag's attitude showed how all

Simes would be once they disjuncted. It was nerve-wracking for Gens never to know when a perfectly innocent act or word would irritate nearby Simes.

She studied the two men, as different as night and day even to Gen senses, and tried to think of appropriate costuming. Zhag had hazel eyes, she saw now. Months of bad transfers could not be wiped out overnight. There was still darkness and puffiness under his eyes, but he no longer squinted as if his head ached, or moved as if he might collapse. Jonmair saw the makings of a handsome man.

Tony was in glowing health, and his face, oddly, seemed more mature than only days before. Perhaps it was taking responsibility for keeping Zhag alive and healthy. Whatever it was, it looked good on him—but his threadbare clothes did not.

"We'll have to go shopping," said Jonmair, "and find the right material for costumes."

Would they really let her do this? In her childhood dreams she had designed elegant ladies' dresses—but wasn't designing costumes even more exciting?

"What's wrong with just a nice shirt and trousers?" asked Zhag. "Dress Tonyo up if you want to—he loves being the center of attention."

"We're a team, Zhag," Tony responded. "Let's hear what Jonmair has in mind. I don't think she'll put you in pink spangles."

Jonmair giggled at the image, but responded, "No—but I would like to put you in complementary costumes if you'll let me. Day and night—the same outfits, but on Zhag's embroider or applique the moon, on Tony's the sun."

"Tonyo," said the Gen.

"What? Why would you let Zhag change your name?" asked Jonmair. "He doesn't own you."

"He didn't change it—*I* did," Tonyo replied. "It's just a stage name anyway. 'Antoine' is the name my mother gave me, the same in either territory. I have a new life in-Territory. So I've taken the in-Territory version of my name."

Jonmair looked at Zhag, who was smiling—but not in the triumph she could imagine on Treavor Axton's face if she capitulated to his attempts to take away the only thing she had left of her former self.

But then, Tonyo had come here of his own accord—he had never been sold into the Pens or been legally less than a person. Jonmair would never give up her name. Furthermore, she determined to parlay the chance Zhag and Tonyo were giving her into the start of a career. One day her name would be synonymous with exquisite design.

Jonmair took the two men into Jax street, to the shops where her mother had always purchased yard goods. She started with the larger store—but the moment Jonmair began searching through the bolts of cloth a sales clerk came running up, saying to Zhag, "Control those Gens! Don't let them paw my merchandise. They'll get it all dirty!"

Tonyo scowled at the clerk, saying nothing—but from the woman's expression Jonmair suspected he had done something very rude with his nager.

The clerk glared at him, but still spoke to Zhag. "Get those animals out of here!"

"I'm certainly not going to spend my money where my friends are not welcome," Zhag responded, and they headed for the door. Behind them, Jonmair heard the clerk gasp, and then begin to sneeze uncontrollably.

Although she could hear the laughter in his voice, Zhag said softly, "Tonyo, stop that! We don't want to give reason for juncts to look down on Gens."

Out on the street, Jonmair asked, "You really made her sneeze?"

"One of the easiest Companion's tricks," Tonyo told her. "Handy for incapacitating a Sime without hurting her."

Zhag said, "You had no reason to incapacitate that woman. She's just ignorant. Ignorance is curable if you don't give her reason to resist."

At the second store the clerk was male, and didn't even allow them to reach the bolts of cloth before he descended on them. "If you please, Tuib," he said obsequiously to Zhag, "we cannot allow Gens or children to run loose in the shop. I have a holding room where they can be perfectly comfortable while I show you—"

Zhag interrupted, "I know nothing about choosing materials. Jonmair is the costume designer for my partner and me. If you like, Tonyo and I will wait in the holding room while she shops."

The man's eyes nearly popped from his head as he sought for polite words to respond. Jonmair joined in the pretense that Zhag was making sense. "No," she said, "I need both gentlemen with me so I can see which colors and fabrics will look best on them," and she moved toward the goods on display as if it were the most natural thing in the world for a Gen to shop for a pair of Sime/Gen partners.

The Sime clerk had to augment to get in front of her—but she won, in a way, because he addressed her directly. And as if she were in charge! "You get out of here, and take those— those—"

"We're transfer mates," Tonyo supplied.

"Perverts!" the clerk retorted, completely losing his composure. "Leave at once, all of you!"

They left, but at the door, Tonyo could not resist turning around to announce, "In case you hadn't heard, perversion is now the law of the land!"

Zhag grabbed his wayward partner by the bicep and yanked him out into the street. "That doesn't help, Tonyo!"

"Well, after we open at The Post, when those lorshes realize that it was Zhag Paget they insulted today, they'll never live it down."

"You may be right," said Jonmair, her momentary triumph fading, "but what are you going to wear for opening night? Zhag, I may be able to find something among the costumes at The Post to alter for you, but everything there was made for Simes. It's all far too small for Tonyo."

"Let's go to the Keon Emporium," said Zhag. "They have everything you could want—and at much better prices."

The large, wealthy Householding had opened stores in Gulf's main cities years ago—and their quality goods at bargain prices had caused many Simes to overcome their prejudices and buy from Householders. Jonmair's parents had not been among them, though, and she had never set foot in the place.

In the big department store there were both Sime and Gen clerks, all wearing Keon red tabards and neat name tags. No one questioned a Sime and two Gens shopping together. Tonyo noticed a display of denim trousers and shorts on special offer. "Look!" he exclaimed. "Both Sime and Gen sizes!"

Indeed, everything in the ready-made department was designed for both larities. These were work clothes and basics— they quickly equipped both men with plain trousers in black and brown, and Tonyo with two pairs of denims to replace the threadbare ones he wore. Jonmair's job would be much easier if she had to make them only shirts and vests or cumberbunds to start out with.

"How about some shorts, Zhag?" asked Tonyo. "Don't Simes feel the heat like Gens?"

"Not as much," Zhag replied, "either heat or cold. But it is the hottest part of the year, and come to think of it, I'm feeling the heat since our transfer." He smiled apologetically at Jonmair. "I was cold practically all the time when I was ill. Do you mind if I take the time to get some lighter clothes?"

"I have all afternoon," she replied. "This is fun, actually." She didn't tell them it was like playing dressup with live dolls.

Jonmair helped them choose shirts, as well—and Tonyo decided to wear one of his new outfits. "Maybe we'd have had a more favorable welcome in those other stores if I didn't look so disreputable."

"Tonyo," said Zhag, "looking is not the first thing any Sime does on meeting *you*!" He paid for their purchases in ready-made and they proceeded to the fabric department. The Sime clerk was available to answer questions, but expressed no surprise that Jonmair knew what she was doing.

There was an amazing selection, from Arensti-winning Zeor

designs down to the least expensive cottons. No wonder even before Unity this place had had junct customers.

Jonmair found sapphire blue silk, which she held up to each man in turn. Like many brunettes, Zhag looked good in blue, while the material picked up and emphasized the color of Tonyo's eyes. "Perfect!" said Jonmair. "I'll make you both shirts from this."

Then she went back to shirt patterns, thinking of how The Post used vests that could be worn over dresses or shirts and skirts or trousers as their livery. "I should make something like that for you two," she said, searching the pattern book for designs that would serve the same purpose but be different from The Post's livery.

She found a kind of waist-length sleeveless shirt. In the hottest weather it could be worn alone, and in cooler seasons over another shirt. She put a pattern for it in Zhag's size on the growing stack of purchases, and then, "Look, Tonyo! Patterns in Gen sizes, too!"

Including, she realized, dress patterns she could adapt for herself. When Zhag noticed her looking longingly at one for an evening ensemble, he said, "That would look beautiful on you. Go ahead and get the pattern and material for it."

"I don't have any money," she said.

"We'll buy it for you," said Tonyo. "You can wear it to our opening night."

Among the imported Zeor fabrics, Jonmair found gold and silver tissue. It was outrageously expensive, but she required only a small piece of each.

There were too many packages even for all eight of Zhag's handling tentacles, but Tonyo pulled a string bag from his pocket and put all the notions into it. "Gen tentacles," he explained, making Jonmair giggle. She had never seen such a self-assured Gen, even at Carre. The Companions were secure enough, especially inside the Householding, but none had Tonyo's brashness. "You should have one of these," he added, glancing around.

Sure enough, string bags in different colors hung on a hook

near the till. Tonyo's was brown, but he picked out a pink one for Jonmair. As she put the materials for her new dress into it, she was forcefully reminded of the day she had first seen Baird, when Mama had been so impatient with her for dropping things while she tried to control her younger brother and sister. How long ago that day seemed now—another lifetime.

When Zhag again paid for their goods, Jonmair wondered if Tonyo had any money of his own. On their way back to The Post, she got up the courage to ask, "Does Treavor Axton have you on the payroll, Tonyo?"

"It's the same as it was at Milily's," the Gen replied. "He pays Zhag and me as an act. We know it's a way of not recognizing me as a person, but for the moment it's not worth making a fuss. But if you're asking why Zhag's paying the bills for both of us, right now he can have a bank account and I can't, so he writes the checks. I just carry walking around money," and he jingled the coins in his pocket.

"But you keep the books, so you know exactly what I owe you," said Zhag.

Tonyo added, "Zhag insists on splitting fifty/fifty with me, which isn't fair, especially now that my meals are included at The Post."

Letting go the strange idea—and then the question of why it should seem strange—of a Gen keeping accounts, Jonmair focused on Tonyo's afterthought. "Why isn't it fair for each of you to get half of what you're paid as an act?"

"Because Zhag has to pay me for my selyn as well. If I get half of our performance money, he ought to get half of our transfer payment."

"I'm the one who can't live without selyn," Zhag said reasonably.

"But this whole selyn-tax thing is a setup for failure," said Tonyo. "Jonmair, you can see it, can't you? Junct Simes already resent being deprived of the Kill, and Gens being set free. Look at our reception in the shops today. On top of that, Gens get paid for both their work and their selyn—how can Simes help resenting it when a Gen can do nothing but donate selyn, and still earn enough to live on?"

"You think all Gens are like you, Tonyo," Jonmair told him, forcefully reminded that she had little control over her own destiny. "We're not. First of all, we're not actually free. We're the wards of whoever owned us the day the Unity Treaty went into effect. That's why people expect Zhag to tell you what to do—they think you're his ward. Treavor Axton is responsible for me. He has to feed and house and clothe me whether he wants to or not, so he collects the payments for my selyn to pay for all that."

Tonyo frowned. "But he makes you work, too. And what is he doing about your education?"

"I finished school before I established. I have as much education as I require for what I planned to do: be a fashion designer."

"Planned?" asked Tonyo, making Jonmair face the reason she had used the past tense.

"As a Gen, I can't run a business," she said as they entered The Post with their packages, and went up to the sewing room on the third story.

"Today," said Tonyo with a shrug. "But the legislature is working on giving Gens full citizenship—although I don't know why they didn't just do it when the Treaty went into effect. Then you could do whatever you pleased."

"And where would I get a start?" she asked. "I have no money—if they had just set me free, the payments for my selyn would barely feed and clothe me. You produce enough selyn for a channel, Tonyo—I make much less. Where would I live? How would I get a job? No one's hiring Gens."

"Oh. You're right," he nodded. "This ward thing is a transition to force Simes to take care of Gens for now. By the time you're granted citizenship, the Axtons will be depending on you for costume design. They'd be fools if they didn't just hire you to keep on doing it."

"I wish that were true," said Jonmair. "Actually, your costumes are my first. I do the laundry and mending, clean rooms, wait tables, and show up at mealtimes to make the customers hungry."

Zhag laughed. "Tonyo's supposed to do that, too. Part of the deal we had to make with Treavor Axton. He drives a hard bargain."

"I don't mind," said Tonyo, "as long as you show up and eat something." He grinned. "Actually, it's about the craziest thing I've ever heard of, getting paid for eating! Just another example of why Gens will own all of Sime Territory in a couple of generations."

"Why do you say that?" Jonmair asked.

"Because Simes pay us for things we do anyway: eat, and produce selyn. In that case, Simes ought to get paid for...how about selyn utilization?"

"We're paid for our work," said Zhag.

"But you have to pay selyn taxes. So Simes will remain perpetually behind Gens financially—Gens will find it easier to buy homes, run businesses, educate their kids—all because they happen to produce selyn. I can't imagine why the Tecton set things up that way. Apparently it's the same in all Sime Territories."

"It's because of the Pen Gens, Tonyo," Jonmair explained. "The Gens nobody would take care of otherwise."

Tonyo blinked. "Of course," he said. Then, "Where are they? The only one I've seen was the one that got killed in the market-place the day of our First Transfer. And he was able to wait on customers and use an abacus—he could have earned a living with something besides his selyn."

"He wasn't a typical Pen Gen," said Zhag. "Probably a breeder—for some reason he had some training. The masses of Pen Gens can hardly talk. They've been raised like animals—even the pre-Gens who change over into Simes have trouble learning how to be...people...after that upbringing. First Year helps, but it can't really compensate for being raised all your life as an animal destined for the Kill." First Year was the period of rapid intellectual growth a Sime experienced immediately after changeover.

Tonyo was frowning now. "Where are all those thousands of Pen Gens? Who's taking care of them, getting them ready to become citizens?"

"The Genfarmers and Penkeepers," Jonmair told him. "Those Simes would be without income right now if they weren't being paid for the selyn of their wards."

"Is there an education program for them?" asked Tonyo.

"For Genfarmers and Penkeepers?" Zhag asked.

"No, Silly," said Tonyo in exasperation. "They can switch to selling some other product. It's the Pen Gens who require training. If they've really been raised like animals...." He shuddered at the thought.

"The Householders will know," said Jonmair, feeling ashamed that she had not given a thought to those masses of Gens who were far worse off than she was.

* * * * * * *

THAT EVENING JONMAIR WORKED IN THE GAMBLING SALON as usual, waiting tables and using her newly learned skills to serve their Sime customers without irritating them. Baird came in soon after her shift started, smiled at her, but did not interrupt her. He went about his own rounds, making certain that all his customers enjoyed themselves.

That was the entire purpose of The Post: to give people a place to have fun. In a few days Zhag and Tonyo would open with their unique blend of shiltpron and nageric performance. She hoped Tonyo would not get annoyed with any of the rowdy customers and play tricks like making that clerk sneeze this afternoon!

How had he done that, she wondered. Did he imagine a tickle in his own nose?

At the table Jonmair was serving, a woman erupted into a sneeze—and so did the man next to her! Startled, Jonmair quickly pulled her field in around her to zlin invisible, as the woman who had sneezed said to another woman across the table from her, "Do you have to smoke that nasty cigar, Shema? Thing stinks like burning rope!"

But Jonmair knew it wasn't the cigar. Was it?

Attempting something less dramatic, she stopped shielding and imagined hair tickling the back of her neck.

In unison, but never taking their eyes from the cards they were playing, all the Simes at the table scratched the backs of their necks.

Again Jonmair pulled an imaginary curtain around her nager, this time to prevent nearby Simes from zlinning her efforts to hold back giggles. She could do what Tonyo did!

But what good was it? She didn't really want to be a nuisance. Most of the time when she was waiting tables she kept her field as neutral as she knew how.

But...that didn't help her customers have a good time, did it? Jonmair felt good this evening. She had enjoyed her afternoon with Zhag and Tonyo, and looked forward to putting the designs she had sketched on the shirt jackets she had cut out and fit to the two men. Her first commission! The beginning of her life-long dream.

And one thing she now realized: the path to that dream would be far easier if she could ease Sime feelings than if she antagonized them. She let her good feelings flow, thinking of how lucky she was to be alive. When she passed by Baird again and he smiled at her, she let herself daydream about being with him, about more days like their ride out into the country, about what he would think when he saw Zhag and Tonyo dressed in her designs.

Maybe Baird would help persuade his father to allow her to design costumes. If she became a free citizen, she was sure Zhag and Tonyo would continue to have her design costumes for them—and she was certain they were going to be a sensation. Her designs would be noticed.

So her life wasn't over. Soon it would be possible for her to make somebody of herself. Even somebody worthy of Baird

Axton.

It wasn't impossible for a Sime and a Gen to marry—there were inter-larity marriages among the Householders, and, she had learned only recently, there were even families with Gen members living in Norlea since before Unity. They lived in the neighborhood near Carre where she had never been allowed to go as a child. Her parents had implied that terrible things happened there. Now she knew it was just that parents there did not sell their Gen children into the Pens, but sent them to Carre to learn how to live safely with their families.

Could she and Baird become such a family? Her heart swelled with hope as for the first time she allowed herself to dream of the possibility.

Letting her happy thoughts affect her nager, she delivered a round of porstan to another table of card players. One of the Simes dropped an extra coin on her tray. "That's fer you, Girlie. Yer cute fer a Gen, y'know?"

"Th- thank you," she stammered, and pocketed the coin, not knowing if she would be allowed to keep it. The Sime waiters were allowed to keep their tips—but no one ever tipped a Gen, just as no one tipped dogs or horses for doing their jobs.

Not wanting trouble, Jonmair again immersed herself in pleasant thoughts and daydreams—but not enough to miss or mix up any orders. When she took another round of drinks to the card players, everyone at the table tipped her! It spread—the people at the next table, and the next, tipped her just as if she were one of the Sime staff. Soon her pockets were heavy with coins. Her spirits rose even higher. If she could just get free of Treavor Axton's wardship, she would be able to make her dream come true!

* * * * * * *

BAIRD AXTON MADE HIS ROUTINE TOUR of The Post, noting that Jonmair seemed happy. He would meet her in the gold salon at the end of her shift, when she would be hungry and perhaps encourage him to eat something despite his state of Need. A week before transfer, he wanted her at his side every minute, but his father would not permit him to keep Jonmair from her work. She would be with him for the night, he reminded himself. He could sleep without Need nightmares.

In the meantime, he stopped to talk with regulars in the bar, and watch the dancers in the main saloon for a while. They were really quite good, but he was glad that an excellent shiltpron player would soon take their place. Attendance was dropping off, as were profits. Zhag and Tonyo would bring in even bigger crowds here than at Milily's, and have customers consuming porstan by the keg.

He worked his way back to the one room that was functioning fully: the gambling salon. Soldiers still mingled with the crowd every night. Baird hoped they were not the only reason that The Post had not yet seen the kind of fights that broke out routinely in other establishments.

In the month that Zhag and Tonyo had appeared at Milily's Shiltpron Parlor, there had been no fights during their performances—in a dive where whip fights and even knife fights were considered normal. He had not included that fact in persuading his father to let him hire them—actually, the only hard part had been persuading Treavor Axton to audition them. One song, and his father put them on the payroll. Baird hoped that once his new act opened not only would business pick up, but they would be able to stop holding their breath for fear of junct Simes taking out their frustrations in a good old-fashioned free-for-all.

As he looked out over the gambling hall, Baird's eye was caught by two soldiers, male and female, sitting together at the bar. There were too many people between him and them to zlin, but he recognized Conta. The other...wore a different uniform. The male soldier was Gen, wearing the uniform of the Gen Army!

Quelling his own surprise so as not to call attention to the pair, he worked his way over to them. Conta was brimming with happiness. The Gen with her was doing Jonmair's trick of hiding his nager so that he was invisible to zlinning.

"Baird!" said Conta. "I couldn't get away, so Robert came to me!"

The Gen soldier grinned and offered his hand, properly waiting for the Sime to choose whether or not to touch him. Baird was getting used to shaking hands with Gens. He had to assess the man visually because his nager was hidden. A healthy adult male Gen, shorter than Baird was, with the muscles Gens developed with hard work. He had straight coarse black hair and brown skin, brown eyes, and those perfect white teeth so common among Wild Gens.

Either because he was hiding his field or because he had a thick out-Territory accent, he sounded far more alien than Tonyo as he said, "Pleased to meet you, Baird. You're Elendra's brother, right?"

"Yes," Baird managed, taken aback by the familiarity.

"She was a good woman, and a hell of a fine soldier," said Robert. It was obvious that he meant it as high praise.

"You were with her when—?"

"You got good reason to be proud of her," said Robert. "She died fightin' fer Unity—and we made sure it wasn't in vain."

"I know," said Baird. "I'd like you to tell my father and me everything...but not here and now."

"Oh, I know," the Gen agreed. "Don't dare let those feelings show in a crowd. I been trainin' up at Keon fer the past month, though most of it I knew already—learnt it under battle conditions." He reached over and took Conta's hand. "I wasn't gonna miss another transfer just 'cause they won't demobilize Conta, so I talked my way into the company sent to Norlea." He looked around. "You don't seem to have much trouble here."

"We've been fortunate," said Baird. "There was a riot and a Kill in the marketplace last week. But Norlea has been lucky compared to what we hear about Lanta."

"I'm glad I'm here," said Conta. "Robert could never have gotten assigned to Lanta."

"Are there...other Gen soldiers assigned to the Gulf Army?"

Baird asked.

"Oh, yeah," Robert replied matter-of-factly. "Musta been two hunnerd of us trainin' up north so's we could join our transfer mates." He winked and leaned forward. "Tell you a secret. Gens may not die for lack of a good transfer, but once we done it, we sure as hell feel as if we'd die without it!"

Tonyo had said something similar—but then he and Zhag were, for all their unorthodox lifestyle, Companion and channel. Conta was a renSime, like Baird, but it was clear that she and her Robert had a similar relationship.

Conta chuckled and stroked her Gen's hand and forearm with her handling tentacles. "It's all right," she said. "When I'm in Need, you'll be ripe and ready for me."

"I'm ripe and ready now," Robert growled, but nothing showed in his field. Then he looked at Baird and blushed. "I'm sorry. I skipped donating 'cause I meant to get here for Conta's transfer—but armies are all alike, Sime or Gen. Hurry up and wait. And wait. For some reason we got stuck for a whole week in Nashul. I was 'bout ready to go AWOL!"

"Well," said Conta, "we're going to have a wonderful transfer at the end of the month."

Baird felt as if the world had turned inside out. Here was a Sime comforting a Gen who...needed...a transfer.

"I'll manage to hang on that long," Robert assured her. "I hope I never even see another channel for the rest of my life! They don't even try to satisfy Gens. How do they expect to get people to donate, except the ones who need the money?" Robert didn't notice when both Baird and Conta winced at his misuse of the word "Need."

Just then Jonmair came up to the bar to pick up drinks and deliver another order. With that uncanny Gen reading of body language, Robert followed the direction Baird was looking. "That your transfer mate?" he asked.

"Possibly," Baird replied, admitting the hope out loud for the first time. "She's training at Carre." He had to control his own nager at the thought of Jonmair as eager to provide him transfer as Robert was for Conta.

"Well, she's handling this room as superbly as any Companion," said Conta. "That young woman is the reason you don't have any tension here tonight. You do realize that, don't you Baird?"

No, he didn't realize it...until he zlinned what Jonmair was doing. As she moved about the room, she left a wake of good feelings. What in the world was she so high on? What had she been doing with Zhag and Tonyo? And how dare she broadcast such feelings to everyone in the salon?

She was supposed to save her feelings for him!

"Baird!" Conta grabbed his shoulder as he was about to lunge in pursuit of Jonmair. "Baird—she's not doing anything wrong."

He shook her off and stalked his wayward Gen.

* * * * * * *

JONMAIR HAD SEEN BAIRD TALKING WITH THE TWO SOLDIERS—one Sime, one Gen, and obviously very much in love. He appeared to be friends with them. She wanted to meet them, find out their story, for she had never seen a Gen in uniform before. Out-Territory army, obviously, but why was he here?

If she were not afraid of upsetting the nageric balance, she would have broadcast her almost painful curiosity at Baird when she came up to the bar. But there were too many Simes around as close to Need as he was—she would have to be more and more careful until Baird's transfer day, which was still transfer day for half the Simes in Gulf. It would mark two months since the Last Kill.

So she curbed her curiosity, and let hope buoy her up once again as she delivered wine and porstan to the table in the far corner where Treavor Axton and Old Chance, the ex-Penkeeper, were playing poker with several other Simes, including Police Inspector Kerrk. She set down the drinks, murmuring "Thank you," and giving a caress of her field to each one who put a coin on her tray.

"I see you still got that fancy Gen," said Chance. "Thought it woulda got itself kilt long since. Accidentally, of course," he added, and everyone at the table laughed except Kerrk. The Inspector carefully kept his expression neutral.

Partly because she knew it would annoy him, and partly to see how much effect she could have on such a jaded Sime, Jonmair smiled at Old Chance and laved him with her happiness as she put down his porstan and said, "Good to see you, too, Tuib Chance. I trust you're enjoying your retirement."

She got an equal amount of laughter, even from Kerrk and Treavor Axton—but Chance didn't think it was funny. "What's the matter with all of you?" he demanded. "You, Treav—you gonna let a Gen control yer feelings?"

Baird's father blinked, and his eyes went unfocused as he zlinned what Jonmair was doing. Then he rose and stared at her. "You little bitch! Another wer-Gen's trick! Get up to your room now!"

Stunned, Jonmair remembered what the channels and Companions had taught her: don't argue when disjuncting Simes have these outbursts, don't try to grasp control, but just get away as quickly as possible. So she did as Treavor Axton told her, pulling her field in tightly and exiting the room at a quick walk.

* * * * * * *

BAIRD AXTON MANAGED TO GRASP CONTROL OF HIMSELF enough not to attack Jonmair when she stopped at his father's table. It gnawed at him more with every passing day that she belonged to Treavor Axton. What if his father decided he wanted her selyn for himself—not just the money he received for it from the channels every month, but the selyn itself?

The transfer Baird wanted from Jonmair.

Treavor Axton's attention was on the Gen, but Old Chance

saw Baird pull up short of their table. "Hey, Baird!" he called. "Aincha gonna go git thet Gen?" And he laughed raucously enough that Simes at nearby tables turned to look—and notice Jonmair scurrying up the staircase outside the salon.

"Yeah—go bring her back, Baird," said one of the patrons.

"She was makin' everbuddy feel good," slurred a man who was far too drunk for porstan alone to be the reason. "Bring that purty nager back here," he hiccupped through a giggle.

"You oughta get more Gens like that one," a woman added. "I never feel this good after turnover."

"Jonmair has just gone to rest a little," said Baird. "She'll be back, I promise." *And I will restrain myself somehow,* he thought, ashamed at another example of his infamous lack of control. Why had he gotten so jealous when Jonmair was merely doing what was good for business?

He sat down across from his father at the table. "That lady is right," he said. "We ought to get more Gens in here, and think about customer satisfaction."

"Them fools?" asked Chance. "I tole you, Treavor, the shidoni-doomed Tecton's gonna have Gens runnin' the territory. Those idiots have bought the Tecton line—you gonna pander to 'em?"

"Shut up, Chance," said Treavor Axton. "Your game or mine, the customer is always right. Baird, was Jonny doing that all over the room tonight?"

"Yes."

"And no one complained?"

"Only me," Baird admitted sheepishly.

His father frowned at him. "The Gen is not yours. Get her back here—I want to watch her work, and if I like what I zlin, then we'll see about getting more Gens to do it."

"Bloody shen!" said Old Chance, kicking his chair back against the wall as he rose with a sneer. "Never thought I'd see you bend over an' ask fer it, Treav. You wait another two, three months and see how you feel!" And he stalked out.

Baird looked after him, shaking his head. "Everybody's going to feel worse in two or three months, but what can Chance do about it? He surely can't think he can get away with arranging 'accidents.'"

Then he noticed Kerrk watching him, listening closely. "The Kill in the marketplace last week was apparently accidental," commented the Inspector, "but they've still condemned the Sime responsible."

Baird swallowed hard, in his mind's eye seeing Jonmair fall limp from Old Chance's tentacles. Or his own. Seeing himself condemned to shedoni—execution by attrition—for killing her. "We have to enforce the law," he said, facing his fears in an attempt to banish them. "If we let people off because they can't control themselves, we'd break the Unity Treaty every day. If that happens, what did we fight the war for? What did Elendra die for?"

Grasping for control, Baird looked across the room to where Conta and her Robert still sat at the bar, a glowing example of what could be. Then he squared his shoulders and went upstairs, stopping in the gold salon on the way to load a plate with Gen portions of Jonmair's favorite foods.

* * * * * * *

ON BAIRD'S TRANSFER DAY, JONMAIR WAS FILLED WITH HOPE. At Baird's insistence, Treavor Axton allowed her to keep some of the tips their Sime customers gave her—enough to buy a beautiful pendant she had seen at the Keon Emporium, to go with the dress she had made for Zhag and Tonyo's opening tomorrow night. The musicians had prevailed on Baird and his father to give her the night off, so she could be their guest.

Even Treavor Axton grudgingly admitted Jonmair had done a good job on their costumes. He also deigned to praise her work in the salons, keeping their customers contented, now treating it as if it were his own idea. Tonyo had easily demonstrated that he could do the same thing, and promised to help Jonmair train other Gens—although where they were to find those other Gens was an unanswered question.

It was only a brief walk from The Post to the dispensary in the Old Pen, now completely converted into a facility for collecting and dispensing selyn. However, this would continue to be the busiest day of the month until people's schedules drifted apart. Quite a few had needed transfer yesterday, as disjuncting Simes used up extra selyn in nervous energy. The Axtons had not come up a full day short yet, but their appointments were now early in the morning. Jonmair walked between them, trying to keep both men comfortable and wishing Treavor Axton had his own Gen.

Although Baird had gone without a Kill twice before and his father only once, Treavor Axton seemed worse off than his son. All Simes got a haunted, haggard look within hours of hard Need, but the lines in Axton's face were drawn deep, his skin grayed beneath its tan. It was true, then, what Jonmair had heard: the older the Sime, the harder it was to disjunct. Many would not survive the process.

Baird had a father who truly loved him, for all his gruff, implacable ways. Jonmair didn't want Baird to lose his father—and to tell the truth, learning her way around Treavor Axton's convoluted mix of business savvy and sense of fair play, she had come to care about him herself. He had built The Post into a Norlea institution on a rare combination of outrageous ideas and common sense. That same combination would eventually allow him to accept her, she was sure.

"Tecton Dispensary," read the sign on the building they approached, but Jonmair had never heard anyone refer to it as anything but the City Pen. It still flew the green pennants, because it was still where any tax-paying Sime was assured of receiving a month's allotment of selyn. Inside, though, the walls had been repainted in soft pastels, and the hallway where they waited turned into an art gallery with bright, cheery paintings. Channels and their Companions circulated through the crowd, balancing the ambient and looking for anyone who should be moved forward in the queue. When a pair came near to the three from The Post, the channel, a woman with iron-gray hair, smiled at Jonmair and said, "Good job. But please let me zlin your Simes now."

Both Simes bristled at being referred to as if they were her property. Jonmair sent soothing thoughts, and then removed her support. The men winced, but Treavor Axton staggered for a moment before he caught his balance. "Please come with us, all of you," said the channel, introducing herself as Sirya ambrov Keon and her Companion, a male Gen who looked the same early middle-age as she did, as Bevin ambrov Keon. Bevin took all of their transfer cards—Treavor Axton provided Jonmair's as well as his own—and copied their information onto forms on the clipboard he carried.

They were taken into a waiting area lined with transfer cubicles. "Now," said Sirya to Treavor Axton, "I want you to shift your focus from Jonmair to me. Can you do that? Just zlin me."

Jonmair could somehow sense when Axton's attention shifted, and only Baird was focused on her. Bevin moved automatically to compensate for the shift in the ambient. Sirya smiled at Jonmair again. "You've done a very good job. Treavor wasn't fixed on you, and the two men are not competing—not an easy functional to pull off."

"I wasn't thinking of it as a functional," Jonmair explained. "I want to give Baird transfer, but I want his father to be comfortable too."

"You did an excellent job of showing them exactly that. Now we are going to take Mr. Axton into a transfer suite." She turned to Baird, and must have done something nagerically because suddenly his attention focused on the channel. "Baird, with Jonmair beside you, you can easily wait another hour. But your father needs his transfer right now. It may take a while. Stay here with Jonmair, all right?"

Baird nodded. "Take care of Dad."

But when the other three had disappeared into one of the cubicles, his logical faculties—slowed by hard Need, when Simes operated on instinct—turned over what the channel had said. "Why should it take a while? Transfer only takes a moment." His eyes widened. Jonmair knew that at this time he could not truly feel anything but Need, but nevertheless he said, "She thinks he's going to shen out!"

He rose. Jonmair moved with him, supporting him as he paced restlessly, shielding him from the Need of two other Simes waiting for their transfers.

"If it's starting this early—only his second transfer—" Baird shook his head, trying to focus through Need. "They said older Simes would have it worst, but Dad's not old. There's a reason shen is the worst word in our language—it feels like dying, only you live through it and then wish you had died. I used to shen out when I was trying to disjunct before— before—"

"Before what?" Jonmair asked, remembering what Old Chance had told her about Baird. Before Unity. He had tried to disjunct before...and failed.

"I wanted to disjunct," he said wretchedly. "I made it through four months, but the third and fourth transfers were bad and worse. And then—"

Suddenly he stopped, staring at her. "No. I shouldn't tell you that! I'm sorry—I don't want to say anything to frighten you."

"It's all right," she said, taking his hand. "I know. I was there. The little girl you saved—that was my sister."

"What?" He stared at her blankly.

"In the square that day. You were trying to help Zhag, and Faleese ran right under your horse's hoofs. You used up the last of your selyn to save her—it was heroic!"

But Baird didn't think it was heroic.

"No," he whispered. "You were there? You saw my shame?"

"What shame? Baird, you saved a child's life!"

"But afterward...I stole some poor woman's Gen, and—"

"It's all right, Baird," Jonmair tried to soothe him. "You were just goaded too far—"

"No!" He pushed her away. "I wanted to stop killing!"

"I know," she said, doing everything she knew to soothe his agitation. "You were so brave, doing what you knew was right when everyone else thought it was wrong."

"I was wrong that day. Genjacking. A public Kill. I acted like a lorsh—and it keeps happening. I can't control myself."

"You don't have to," Jonmair reassured him, "not when you're in Need. I'm here for you." She thought of him depending on her as Zhag did on Tonyo.

"You think I'm going to let a Gen control me?" Baird looked around wildly. "I have to control myself!"

He flung off her hand on his arm and ran, augmenting through the small waiting area. He tore open the door into the crowded hallway, and bolted into the crowd of Simes in Need. Jonmair pounded after him, parting the Simes with a flick of her field, but Baird remained ahead of her. He bludgeoned his way, raising cries of outrage as he jostled sensitive forearms with their swollen ronaplin glands.

There were other channel/Companion pairs working through the crowd as Sirya and Bevin had been doing. One such pair moved to intercept Baird. In a flash, the channel, a red-haired man as tall as Baird, grabbed the fleeing Sime, intertwined their tentacles, and pressed their lips together.

A shock went through the ambient—Jonmair could not have said whether what she felt was the forced transfer, the reaction of nearby Simes, Baird's shock, or her own outrage. But as tentacles retracted and hands dropped, as Baird stared clear-eyed into the gaze of the intercepting channel, he and Jonmair, half the length of the hall apart, wailed in unison: "No-ooooh!"

Jonmair dashed up to the channel, raising her fists to pound on his chest. He grasped them before she could jolt the sensitive node she knew lay behind his breastbone. Struggling against Sime strength, she gasped, "You had no right! You had no right! He's mine!"

CHAPTER SEVEN
GRAND OPENING

ONCE AGAIN, BAIRD AXTON CAME TO HIMSELF BURNING WITH SHAME at a public loss of control. The channel who had intercepted his blind rush away from Jonmair now held the Gen woman at arm's length as she cried, "He's mine! You had no right!"

People were staring, but several channel/Companion pairs converged to insulate those in Need from the nageric shock of high-field Gen fury.

"It's all right," the channel told Jonmair in a soothing voice. "It wasn't your fault."

"Of course it wasn't!" she shouted. "It's *your* fault, you lorsh! He needed me, and you took him. Simejacker!"

The channel's Companion, who looked about Tonyo's age, burst out laughing at the word Jonmair coined. But then he pulled himself together and said, "Let's get some privacy."

Shocked to realize how badly Jonmair had wanted to give him her selyn, Baird let them lead him back into the now empty waiting area.

The channel introduced himself as Vent Gascon, not a Householding name, his young Companion as Mern. Mern told Jonmair, "You and I were in the Pen together, Choice Kills. I saw you sometimes in passing."

Somewhat calmer now, she nodded. "I suppose your story's pretty much like mine. You established and your family sold you into the Pens."

"Yeah. But I was lucky. The Householders bought up as many of us as they could afford, 'cause they knew we'd be easier to train than Pen Gens. I just gave transfer for the first time a couple of days ago." He smiled. "I don't blame you for wanting it."

"But she couldn't control the Sime in her charge," protested Vent. "I couldn't let him leave the dispensary."

"We're gonna catch shen from the controller," said Mern resignedly, "but shidoni, what does the Tecton expect? We've got two whole days of experience!"

"You did fine," said Baird, realizing that while not as satisfying as a Kill, the transfer had been his best one yet.

"Thanks," said Vent, easily understanding his meaning. "That's because I'm junct." He shook his head. "Two months ago I took my Last Kill, shenning the Tecton with every breath— and a few days later I got a notice that my selyn consumption profile indicated that I was a channel. Now here I am working for the shenned Tecton!"

"Crazy world," said Mern. "If Vent had bought me for his Last Kill, I'd be dead. Instead, two days ago he gave me the best experience of my life. Now we're partners." He turned to Baird. "Are you all right now?"

"Fine," Baird answered. "I'm sorry I caused a scene."

"My fault, not yours," said Vent. "An experienced channel should have been able to get you to privacy, at the least." He looked at Jonmair and shook his head. "I can't tell if it would have been safe to let you have direct transfer. Mern and me shoulda had months of training for this duty. I don't know how we're managing not to have Kills in the streets."

"You can kill me again any time you've a mind to," Mern said with a suggestive flick of his nager. He was nearly as post as Tonyo had been the day after his transfer with Zhag.

"Stop that!" Vent said, directing a nageric slap at the boy.

Mern laughed. "Can't hurt a Gen that way!"

"Then how do you know what I did?"

The Gen merely laughed louder. Vent tried to scowl at

him, but couldn't maintain his annoyance in the face of his Companion's good cheer and his own post reaction. "We'd better take Jonmair's donation and get back out there before something else happens," said Vent. "The Tecton has enough trained personnel for most of the month, but these couple of days we don't."

Jonmair was taken into one of the cubicles, and returned in moments to sit beside Baird as Vent and Mern went back to their crowd control. After a moment, Baird said, "I'm sorry. I didn't mean to run from you, Jonmair."

He could zlin that she was far from post—it was beginning to seem normal to think such things about Gens—but she seemed stable. She turned to look at him. "You were upset about your Dad. I'm worried about him too, Baird. It's taking too long."

And it was nearly twenty minutes more before the door opened and Bevin called them in. Treavor Axton lay on the transfer couch, eyes closed.

"He's just sleeping now," Sirya said. "Let him rest until he wakes by himself, then make him take it easy the rest of the day. He's got a pretty bad nerve burn."

Bevin poured fosebine into a vial. "We gave him a dose that will wear off in a few hours. Have him take this if his pain returns."

"How would a Sime get a burn?" asked Baird. Nerve burn, not being drained of selyn, was what Gens died of in the Kill.

"Sirya had to force the transfer on him," Bevin explained.

The channel said sadly, "Baird, your Dad has lived almost twenty-five years past changeover. Juncts rarely live that long, even without the strain of disjunction."

"What are you saying?" Baird demanded, zlinning his father to make certain he was truly asleep and would not hear the answer. "What will happen next month?"

"I don't know," Sirya said flatly. "He may survive another transfer...and he may not. Baird...he needs direct Gen transfer—a matchmate."

Baird felt his teeth clench. He fought down his denial and

managed to ask, "Can Jonmair do it?"

He hated the surge of relief that went through him when Sirya shook her head. "She might have if he were the Sime she had spent her time with since she was released from the Pens. But she is committed to you, Baird—your field and hers have been interacting all this time. Furthermore, she is emotionally committed to you—Gens can become fixed on Simes just as Simes do on Gens."

"Yes," he said. "I...just witnessed that."

Sirya said, "You, too, are ahead of schedule—I would have expected you and Jonmair to have achieved transfer today. I want the two of you in my office day after tomorrow, first thing. I wish I could start counseling you today, but—"

"We understand," said Jonmair. "We'll be there. I have to learn how to keep Baird from running from me next month."

Baird fought down annoyance at Jonmair's responding for him, to focus on a more immediate problem: "Where do we find a Gen for Dad?"

"All of the am Keon or am Carre Gens either overmatch your father or are in committed relationships. We have a handful of new Gens in training at Carre, though. Can you persuade your father to come and meet some of them?"

"Am" Keon or Carre meant "under the protection" of the Householding—it had been Baird's goal to become one of those Simes, who did not retreat within the walls of the Householding but lived in junct society without killing. Practically everyone in the city of Laveen, near Keon in the north end of Gulf Territory, was am Keon, and there had been a growing community of am Carre in Norlea before Unity.

The Gulf Householders believed that over time they could have disjuncted the Territory family by family. Their plan, though, was formed without the knowledge that Norwest Territory was on the brink of collapse, and Nivet not much better off. Now the Unity Treaty had thrown them into this make or break situation.

"What's wrong with matching Mr. Axton with a Gen who overmatches him?" asked Jonmair.

"We'll try that if it's the only way to get a transfer into him," Sirya said, "but it's not a long-term solution."

"But there is an alternative to channel's transfer if we can't find a match for Dad by next month?" Baird demanded.

"Yes," Bevin said gently. "Baird, while some Simes are going to die, we will attempt to save everyone. The very best thing for your father is a matchmate. Don't give up hope of finding him one—after all, nature didn't stop the day the Unity Treaty went into effect."

"All new Simes except channels are being started off on channel's transfer," said Sirya. "That leaves all new Gens as potential matches for the Simes who most need them. Your Dad is high on that list. We *will* find him a match."

* * * * * * *

THAT EVENING BUSINESS WAS SLOW AT THE POST. Customers who had had transfers from the newly-trained junct channels were post, as were most younger Simes. Baird actually felt good for once—but Jonmair was unsatisfied, and Tonyo unavailable to cheer up their customers, as he and Zhag were playing their final evening at Milily's.

They'll be here tomorrow night, Baird reminded himself. Conta and Robert were at the bar. Since Jonmair and Tonyo had begun balancing the ambient they were frequently the only soldiers on the premises.

Most customers in The Post tonight were regulars: people who could afford to frequent such an establishment had always been secure that they could buy a Choice Kill if Pen shipments were late. Those less well off now had security under the Tecton. Even if it meant pressing channels with two days' training into service, the Tecton was keeping its promise that everyone would be supplied with selyn. People who had never had that security before were relaxing and experiencing postsyndrome…and not coming to The Post to celebrate it.

But Zhag and Tonyo would bring them in.

Low field and not post, Jonmair made a laudable effort to be soothing to the customers, but Baird could zlin that it was a duty rather than a pleasure. Many regular customers understood exactly how she felt, and sympathy flowed in both directions.

Baird had persuaded his father to remain upstairs. When he went up to report, he found him dozing in his chair, feet up on an ottoman. The difficult transfer he had endured showed in the drawn lines of his face.

The daily newspaper, which Treavor Axton normally read over his morning kafi, had fallen from his lap, open to the obituary page. That page was longer every day now—longer than any days Baird could remember other than ones on which war casualties had been reported.

Baird picked up the paper, noticing as he did so the lax hand it had fallen from. The knuckles were enlarged, age spots marred the skin, and veins stood out against the bone and tendon where the flesh had dwindled away. Tentacle sheaths stood out in relief on his forearm.

Baird's throat tightened. *I've lost my sister, and now I'm going to lose my father.*

His father opened his eyes. "Baird."

"Hi, Dad. Feeling better? Shall I send for tea?"

"No." He pushed himself up in the chair, wincing. "Fosebine makes me do nothing but sleep! I'm not taking any more of it."

Baird zlinned him before saying, "You don't have to," for although his father felt stiff and somewhat achy, his transfer burn had healed.

"Well?" Treavor Axton demanded after a moment. "How's the house? Or do I have to come down and zlin for myself?"

"It's just what we expected—fewer customers than usual, but with the main salon closed the saloon and gambling hall are full."

"And the ambient?"

"Very few of our customers are post. Everyone who is went to Milily's. Starting tomorrow, they'll come here."

"Any trouble?"

"No. There's a sort of camaraderie—we're all going through the same thing together, uncomfortable, but with good reason to endure it. Like soldiers in the field."

"What would you know about that?" his father asked.

"I was thinking about something Elendra wrote to me. When the Sime and Gen armies had to join together against the Freebanders, she got to know some Gens."

"That Robert who hangs around her friend Conta," Treavor Axton agreed.

"Yes—but other Gens as well. Robert's had training at Keon now. In the field, they were side by side with untrained Gens— and not killing them. Even under battle conditions."

"I've heard the stories. It makes sense not to kill your allies against a common enemy."

"Dad—they had to overcome primal instinct, just as we're being asked to do. And...the Gens had to overcome it too. They had to stop being afraid. And the way they did it, both Simes and Gens, was to become friends."

"So?" his father asked.

"So...you can't be friends with some Gens and kill others. Dad...Elendra had already started disjunction when she died. She would have come home disjunct, just as Conta did."

Baird could feel his father zlinning him, trying to comprehend. Then he said, "Why didn't she tell me?"

"Why didn't you take me to Carre when I went into change-over?" Baird countered.

"Because I'm not a shenned fortune-teller!" his father snapped. "Shen it, Baird, how was I to know the world would turn upside down? Yes, you'd be better off nonjunct as things turned out. But if the Tecton hadn't made that insane promise to disjunct all Simes you'd have been better off junct, Son. You'll never get the chance to know it, now—but junct is the natural Sime lifestyle. It never pays to go against nature."

"How can you say that? You've zlinned Conta and Robert together. And Zhag—he almost died before Tonyo came, but zlin him now. How could anyone zlin Sime and Gen transfer mates and think them unnatural or unhealthy?"

Treavor Axton shifted his weight uneasily. "It's what you have to live with, so I suppose it's best that you think it's normal."

Shen. This was not going well. How could he get the subject around to having his father accept a transfer mate?

In the street below, a newspaper seller began to bellow, "Special edition! Riots in Lanta! Raid on the Lanta Genfarm! Martial Law in the capital!"

A chill went through Baird.

"Go down and get a paper," his father ordered.

The news was even worse than it sounded in the terse headlines. As Baird skimmed the front page his heart sank.

Jonmair came to his side. "What's wrong?" she asked. Customers gathered around those who had gone out to get papers.

"Lanta," Baird said grimly.

It was the two-month anniversary of the Last Kill all over the Territory, of course—but in the capital there was wide-spread defiance of the anti-Kill laws. Not only were there more than twenty "accidental" Kills of Gens all over the city—several of them new and poorly-trained Companions like Mern—but a mob of Simes had turned Raider and attacked the Lanta Genfarm, source of selyn for the capital. More than a hundred Pen Gens had been killed, and three channel/Companion pairs working on the premises murdered. As the story went to press, it was not known whether the owner of the Genfarm and his family, who had not been hurt, were innocent victims or part of a conspiracy to break the Tecton hold on Gulf.

The Legislature immediately met in emergency session. Ambushes of legislators from Laveen and Norlea—those who most strongly supported Unity—were narrowly averted. Martial Law was declared in Lanta and its environs.

Waves of sick feeling traveled through The Post as copies of the paper were passed around. *We should close,* Baird thought, *before—*

Then he realized what he was zlinning: people were horrified, sick at the thought of what had happened in Lanta. But no one was applauding it!

Which made him realize who was not here tonight: Old Chance and his usual cronies, or any other influential proponents of the old ways.

Outside, though, there was shouting in the square. "Shen the Tecton!" "Back to the Kill!" "Kill! Kill! Kill! Kill!"

A fire blazed up on the other side of the square.

Baird didn't wait to see what had been set ablaze, but closed the front doors and locked them, shouting to the waiters to lock the side and back doors as well. Then he went into the gambling salon, Jonmair at his side.

Outside, the shouting escalated, punctuated by police whistles and the clang of a fire engine.

"Friends," Baird announced, "we don't know what will happen in Norlea. I think you're safest right here—you're welcome to stay the night if things don't calm down."

"My children!" exclaimed a woman. "I have to get home!"

Conta and Robert joined Baird. "Just wait a few minutes, please," said Conta. "Norlea's troops are on alert. Wait, and you will have an escort."

Sure enough, even as people were tensely discussing what to do, there was a knock at the front door.

Conta and Robert flanked Baird as he opened it—to find uniformed soldiers under charge of a Norlea police officer. "Is everything all right in here, Sir?"

"Yes—but what about out there?"

Their customers poured into the foyer to hear.

"Norlea's prepared. The army and the police are patrolling—it's safe to return to your homes if you folks want to. If you suspect trouble, ask any officer for an escort."

Many of their customers left, but almost half stayed behind, including Conta and Robert. "This is your station, isn't it?" Baird asked them.

"Some nights it is," Conta replied. "Tonight, yes, we're on duty."

"And tomorrow night?"

"The grand opening? The whole troop wants that duty! Milily's is too small for Zhag and Tonyo now. You'd better be prepared for standing room only."

"You don't think we'll be closed down?" Baird asked.

Conta chuckled. "Look out there."

Looking out at the square was what Treavor Axton was doing when Baird went upstairs again. "You took long enough!" his father told him.

"You had a better view than I did," said Baird.

"Yeah—just a few rowdies blowing off frustration. The whole shenned army was out there to round 'em up!"

"Better than being unprepared, like Lanta," Baird said, handing his father the newspaper.

Treavor Axton frowned as he read. "That's gross negligence! They should have expected something like that!"

"Perhaps, but not now. All the predictions have been for serious trouble four to six months after the Last Kill."

"Householding stupidity." He shook his head. "Why would people wait to get really sick before fighting back? Shen it, they're fighting for their lives!"

"Dad...you sound as if you agree with the Raiders."

His father sat down in his armchair once again. "Baird... you're sick, too, Son, young and strong as you are. You started making yourself sick when you first tried to disjunct, and you're doing no better this time. Don't try to deny it—you're no more post than I am."

"Actually," Baird said bluntly, "it's Jonmair who had a bad transfer. Mine was pretty good this month, but I'm reacting to her mood. Next month we'll have transfer—"

"I'll send her across the Mizipi first!" Treavor Axton threatened.

"No you won't," said Baird. "I need a matchmate, and so do you. You won't endanger my health, and I'm going to find a match for you before your next transfer."

"No. The channels are bad enough. I will not have a Gen

pushing me around."

"Dad—"

"No, I said! Look at them, running roughshod over Simes, getting anything they want with a flick of their nager. Look at you, telling me that your post reaction is controlled by that Gen! You're not even resisting!" He held up the newspaper. "Those Simes who went killing today are right. Oh, they're martyrs to a lost cause, because if they succeed, there's no way to prevent Zelerod's Doom. So we have to have the Martial Law and we have to have the channels, sick as that system is. But what we don't have to have—what no Sime in his right mind should stand for—is dependence on Gens for anything other than the production of selyn!"

* * * * * * *

BY THE NEXT DAY, JONMAIR HAD GOTTEN OVER the disappointment of her transfer and determined to woo Baird into sharing with her next month. After all, things were going well otherwise in her life, and in Norlea.

The news from Lanta was frightening, but there had been no Kills in Norlea. Several fires had been set, and a few gangs of frustrated Simes had been held overnight for disorderly conduct, but the morning revealed only a little property damage, and no loss of life or limb. Norlea congratulated itself on its sensible and law-abiding citizens.

The opening of Zhag Paget and Tonyo Logan at The Post was to go on as scheduled, despite the fact that they had been attacked on their way home from their final performance at Milily's. The story preceded them, growing with every retelling, so when they turned up at The Post at noon, Jonmair was astonished to see that they appeared completely normal.

Tonyo and Jonmair were expected in the kafi lounge, where that beverage was dispensed along with varieties of tea and juices. Jonmair didn't know why Gens were supposed to be so fond of kafi, which she found bitter and unpleasant, although many Simes apparently enjoyed the stuff.

It was her job to persuade the Sime customers to eat as well as drink. Small notes had been placed on the menus touting the health benefits to Simes of eating twice each day, and the pleasant atmosphere provided at The Post to encourage them to do so. The "atmosphere," of course, was simply Gen hunger on the ambient.

Just past turnover, Zhag had no appetite. Although he made no attempt to feed his partner the crusty bread and cheese the Gens were eating, Tonyo peeled a mango and sliced it, offering pieces to Zhag as they talked. Jonmair noticed that, distracted with conversation, the Sime ate nearly a third of the fruit, sliver by sliver. It was no problem to get Baird to eat—he was still post.

"We heard some ruffians attacked you last night," said Baird. "You don't look as if you were in a fight."

"I wasn't," said Zhag. "Tonyo did all the fighting."

"Well, they were Simes," said Tonyo, as if that explained it all.

"Someone said ten Simes attacked the two of you, and you left them bleeding in the road," said Jonmair.

Both men burst into hearty laughter—the kind of laughter Zhag should not have been capable of after turnover. "First of all," he said, "there were only four of them."

"But only two of you," said Baird.

"They probably could have taken us if we were both Sime," said Zhag. "But they never even got near us."

"They got too near," Tonyo corrected. "I was concentrating on keeping Zhag from falling off the planet, so I was blocking them from Zhag's attention, and didn't notice them creeping up on us myself."

"What do you mean, falling off the planet?" asked Jonmair.

"Turnover," chorused all three men.

"That's a good description," said Baird. "It does feel as if all support is gone, even the ground under your feet." He smiled at Jonmair. "When you're with me, I don't feel it."

"But I don't do anything," said Jonmair. "Tonyo, why did you have to concentrate?"

"My fault," Zhag said. "He had just experienced his own first turnover, and I was fool enough to tease him about it."

"I still shouldn't have let you fall," said Tonyo contritely. "But shit, I was embarrassed!"

Zhag chuckled. "Next month you'll know better."

When Baird looked at her with a puzzled expression, Jonmair shook her head. She didn't know any more than he did what the musicians were talking about. "Gen turnover?" she asked. "I've never felt anything."

"You haven't given a real transfer yet," said Tonyo. "I had no idea it was going to happen. I felt it hit Zhag in the middle of the performance, but he never missed a note."

"What did you feel?" Jonmair asked curiously. She had learned to "balance the ambient" by letting herself move to wherever she was most comfortable, but she couldn't for the life of her distinguish that she actually felt anything.

Tonyo frowned, searching for words. "It's...sort of the way it feels when a Sime is in Need. You know, how you want to give him your selyn?"

Oh, yes, Jonmair knew that feeling, and the screaming frustration when Baird had run from her.

"Well," Tonyo continued, "it's something like that, except that it's not about transfer. He just needs you to be there—you want to move close, see that no one gets in between you. It was only bad for a moment."

"Because you were there to support me," Zhag agreed. "But then you forgot all about me...as usual."

Suddenly Baird got it. "Oh, no," he laughed. "Tonyo, you didn't go on flirting with the women in the front row?"

Tonyo winced. "Well, I have a certain reputation—"

"Gens are always post!" chorused Zhag and Baird, while Tonyo blushed.

Then he said, "I learned last night that we're not. After the show, backstage with those women, well—"

"You're too good an actor," said Zhag. "They wouldn't have been all over you if you'd just let them feel what you were really feeling. Or rather weren't."

"I thought I was over getting culture shock every time I turn around," said Tonyo. "Back home, it's not normal for a healthy man of my age to have three beautiful women coming on to him and not be able to...uh...."

By this time both Baird and Jonmair were trying helplessly to stifle guffaws. Tonyo glared at them. "That's what *he* did," he said, pointing a thumb at Zhag, "so I pulled the rug out from under him."

"Tonyo," Zhag said soberly, "I honestly had no idea you didn't know you'd be affected." Then, with a quirky grin, "I was trying to imagine how you thought you were going to fake it."

"And I didn't know how hard it would hit you to have me suddenly withdraw support." He looked over at Baird and Jonmair. "He fell over in a dead faint. Certainly took my mind off *my* troubles!"

"Zhag?" asked Jonmair in concern. "Are you all right?"

"I'm fine. If I survive a few more transfers with this one, I'll stop reacting to every shift in the ambient like some finicky Farris."

"I forget how sick Zhag was only two weeks ago," Tonyo said contritely. "He seems so strong and stable now."

"Any other day," said Zhag, "I wouldn't have reacted so strongly. But that was within an hour of my turnover—and you're my matchmate. Anyway, I wasn't hurt, just out of it for a few seconds. No convulsions, no voiding—I'm well, Tonyo, just not back to full strength yet."

"Are you sure you're strong enough to perform tonight?" asked Baird.

"Baird, I need music as much as I need selyn," Zhag said solemnly. "The day I can't perform is the day I die."

"You were strong enough to fight off attackers last night," Jonmair said.

"I really didn't do anything," Zhag insisted. "If those Simes claim I beat them up, it's because they don't want to admit that a Gen laid them out in the road without even getting his hands dirty."

"All I did was Genslam them," said Tonyo. "By the time I noticed them, that's all there was time for."

Jonmair had only recently learned the nageric trick of shocking a Sime with her field, a dangerous practice that could easily backfire. "How could you slam them without slamming Zhag at the same time?" she asked.

"He knocked me hypoconscious first," said Zhag. He shook his head. "I was focused on Tonyo. Suddenly I couldn't zlin— there were Simes coming at us from all directions—and then they fell, I could zlin again, and Tonyo was apologizing for not having time to warn me!" He laughed again. "If I can survive life with Tonyo, I can survive anything!"

* * * * * * *

BAIRD LISTENED TO THE STORY, and watched Tonyo manipulate Zhag, with growing revulsion. How could Zhag not mind what the Gen did to him—even controlling whether or not he could zlin! He wanted to squirm in his seat as he watched Tonyo peel another section of mango with a sharp knife, slice off a piece, and offer it to Zhag speared on the blade.

"No more," said the shiltpron player, waving the fruit away with a casual handling tentacle. He never seemed to worry about sharp instruments in Tonyo's hands, even in proximity to Zhag's forearms. How could he place that kind of trust in anyone, let alone a Gen?

Tonyo didn't argue, but simply asked, "Want some cake?"

Zhag shook his head. "I'll just have a bite of yours."

Tonyo used his nager to summon a waiter, and ordered cake and kafi.

"You're still hungry," Zhag observed.

"You can have anything you want," said Baird.

"I'll eat after the show. Better warn your cook, Baird—I'll

be hungry."

Baird laughed. "I'll be sure to do that. You cleared the buffet last week—but when they replenished it, our customers cleared it again."

"You eat even more than I do," Jonmair observed.

"I'm a lot bigger than you are," said Tonyo.

"Is that the reason," Baird asked, "or is it that Tonyo produces more selyn?"

"Probably both," said Zhag as the kafi arrived. "Tonyo, are you sure you want a stimulant?"

"I miss coffee," the singer replied. "This kafi is different from the coffee we had back home, but it has the same kick—maybe even more. Will it affect my selyn? If so, I won't drink any on our transfer day."

"I think he meant because you're so full of energy as it is," observed Baird.

"Of course I'm full of energy," said Tonyo, taking a sip of steaming kafi. "I'm Gen!"

The kafi was very hot. Baird could zlin it burn the roof of the Gen's mouth, and yet he swallowed it and took another mouthful, savoring it. Baird zlinned Zhag, who, past turnover, would have to deliberately concentrate not to zlin.

"Oh, that's good!" Tonyo said blissfully.

Zhag echoed the Gen's satisfied smile.

"You wouldn't be allowed to do that in a Householding," said Baird.

"Do what?" asked Tonyo. "Drink kafi? They served it at Keon."

"No," said Zhag, "you wouldn't be allowed to drink it that hot."

"Who wants lukewarm kafi?" asked Tonyo.

"Gens who don't want to burn nearby Simes," Jonmair told him.

Zhag zlinned Baird. "Did Tonyo hurt you?" he asked.

Tonyo put his cup down and began to say, "I'm sorry—" but Baird held up his dorsals.

"No—I zlinned what you did, Tonyo. To you it felt and tasted good, so it did to me, too. I guess...it's something Simes and Gens have in common. Something that's just a little bit painful actually feels good."

"Then it's not a junct reaction," said Zhag, relief in his voice and field. "Thea is worried about our act—that we're playing to the junctness of the audience. She's afraid it will get out of control." Thea was the Carre channel Zhag had a romantic interest in. Baird couldn't help wondering if his friend was setting himself up for heartbreak.

"Sime or Gen," said Tonyo, "there's no life without pain. Our act is about life. I don't think people want just sweetness and light."

"What you've been doing certainly draws the crowds," said Baird, "so don't change it!"

"We're just adding to it," said Zhag. "Wait till you hear the new song Tonyo wrote."

"Tonyo wrote?"

"Only the lyrics," Tonyo explained. "After our transfer, Zhag composed this great melody. I just put words to it."

Zhag said, "It's more than that. You'll see. I hadn't been post in a year, and all my feelings came pouring out in the music. But Tonyo—" he shook his head "—somehow he knew where the music came from. Wait and zlin."

After they had eaten, they went to the main salon, where Zhag made certain that his shiltpron was set up correctly, all the strings in tune. Then he and Tonyo put on the clever vests that Jonmair had made, and they tested the lighting from various positions on the stage.

Then Tonyo asked the lighting director, "Can you keep one spot on Zhag, and follow me into the audience with the other?"

"Into the audience?" the woman asked.

"We shift the ambient in performance," Zhag explained. "That way everyone gets to zlin Tonyo up close, too."

"Isn't that dangerous?" Baird asked without thinking.

"Just because he's singing instead of serving drinks?"

Jonmair asked.

"Sorry," Baird replied, flustered. *She controls our customers all the time. Do I even know how often she controls me?*

Tonyo's request required repositioning one of the spotlights. By the time that was finished, the grand opening was only three hours off.

"Zhag," said Tonyo, "if you come with me, do you think we can find a barber shop that will take a Gen customer, or do I have to go all the way to Carre to get my hair cut?"

"No!" exclaimed Zhag, Baird, and Jonmair on one breath.

"Huh? It hasn't been cut since I came in-Territory," he said, pushing unruly curls off his forehead. They tumbled right back down into his eyes.

"You'd look like a Pen Gen!" Jonmair exclaimed. "Tonyo, your hair is only starting to get long enough."

Tonyo looked from Baird to Zhag. Gulf Territory men typically wore their hair collar length, or even brushing the shoulder. "But mine curls," he pointed out. "In this humidity it frizzes. I've cut it short ever since I got my Mom to realize I was too old for ringlets."

"Your hair is beautiful," said Jonmair. "All it requires is proper treatment. What do you use to wash it?"

"Just soap."

"Well, get some proper shampoo. Wash your hair, and then rinse it with sugar water—that's how my mother tamed my little sister's curls."

"Sugar water?" Tonyo asked doubtfully.

"That will give it body," Jonmair explained, "so it won't frizz."

When the four of them went barging into the kitchen, Baird expected the wrath of their temperamental chef, who had his staff preparing delicacies for the evening. Instead, he watched Jonmair appease the man with a soft brush of her nager, watched him leave his work to examine Tonyo's hair, nod, and mix up a small pitcher of water and sugar. Then he added a squeeze of lemon juice, saying, "That will keep your hair shining as brightly as your field."

Tonyo took the mixture and stared into it. "You're all playing a joke on me, right? You want me to wash my hair with lemonade!"

Jonmair chuckled. "Taste it—there's not enough of either sugar or lemon to make lemonade. It's not a joke, really, Tonyo! Come on—let's get out of Chef's way, and I'll show you."

Upstairs, Jonmair gave Tonyo some shampoo and sent him to shower. "The last thing, after you've rinsed out the shampoo, is to pour the sugar water through and leave it in," she instructed. "Then come back and I'll style it for you."

With Tonyo behind the insulated bathroom door, Zhag lost his good cheer, but not his stability. If Baird had not seen him with the Gen, he wouldn't have zlinned anything but a normal post-turnover Sime. Were the good feelings worth being dependent on a Gen?

On the other hand, was keeping Gens around any different from drinking wine or porstan to release inhibitions and enhance feelings? Baird pretended interest in the costume designs Jonmair was showing them. Why had he run from her? She was just a Gen. He didn't have to hand control over to her the way Zhag did to Tonyo.

People made choices about wine, porstan, or gambling, didn't they? Baird and his father earned their living from those choices. A few people could not control themselves and became addicted to one or the other. But most people were perfectly capable of using The Post's offerings as recreation, and not having them take over their lives.

So most Simes ought to be capable of interacting with Gens, using them for their selyn, and not letting them take over their lives. *I can do that. I don't have to run away from Jonmair.*

Tonyo rejoined them, hair damp, announcing, "At least it's not sticky."

"I told you it wasn't lemonade," said Jonmair. "Now come here and let me comb your hair."

Baird watched her fuss over the Gen, placing him before the

sewing room mirror, combing his hair in different ways, snipping a few recalcitrant strands to make them blend with the rest. Zhag and Baird were at the other end of the long sewing table, the shiltpron player cheery now that his pet Gen was back in the room.

Tonyo was amusingly concerned about his appearance. "Doesn't he know all the audience cares about is how he zlins?" Baird said softly to Zhag, while Jonmair dispensed hair care advice to Tonyo.

"He's still learning," Zhag replied, "but so is our audience. After all, we want them to hear Tonyo. He does have an amazing voice, too."

That was true. That first night he had performed with Zhag at Milily's, Tonyo had shown power and range beyond any singer Baird had ever heard. Six weeks under Zhag's tutelage had given him greater control over his voice and a far better understanding of the meanings of their songs.

Duoconscious—both zlinning and watching the two Gens at the other end of the table—Baird noticed how interested Tonyo seemed in the costume sketches Jonmair was showing him...and in Jonmair. Tonyo couldn't do anything beyond flirting until his next transfer, but nonetheless—

Zhag was also watching the Gens. "Jonmair has artistic talent, too," he commented. "And they get along together. Maybe we should breed them."

The shock that went through Baird was so strong that Jonmair looked up sharply. Tonyo, though, said to Zhag, "I heard that. Gens don't go deaf and blind when we concentrate, you know."

Zhag, usually ultrasensitive to other Simes' feelings, ignored Baird's discomfiture as he replied, "Well, you should think about settling down, Tonyo."

"When I'm ready," the Gen replied, "I won't interfere with someone else's relationship. How would you feel if I tried to court Thea?"

"I'd rather you courted Janine," Zhag replied. Janine was Thea's Companion.

"I like Janine," said Tonyo, "but I don't think we could ever be more than friends."

Baird sensed something Tonyo wasn't saying, and zlinned that Zhag did too.

"Besides," the Gen added, "I'm younger than you are. I'm having fun. You don't have to tie me down with a wife. I'm not going anywhere."

* * * * * * *

JONMAIR HAD ALSO HEARD ZHAG'S REMARK, even uttered in his soft voice. It was uncharacteristic—of all the Simes she knew, Zhag was the most accepting of Gens as people in their own right. At Baird's reaction, though, she realized that she had an ally, not an enemy: Zhag had made the outrageous remark to test Baird's feelings. Carefully, she controlled her field so that her joy would not show.

Still, Zhag gave her an understanding smile: the channel could zlin through her control when renSimes could not. She couldn't affect him, either, as she could most of her customers, and testing her abilities on Inspector Kerrk had shown her it was that they were channels, not whether they had their own Gens, that gave them immunity to her talents. It didn't matter: as long as she could soothe Baird and her renSime customers, she was happy.

When Zhag and Tonyo left, Baird went downstairs to supervise last-minute preparations, and Jonmair was left to get ready for the evening. She arranged her hair in an elegant updo, and put on the dress she had made from the iridescent silk Zhag had picked out for her. She loved the material, the way the color shifted between black, dark blue, and a deep wine color that nearly matched her eyes.

If it were not already obvious to everyone that she was Gen, though, the dress revealed her increasingly rounded bosom and flowed outward from her slender waist over curves like no Sime woman's. *If I were Sime,* she reminded herself as she studied her image, *I would not be able to give Baird what he needs. I couldn't even dream of giving him transfer.*

She had no model for Gen beauty. But as she went down the staircase, Simes turned to her, laterals extending to zlin her...and she had to laugh at herself, and Tonyo as well. Among Simes, it hardly mattered what a Gen looked like.

There were a number of troops in uniform among the people already gathered, but Conta and Robert were for the first time dressed in civilian clothing. Conta wore a pale yellow dress with a tulle shawl, and her hair lay loose on her shoulders, fastened back with gardenias. Jonmair had had no idea the tough soldier could look so pretty. Robert, in a new suit of in-Territory cut, beamed with pride.

The opening was calculated to take advantage of as many post reactions as possible—even if the performers were not post themselves. Jonmair found Zhag and Tonyo in the dressing room, arriving just in time to stop Tonyo from taking a brush to his now-dry hair. "You can't brush curly hair," she told him. "In this climate it will frizz."

"Then how—?" he asked, puzzled.

"Just run your fingers through it," she told him.

When he did so, his hair sprang into soft curls around his face. He laughed. "That's neat! How did you know that?"

"From watching my mom with my little sister," she said. At the memory of her mother running her tentacles through Faleese's strawberry blonde curls the ache in her heart—that aloneness, desertion, betrayal she had felt so strongly in the Pen—suddenly reopened wounds she had thought healed.

Tonyo saw her face in the mirror, and Zhag must have felt her pain directly, for Tonyo hugged her, and Zhag came up behind her, wrapping gentle fingers and tentacles about her upper arms. The feel of those appendages brought tears again, tears she had thought she had used up forever in her first days of captivity.

Tonyo gently wiped her tears away with tissues from the dressing table. "It's all right," he said. "I didn't realize—of course you miss your family." Then he added, "But now—can't you go home to them if—?"

Zhag's hand moved swiftly from Jonmair's arm to Tonyo's, squeezing him to a halt. The Gen was bewildered. "What?" he asked. "What don't I know this time?"

"My parents," Jonmair managed to choke out, "s-sold me into the Pen."

"Bloody shit!" Tonyo exclaimed. "I'm so sorry. I didn't know—Jonmair, I never dreamed— How could anybody sell their own child—?"

"Tonyo," warned Zhag, "quit while you're ahead."

Jonmair looked into Tonyo's puzzled blue eyes and told him, "They only did what was expected of them."

Tonyo paled, and Zhag drove the point home. "That is what it means to be junct."

Tonyo stared at his partner over Jonmair's shoulder for a moment. Then he shook his head. "Not everyone did that," he said firmly. "Not you. You tried to take your brother to the border. My mom's parents did get her to the border, or I wouldn't be here. Not all junct Simes stop loving someone just because they turn Gen."

He looked back to Jonmair. "Please forgive me. I didn't know—"

"And you don't know that Zhag and your grandparents are the exception, not the rule," said Jonmair.

"I don't think so," said Tonyo.

"You didn't live here before Unity," she told him. "Zhag and I did."

Tonyo shook his head. "I can believe most people obeyed the law. Out of fear. I understand why the law had to punish them if they didn't turn over their Gen children—as long as the Kill continued. But I can't believe that most people didn't suffer for it—and are suffering still."

Jonmair met Zhag's eyes in the mirror, and saw kinship. He understood, as she did, what Tonyo could not. At least not yet. Culture shock, he had called it. This one appeared to be his worst yet.

"Tonyo," said Zhag, "we're on in ten minutes. Are you going to be all right?"

"Of course I am," his partner replied. "Jonmair?"

"I'm fine," she said, forcing a smile that she knew fooled neither man, but they accepted it. "Let me make sure your costumes are all in order."

They were now wearing the identical black trousers they had purchased at the Keon Emporium and—because it was stiflingly hot with both the native heat of midsummer and the crowd—just the shirt-vests that Jonmair had made for them, without shirts.

The effect was to emphasize their Sime/Gen differences, especially as Zhag was still too thin, his tentacle sheaths making cords down his forearms with no flesh to hide them. Jonmair noticed that Zhag's ronaplin glands seemed far too swollen for his negligible state of Need.

"It's normal for me," he insisted.

"It is," Tonyo agreed. "You'll see why when he performs."

Jonmair went out to the table near the stage where Baird and Treavor Axton were talking to people being seated at the front tables. The big salon was nearly full already. She saw Robert and Conta seated with two Simes in dress uniform several tiers back. Another table of soldiers made a dark patch amidst the bright clothing toward the back of the room.

The Post's efficient staff were serving drinks, and people talked and laughed while waiting for the show to begin. A stir went through the crowd, though, as six people entered: three Simes and three Gens, all in formal floor-length capes with the insignia of Householding Carre.

Jonmair recognized the channel Thea and her Companion Janine; the Sectuib in Carre, whom she had met only once when he spoke to her training class; his Companion; and two other women she didn't know but assumed one of them to be the Sectuib's wife. As they were Householders, she did not know whether it was the Sime or the Gen!

People stared and whispered as the Householders were

escorted to a table next to the Axtons. As they removed their cloaks and introductions were performed, Jonmair learned that the Sime woman was the Sectuib's wife. Like the Sectuib, she and her Companion were of Baird's father's generation. But the Sectuib's Companion was hardly more than a girl, in a sprigged muslin dress, bursting with excitement at being here. "This is our daughter Laweez," the Sectuib introduced her, "performing her first public duty as my Companion this evening."

"She just established three months ago," her mother said, beaming with pride. "But she has already given transfer, and is developing into a fine Companion."

Jonmair fought down jealousy of this young woman whose parents not only loved her despite her becoming Gen, but would never think of it as "despite."

Laweez smiled at Jonmair and asked, "Do you know Zhag and Tonyo? I've heard so much about them. I know they've been at Carre, but I've never had the chance to meet them."

"I'll introduce you after the show," said Jonmair.

"If it doesn't interfere with your work," Treavor Axton said warningly.

Jonmair did not reply because Baird's father was capable of sending her to her room for talking back. He was already annoyed at having Householders in the best seats, but they were Zhag and Tonyo's guests.

The lights dimmed, and the huge room hushed expectantly. Then they went out entirely, a few throbbing chords of music played, and when the stage lights came on to a gasp from the audience, Zhag was seated behind his shiltpron in the spotlight, Tonyo sitting tailor-fashion on the floor just at the edge of the light.

* * * * * * *

BAIRD WONDERED WHAT THE GENS IN THE AUDIENCE MADE of the beginning of the performance. Were they aware that to Sime senses, Tonyo Logan wasn't there?

It was a common Companion's trick, of course—even Jonmair knew how to disappear from the ambient. But translated into showmanship the simple function was highly effective: the Simes in the audience had to remain duoconscious in order to absorb the nageric nuances of Zhag's playing and at the same time see what the Gen performer they had heard so much about was doing.

Which for the moment was nothing at all.

Zhag performed solo for only a few bars, however. Then Tonyo rose to his feet, remaining near the back of the stage beside Zhag, and began to sing.

Using only his voice, without words, Tonyo sang harmony with the melody Zhag played. They exchanged parts, Tonyo taking the melody and Zhag the harmony—and then moved on to counterpoint, a performance of pure sound.

It was elegant, it was beautiful, and it was totally unexpected—absolutely nothing like the raucous songs they had performed at Milily's. When the piece ended, the audience sat in rapt appreciation for a moment before exploding into cheers.

Tonyo bowed, and gestured toward Zhag, who gave a shy grin, settled his hands over the strings, and plucked the opening notes of an old saloon song. The audience recognized it, cheered louder for a moment, and then quieted as Tonyo began to sing— this time with nageric accompaniment.

"Taxes goin' higher,
Last month I sold my horse.
Border's too far for raiding—
How could things get worse?
Ol' Mizipi rising—
Flood and hurricane—"

It was one of the songs Tonyo could not get right when he had first started performing with Zhag. By now, though, he had developed enough understanding of what it meant to be Sime to produce a realistic nageric accompaniment. He soon had every Sime in the room shuddering at the specter of frustrated Need.

The song might have been traditional, but where Zhag and

Tonyo then took it definitely was not. Baird sensed growing concern at the next table as Tonyo began to project quintessential Gen—Wild Gen, at first merely wary, then frightened.

Zhag played variations on the melody, Tonyo again vocalizing. They had run out of lyrics, for this was never part of the original song. Zhag picked up mallets, hammering as well as plucking strings, keeping time with the Gen's increasingly frenzied heartbeat. He began to project a Need Baird knew he did not really feel—a channel's trick, he reminded himself, wondering if it were possible for Zhag to become so wrapped up in his own performance as to lose control. Ronaplin dripped from his extended laterals as if he were in hard Need.

The Sectuib in Carre slid quickly over to the Axton table. "Mr. Axton," he whispered sharply, projecting urgency with his nager, "you have to stop the performance!"

Clearly annoyed at having his own concentration broken, Treavor Axton looked around. Every Sime in the room was spellbound.

"Why should I?" he growled. "This is what folks're paying for."

"Because if it continues," the Sectuib replied, "it's going to provoke a Kill!"

CHAPTER EIGHT
POSTSYNDROME

BAIRD, WHO HAD SEEN ZHAG AND TONYO CONTROL MOBS of rowdy juncts at Milily's without provoking so much as a fist fight, said, "Hush. They know what they're doing."

The Sectuib insisted, "They can't. Zlin the ambient!"

"Shut up!" Treavor Axton whispered. "If you disrupt the performance, I'll have you and your whole gang thrown out!"

For a moment, Baird thought the channel would walk out, but then he moved back to his table and gathered the attention of the Householders, preparing to act if there was trouble.

On stage, meanwhile, the performance became a musical chase. Zhag's playing took on the sound of running water—first metaphorically, then as close to the actual sound of a rushing river as the shiltpron could produce. The Gen apparently took to a boat—and suddenly the Simes in the audience felt as if they'd been doused with cold water! The frustrated Sime was left floundering.

The sensation lasted only for a second or two, followed immediately with the triumphant relief of the escaping Gen fading into the distance.

The audience burst into laughter.

The music went back to the chorus, the poor Sime wondering, "How could things get worse?"

The laughter, Baird realized, was relief. Although the Sime in the song was a stereotype, there had frequently been people in that very situation...and whole Territories faced it if the Pen system collapsed. *There, but for the grace of God—*

The cheering for this unique performance was even stronger—the junct audience loved Zhag and Tonyo, whatever the Householders might think. The musicians next launched into traditional barroom songs, sung pretty much as they had done them at Milily's. Tonyo stepped down off the stage, wandering from table to table, focusing his attention on each member of the audience in turn.

As they brought their medley of songs to an end, Tonyo moved to the Axton table, laved them with his field as he had been doing for all the Simes, and after the song ended took Jonmair's hand and drew her to her feet. "I want you to meet someone," he announced. "This is Jonmair, who has a lot more talent than just a beautiful nager. She designed these great costumes for Zhag and me."

Jonmair blushed. Baird felt proud of her, and it occurred to him that he had never questioned his father's assigning her to menial tasks. What other talents might she have?

After a pause to drink some water, Tonyo took center stage, saying, "The next songs may not be familiar to some of you. They're Gen songs—Wild Gen songs, if you prefer."

Some uncertain giggles.

"Oh, I know what you think about Wild Gens," said Tonyo. "Used to be a Wild Gen myself, you know."

Derisive snorts.

"Hey—what you've heard about Wild Gens is true!"

Skeptical chuckles.

"I guess I've been tamed now. All *his* fault," he added conspiratorially, pointing at Zhag from behind his hand.

The laughter became a bit uneasy, as Simes wondered where this monologue was going.

"The songs we're about to perform are about what it's like to be a Wild Gen. Which I will be again in about—" He began counting on his fingers, looking puzzled when he had used them all up. Then, with a flick of his nager as if he had just had an inspiration, he went to Zhag, lifted one Sime arm, and finished counting on Zhag's handling tentacles, concluding triumphantly, "—about thirteen days from now!"

The audience exploded into laughter.

Tonyo's humor was crude, but it was effective. Baird wondered how many Simes realized that Tonyo was playing on all the stereotypes of Gens, always post, not very intelligent? Did they realize how he was manipulating them?

No matter what level they got it on, he zlinned that everyone enjoyed it. Even his father was laughing.

"This next song is supposed to have come down to us from the Ancients," Tonyo continued. "I'm not so sure about that, though—because it's pretty obviously about being post!"

Zhag's shiltpron exploded with pounding rhythm and wailing chords. Tonyo met it note for note, his voice sailing through sounds like nothing human, his field berserk with raw sexuality.

Baird knew enough of the Gen language to recognize that he was not distorting the meaning of the song—it *was* about raw sexuality! He zlinned Jonmair responding to the primitive Gen rhythms. Finally, she was becoming post.

So was everyone in the salon.

It would not last, Baird knew, for anyone past turnover, but by far the majority of their patrons had had transfer within the past couple of days. With Zhag and Tonyo performing this way, he realized, The Post could once again live up to its name.

To rousing cheers, the musicians bowed, and took a brief break. In the interval, people came to the Axtons' table to congratulate them. Treavor Axton told everyone, "My son found them. He has a fine lateral for talent." Baird basked in his father's rare approval, and traded smiles with Jonmair, thinking of getting away with her—

But just then a woman approached…and spoke directly to Jonmair!

"You designed the performers' costumes? And the dress you're wearing, too?"

"I made them," Jonmair replied, "but they're all based on patterns I got at the Keon Emporium."

"May I?" the woman asked, and turned back the edge of Jonmair's sleeve to examine the stitching. "Fine workmanship," she said. "Perfect fit. Are you interested in another commission?"

Baird restrained himself, hard, to keep from threatening another Sime touching his Gen.

But his father had no such compunction. "The Gen works here, Miz Delancy. It has plenty of work."

The woman gave him a smile. "Well, you can't blame me for asking, Treavor. You can't keep all the best talent in Norlea tied up forever." And she turned once more to Jonmair. "If you're ever looking for work, I own Delancy's Dresses."

Jonmair's field glowed with both pleasure and confidence, and for once Baird blessed his father's competitive spirit. The more he realized the woman's potential value, the harder he would hang on to her. After tonight Baird could dismiss the threats to send Jonmair to the other end of the Territory.

* * * * * * *

JONMAIR COULD NOT BELIEVE IT! Miz Delancy had approached her as if she were Sime, able to choose whom to work for. Despite Treavor Axton's warning, "Don't you get any grand ideas!" she indulged in grand ideas indeed. The new laws were not completed—but when they were, surely they would include some way for Gens to choose their work. She could have her long-cherished dream of becoming a fashion designer! And if she could do that...then it might even be possible to marry someone like Baird Axton.

As Jonmair sat thinking of how she could turn her dream into reality, Zhag and Tonyo came back, and Zhag spoke to the audience for the first time as he carefully disconnected the central stringed part of his shiltpron—the essential instrument—from its peripherals and amplifiers. He sat on a chair Tonyo set out for him near the front of the stage to one side, his instrument on his lap.

"Now we're going to perform a song that Tonyo wrote," said Zhag as he tested the tuning of his shiltpron and tightened a string.

"Just the lyrics," Tonyo said. "Zhag wrote the melody. It's a real Sime/Gen collaboration."

Jonmair had had no idea Zhag and Tonyo were this talented. Not only were they brilliant performers, but they could compose new music, too. *Just as I can not only sew, but design,* she thought. *People will learn that Gens can be just as talented as Simes.*

The music began with Tonyo seated cross-legged on the floor again at the far side of the stage as Zhag played a soft, haunting melody. Then the Gen began to sing.

"My brother, he turned out wrong—
Had to run for the border.
And I will never see his face again—
Never see him again."

People gasped, listening to a story every Sime knew, but never, ever talked about.

"My sister, she turned out wrong," Tonyo sang next.
"The Sheriff came to shoot her—
And I will never see her face again—
Never see her again."

The realization that turning out the wrong larity had been equally a death sentence on the Gen side of the border rang through the room—Jonmair could almost zlin it.

"My daughter, she turned out wrong—
I don't know where they took her,
But I will never see her face again—
Never zlin her again."

Jonmair wondered if there were indeed parents who had cared when they allowed their Gen children to be taken. Had her own parents felt a twinge of loss?

"My son, he turned out wrong—
And I dared not to touch him."

The musicians remained on opposite sides of the stage as the song continued with variations on the sweet, sad melody, voice and instrument taking different, clashing paths that mimicked the poignant reality that had existed until so very recently. Then, melody and counterpoint began to move toward one another as Tonyo rose and moved toward Zhag, circling, backtracking, hesitating—and finally moving behind him to stand with his hands on the Sime's shoulders as once again he sang without words, instrument and voice meshing in beautiful, soaring, blended chords of hope.

When the music ended, there was total silence. Jonmair tried to swallow the lump in her throat, then dared to look around. People all over the room were wiping their eyes.

A voice from the back called, "Again!"

"Sing it again!" someone else cried in a choking voice.

"Again!" "Again!"

Zhag and Tonyo looked at one another in amazement—clearly they had not expected this reaction. Then Zhag nodded, and Tonyo, after taking another drink of water, moved once again to the far side of the stage.

No one in the audience moved. The waiting staff retreated to stand by the bar. Utter stillness reigned as Zhag and Tonyo performed the song again.

By the time it was over, every person in the room was crying. The performers remained in stillness as the silence told them more than any applause how much the audience had been moved.

Jonmair dabbed at her own tears, and looked over at Baird. He reached out a hand, and she took it, feeling at last that he understood, and that next month he would accept transfer from her. She wanted it so badly—it had to be how Need felt for a Sime.

Finally Zhag got up, cradling his shiltpron, while Tonyo moved his chair to center stage. Zhag sat down again, and Tonyo spoke to the audience.

"We have with us tonight soldiers, both Sime and Gen, who fought in the battle against the Raider bands who almost brought on Zelerod's Doom. They tell me that in that campaign Simes and Gens had to learn to fight side by side, shoulder to shoulder, comrades rather than enemies."

"That's true," said Conta. "I was there." She took Robert's hand across their table.

"That was when you learned that Unity was possible," said Tonyo.

"It was," called some of the soldiers at other tables.

"And you tell me," Tonyo continued, "that after the battle was won, Simes and Gens who had fought together, had shared food and selyn, did not separate back into Sime and Gen units, but celebrated together."

"Aye!" "We did!"

"And there was a song everyone knew," Tonyo added. "They say the music goes back to the Ancients, but the words are different in different times and places. I know it, Zhag knows it. You know it—and it doesn't matter if we all sing different words. We all know the same tune. Join me!"

The shiltpron crashed into a vibrant marching rhythm, and everyone began to sing, growing louder as they gained confidence. Tonyo was right that everybody knew different words to the verse—but whatever they had once sung for the chorus, there were new words now, spread throughout the territories by those who had been there:

> "Peace to Sime and Gen forever,
> Hope for Sime and Gen together,
> Peace to Sime and Gen forever,
> Together one and all!"

When the song ended the cheering and whistling were loud enough to raise the roof. Everyone rose to their feet in acknowledgment of the catharsis they had experienced, Sime and Gen alike.

The performers bowed, holding hands, Zhag's tentacles sealing Sime and Gen hands together. Zhag's laterals dripped ronaplin all over Tonyo, who didn't seem to mind or even notice.

But on the stairs up to the Gold Salon, both performers wiped sweat and ronaplin off themselves as the mob surrounded and carried them upward, the entire audience trying to crowd into the small room where supper was laid out.

Baird and Treavor Axton signaled to their staff, and waiters quickly began circulating with chits for the gambling tables and promises that after they had eaten, Zhag and Tonyo would circulate through all the rooms so everyone would get the chance to see them again.

The near riot averted, Treavor Axton turned to Baird. "You made a real find, Son. That's the most amazing act I've ever zlinned, and I've been in Norlea all my life. Offer Zhag a raise and a year's contract before someone snatches them from us the way you snatched them from Milily. Give them free rooms into the deal! People will come in at all hours if there's a chance of running into our star attraction."

When Baird and Jonmair reached the Gold Salon—by the back stairs that were not open to the public—they found their "star attraction" holding court.

Zhag and Tonyo sat behind the largest table in the room, drinking porstan and talking to people who had formed a receiving line. Jonmair saw a Sime woman surreptitiously pick up the ronaplin-soaked towel one of them had left draped over the back of a chair. A rather odd choice of souvenir.

Someone brought Tonyo a plate of food and he ate heartily, trying to entice Zhag. Suddenly Zhag gasped and grabbed for the canapé Tonyo was about to bite into.

"I thought you weren't hungry," said Tonyo.

"That's poison to you!" said Zhag, turning pale. Then he looked up at Baird. "Doesn't your chef know brown dagger mushrooms are deadly to Gens?"

Baird seemed taken aback. "Probably not. I didn't know it." He looked helplessly at Jonmair.

"It's on the list we got at Carre," she said. "Tonyo—didn't you learn what to watch out for?"

"Yes—but I just assumed food would be safe here."

"You'd pay attention if you stopped breathing!" said Zhag, his fear for his partner and Companion turning to anger.

"All right," said Tonyo, "I'll be sure to look under the toppings before I eat anything."

Zhag said to Baird, "Gens can't zlin. How are they supposed to know if some ingredient in a sauce or a salad is poison to them?"

He took Tonyo's plate, zlinned it carefully, removed a small sandwich made of many layers of colorful ingredients, and handed the rest back.

"I'll make certain Chef gets the list from Carre," said Baird.

"Chef likes Tonyo," said Jonmair. "He'd never deliberately—"

"I know it wasn't deliberate, but if he had eaten that he'd be just as dead. You have Gen patrons now," said Zhag. "You don't want them to have to worry about whether they dare eat your food."

"Just label it," said Tonyo, "the way they do in Householding refectories. Simes Only, Gens Only, and if it's unlabeled it's safe for everybody."

Jonmair could see Baird trying to assimilate the idea of Gens as patrons. If it sounded strange to her, how much more difficult must it be for him?

How could it be so easy for Zhag?

The Householders arrived just then, and Zhag and Tonyo invited them to sit with them. Jonmair realized that that was why the two had commandeered a table for eight. She enjoyed seeing the way Zhag and Thea, although neither was post, lit up when they saw one another. Baird told Zhag and Tonyo about his father's promise that they would circulate through the salons, and left them to their friends.

"Come on," he said, taking Jonmair's hand as they left the crowded salon. But when they reached the back stair again, he led her up, not down, to a landing where they would not be seen, nor zlinned through the post-heavy ambient below. Baird drew her into his arms and kissed her. *At last!*

Jonmair kissed eagerly back, loving the feel of his hot mouth exploring hers as his arms supported her, one hand cupping her head, handling tentacles sliding into her hair. In a moment he drew back, gray eyes luminous with promise. Then he took her hand again and led her to his room.

Her breath coming rapidly, Jonmair turned to Baird the moment the door closed, and began unbuttoning his shirt. His tentacles dealt with the fastenings of her dress, and they laughed as they stripped one another and fell onto the bed.

Their mating was swift but sweet, Baird grinning up at Jonmair as she straddled him, working her hips to pleasure herself while she saw in his eyes that she was carrying him away. He caressed her with hands and tentacles, even extending his laterals to tingle her nipples with ronaplin.

By now they knew many of each other's quirks, but there were still little surprises, such as Baird's helpless gasp when Jonmair held him suspended with her field as she built her own desire to its peak before she released him to share the moment of perfection.

Panting, Baird pulled her down into his arms, kissing her aggressively. "You are incredible!" he whispered.

"So are you," she responded. "I wish we could stay here forever."

He sighed. "Don't tempt me, sorceress."

And then something wary entered his eyes, and he frowned. Sitting up, he said, "Why did I let you do that? I have duties, and so have you, Jonmair."

"No one missed us," she said, putting a hand carefully on his forearm, knowing now exactly how to torment him with her field without hurting his delicate laterals.

"Don't!" he said, pulling away. "Get dressed," he said, pulling on his own clothes. "We're expected downstairs."

His laterals were now tightly retracted, so her field could have no effect on him. They did have to go back downstairs, but Jonmair was certain that their few stolen moments had hurt nothing.

Still, she didn't argue, but found her own clothes and put herself back in order. Her carefully-coiffed hairstyle was a casualty, though. She brushed it into shining waves and followed Baird out of the room.

The Post remained crowded, the biggest house Jonmair had seen since she had come to work here.

"It will be even more crowded once word gets out," said Baird, all business once again. "We'll take out the back tables in the main salon tomorrow, and put more chairs in. We're going to be sold out for the foreseeable future."

In the gambling hall, Jonmair saw a greater bustle than any night since the Last Kill. All the tables were crowded, and at the bars at either end Emlu's girls plied their trade successfully for the first time in two weeks. As Jonmair watched, three of them led customers out. She refused to let herself think of the torn sheets to mend tomorrow.

Zhag and Tonyo were circulating through the hall, accepting congratulations on all sides. They had changed from their costumes into casual shirts and denims. Jonmair held her field tight so her moment's amused speculation would not show—but the musicians were not post. They would have changed clothes only so their costumes could be cleaned for tomorrow's show, not because of any hasty, sweaty encounters with the opposite sex.

The performers were alone—not surprising that the Householders had left, as so many channels and Companions could not have time off at once. Thea would probably save her free time until she and Zhag were post again.

The musicians settled on stools at the end of the bar, where they continued to charm everyone who approached them. When the crowd finally thinned out, Zhag and Tonyo got up to leave. Tonyo staggered slightly, and Zhag righted him. Drunk?

"Nah, just tired," the Gen reassured them with a sleepy grin. "Great night. Don't want it to end." But his words were smothered in a yawn.

Zhag laughed. "I'd better get you home, before I have to

carry you!"

"I want to talk to you about that," said Baird. "Come into the front office for a minute. Tonyo, you can take a nap if you like." He gestured to the couch as they entered the office.

But Tonyo elected to remain standing. "If we're gonna talk business, I'd better stay awake." His eyes widened, and then he glanced at Zhag. "Thanks."

"What did you do?" asked Jonmair, who had sensed a change in the ambient that caused her to shift position to shield Baird, but couldn't say what it was.

"I'm projecting Need," Zhag replied, "and just a hint of interest in you. It puts my Companion into alert mode. Now, Baird, what did you want to talk about?"

"We'd like to offer you a raise and a year's contract," said Baird.

"Six months," said Zhag as if he negotiated such things daily, "extendable for six more if both parties agree, payment to be renegotiated quarterly."

Jonmair choked back a giggle. She hadn't expected the shy artist to turn abruptly into astute businessman.

But, "Agreed," said Baird. "Fifty percent increase over what we're paying you now."

Zhag looked at Tonyo, who nodded.

"Agreed," said the shiltpron player. "Draw it up, and we'll sign it."

"Wait a minute," said Baird. "It still includes Tonyo eating lunch and supper in our public dining rooms."

"As long as they don't try to poison me," said Tonyo.

"I'll get Chef the lists of foods from Carre in the morning," said Baird, "and we'll start labeling immediately."

"Payment," said Zhag. "Half and half between Tonyo and me."

Baird shrugged. "I don't care how you split it."

"No—hold off on the contract for a few days. Tonyo will take the citizenship exam as soon as the office opens in Norlea," Zhag explained. "Then he can open his own bank account, and sign his own contracts. It's important, Baird. People have to get used to Gens handling their own affairs."

"What difference does it make?" Baird asked in annoyance.

"It makes a difference," Jonmair put in. "Take my word for it."

Baird scowled at her. "Zhag and Tonyo are an act," he said. "Zhag's managing it. It's routine to pay the manager rather than the individual performers."

"Then put Tonyo down as manager," said Zhag. "There's a point to be made, and we have an obligation to make it."

Baird sighed. "All right—I'll have our bookkeeper split the payment. Now—one more perk. We want to give you rooms here."

"No," chorused Zhag and Tonyo, without the consulting glances.

"But why?" Jonmair asked. "It's so much nicer here than that old house you're living in."

"Privacy," said Zhag. "We're not just Sime and Gen—we are channel and Companion. You don't have a suitable suite of rooms. When we have transfer, we don't want to have to traipse over to the Old Pen or to Carre to use one of their antiseptic cubicles, or else have to use your—" distaste in his voice "—old Killroom in order not to have every Sime in the vicinity zlin what we're doing."

"But your house isn't selyn insulated at all!" said Baird.

"It's far away from everything and everybody," said Zhag. "Besides, we're looking for better quarters. We also require musical privacy—someplace we can compose without being overheard."

"My father really wants you on the premises," said Baird.

"Not gonna happen," said Tonyo. "Baird, I don't know exactly what relationship you and Jonmair may have," although the way the corners of his mouth turned up as his eyes went to Jonmair's loose hair indicated that he knew perfectly well. "However, it's obvious she Companions you. I nightward Zhag when he's in Need—but when we're post, we both require privacy. We are neither sexual partners nor voyeurs," he said bluntly.

"So?" said Baird. "No one cares, Tonyo."

"Well, we do," the Gen explained. "We have to have a house or an apartment that allows us to be together during Need and have privacy when we're post—yet always be within reach. The Householdings build suites for Simes and Gens to accommodate the Need cycle. There are houses built on that design for mixed Sime~Gen families over near Carre. We're looking for something like that, with far more insulation than average, but we're not going to ask you to remodel for us."

"Tonyo requires a place where he doesn't have to control his field every minute," Zhag added. "If he overwhelms me at times, think how careful he has to be among renSimes."

"I can handle the ambient in public," said Tonyo. "But, well, it's really hard to find a place to relax. Think about it—you wouldn't want me sleeping in the room next to yours. If I had a nightmare, I'd spook every Sime on the floor!"

And you wouldn't dare lose control during your sexual escapades, Jonmair realized. She hadn't thought of a field as strong as Tonyo's was reputed to be as a liability.

"I see," said Baird. "All right—we won't make residency a requirement. But don't be late for lunch. And we do have a sound-insulated rehearsal room you can use."

The terms were agreed to, Zhag and Tonyo left, and Baird and Jonmair were free for what was left of the night.

Jonmair was not as tired as Tonyo, as she had been off duty most of the day. They walked through the gambling hall, which stayed open all night. Inveterate gamblers were still at the tables—there was never a time when this room had no patrons.

Less than half the tables were occupied at this hour. At one of them, Robert and Conta played poker with a group of Simes who, she deduced from the pile of chips in front of the Gen soldier, were learning that a poker field was a greater advantage than a poker face.

At the back of the room, Treavor Axton played cards with a group of Simes his own age. He looked better tonight than he had since his rough transfer. If Zhag and Tonyo could keep making Simes—and Gens—feel post even after poor transfers, the Axtons should consider expanding their main salon!

Jonmair moved nearer to Baird as they climbed the stairs, letting her anticipation show. When they entered his room, she turned into his arms.

Tentacles tightly retracted, he grasped her upper arms and pushed her away, saying, "Stop that!"

"Stop what?" she asked, letting honest puzzlement show in her field.

"Stop controlling me!"

"I'm not!" she protested. "I'm only letting you feel what I feel."

"So you can get what you want from me!"

"I thought we wanted the same thing."

"How does Zhag stand it?" Baird asked.

Jonmair tried to follow his train of thought. "You mean how he lets Tonyo protect him from the ambient?"

"I mean how he lets Tonyo run his life!"

Jonmair frowned. That was not how she saw the two musicians. "They're partners—equal partners. It's hard for people to think of Gens as fully human, but we are. Zhag makes sure he treats Tonyo that way because they are in the public eye, setting an example."

"That's what you want us to think, isn't it?" asked Baird.

"Us? What do you mean, Baird?"

"Us—Simes. You Gens want us dependent on you. You already have the power of life and death. Why do you have to control our thoughts, too? Is it revenge?"

She fought to control her emotions, although she could tell Baird was deliberately not zlinning. "Baird, you know I can't control your thoughts," she said reasonably. "I can influence your feelings only if you let me. What you're doing right now is all you ever have to do to escape Gen influence."

"Right," he said, "just give up one of my senses!" He shook his head. "Get out of here, you whore! I know what you are now.

How I could have let you use me earlier—"

"Baird, no!" she gasped, cut to the quick.

"I said go!" he insisted. "Go away! Leave me alone!"

Tears blurring her vision, Jonmair fled.

CHAPTER NINE
CITIZENSHIP

JONMAIR DRESSED IN HER WORK LIVERY THE NEXT MORNING and came down to breakfast. Baird was nowhere to be seen, nor was his father. She was over an hour late, having cried herself to sleep near dawn, but Chef was only beginning to lay out the makings of lunch. She saw him studying lists of foods, frowning. "How am I supposed to prepare foods for Gens that are poisonous to Simes?"

"Hire a Gen cook?" Jonmair suggested before she even thought.

He stared at her indignantly for a moment, and then shook his head. "Why not? Can you cook, Jonny?"

It was useless to protest Treavor Axton's name for her with his staff, so she replied, "All I know is cooking for Simes or children."

He grinned. "Of course. And I don't know where to get these ingredients anyway. White cloud mushrooms? Cheltenham flour? Strawberries? There's none of that in the market."

"Did someone say strawberries?" Tonyo asked, barging into the kitchen and helping himself to a cup of kafi and an orange. "Where'd you get strawberries out of season?"

"I didn't," Chef told him. "They're on this list of Gen foods." He showed Tonyo.

Tonyo said, "My dad has a strawberry patch in the back yard. Maybe the Householders grow them. I love strawberry short-cake." He studied the list. "I can help with the mushrooms. My dad taught me the safe ones when we went camping. I don't know what Simes call most of them, but I can show you in the woods. I ate lots of mushrooms and blackberries on the road between Keon and here."

"Blackberries are safe for both larities," said Chef. "Until I can add a Gen cook to the staff, I think we'll have only two kinds of food, 'Simes only,' and 'Safe for everyone.'"

"That'll do for now," said Tonyo, opening the bread cupboard and slicing himself a big chunk. "Jonmair, you want some bread and jam?" he asked.

"Don't go spoiling your appetite for lunch!" Chef warned. "You're both due in the kafi shop in an hour."

"That's why this is all I'm having now!" Tonyo replied, smearing his bread with marmalade. Then, "I wonder if Miz Coyt would want to work here."

"Who's that?" asked Chef.

"Penta Coyt am Carre," said Tonyo. "She's Gen, but her husband's Sime. She works at the Keon Emporium, but they've got a son just established they want to send out-Territory to learn Gen engineering. That's going to cost more than the two of them are making right now."

It was clear to Jonmair that Chef was taken aback at actually hearing of a candidate for the position of Gen cook—he had probably thought he could use the lack of staff not to deal with providing a Gen menu. But he quickly melted under Tonyo's innocent gaze, and no doubt the effect of his field.

"Tell her to come and see me—and remember, if I hire her, what she cooks, you have to eat!"

Then he shooed Tonyo and Jonmair out of the kitchen. "Why are you here so early?" Jonmair asked Tonyo. "And where's Zhag?"

"Asserting his independence," Tonyo responded. "Actually he's fine on his own. No matter what people say, I don't want Zhag dependent on me between turnover and transfer."

"Simes got along without Gens at their side before Unity," Jonmair agreed.

"Yeah, but Zhag's a channel. From what they tell us at Carre, I ought to keep him on a leash two weeks out of the month! It's ridiculous. The man has so much control I'd swear he could levitate if he just put his mind to it."

"They're afraid he'll hurt somebody?" Jonmair asked.

"Isn't that crazy? The Householders are paranoid about protecting Gens, when with the proper training we're perfectly capable of protecting ourselves. Oh, well, people will get used to us." He pulled a pamphlet from his pocket. "Will you help me puzzle out some of this legal language?"

The pamphlet contained instructions for applying for citizenship—and although Jonmair had spoken Simelan all her life, she found it as confusing as Tonyo did. "That's deliberate!" she said. "They don't want Gens to understand it."

"I wonder if Simes can," said Tonyo.

"Ask Zhag."

"I will. He hasn't seen it yet—I picked it up on my way here this morning. But come on—let's see if we can work it out."

The language was deliberately convoluted, but the two Gens took it paragraph by paragraph, and had worked out the requirements by the time Baird Axton entered the kafi shop.

* * * * * * *

THE FIRST THING BAIRD SAW AND ZLINNED was the table near the entrance where two hungry Gens sat side by side, bent over some papers. He was about to scold them and tell them to eat when he realized that Sime customers were being affected by Gen hunger even when the Gens weren't. There were more customers than the day before, and the staff were already making fresh pots of tea and kafi. As he watched, honey cakes were brought from the kitchen to restock the empty shelf.

So he forced down the annoyance he felt as he approached the Gens' table, wondering why he was displeased to find Jonmair trying to work her sorcery on a fellow Gen. Tonyo looked up with a grin as Baird approached. "Hello! Just the man I want to see!"

"Oh?" Baird asked suspiciously.

"Do you have any of your old school books I can borrow, Baird? I can read and write and do arithmetic, but I have to study up on Gulf Territory history and government before I take the citizenship test."

"You're serious about that?" Baird asked. "Why would you want to become a Gulf Territory citizen?"

"Because I live here!" Tonyo told him. "Zhag and I can work together here. It'll be years before Simes will be allowed into Gen Territory. Besides, I like it."

What harm to let the Gen try? "Sure, Tonyo—I think my old schoolbooks are in the library. After lunch I'll help you find them."

Jonmair had said nothing so far. She seemed subdued today, her field as neutral as she could hold it without doing her disappearing act. Now she looked around. "Oh—it is time to eat, isn't it? I'll get us some food."

Tonyo watched her go with a puzzled frown. "Lovers' quarrel?" he asked. Then, "Sorry—none of my business." He turned his attention on Baird, who almost squirmed as the focus of that overpowering field. Tonyo pulled it down several notches and said, "I thought you approved of Unity."

"I do," Baird said. "It's just...I don't think any of us considered all the consequences."

"Like the possibility of Gens in the legislature?" Tonyo teased.

"Like the possibility of Gens everywhere," said Baird. "Chef wants to hire a Gen cook. Pretty soon there won't be anywhere a Sime can go to escape Gens."

Tonyo looked at him, eyes candid, field candid, and asked, "Why would you want to? I feel no desire to escape Simes— ever since I set foot in-Territory it's felt right."

"Just last night you claimed you couldn't live here at The Post because you require privacy," Baird pointed out.

"Well, there are some things no one wants to broadcast to the world," Tonyo said reasonably. "Most of the time I'm perfectly comfortable being zlinned."

Tonyo's field indicated that, in fact, he enjoyed it.

"Yes," the Gen disconcertingly answered his thought, "I do enjoy it, especially when I'm post and the Simes zlinning me are beautiful women. But when I'm in Need—"

"High field," Baird corrected. "You can't feel Need, Tonyo."

"Really?" the Gen asked, and washed him over with a poignant yearning that was only an echo of what Baird had zlinned in Jonmair when she had pursued him—stalked him, he realized—on his transfer day.

Tonyo shielded the feeling immediately, and said, "That's nothing to what I felt when Zhag was in hard Need, and now that I've actually experienced transfer I expect it will be nearly unbearable to be apart at the end of the month. And you tell me it's Zhag who's dependent on me?" He sat back, looking Baird up and down as if he might see what a Sime would zlin. "You brought Zhag and me together, Baird. You knew—you zlinned me and immediately sent for Zhag. Why can't you zlin that you and Jonmair belong together?"

Baird watched Jonmair, who had finally reached the front of the queue, loading a tray with food and drinks. "Why can't Jonmair see what you see? You don't have to watch Zhag all the time. To tell the truth, the way you control him sets my teeth on edge, but today he's in Need and you're not dogging his foot-steps. Or did he send you away?"

"No—he didn't invite me along today, so I let him go. And Baird...I don't control Zhag, any more than Jonmair controls you. We could, because in both cases we're matchmates— but you and Zhag could control us, too. But life shouldn't be a contest of wills. I think the reason Zhag doesn't sense my support as control is that he knows it goes both ways. Try zlin-ning how much what you do and feel affects Jonmair. I think you'll see she has no advantage."

Remembering again the selyur nager—the Need to Give— with which Jonmair had pursued him on his transfer day, Baird had to agree. Why had it frightened him? Wasn't Jonmair doing exactly the same thing Tonyo was today, staying away from him because he hadn't invited her?

I drove her away, he reminded himself, regretting his harsh words.

In the cold light of day, he realized that their lovemaking last night had not happened only because Jonmair was Gen. Every available room in The Post had been taken after the concert—if he had been with a Sime woman, the same thing would have happened. If anyone was at fault, it was Zhag and Tonyo! But no one else considered their good feelings after the concert a bad thing.

As Jonmair brought her loaded tray back to the table, Baird rose and took it, saying, "I'm sorry about last night, Jonmair. But...I can't promise it won't happen again."

She gave him a puzzled frown. "Why?"

"Because...I just realized why Zhag doesn't have control issues with Tonyo."

"Because Tonyo knows when to back off and I don't?" Jonmair asked, eyeing the other Gen.

"No," Baird assured her. "Jonmair, it's not your fault—it's mine. The difference between Zhag and me is that he has completed disjunction, and I haven't."

* * * * * * *

JONMAIR TOOK BAIRD'S STATEMENT SERIOUSLY ENOUGH to ask about it the next time she was at Carre. The channels assured her that Baird's behavior was not unusual during disjunction. Jonmair looked forward to the weekly lessons, glad that she was in one of the smaller classes that had started immediately after Unity. Now that no Gens could be sold into the Pens, a new and larger class began each month. It was strange to see the newly-established Gens, only a few months younger than she was, and wonder, *Did I ever look that young? That innocent?*

The new Gens were ill at ease, as they were almost all the children of Simes. They believed themselves inferior somehow, a disappointment to their families.

Jonmair realized...she no longer felt inferior to Simes. As she did her work, including making new and intricate costumes for Zhag and Tonyo, she didn't even yearn for the convenience of tentacles.

But outside the Householding, most Simes saw her as less than human. She felt safe walking or riding through Norlea by herself now, but most shopkeepers still would not wait on her. If she was in her Post livery, vendors would sell her food and supplies, assuming she was on a servant's errand—but Sime customers expected her to step aside and let them go first.

At The Post, Jonmair was now accepted as part of the staff, there to see that customers' desires were met—but she was tired of waiting tables, doing laundry, cleaning guest rooms, and mending linens. Treavor Axton adamantly refused to let her design costumes for any act other than Zhag and Tonyo—and then tried to keep her too busy to accept their private commissions. Performing every evening, they required more elaborate outfits as their reputation spread and the waiting lists for tickets to their performances grew longer. She stayed up late, sometimes falling asleep over her work, rather than give up the one creative task she was allowed.

She was still not in charge of her own destiny. Her larity had decided for her: she would always be considered a little less than human, always have someone ordering her around. Tonyo might think Gens had the advantage over Simes, but what did a Wild Gen know about it?

Zhag and Tonyo arrived at The Post one morning, grinning. "I passed the test!" Tonyo announced, waving a parchment with an official seal attached. "I'm a citizen of Gulf Territory, with all rights and privileges pertaining thereto!"

Zhag was as proud as could be of his partner, but Jonmair saw the disconcerted look that crossed Baird's face at the news. He covered it quickly with a smile, though, and said,

"Congratulations, Tonyo! I suppose this means you'll be running for Mayor of Norlea?"

"Not this year," Tonyo replied. "Maybe someday, though." He showed his certificate to Chef, who managed to sound sincere in congratulating him. The kitchen staff followed their supervisor's lead.

All except Penta Coyt, the new Gen cook, whose enthusiasm was unforced as she kissed the boy and said, "Good work, Tonyo! I knew your studying would pay off."

"What about you?" Tonyo asked her. "When are you going to take the test?"

Only the Householding Companions had been declared citizens on the first day of Unity. All other Gens, including those under the protection of a Householding, like Penta, were wards of whatever Simes had previously owned them—her husband, in this case.

"I have an appointment the end of next week," Penta said. "When word got around that you had taken the test, every educated Gen in Norlea rushed to sign up—so now there's a waiting list."

Jonmair said nothing. The first day she had been allowed out alone, she had gone to the registry office, relieved to find that taking the citizenship test did not require the consent of Treavor Axton. The legislators obviously recognized that such a restriction would have prevented most Gens from having a chance at freedom. Her appointment was in two days, deliberately chosen because no one would question what time she returned from her weekly lesson at Carre.

Tonyo had told her the test was easy as long as she could read and write, and had taken him less than an hour to complete. If a Wild Gen could pass it, she felt even more determined.

Tonyo carefully rolled up his certificate and retied the ribbon around it.

"Show them your tags," said Zhag, in tones of annoyance.

"Zhag, it's not important," said Tonyo, taking out two green enamel tags inscribed with his name and tax number. "It's easy enough proof to carry, until eventually everybody simply assumes that an adult Gen is a citizen."

"No," said Penta, examining the tags, "it's an insult, Tonyo. They've copied the registry tags in the Pen system. You didn't grow up seeing those tags on the collars of Gens being led through the streets to their death."

"Oh," said Tonyo, closing his hand over the tags. "Then... Zhag—what can we do about it?"

"Keep them in your pocket, and only show them if you're questioned," said his partner.

"But that won't change anything!" said Tonyo. "How do we get the government to choose a different symbol? We have to protest this one."

"The Householders already have," said Penta. "They were told they've already been given everything they wanted, so if they insist on designing different identification it will delay offering Gens citizenship by at least a year."

"Politics!" snorted Zhag. "Let it go, Tonyo. You're a citizen under the law. That's all that matters."

"Not to me," said Tonyo. Then, "Shen it, I'm proud to be a citizen of Gulf! It's not something to be hidden as if it were shameful. Let's do with these tags what Keon did with the white-painted chain."

Householding Keon used that chain as its symbol, worn by all members, both Sime and Gen.

"I know what to do," said Zhag thoughtfully. "It will probably take a few days to get ready, but I know some other people who will join in."

Meanwhile, Conta came to The Post that evening cheering Robert, for he, too, had passed the test. Then they trumped Tonyo's news by announcing their wedding date.

Their glowing happiness only made Jonmair more determined that she would win both her freedom and transfer with Baird before the month was out.

* * * * * * *

THE DAY ZHAG AND TONYO HAD THEIR NEXT
TRANSFER, The Post bulged at the seams with customers
wanting to ride on their post reaction. Therefore, that night the
musicians chose to implement Zhag's plan to spite the junct
legislature's tagging new Gen citizens like Pen Gens.

Just the day before, Jonmair had received her own tags and
certificate. The certificate was hidden under her mattress, the
tags in her pocket, while she waited for the right moment to
inform Treavor Axton that she was no longer his ward. She
wanted to tell Baird first, but he had been away on a purchasing
trip, and returned only an hour before Zhag and Tonyo's performance.

Today was definitely not the time to tell Baird's father. He
was at the breakfast table when Jonmair came downstairs,
reading the paper and drinking kafi.

Treavor Axton had not recovered well from his bad transfer.
Although he was functioning, his face was drawn, and despite
Jonmair's bringing her hunger into his presence every day, he
was not eating. Jonmair wished she knew how to get past his
resentment so she could help him.

"Stop that!" he snapped.

"I'm not doing anything," she replied. "You can't expect
Gens not to have feelings."

"You'd better not go around pitying Simes, or one of 'em is
gonna slit your throat."

"Then you think I can't be killed?" she asked.

"I'd never trust your hands anywhere near my laterals!"

"You've heard what they're teaching new Gens," she said. She
referred to the fact that normal—instinctive—Kill or transfer
position put a Sime's vulnerable lateral tentacles right where the
Gen could do serious, even fatal, damage with a sharp squeeze.
All the Gen had to do was overcome the reflex to pull away.

But Jonmair could not imagine inflicting such agony on any
Sime, and was learning less harmful ways to abort an attack.
"Don't you realize that any Gen allowed out alone is too sympa-
thetic to Simes ever to hurt one?"

"Don't you realize that Simes don't want their life in a Gen's hands?" Axton retorted.

"It's already there," she replied. "It's what nature intended: Gens are meant to produce life energy for Simes. But there's no reason to die to do so. If we can just find the right Gen for you—"

He got up, crumpling the newspaper impatiently, started for the door, and fell.

Jonmair dashed to his side, supporting him with her field and sending a nageric as well as vocal cry for help.

Chef and his staff ran in from the kitchen. "Bad turnover," said Chef. "Jonny, keep doing what you're doing."

For the moment her field might be soothing Axton's, but as soon as he came to—

"Get away from me!" Treavor Axton tried to growl, but it came out a choked whisper.

Penta Coyt knelt on his other side. "It's hard," she said, "but you'll be all right. Let us help you to your room, and I'll bring you some trin tea. You really shouldn't drink kafi on your turn-over day—didn't anyone ever tell you that?"

Axton scowled, but for some reason Penta's attention didn't seem to irritate him as much as Jonmair's, so she carefully relinquished to the other Gen and let Penta and two of the Sime staff take Baird's father upstairs.

When Penta returned for the tea, Jonmair asked, "What did you do different from what I did?"

"Nothing, really. I just wasn't arguing with him when he hit turnover. You'll learn to keep track of the cycles of Simes you interact with every day," she explained.

"I do," said Jonmair. "Mr. Axton is early, by almost a day."

"Ah," said Penta, "that's a bad sign. Unless he's been augmenting?"

"I don't think so," said Jonmair. "They say the older the Sime—"

"No," Penta stopped her. "We can't lose an entire genera-tion. If Mr. Axton would only cooperate, it wouldn't be hard to find him someone. Look how many soldiers found matchmates on campaign—from among Wild Gens yet! It's the channels who are hard to match. If the government would just set up a program—"

"There aren't enough Gens," said Jonmair.

"Not enough awake and aware ones," Penta agreed. "But you've got your hands full with Baird, so we will just have to set ourselves to find someone for his father."

Jonmair was scheduled to serve in the Main Salon that evening. Every Sime with access to a Gen had brought that Gen along to heighten the experience. Zhag's friend Thea and her Companion Janine were in the front row, both women dressed in pretty summer frocks, only their Householding rings indicating their affiliation.

At the back, in the cheapest seats, Jonmair spotted Vent and Mern, the young channel/Companion pair who had intercepted Baird at his last transfer. They were not Householders, and Jonmair wondered whether Mern was also forced to take the exam to earn the citizenship that should have been his by right.

The costumes Zhag and Tonyo had chosen for tonight were new, elegant, but plain. Zhag was in black and Tonyo in white form-fitting trousers and shirt-vests with gold buttons. Zhag fastened his, but Tonyo wore his open almost to the waist. In the early autumn heat they wore no shirts under the vests, so everyone could see that Zhag had almost recovered normal Sime physique, while Tonyo displayed the defined muscles of a healthy Gen. It didn't require zlinning to see that they had had a grand transfer and were, if possible, more post than the month before.

Jonmair had wanted to embroider the vests, but the two men insisted that, at least for tonight, they remain plain. When she went to the dressing room before the show, she learned why.

"Do you have your citizenship tags yet?" Tonyo asked her.

"How did you know?" she asked, fishing them out of her pocket.

He laughed and took them from her. "You're too smart not to

take the test. Haven't gotten up the courage to tell Baird?"

"He's been away."

"If you'll join us," said Zhag, "you can tell everyone at once."

He picked up a box from the dressing table and showed her its contents: metal collars resembling the one she had worn in the Pen—but thinner, more flexible, and executed in what certainly looked like gold. Green tags set into gold frames dangled from both. One set were Tonyo's citizenship tags. Another set bore Zhag's name and tax number.

Jonmair stared at the Sime. "You had these made—?"

"To turn the tables on those lorshes in Lanta. After all, I'm as proud to be a Gulf citizen as Tonyo is."

"We had this one made for you," said Tonyo, picking up a third gold collar. "If you don't want to wear it, we'll certainly understand."

"If it helps," said Zhag, "there will be other Simes wearing them tonight."

"Conta?" Jonmair asked.

"Yes," said Zhag, "and Thea, and all the soldiers who could get in—we have a full house and then some. We're running ahead of the turnover curve by a few hours, so everyone will be feeling as good as we can make them. It's the right time to do this."

"We're going to put them on just before 'My Brother He Turned Out Wrong,'" Tonyo told her, picking up a pair of small pliers from among the coins, pocket knife, comb, string bag, and other odds and ends that he had emptied from his pockets into a box on the dressing table. With fingers as deft as a Sime's tentacles, he fastened her tags to the gold collar and handed it to her. "You can decide from the mood of the room whether you want to join in."

She slipped the collar into her pocket, thinking that if she didn't know what it was modeled after it could easily be taken for elegant jewelry.

Zhag and Tonyo's shows always went splendidly, but tonight was the first time they had been post at The Post. If their first performance had sent the audience wild, this one transported them to another world. There was no uncertainty tonight—everyone was ready for the experience of their lives.

As usual, Tonyo did most of the talking, but when it was time for the highlight of the show, Zhag came forward and spoke to the audience. After the first night, they had moved their intermission to after what had become their signature song.

Zhag explained, "We're about to perform the first song Tonyo wrote, after he and I became transfer mates. As some of you know, Tonyo recently became a citizen of Gulf Territory."

There were cheers, and shouts of "Welcome, Tonyo!"

Zhag continued, "I'm sure all of you know that our new Gen citizens are being given tags to mark that fact."

An uncertain murmur, but Jonmair could hear disapproval in quite a few voices.

"Exactly," said Zhag. "It doesn't seem right that Gens wear proof of citizenship and Simes not, so...."

Both Zhag and Tonyo produced their gold collars with the green tags dangling from them, and put them on.

There were gasps from the audience—and then people began to look around as other Simes and Gens took out similar collars and put them on: Thea and Janine, Robert and Conta, Vent and Mern, some Sime~Gen pairs Jonmair didn't recognize—but also here and there Simes not with Gens tonight. Several soldiers donned collars and waved to Conta and Robert. Two young Sime women who had been flirting with Tonyo all evening. And here and there other Simes all through the audience.

There must have been thirty people, most of them Simes, wearing collars dangling the green tags. Very few were the elegant gold of Zhag and Tonyo's, but all were the same design and all bore the green enamel tags.

Wishing desperately that Baird were there and doing the same, Jonmair took out the collar Zhag and Tonyo had given her and fastened it around her neck. She shivered at the memory of Old Chance fastening the cold, stiff, unyielding one when she was taken from her parents' home—but this was different, she reminded herself. This collar she could put on or take off at will—it was her decision, and the tags on it said she was a free citizen, not an animal marked for death.

As the crowd settled, waiting for Zhag and Tonyo to begin to perform again, she suddenly realized how Tonyo felt about changing his name: when it was his choice to mark a passage in his life, it was completely different from being forced.

No one in the salon ever moved during "My Brother, He Turned Out Wrong." Jonmair and the other waiters retreated to the bar and let the emotion wash over the audience. As had become ritual, the audience demanded that the song be repeated, and at the end tears fell all through the house.

After a break, the musicians played their usual variety of songs, and during the Unity Hymn with which they ended their performance everyone stood and sang triumphantly. Afterward, the audience filed out into the other crowded rooms, while Zhag and Tonyo went by the back staircase to the Gold Salon to eat and hold court.

It was still Jonmair's duty to join them, adding her hunger to the ambient so that the guests would enjoy the buffet now laid out with dishes marked "Sime," "Gen," and "All Larities." Jonmair wondered what larities other than Sime and Gen the sign painter had had in mind. Although foods suitable for everyone took up most of the buffet table, there were as many special dishes for Gens as for Simes. She tasted them cautiously—growing up in a family of Simes, she had never had Gen foods before.

Thea and Janine joined the musicians, Zhag and Thea flirting discreetly while their Companions urged them on. Delivering drinks to the table, Jonmair overheard Tonyo tell Zhag, "Go ahead and leave. You deserve some private life. I'll cover for you."

"Robert and Conta will escort me home," Janine added.

Jonmair wondered, not for the first time, why Thea's Companion seemed to have no one to share postsyndrome with. Or perhaps she did, back at Carre.

When the crowd finally thinned in the Gold Salon, Zhag and

Tonyo went to their dressing room and Jonmair reported to the gambling hall. It was still crowded with people waiting for Zhag and Tonyo to make their usual appearance.

Most of the soldiers who had attended the concert were now at the gaming tables—Jonmair had noticed that the veterans of the Western War preferred either the dice games or poker, and that Simes and Gens seemed equally likely to come out winners.

All the soldiers wore the collars with green tags, even those who had not been at the concert. The Gen soldiers brave enough to follow their Sime matchmates into Gulf were all as popular with their fellows as Robert was, and their friends resented anything that proclaimed them second-class citizens.

The soldiers who had saved the continent from Zelerod's Doom were heroes to most people. The vast majority of Simes populating The Post tonight had known nothing about Zhag's idea—but naturally people asked what the collars meant.

Someone found scissors and colored paper, and soon more than half the Simes in The Post wore makeshift collars with green paper tags dangling from them, ID's and tax numbers penciled on. Jonmair served drinks and collected tips and congratulations, basking in the friendly atmosphere.

All that was missing was Baird. She had seen him in passing when he arrived home, but he had disappeared upstairs with hardly a word. Was he still with his father? How ill was Treavor Axton?

Jonmair could not dwell on her concern, for it was her duty to keep up the good spirits of their guests. Tonyo entered the salon with three pretty Sime women, but no sign of Zhag. No one seemed to care, though, as people flocked to talk with the young Gen and bask in his postsyndrome.

Eventually the crowd thinned, Tonyo left with his entourage, and only inveterate gamblers remained at the tables. Jonmair's duties were over for the night. Baird would know where to find her if he wanted her, so she went up to her room.

She had forgotten about the gold collar, which, unlike the one she had worn in the Pen, did not bind or chafe. It was flexible enough to roll up and go into her pocket.

That was where it was when she went downstairs the next morning. Once again the breakfast hall was empty, but in the kitchen Penta was preparing a tray with trin tea and cereal with a few berries. "I'll try to get Mr. Axton to eat a little," she said.

"Take him kafi," said Jonmair.

"But he's in Need—"

"Only the beginning of Need," said Jonmair. "He drinks kafi all month long, Penta. You're never going to turn him into a Householder."

The other Gen woman nodded. "I know. The idea is to keep him alive long enough to find him a matchmate."

"You actually like him, don't you?" asked Jonmair.

"I don't dislike him—he's willing to let me work here."

"Only because having Gens around increases profits."

Penta chuckled. "What's wrong with that? Last night was amazing. Who would think that a place like this would take the lead in promoting Unity?"

Jonmair took some of the cereal with berries and tea, but without company she didn't feel very hungry. Baird did not put in an appearance, and now that he was no longer studying, Tonyo would not show up until lunch time—especially today.

She completed the cleaning tasks on her list, then showered, and went to the sewing room. Once again her basket was filled with torn linens, tribute to last night's revels. How she hated the boring work that kept her from the designs she wanted to make! She would even be willing to make new dresses for Emlu's girls, something that would make them look just as sexy without appearing so...cheap.

But she was free now, although she had not told Treavor Axton yet. She could leave here today—Miz Delancy would be happy to hire her. So why didn't she just go?

She knew the answer, of course: Baird. If she left The Post she might never see him again, never become his transfer mate. Besides, she liked life at The Post—all but the endless laundry, cleaning, and mending.

A memory entered her mind, unbidden, for she tried never to think about her family. Yet...about four years ago, her father had asked for a raise at his job, but his boss had turned him down. So he had gone out looking for a better job—and when he found it, he returned to his boss with the news, and was promptly given the raise he wanted if he would stay.

Perhaps, if she could come to Treavor Axton saying someone else was willing to hire her to do more challenging work than cleaning rooms and mending linens, he would allow her to give up those tasks and take on designing.

By the time she met Tonyo in the kafi shop, she had decided to talk to Miz Delancy. "You're looking determined," he told her. "What's going on?"

He was wearing his gold collar and enamel tags, and looked as if he had not had enough sleep last night, for pleasant reasons. It was a feeling Jonmair had known a few times herself.

"I haven't told Baird or Mr. Axton about my citizenship yet," she explained. "I'm going to ask for better use of my skills here... or else I'm going to look for work elsewhere."

"Good for you!" said Tonyo. "Zhag and I will give you references—but I can't imagine the Axtons being crazy enough to let you go."

I hope you're right, she thought, just as Baird joined them. He looked terrible. Jonmair could tell from the way she was drawn to him that he had passed turnover without her help, but that alone did not account for his pallor, or the drawn look about his eyes.

He glanced at Tonyo's collar and frowned. "What's that? I've seen half a dozen people wearing them this morning."

"Moral support for Free Gens," Tonyo replied.

"Huh?" Baird replied blankly. He looked too tired to think. "What are Free Gens?"

"Gens who have passed the citizenship exam," Jonmair supplied.

"Oh, that," he dismissed it. "If they've got the guts and the ability to do it, why do they need moral support?"

Tonyo took off his collar and showed Baird the tags. "Because these are what they're giving out to those who pass."

Baird squinted at them, and rubbed his forehead with his fingers while his dorsals massaged his temples. "Oh, shen," he said softly, recognizing what the tags represented. "On a collar like that?"

"No—the collars are to protest the tags," Tonyo replied. "Reverse psychology, like Keon's chain."

Baird nodded. "Count me in, but please don't bother my dad about it. I've never seen him have such a bad turnover. He... doesn't expect to survive his next transfer. I've been with him and his lawyer all night, setting his affairs in order."

"Oh, Baird!" Jonmair whispered, taking his hand.

He stared at their joined hands, and then at her face, something dawning in his eyes. He looked from her to Tonyo and back, his laterals out to zlin, leaving pleasant little tingly trails where they touched Jonmair's skin. "Thank you," he said. "Both of you."

"For what?" asked Tonyo.

"For letting me feel what I'm feeling."

"That's what we're supposed to do," said Jonmair. "I wish I had been there to support you."

"Dad didn't want you there. I'm sorry. I could have used your support, but he would not have Gens present while he set everything up just in case...."

Jonmair didn't say anything—what was there to say? Treavor Axton would not allow a Gen to help him, and without a transfer mate he probably would die soon. She didn't love the man the way his son did, but she didn't want him to die. What she wanted was for Treavor Axton to accept her as a person, as an equal, and one day...as his son's wife.

* * * * * * *

FOR THE NEXT TWO WEEKS, BAIRD AXTON tried merely to maintain his sanity. He kept Jonmair with him as much as he could, but his father would not tolerate her near him, and she still had her work, while he had his and his father's as well. After a couple of days, Treavor Axton declared he would have no Gens in his presence at all, ending attempts by Penta Coyt and Tonyo Logan to ease his painful descent into Need.

Twice, Treavor Axton tried to come downstairs, and both times nearly passed out in the ambience of The Post's crowded rooms. Baird did not miss the irony of his father's not only being unable to enjoy the greatest success the establishment he had built had ever known, but resenting vehemently that the success came from the incredible combination of Sime and Gen that was Zhag and Tonyo.

The Post was now known as Gen-friendly, so at any given time, besides Jonmair, Tonyo, and Penta, there were likely to be other Gens on the premises. Simes were learning that being around Gens who were comfortable in the presence of Simes eased their Need nerves, and The Post was packed, day and night.

Baird was beset by guilt when, after considering hiring more am Carre Gens like Penta to enhance the ambient, he realized that he could do so only over his father's dead body.

Treavor Axton's friends visited often—holding death vigil, Baird was afraid, but if his father didn't protest he decided that anything that kept his mind off his Need had to be good. So Old Chance and Treavor Axton's other gambling buddies visited daily, none of them as sick as his father, but all showing signs of the Need anxiety gripping Norlea.

When most of the city had passed turnover, the crowds thinned. Gens or no Gens, food consumption dropped, and only the most inveterate gamblers could concentrate well enough to enjoy the games. Nevertheless, Zhag and Tonyo's shows remained packed with Simes seeking relief from the nagging ambient everywhere else in town.

After working separately from Jonmair most of the day, it was blissful relief for Baird to hold her in his arms at night and feel her growing desire to assuage his growing Need. At last, the channels said it was safe for them to attempt transfer. The appointment was made, and Baird was determined that this time he would not flee. Basking in her growing field, he could not understand where that terror had come from last month, to send him hurtling away from her when all she had wanted to do was give him life.

If only there were a Gen who felt that way about his father. If only his father would permit a Gen to get that close to him.

His mind circled endlessly, trapped in anxiety that only increased as the end of his cycle approached.

One day he heard angry shouting from his father's room, and rushed in to find Old Chance standing by the window, Treavor Axton facing him on unsteady feet. But he was too weak to shout anymore, and dropped back into his armchair, passing a withered hand over his eyes. "Oh, shen, Chance," he said in a voice like ash, "you're right. But you shouldn't be. You shouldn't be."

"I didn't design the Sime larity," the ex-Penkeeper replied. "You can't fight nature, Treav."

That night when Baird came to give his father the house report, Treavor Axton told him, "When I'm gone, this place will be yours."

"That won't be for a long time, Dad."

"Perhaps," his father told him. "But I want you to know that I'm proud of you, Baird. You will adapt to whatever life brings—so do what you have to do to stay alive and keep The Post running—understand? No matter what happens to me, no matter what happens to you. The important thing is to keep going for as long as you can. Do...whatever is necessary. Understand?"

Baird understood that his father expected to die the next day. "Yes, Dad," he replied solemnly, glad he was too close to Need to feel strong emotions. "I'll do what I have to—I promise. But tomorrow you're going to do what you have to."

A weary smile, more of a grimace. "Yes. We'll both do what we have to, tomorrow." Baird didn't bother to correct him about his own transfer date, which was a day later—no reason to remind his father of his shortening cycle.

But the next morning when Baird went to help his father get up and get dressed, he found Treavor Axton's room empty. A frantic search through The Post brought the information that three of his old friends had come to get him early that morning.

Jonmair, sticking to Baird's side as if on an invisible chain, allowed him to rest on her field as he realized, "He's going to die—and he doesn't want me there!"

She remained silently sympathetic as Baird tried to decide what to do. He could not live with himself if he didn't try to find his father.

But as he and Jonmair walked out the front door of The Post a wagon pulled up...and Treavor Axton climbed down from his seat beside Old Chance. On his own power, he walked up the steps and into Baird's arms, the three Simes on the wagon laughing and yelling encouragement.

"Dad!" Baird exclaimed, unable to feel the joy he wanted to feel, just as he had been unable to feel sorrow last night. "Dad— you're alive! You're better!"

Treavor Axton set him aside, saying gruffly, "Of course I am. I told you I'd do what I had to. So will you." He turned, saying, "I got a good bargain on some rare wine." He lifted a cask out of the wagon and thrust it into Baird's arms. "Put that in the fourth cellar for now. It has to rest a few days." Then he brushed past, ignoring Jonmair, merely adding, "Somebody get me some kafi—I'll be in my office."

Arms around the wine cask, Baird stared after his father's retreating back. "What just happened?"

Behind him he heard the wagon pull out—he wasn't going to get the answer from his father's gambling buddies, who all zlinned high-field and full of themselves.

Jonmair answered him. "They must have matched him with a Gen, and he doesn't want to admit it."

It was all Baird could think of to explain his father's recovery— but he didn't really care how the channels had managed those four recalcitrant old Simes. They had saved their lives!

With Jonmair by his side, Baird concentrated on getting through this day to the moment tomorrow when she would give him her selyn and he would be disjunct at last.

She came with him to put the wine cask in the fourth cellar as instructed. It was a new cask—but his father had said the wine was rare, not old. There were no markings on the cask, and the contents didn't slosh as he was accustomed to. Could it be Gen manufacture? Had his father procured a new import?

When he tried to zlin the contents, he found it as opaque as a private lock box, the cask lined with some kind of insulating material. He had only ever heard legends of vintages so precious that their very existence had to be screened from potential thieves. Where in the world had Treavor Axton found something so rare and potent? He was willing to bet it was Gen made and smuggled across the border without paying full duties—his father had always found it worth paying fines for the once in half a dozen times he got caught serving high-priced contraband to special customers. The times he wasn't caught far more than paid for it. Baird looked forward to trying out whatever his father had found this time. Meanwhile, he had a business to run.

Most Simes were feeling as Baird did today. The Last Kill cycle was drifting month by month, but still more than half the Simes in Norlea were scheduled for transfer within the next three days. Zhag and Tonyo would have their work cut out tonight, especially with this being Zhag's turnover day.

Jonmair knew better than to try to make Baird eat, though under the impact of both her hunger and Tonyo's he drank the juice she put in front of him instead of kafi. Zhag came to lunch with Tonyo, not wanting to risk stepping off the precipice into Need without his Companion at his side. Baird didn't blame him—without Jonmair, his own turnover had been particularly nasty this month.

There were more and more collars with green tags now, jewelers making a nice profit from creating enamel tags for Simes and selling elegant collars to both larities. They were seen most often on patrons of The Post, in far fewer numbers among the population at large. Baird didn't have one, he realized—and also remembered that Treavor Axton hadn't yet seen Jonmair's, didn't know she was no longer his ward.

"Let's tell him after our transfer," said Jonmair.

"Good idea," said Zhag. "Once you've actually shared a good transfer, Baird, you'll have none of that anxiety that Gens are going to deprive you."

"As if we'd deprive ourselves!" Tonyo agreed, grinning at Jonmair. "I am so glad you two are finally going to do it."

Jonmair zlinned completely confident. Baird pushed down the trickle of fear that she could control him any time she wanted to. He understood, now, that such feelings signaled disjunction crisis. Welcome them, the channels told him, but, paradoxically, don't fall prey to them.

Would understanding what was happening get him through it this month? Or would he go as mad tomorrow as he had last month?

He saw Tonyo reach over and take Zhag's hand just as the shift in the ambient signaled that the channel had hit turnover. Jonmair edged closer to Baird, and Zhag smiled at Tonyo, wrapping handling tentacles around his hand for a moment. *That's the way it ought to be,* Baird thought. From now on he would never go through it without Jonmair.

As if she could zlin his feelings, Jonmair smiled and took Baird's hand the same way. *From now on,* he could feel her promise. *From now on we're going through it together.*

That evening Baird returned to Jonmair's side between each of his routine checks of the various rooms. There were Gens scattered throughout the salons, off-duty soldiers gambling as usual, Robert and Conta among them. Old Chance and a number of other older Simes had commandeered the largest poker table, playing the highest stakes the room allowed. Baird wasn't worried—they could all cover their bets.

His father had retreated once more to his office. Baird could not gather the emotional energy to demand an explanation of how the channels had managed to match him with a Gen. After his transfer tomorrow he would be up for the confrontation.

What had happened to the Gen? Unless he or she were one of the Companions, Treavor Axton had to be talked into asking that Gen to be *his* Companion. It was probably one of the young Gens who had recently established into a world of unexpected safety, and had simply gone back to his or her family after transfer. Baird hoped it was someone with skills they could use at The Post, but then, it really didn't matter much. They could train anyone to serve food and drinks, and Gens quickly developed instincts to keep the ambient serene.

* * * * * * *

IN THE MAIN SALON, JONMAIR SERVED DRINKS as Zhag and Tonyo's show got under way. They opened with the same song every night, and the centerpiece of the performance didn't change. Otherwise, though, they played an ever-growing variety of pieces, including tunes from out-Territory. Jonmair wondered if they got tired of playing the same thing all the time, or if they varied it because of all the repeat customers.

Tonyo had a habit of dropping snatches of other songs into whatever he was singing—she didn't know how Zhag could keep up with him, but the shiltpron player always did.

The salon was packed. Jonmair had to squeeze between rows of customers to hand out mugs of porstan—no delicate breakable glasses in here. She knew how to ease through with her field, no more intrusive than the Sime staff despite not having their inherent grace. Her tips told her the customers found her presence more than acceptable.

Except for one group of Simes by the door, and a couple who had come early and snagged two of only four stools at the small bar.

Jonmair couldn't help noticing that while the woman was post, the man was in Need and agitated, not getting into the music at all. As she had to pass them repeatedly to pick up drink orders, it crossed her mind that she had never seen these two before. Odd that they hadn't bought tickets for the next night, when both of them would be post.

She came near them again when she approached the bar with an order for porstan, lemonade, and brandy. Lukis, the bartender, found the brandy bottle empty. He glanced at his assistant, who was mixing cocktails, and turned back to Jonmair. "Run down to the cellar and get another bottle, Jonny." He tossed her the key to the wine cellar door.

She caught it, controlling her delight when she realized Lukis was treating her exactly as if she were a Sime! She had never been entrusted with the key or sent to the cellar alone before—Simes were always sent for heavy porstan kegs—but she knew what to do.

Jonmair unlocked the door down the hall from Treavor Axton's office, took a lamp to navigate the old wooden stair-case, and paused at the foot to think which room held brandy.

She had only been down here twice before, once when Lukis showed her how the records were kept, and then this morning with Baird. There were racks of porstan kegs behind the first door she opened. The next one, though, revealed wines and liqueurs. A brief search brought her to two bottles of brandy like the one just emptied. She took one, and before returning to the salon followed protocol to record that there was only one bottle left. But the pencil beside the inventory book was broken, and she had no knife to sharpen it.

Jonmair looked around, but there was no one in the corridor who might have a pen or pencil. Why had she left hers on the bar? There were customers waiting for drinks, but if she didn't record what she had taken there would be trouble at the next inventory.

So she went to Treavor Axton's office. He wasn't in—probably at the poker table at this time of night. She took the pen from his desktop, made the entry, locked the cellar door, and returned the pen to its proper place.

As she stepped back into the hallway, she came face to face with Treavor Axton. "What are you doing in my office, Gen?"

he demanded.

Jonmair held up the bottle of brandy. "I borrowed your pen to write down that I took this from the cellar."

"What were you doing in the cellar?" he bellowed.

"I told you—getting a bottle of brandy for Lukis."

"I don't want Gens poking around the cellar or spying in my office!"

"I wasn't spying. I left my pencil and pad in the Main Salon when Lukis sent me—"

"No excuses! You don't belong in either place!"

"Dad! What's going on?"

Baird came up and put a protective arm around Jonmair.

"Keep that Gen from snooping around my cellars!" His father went into his office and slammed the door in their faces.

"What was that about?" Baird asked.

"I don't know. He would've yelled at me if I hadn't recorded taking the brandy, especially as it's time to reorder."

Baird shook his head. "I'm afraid he's not as well as I thought. Though we have occasionally had employees help themselves to the stock. You'd better get back to work, Jonmair."

"Come with me," she suggested. "Why can't your dad do the house inspections when you're in Need?"

"Because it's my job. I'll join you in the Gold Salon right after the show," he promised. "Go on now—Lukis is waiting for that brandy."

Jonmair had to push close to the odd couple of Simes at the bar, in order to hand Lukis the bottle and the key.

"You—Gen!" the man hissed at her. "You stop starin' at me!"

"Shut up, Rark!" the woman said. "You'll get yours soon enough."

Jonmair, who had not been staring, deliberately took her attention away from the couple. But when she stopped to see if the group by the door wanted fresh drinks, "Not from no Gen, we don't," one of them sneered, while another growled, "Animal!" as she passed. Something besides the arrant prejudice bothered her. Why would such people pay to see Zhag and

Tonyo? By this time, she could tell from her body's response to them, especially high-field as she was, that like the couple at the bar, they paired Simes who were freshly post with Simes in hard Need.

Suspecting they were there to make trouble rather than to enjoy the show, she decided to warn Zhag and Tonyo at intermission, and then find Baird. The Post did not allow brawling, and these Simes seemed to be itching for a fight.

There were only two Gens in the main salon tonight besides Tonyo and Jonmair, but at least a dozen Simes besides those with the Gens wore collar-and-tags. None of the roughnecks did, of course—she suspected they had come to pick a fight with the "Genlovers."

Unless, of course, the music and the ambient changed their minds.

Just before intermission, Jonmair and the other serving staff went to their positions along the sides of the room for "My Brother, He Turned Out Wrong." Zhag came out from behind his shiltpron to begin his introduction of Tonyo's song—but before he could speak, the female Sime at the bar pulled something out of her pocket, did something to it that Jonmair couldn't see, and then lobbed it onto the stage.

In the hushed moment it landed with a clunk, and a hissing sound.

The object fell behind Zhag, between him and Tonyo. The shiltpron player turned, gasped "Bloody Shen!" and leaped over the object to give his partner a vicious shove toward the stage door. "Run, Tonyo!"

Tonyo stumbled, saying, "What is that?"

Zhag stripped off his jacket to cover the object as he cried, "Just go! Get all the Gens out of here!"

Although Zhag was trying to wrap up what Jonmair now realized was a small canister, she could smell a faint odor that made her heart start to race. It must have meant something to other Simes, for several ran forward, grabbed her and Tonyo, and carried them toward the stage door.

Other Simes were trying to take the Gens in the audience out through the front entrance, but it was blocked by the group of Simes Jonmair had noticed earlier—and they were flinging more canisters!

"It's fear gas!" Zhag shouted. "Don't let Gens breathe it!"

Tonyo was out the door now. Jonmair cooperated with her rescuers as they augmented to try to get her out of harm's way—but another canister landed between them and the door as the couple who had been at the bar loomed before them, barring their way to safety.

Safety?

Outside, Jonmair heard shouting—and then screams!

She gasped, unable to hold her breath any longer. Acrid fumes burned her lungs.

Zhag threw the male Sime aside, but the woman lunged through the door and slammed it shut in his face. When he reached for the handle, it came off in his hand.

Jonmair was shaking, her heart pounding. She wanted to control, but cold sweat broke out on her skin as her nerves tingled with anxiety.

Doors at The Post were sturdy oak. Three augmenting Simes launched themselves repeatedly at this one before it came off its hinges—only to reveal screaming, fighting people, crashing noises, and more of the acrid smell.

Jonmair couldn't breathe. Someone was dragging her—

Simes reached for her! Her heart beat so fast it hurt.

Frantically screaming, she pulled away from grasping tentacles, knowing that the Sime who caught her was going to kill her!

* * * * * * *

BAIRD WAS ON HIS WAY TO THE GAMBLING SALON when he heard a crash in the kafi shop. Hardly anyone was in there at this time of night—but when he entered he saw the window shattered and a canister lying in the midst of the shards, giving off a hissing noise and odd smell.

Through the broken window came screams and swearing from the square—then screeching Gen fear, followed by the unmistakable jolt of the Kill.

Jonmair!

He had to get to her. He had to think—and to be able to think, he needed Jonmair!

He ran toward the main salon, past the door of the gambling hall. Shouts and crashes erupted, and people came barreling out.

"Fear gas!" someone shouted. "Get the Gens outside!"

"No!" Baird replied. "There's more gas out there!"

The stuff burned his eyes and lungs.

Gen fear sliced through the ambient from the gambling hall. Sime fear accompanied it—fury—rising Need.

Baird forced himself to focus. He needed Jonmair, needed her now. She was in the main salon—

Killbliss erupted from the gambling hall.

Baird's knees gave way. *Mustn't zlin. Find Jonmair. Lean on her field.*

He fought for sanity, and pushed his way down the crowded hallway just as the stage door to the main salon opened and Tonyo Logan was hauled through by two renSimes, one of them a Post staff member named Gus.

Gus zlinned, and gasped, "It's everywhere! Where can we put the Gens?"

"Where's Jonmair!" Baird demanded, trying to push past and through the door. He saw and zlinned her, on the far side of the stage, Simes converging—to help her or to kill her?

Zhag knelt on the stage, covering something with his jacket—one of the canisters, Baird realized—but even as he thought it, another one clunked down, hissing, and a woman launched herself through the door and slammed it shut behind her, blocking his view.

Baird leaped forward, only to see the door handle fall off as the door was shaken from the other side.

Sabotage!

As he prepared to batter the door from his side, though, he heard and zlinned augmenting Simes hitting it from the other. The sturdy door finally gave way, and three Simes barreled into the hallway, followed by two Simes dragging Jonmair—

Who screamed in abject terror!

Tonyo rushed from one side and Zhag from the other to try to shield her—but she was as terrified of them as of everyone else, including Baird.

Her fear, carried on her perfect field, triggered Baird's Need as he had never felt it before.

People shouted at him, but he could not hear them, using only Sime senses to stalk his perfect prey. Jonmair. Jonmair! *Jonmair!*

She cringed, whimpering in the purest fear he had ever zlinned, his for the taking. He would strip that exquisite selyn from her nerves in the best Kill ever!

NO!

Baird stumbled back, tearing himself away from the temptation. He wanted her selyn, not her life!

Fire seared every nerve as Baird tried to move away from Jonmair. He was paralyzed, supported by nothing but pain, unable to kill Jonmair, unable not to.

Somewhere, he found his voice. "Zhag," he croaked. "You're...a channel. Help me!"

"Go on!" he heard Tonyo say, and then his old friend was there, entwining their tentacles, ready to give him the transfer he needed.

But he didn't want channel's transfer, even from Zhag. He wanted Jonmair!

He turned his face away before Zhag could touch lips, strength he had not known he had coming from somewhere. "No—protect her. Get the Gens...to safety!"

But there was no safety. Tonyo's powerful field, shielding Baird from Jonmair's terror, vibrated with anxiety as he could not help breathing in that foul stuff.

Zhag interposed his channel's field, but had no protection

himself from his Companion's increasing anxiousness. If Tonyo panicked, they were all doomed!

Baird staggered and would have fallen were it not for Zhag's support—but with the channel managing the ambient he found himself capable of thought.

Horror raged in the crowded corridor. Jonmair cringed, her field a beacon no Sime could resist—

Except that on every side, Simes were resisting, high-field Simes placing themselves to protect their low-field friends.

Gus and Emlu, both post, took Jonmair's arms on either side, refusing to zlin her terror.

Baird wanted to tear his Gen from the other Simes—but Zhag grasped his bicep, and from somewhere the voice of reason told him, *You don't want to kill Jonmair!*

The ambient rang with postkill mingled with Gen terror—not just Jonmair's. The brave resistance of nearby Simes could not last—did not last. Behind Baird, another flare of Killbliss shattered the ambient.

Two soldiers came running up. "It's worse out in the square! They've attacked the dispensary—the Old Pen—with that stuff. It's chaos! No one knows where to take Gens to protect them."

"I know," said Baird, teeth gritted so hard his jaw ached. "Get them into the Killroom!"

Zhag winced, but then agreed. "Pass the word," he told the soldiers. "Killrooms are insulated. Come on, Tonyo," he said.

"Huh?" his Companion said. "I'm okay."

"You're running on nothing but courage," Zhag told the young Gen, who didn't seem to realize that he was trembling with the effort to remain superficially calm. Everyone could zlin his increasing fear. "Stay out here, and you'll breathe even more—can you imagine pure fear carried on *your* field?"

Jonmair had to be dragged, as did most other Gens lucky enough not to have been killed.

Yet.

The Post's Killroom was designed to accommodate half a dozen Gens in the little comfort they had ever been afforded before Unity. Tonight, by the time they had saved as many Gens as they could, it held fifteen, all in panic except Tonyo, who reeked of free-floating anxiety by the time they pushed him in and shut the door.

When the tempting fear was at last shut away, Baird almost collapsed. He wanted to tear the door open, pull a Gen out, and kill—

But he didn't.

Somehow, he didn't, just as the other Simes didn't...although those precipitated into hard Need converged on Zhag, the only channel available. Baird, though, pulled himself together. He was not due for transfer until tomorrow. Tomorrow Jonmair would be recovered. He could do this—he had waited out the last hours before his transfer every month of his life since his changeover.

He left Zhag and the Simes rigging up a transfer room, and went to see to his guests.

There were ten Gen corpses in various rooms of The Post, and more than ten Simes grieving over them.

The main salon and the gambling hall looked like the aftermath of a battle, where Simes had fought to protect Gens against those determined to kill them. But most of the Kills had not been made by those who had smuggled in the fear gas. The poison had served its purpose: many Simes had killed Gen friends.

When Baird found Conta weeping uncontrollably over Robert's body, he at first thought she had killed the man she loved. But she looked up at him and told him, "I couldn't save him! It wasn't Jaik's fault—I know it wasn't! But—"

"Jaik?" Baird asked.

Conta nodded at another corpse, this one Sime, an army-issue utility knife protruding from his chest. "I was at the bar, getting drinks. The gas was released, and everyone started fighting. I couldn't reach the table. I tried—"

"Of course you did," said Baird. "It wasn't your fault, or Robert's."

"Or Jaik's," she said in anguish. "Jaik killed Robert. And I...I murdered Jaik."

Baird thought, *You saved him from execution,* but he didn't say it. Such Kills would probably be ruled the fault of those who released the fear gas. And Conta was in enough pain.

She zlinned him. "Jonmair?" she asked.

"She's safe. I—I couldn't kill her, but I couldn't let her go, either. I had to ask Zhag to help me. Then he and Tonyo shielded her."

Awe broke momentarily through Conta's grief. "You asked?"

"It was the only thing I could think of," he admitted.

"You thought? Oh, Baird, then something good came out of this horrible night. Don't you realize? Your matchmate was in terror under your tentacles, and you resisted killing her. You could only do that if...you're disjunct."

But her moment's thought for him could not last, and she turned back to the dead men, weeping once more.

Baird had no time to think about what Conta had said as he went back to assessing the results of the attack on The Post. Three attackers were dead, but two others had been captured by some of the soldiers, who now struggled to keep other Simes from murdering them.

But there had been more than five. Most had escaped in the panic—escaped to plot new attacks against Unity.

Before this night, many Simes had believed fear gas to be a myth. Baird had known it was real, both its manufacture and its possession capital offenses. Invented for use by the most jaded of Simes, its very existence was outlawed because of its potential to disrupt the always precarious selyn delivery system.

Someone had managed to manufacture enough fear gas to attack the Square, The Post, and the Old Pen. And, he learned as reports came in through the night, the attacks had reached Carre, and the neighborhood around the Householding where mixed Sime/Gen families lived.

It was a well-orchestrated, devastating attack on Unity itself.

Baird could not feel anything in his encroaching Need except increasing anxiety. What would happen to Jonmair now? How could he protect her against this kind of guerilla warfare? Even if she recovered physically, how could she recover emotionally from such an assault? Would she be able to give him transfer now?

And what about Norlea, or any city in Gulf? How many Simes suffering through disjunction would give up? Up to now, many had been willing to endure increasing agony so that they, or their children or grandchildren, could live without fear. What if these terrorists tipped the balance, made most Simes believe that the Sime killer instinct could never be quelled? Could a handful of determined criminals undo all the hard work accomplished toward Unity?

After the police and militia had carted the surviving attackers off for interrogation, Baird saw the last of their guests out of The Post and locked the doors. He turned to find his father standing in the hallway outside his office.

Treavor Axton had been nowhere to be seen through the attacks and their aftermath. He told the police that he had been in his office, working with his accountant on quarterly tax forms, and everything had happened so fast that by the time they realized there was an attack the worst was over.

Baird found that hard to believe. The accountant for The Post was Anbel Reevs, another of Treavor Axton's card playing buddies. He supposed it was possible that she had joined him immediately after he and Jonmair had seen Treavor Axton go into his office—but how could they have ignored the noise?

Anbel and his father alibied one another. Old Chance and the rest of the gang had been playing poker in the gambling hall, witnessed by dozens of people at nearby tables. None of them had thrown a canister, and none of them had killed in the ensuing panic.

Baird felt his father zlin him. "So," he said, "you are still in Need. You could have taken a Kill."

"Broken the law and been punished with shedoni?"

"No one will be charged with taking an illegal Kill over what happened tonight." His father looked around at the crew cleaning up the mess. "You showed unexpected strength, Baird."

"Yes, I did," Baird told him. "So did other people. Most of the Gens on the premises were not killed. We can be proud of the staff and the clientele of The Post."

"Oh?" Baird felt his father again zlinning him, trying to read in his field what he was holding back. "Despite your Need, you zlin healthy."

"As do you," Baird replied. "Dad, there's no way you could be in the shape you're in after channel's transfer."

"Baird, I wouldn't have held it against you if you had killed a Gen that belonged to me."

"But I didn't," Baird told him. "Yes, Jonmair was panicked by the gas. I did what I had to do: turned away from her to a channel, so I wouldn't take a life. I'm disjunct, Dad." He said it proudly, beginning to believe it now as he had not when Conta had said it earlier.

He zlinned the way his father's field went flat. "You didn't kill her when you had the chance? But you didn't take channel's transfer, either."

"My scheduled appointment is tomorrow. If Jonmair hasn't recovered by then, I'll be all right on channel's transfer for another month. I'm certain now, Dad—if I didn't kill tonight, I will never kill again."

"Then you are quite simply a fool, Boy. The Unity Treaty won't last the month."

"You'd better be wrong, Dad," Baird told him. "Because if you're right, and we break our word of honor, then the Gen army will be on our doorstep in no time. We won't have to wait to die in Zelerod's Doom."

CHAPTER TEN
AFTERMATH

BAIRD WAS STILL TRYING TO FIGURE OUT what felt odd about his father when there was a sharp rapping at the front door.

"We're closed!" he called.

"Please—it's Bran Coyt. My wife Penta works here."

Realizing that the man didn't know whether she was dead or alive, Baird hurried to open the door. "Penta's safe—just scared. Come in! Stay here tonight—don't try to take her home."

"Thank you!" Coyt said, his field ringing with relief. "Where is she?"

"We put all the Gens in the Killroom because it's the only room with the insulation to block their fields."

Coyt winced, but nodded. "Good thinking. I got our son to Carre—Penta will want to know he's safe."

"What happened at the Householding?" Baird asked.

"Someone lobbed canisters of fear gas over the walls. It affected a few Gens, but the channels rushed them into insulated rooms. There were no Kills. The Dispensary's another story, though. I heard it was pure shen there tonight."

Treavor Axton trailed them as they skirted the kitchen and took the other passage to where the insulated Killroom stood at the end of the corridor. In front of it, the hallway was partly blocked by an impromptu dispensary, insulated curtains over a pair of ladders with a plank running between them. In the small tent thus created, Zhag Paget, the only channel on the premises, had given transfers to those Simes brought to desperation dragging terrified Gens to safety.

Zhag sat against the wall now, exhausted. When they approached, he looked up and zlinned them, saying, "Thank goodness none of you needs a transfer. I don't know how the working channels do it!"

"Can I get you something?" Baird asked his friend.

"Tonyo," Zhag replied. "Shen, but I'm cramping." He gritted his teeth, but managed to stay hypoconscious until the spasm passed, so as not to broadcast his pain to the other Simes. Baird knew cramps in the selyn-conducting nerves were a problem channels sometimes experienced, and their Companions could somehow ease it.

"If you think it's safe to let them out—" said Baird.

Zhag nodded. "No one's screaming anymore, and none of us are in Need. They're likely to be pretty shaky, though."

The Gens were, quite literally, trembling—but all were back in their right minds now. Jonmair looked up in startlement at the opening door, but the moment she saw Baird she jumped up and flung himself into his arms, clinging to him for dear life.

He could hardly move out of the way before Penta ran to her husband, sobbing, "You're all right! But where is Kev?"

"He's fine. I took him to Carre," Coyt replied. "I was so worried about you!"

Tonyo hurried to kneel beside Zhag. "You're hurt!" he gasped.

"It's just vriamic fibrillation. Deep breaths, Tonyo. Get that stuff out of your system so you can calm down and help me."

All the Gens radiated anxiety, and Baird could feel Jonmair's body trembling as she tried to breathe deeply when her diaphragm was seized up with stress.

"Dad," said Baird, "please go make sure the courtyard is clear of anyone in Need. We should take the Gens out in the fresh air." He could smell the fear gas in Jonmair's hair and clothing.

In a few moments they were out in the night air. Other Simes, hearing that the Gens had been released, came to receive the same reception Baird and Zhag and Bran Coyt had received. Soon every bench in the courtyard contained a Sime and a Gen reassuring one another.

The attacks were apparently over. The night breeze dissipated the gas, and Jonmair's shivering subsided as she remained plastered against Baird, drawing warmth despite the warm night. He took her cold hands, and when she clasped his willingly, wrapped tentacles about them as well.

As Jonmair calmed, she asked, "Do you want to take transfer now, Baird?" Her field combined enticing residual anxiety with a powerful Need to Give. Oddly, it didn't overwhelm his control.

"Tomorrow," he promised, awash in delicious anticipation.

He watched Zhag calming Tonyo, who finally detached himself from the channel, stood, and shook himself like a puppy coming out of water. Then, with a smile no longer forced, he turned again to his partner, saying, "Let me help you now, Zhag."

Roles reversed, the shiltpron player took Tonyo's forearms in transfer position, but instead of touching lips he laid his head on the Gen's shoulder and gave a sigh of pure relief. "Thank you," he said softly, as he let go the shielding he had been holding over his painful field. His blessed relief poured over the Simes in the courtyard.

"No," said Tonyo, "thank you, Zhag. You saved my life."

"I think that makes us even," said Zhag with a smile at his Companion. "Until the end of the month."

"What's…vriamic whatsis?" the young Gen asked.

"Spasms in the vriamic node from providing several transfers in a row. Normally I don't perform that particular function at all. It's nothing serious — it's like the cramp you get in an unused muscle if you suddenly exercise hard. Working channels get proper training in First Year, and then keep up the exercise daily. Playing shiltpron doesn't use the same…muscles, as it were."

"As long as you're all right." Tonyo appeared to have recovered completely. "What was that gas," he asked, "and how do we protect Gens from it? I didn't get the full effect, but the anxiety attack it gave me was bad enough."

At Tonyo's words, Jonmair shuddered again. "I'm so sorry," she said, fighting back tears. "I— I couldn't control my fear, Baird!"

"Of course you couldn't," he replied, stroking her hair as he knew she found soothing. "It's all right now."

"No it isn't," said Tonyo. "I'm not afraid of Simes, but I sure am afraid of that gas! Bloody shen—the first canister was meant for Zhag and me. They thought they could make him kill me. But not all Simes have Zhag's control. If we're attacked again, how can Gens keep from losing control?"

"You can't," said Zhag, "any more than you can keep from losing consciousness if you're hit over the head. It's a police matter now—maybe an army matter. They'll get the people who did this—count on it."

"You mean the gas is not something new?" Tonyo asked.

"No," Baird told him. "It's the stuff of legend, but obviously it actually exists."

"But...before Unity what use would there be for it? A weapon against the Householders?"

Zhag said, "Certainly not the kind of direct attack we had here tonight, because the stuff was banned the moment the Sime government found out it was real. The people responsible for these attacks will be executed. Simes are just as terrified of fear gas attacks as Gens."

"But why?" the boy asked. "Simes didn't panic. It's obviously geared to Gen metabolism."

"True," said Baird, "but Sime Territories have never had enough Gens to afford the possibility of fear gas set off in a pen or on a Genfarm. Think about it, Tonyo. The sole reason Simes have agreed to disjunct is that the only other option is Zelerod's Doom."

"And that," said Bran Coyt, cradling his wife the way Baird still held Jonmair, "is why fear gas has always been illegal and illicit. In a junct territory, set loose among pen Gens, it would produce enough off-schedule Kills that there would not be enough Gens to go around that month. I don't care how junct the leanings of the legislature are: even those who secretly dream of a return to the Kill know they can't allow another such attack. We're on the road to suicide if we don't prevent it."

"What was fear gas ever invented for?" Tonyo asked.

Zhag looked at his partner. "There are Simes who...just don't get enough thrill out of the Kill of a pen Gen."

"I know about Choice Kills, Zhag," said Tonyo.

"Yes," said Baird, "but most Simes could never afford one, or only on rare occasions. Fear gas could spur a pen Gen into a panic that might satisfy a jaded Sime."

"Of course that was illegal, too," added Zhag. "It would be disastrous to have a large number of Simes hooked on such Kills. As if every Sime were a Freeband Raider, seeking more thrilling Kills until they burned themselves out."

"So it's not likely they'll try again tomorrow night?" asked Tonyo.

"You surely don't think you can perform tomorrow night!" said Treavor Axton, who had remained standing near the entranceway. "We can't allow you—"

"We can't allow them to stop us!" said Tonyo.

"Tonyo's right," said Zhag. "We must not let the people who did this win. If you keep The Post open, we'll perform."

"And if you don't," added Tonyo, "we'll give a concert in the square."

The same sentiment prevailed all over town. In the morning shops were open, and there were even more Gens in the streets than usual, albeit none without Sime escort. Seeking news of just how bad things had been, Baird, Zhag, and Tonyo went out at daybreak. The dispensary in the Old Pen was open, green flags flying. A long line of edgy Simes who had held themselves in control all night waited for their transfers.

The corridor was nearly empty of furniture today. Baird might have thought the chairs had been removed to make more room for the lines of people, except that the few that were left showed signs of hasty repair, the posters had been ripped down, and gashes on walls and doors indicated how the missing furniture had been broken.

They went into the controller's office to allow Zhag to report his activities as a channel the night before.

Thea ambrov Carre was acting controller today, her Companion Janine quiet at her side. Thea's plain heart-shaped face broke into the smile that made her pretty when she saw Zhag and Tonyo together. "I heard you didn't succumb to the attack," she said, "but it's a relief to zlin for myself."

Tonyo laughed. "Zhag saved me and at least half a dozen other people," he said. "He's been channeling all night."

"Oh, dear," said Thea, obviously proud of the man she loved, but still concerned. "Zhag, you're not in practice—"

"—and my vriamic node let me know it!" he responded. "But I'm fine now. We won't keep you, but you have to have the information for your records." He gave her the names of the Simes he had given transfer to, and the amounts of selyn.

"Well," she said, "at least it eases today's schedule by that many." She zlinned him. "Do you think you could help out here for a while? Even just an hour would ease the load. So many people have come up short, resisting fear last night."

"Of course," said Zhag. "Tonyo and I will be happy to help."

When Zhag and Tonyo had gone to their assignment, Thea turned to Baird. "Where is Jonmair?"

"I left her sleeping. She was pretty badly affected by the fear gas, but she still wants to give me transfer today."

"Oh, Baird, you can't ask that of her!" exclaimed Janine.

"It's what she wants," he protested.

"I know it is," said Thea's Companion. "I understand how badly she wants it—but out of desire to have it behind her, to not disappoint you, to keep her promise. For Gens, courage kills, Baird."

Courage kills. He had heard that often enough at Carre: a Gen fighting down fear could not give transfer. A Gen had to truly feel no fear in order to give up selyn in pleasure rather than pain.

"All right," he agreed. "My appointment is this afternoon. I'll bring Jonmair, and one of the channels can decide whether it's safe."

"No—don't come ready to be disappointed when you're told no." Thea zlinned him. "Baird, you are remarkably stable this morning. You resisted Jonmair's fear last night?"

"I had to," he explained. "If I hadn't protected her, someone would have killed her."

"How did you protect her?"

"We put all the Gens in the Killroom," he admitted. "There was no other insulated room—"

"Baird, don't apologize!" Janine interrupted, eyes shining. "That was brilliant thinking, and I'm sure none of those Gens feels anything but gratitude."

"But Baird," Thea persisted, "how did you get the Gens into the Killroom?"

"Drag, carry—whatever we had to do, we did. There was no time to be gentle."

"Did you—yourself—touch Jonmair?"

He frowned, puzzled. "I—didn't dare. If I had touched her, I might have killed her. She couldn't help herself—she was hysterical from the fear gas."

"Then you actually weren't near her?" Thea asked.

"I was as close to her as I am to you," he said. "It was so hard. I had to ask Zhag to help me break away."

"You...asked? It wasn't that Zhag intervened because he saw what was happening?"

"No. I had to ask him. He would have given me transfer if I'd wanted it, but I didn't. I only wanted Jonmair—but for transfer, not the Kill."

"Oh, Baird," Janine whispered, tears filling her eyes. "Your matchmate, flaring fear, and you less than a day from hard Need—"

"All the more reason," said Thea, raising a handling tentacle to stop her Companion's outburst, "to make certain that nothing goes wrong today. Baird, it's obvious that Jonmair is a person to you—that you now see Gens as people just as much as Simes. If we don't risk residual fear causing Jonmair to panic today, I am certain that next month you can complete your disjunction."

Baird saw Janine frown and start to say something, then think better of it. From somewhere beyond his nagging Need, Baird found a smile for her, knowing it was what Conta had said: that he was disjunct, that last night had proved it.

But Thea was right—Jonmair's safety was more important than Baird's comfort. No sense risking his disjunction and Jonmair's life when just one month would guarantee them both. He accepted the appointment Thea assigned him, almost three hours later than his original one because of the long lines still to serve from last night. Trying to take it as a compliment to his control and not a punishment, he left the controller's office.

On his way out, he learned more of what had happened at the dispensary last night. Someone had set off canisters of fear gas amidst the lines of Simes in Need. The only Simes not in hard Need were channels. The only available Gens were Companions, Gens with fields like Tonyo's. Helplessly, they had succumbed to the gas. Four Companions, stripped of their defenses, had been killed before the rest were shut up in the insulated transfer suites, channels fighting hand to hand against Simes trying to reach the remaining Gens.

The police had had no choice but to shut down the dispensary until the gas was cleared and it was safe to bring in more channels and Companions from Carre to cope with the growing numbers of Simes in hard Need.

They were still coping, but although there was much free-wheeling anxiety among the Simes waiting in the long lines this morning, there were no complaints. But there were Thank you's to the Companions circulating among them to ease their stress while they waited.

All over Norlea, there was a new appreciation of Gens. They had always been important, of course, as the source of selyn. But something had shifted in the community's attitude: more and more Simes shocked into perceiving Gens as people.

Baird saw signs in shop windows that had not been there yesterday: "Gens welcome," and "All larities served." When he passed through the square on the way home, he saw a vendor with cheap copies of the Gen collar necklaces Zhag and Tonyo and Jonmair wore, selling them hand over tentacle. Even as he watched, the woman ran out of her supply, and closed up her stand.

The attacks meant to drive Sime and Gen apart had only succeeded in bringing them together.

The newspaper was late today, but by midmorning a special edition appeared, with stories of the horror visited on Norlea. Baird took a few copies back to The Post. There was a special featured story on the front page.

Bran Coyt, it turned out, was a reporter for the Norlea Tribune. "Last night," he wrote, "Gulf Territory witnessed something no one ever thought to see: frightened Gens turning for protection to the arms of Simes."

Baird watched his father's lips thin as he read the paper over his morning kafi. Then he deliberately turned it over to read the story below the fold—about the devastation in the Gulf capital of Lanta.

Gulf's largest city, where there were no Households and no mixed-larity families, was once again under martial law. There were four dispensaries in the city, and all had sustained fear gas attacks. The pen Gens kept on the premises for the channels to strip for selyn had been killed, as had more than a dozen Companions, some by their own channels.

"I'm glad we live here, rather in than in Lanta," said Baird.

"You enjoy being perverted?" his father asked.

"Dad—we're not perverted. Juncts are perverted."

Treavor Axton put down his newspaper and stared at and zlinned his son. "What's happened to you?"

"I told you—I've disjuncted," Baird replied confidently. "I didn't want to kill last night. I'll need selyn every month, but I'll never want to kill again. I feel free, Dad. You'll understand in a month or two."

"No," his father said.

"Dad," Baird ventured, "it's nothing to be ashamed of! I know the only way you could be so much better after just one transfer was if—"

"You don't know anything!" his father said, rising from the table. "I don't want you talking about it—understand? No speculation, no discussion. It doesn't go outside the family." And with that he walked out.

Baird wished his growing Need didn't keep him from feeling the contentment he should have. Once his father completed his disjunction he wouldn't feel ashamed, or dependent on Gens. He, too, would come to understand that Simes and Gens depended on one another equally.

And Baird picked up the paper to read Bran Coyt's article again.

* * * * * * *

WHEN BAIRD TOLD HER OF THE CONTROLLER'S DECISION, Jonmair felt deprived of the transfer she should have had with Baird, and of the post reaction that would have followed. She wished he had wakened her and taken her along— any Sime could zlin she wasn't afraid! *Next month,* she promised herself yet again, joining Zhag and Tonyo in the kafi shop.

They had come back from the Dispensary late for lunch, Zhag weary from performing transfers for over two hours before Tonyo dragged him away to ply him with trin tea and try to get some food into him.

"We have to go back tomorrow," said Tonyo. "I understand, but Zhag, you have to be up to performing tonight, and then channeling tomorrow."

"I can do it," said Zhag. "I'm in good health now, Tonyo."

"Thea says it'll take a year to build you up to full strength. So you're going to take a nap this afternoon."

Zhag laughed. "Tonyo, you are so sleepy that I won't be able to help taking a nap!"

"Good! But food first."

Jonmair sipped her tea and nibbled at fresh bread and cheese. Like most establishments, The Post had opened late this morning, so Chef had not had time to make the usual variety of pastries. It didn't really matter, though, as the kafi shop was nearly empty. Probably most people didn't expect them to be open.

"How bad were things at the Dispensary?" Jonmair asked as Tonyo brought a tray laden with fruit, bread, honey, and cheese.

"It was the worst there," Tonyo told her. "Four Companions were killed."

"I thought they couldn't be killed," said Jonmair.

"Not ordinarily. But you got the fear gas worse than I did last night. If we hadn't been protected by the Simes here...." he let the thought trail off.

"Didn't the channels protect their Companions?" Jonmair asked.

"Of course they did," said Zhag. "There were fifteen Companions out in the public areas, and the channels got eleven of them to safety. But there were over a hundred Simes in hard Need waiting for transfer. Some of them were able to reach the Gens first."

Jonmair shuddered, remembering how hysterical she had been. It must have been even worse for Companions, to lose the control they worked so hard to learn.

"Did you know a channel called Vent, and his Companion Mern?" Tonyo asked.

"Yes," said Jonmair. "Vent gave Baird his transfer last month." She didn't elaborate.

"Oh," the young Gen said, and fell silent.

"What's wrong?" asked Jonmair. "Was Mern one of the Companions who got killed?"

Tonyo nodded, his mouth full of bread and cheese it seemed he was having a hard time swallowing.

"You'll hear about it," said Zhag, "so we may as well tell

you."

"Vent killed Mern," Jonmair said. "Nothing else could make you hesitate to tell me."

Both men nodded. "Of course that was what the attackers wanted to happen to all the channels and Companions," said Zhag.

Jonmair remembered the young Gen teasing the channel. "Oh!" she gasped.

"What?" Zhag asked her.

"Something Mern said to Vent—he actually said, 'You can kill me again any time you've a mind to.'"

"Vent was junct?" Zhag asked.

"Yes. The Tecton had just recruited him and Mern, and they were put to work after their first transfer. They had had only two days of experience when we talked with them."

Tonyo nodded. "It's a dangerous situation—but there're not enough channels to go around. I'm sorry it happened, though."

"What will become of Vent?" Jonmair asked.

"He— Well, Janine thinks he committed suicide," said Tonyo. "He threw himself into the fighting to protect the other Companions, and someone knifed him."

"Once he realized what he had done," said Zhag, "I doubt he cared."

"Conta's fiancé, Robert, was killed, too," said Jonmair. "Then she murdered the Sime who did it."

Tonyo pushed aside most of his food. "The attackers didn't achieve what they wanted to, but they sure caused a lot of suffering."

"Baird says they caught some of them," said Jonmair.

"Who was behind it?" asked Zhag. "I heard there were attacks all over the territory. Somebody had to organize it."

"Right now," said Jonmair, "no one knows."

The police, though, were trying to find out. They had interviewed Sime witnesses last night, but today they were questioning surviving Gens. Just as the three friends finished lunch, two Simes came into the kafi shop. The younger Sime, female, wore police uniform, while the older, male, was Police Investigator Kerrk.

"If you please," the woman, whose name was Gabi, said to Jonmair and Tonyo, "we would like to get your stories separately. You were both present at the first attack, yes?"

"My partner was the object," said Zhag. "Obviously the attackers hoped he would panic and I would kill him."

Inspector Kerrk said, "If you please, Mr. Paget, we already have your statement, and right now we don't want interpretations, just facts."

He turned to Jonmair. "Do you feel up to talking with us alone?" he asked.

"Of course," she replied. "The fear gas has worn off."

"Good. Is there someplace we can have privacy?"

Jonmair took the two police officers into the small private bar that wouldn't open until late afternoon, and told them everything she could remember about the attackers in the main salon. Gabi wrote everything down, while Kerrk zlinned Jonmair as he questioned her.

"Excellent observation," he said as Jonmair described the man and woman at the bar in the main salon last night. "Simes keep trying to describe the ambient, but Gens give us physical descriptions." Jonmair heard respect in his voice, something he had not had for Gens only a few weeks before. "How old were these two people?"

"At least ten years past changeover," she said. "The woman may have been older—she was well-dressed, her hair carefully styled and possibly colored."

"What do you mean by well-dressed?" Kerrk asked.

"Well, I think she meant to blend in. She probably picked the simplest evening dress in her closet, but it was still perfectly tailored, a design to flatter her figure," Jonmair explained. "It was the finest material, too—it would have been very expensive."

"What you're saying is that she didn't fit in at all?"

"Not exactly—everybody comes to The Post. But the man

TO KISS OR TO KILL | 255

with her was wearing a nice but ordinary suit—not the same quality at all. I now know that they were part of a widespread plan to attack Gens with fear gas. But if that hadn't happened, I would have thought from looking at them that—well, that the woman was cheating on her husband with a younger man. Except that she was post and he wasn't."

"You noticed that?"

"It seemed strange. They were obviously together, but couples generally try to come to Zhag and Tonyo's performances both post."

"You were suspicious?"

"You mean, did I think he was there to kill someone? No, of course not. I just thought it was odd, that's all."

"What else can you tell us about them?"

"The woman had dark brown hair, brown eyes, and olive skin. And she wore a beautiful ring on her right hand. I noticed it when I was at the bar waiting for a drink order. She kept pushing it back and forth with her dorsal tentacles. She wasn't in Need, so I guess I thought she was nervous about being seen with her escort."

"What did the ring look like?" Gabi asked.

"Gold, with a green stone, and kind of sculptured sides that held the stone up so the light could get into it. Large—she had large hands for a Sime, but graceful. Her nails were manicured, all perfectly even and buffed."

"And the man?"

"Curly reddish brown hair, blue-green eyes, sallow complexion. Taller than I am. Oh—he had a mole beside his mouth, on the left side."

Kerrk smiled at her. It made the lines in his leathery cheeks even deeper. "That's very helpful. Anything else you remember?"

"He had a red money pouch that looked new. I saw it when he bought drinks. And...maybe it was because he was in Need... but the skin of his tentacles looked darker than the skin of his arms and hands."

Kerrk shook his head. "It's so different working a case with Gen witnesses. Simes go hyperconscious and don't see anything—I get sick of being told, 'I'd know him if I could zlin him.' But on this case we've got detailed descriptions of a dozen people, all from Gens."

"I hope you're nearing the end of your investigation," said Jonmair.

"Why?" he asked.

"Because you're in hard Need, and I think you're not taking your transfer so that you can be sensitive to every nuance you can zlin."

Gabi laughed. "She's got you pegged, Kerrk."

"How?" he asked. "Gens can't zlin."

"We're attracted to Simes in Need," she explained. "I couldn't serve your Need, but that doesn't keep me from being drawn to it. You really should have a Companion."

"I've been telling him that since I started working with him," said the female officer. "I'm nonjunct," she explained. "It's Gabi ambrov Carre. I've been trying to match Kerrk up with a Companion since I found out he's a channel."

"Gabi's right," said Jonmair. "Talk to Zhag about what Tonyo does for him."

"Runs his life," muttered Kerrk, then visibly pulled himself under control. "I'm used to living without Gen help. My job is to uphold the law, which includes protecting Gens. Protecting them, not being protected by them. If you don't have anything else to tell us, then we'll get on to Tonyo."

Kerrk's attitude reminded Jonmair very much of Treavor Axton's, little wonder since they were friends. Still, he clearly respected Gens as witnesses... probably the way Baird's father grudgingly respected the entertainment abilities of the Gens at The Post. It appeared that one way for Gens to gain respect from Simes was to prove their value to whatever work the Simes did.

It was quite some time now since she had seen Kerrk playing poker with Mr. Axton and his cronies. Perhaps they didn't want to hear that Gens made good witnesses.

Jonmair left the little bar and sent Tonyo in, then started upstairs to face her daily pile of mending. On the way, she encountered Baird, who said, "Dad wants to talk to you."

"What about?" she asked.

"He noticed your citizenship tags."

Jonmair's hand went to her throat. She had forgotten that she had yet to inform Treavor Axton that she was no longer his ward.

Well, no time like the present. Squaring her shoulders, she went to Mr. Axton's office.

He looked up when she entered, and said, "I hear congratulations are in order. That you are a Free Gen now." But he didn't sound happy for her.

Still, "Thank you," she replied politely. "I've been meaning to tell you, and discuss remaining as an employee."

"Oh, no necessity for that," he told her. "I'm sure you'll be glad to leave—and I will be happy to have my son free of your influence. Go on now—pack your things. It's no longer my responsibility to provide for you."

His words hit her like an icy shower, but she controlled her field, too proud to let him know he had hurt her.

"Very well," she replied, calling on all her self-esteem to say stiffly, "Thank you for everything you've done for me. If your kindness can extend to a letter of recommendation—"

"Recommendation? For an ungrateful Gen who didn't even tell me it was plotting to leave? Put those clothes back where you got them, and get out of here."

Although she was still in shock, Jonmair remembered that she had friends. Miz Delancy would hire her. Zhag and Tonyo would take her in for a few days, or Penta Coyt's family, until she could find a place of her own.

"I'm sorry you feel that way," she replied. "I will be gone as soon as I pack my things."

Treavor Axton rose from behind his desk. "Just one more thing," he said, picking up a sheet of paper. "Here is what you've cost me, Gen. I expect repayment within the month, or I'll have the law on you."

She took the paper, and felt her limbs go numb as she stared at the figures.

It began with what Treavor Axton had paid for her as a Choice Kill, and continued with charges for her room, food, and clothing for all the time she had been at The Post.

The final total was staggering.

What little money she had saved from her tips was not a tenth of what she owed. There was no job that would allow her to earn that much in a single month!

What was she going to do? She understood that Baird's father was angry at her because he hated his son's dependence on her. He would invoke the law if she didn't pay.

What if it meant she wasn't available for transfer with Baird next month?!

As tears blurred the figures on the paper she held, she turned and fled from the room. The most she could manage at that moment was not to allow Treavor Axton the satisfaction of zlinning the feelings she could not control. He had not only succeeded in separating her from Baird, but he had destroyed any life she could have hoped to build—for how could she ever make her plans come true if her so-called freedom began with an arrest for unpaid debts?

CHAPTER ELEVEN
RESISTANCE

JONMAIR RAN FROM TREAVOR AXTON'S OFFICE and up the stairs—but before she got past the second-floor landing Baird caught up with her. "What's wrong?" he asked. "I've never zlinned you this upset without fear gas."

She thrust the paper at him. "I'm ruined!" she said. "I can never pay this!"

He read it, and put his arm around her shoulders. "You don't have to pay all this," he said. "My father just wanted to upset you."

As Baird led Jonmair back toward his father's office, she pulled herself together. Baird was right—there were new laws governing Free Gens so that they could get a start in life. She had not taken the time to read through the thick packet of fine print she had been given with her citizenship papers—but she realized that she knew one way the bill he had presented her was grossly unfair.

"Do you want me to take care of it?" Baird asked.

"No, I can do it."

When they returned to the office, Jonmair stepped forward, saying, "I'm afraid you made an error in figuring what I owe you, Mr. Axton."

"I don't think so," he replied flatly.

"Yes, sir, you did. You forgot to deduct what you were paid for my selyn for each month I was your ward."

Baird grinned. "She's right, Dad."

"You can't have it both ways," Jonmair pointed out. "You were paid for my selyn, so I owe you nothing for room, board, or clothing." She put the sheet of figures on the desk, picked up Treavor Axton's pen, and deducted the selyn payments. That wiped out the costs for her care and a quarter of the Choice Kill sum.

"I haven't donated this month yet," Jonmair added. "I can give you that payment as soon as I get it."

"Under the law," said Baird, "the most you owe is half your selyn payment each month until the purchase price is paid off. And," he added, "former warders are encouraged to reduce it to a quarter of the selyn payment in order to allow Free Gens to become productive taxpaying citizens."

"Taxpaying!" his father sputtered. "They get *our* tax money!"

"Gens still have to pay income and property tax," said Baird. "You don't want to keep them so deep in debt that they never have income or property to pay taxes on, do you, Dad?"

Both Baird and Jonmair knew that that was exactly what he wanted, but he wouldn't say it. Instead, he said, "All right. But she leaves. Now."

"I'll pack my things," said Jonmair.

"And I'll take you over to the Jax," said Baird. "Binni Dodson has been hunting for a Gen to do for her guests what you've been doing for ours."

Jonmair was about to protest that she planned to go to Delancy's when Treavor Axton demanded, "You'd take her to our biggest rival?"

Jonmair decided to play along with Baird. "You said you wanted me to leave. I'm free to take another job."

"Binni won't expect her to clean rooms or mend linens, either," said Baird. "Jonmair will be able to design costumes for Zhag and Tonyo in her free time, and take on other clients, too."

"I won't have her going to our rival!" exclaimed Treavor Axton.

Jonmair seized her opportunity. "Then what will you offer to keep me here?"

"You dare bargain with me, Gen?"

"For one thing," she replied, "you will call me Jonmair if you want me to stay. I want room and board, and the same wages as the rest of the staff."

"Plus 15%," said Baird, "for her special abilities as a Gen."

"No cleaning rooms or mending linens," added Jonmair. "I will eat meals among our guests as usual. I will serve food and drinks. And I will accept clothing and costume design commissions on my own time."

Baird's father stared from one to the other of the two young people facing him. "Are you through?" he asked warningly.

"For now," said Jonmair. "Anything else can be negotiated later."

"And her salary will be renegotiable in six months," Baird put in.

"No," said Treavor Axton. "Room, board, and tips, no salary. And she does any job I tell her to, including cleaning the guest rooms."

Jonmair turned to Baird. "Shall we go over to the Jax?"

"I'll help you pack," he replied.

Treavor Axton scowled. "It'll be worth it to get that Gen out of your bed, Baird,"

"There will be a bed in my room at the Jax," Jonmair said boldly.

"And it's less than five minutes away," Baird pointed out.

"All right, all right, shen you!" his father exploded. "You may think you've won, but no good can come of this. Back to work, both of you!"

"Are we agreed on terms?" Jonmair asked.

"We are. Now get out of here...Jonmair."

* * * * * * *

UNDER HER NEW TERMS OF EMPLOYMENT Jonmair was on her own time until her evening duties. As for Baird, he had no specific duties until that same time. So he took her hand, zlinning her triumph.

"I'm proud of you," he told her.

She smiled back, especially beautiful now, confident, head held high. He led her to his room, where they could have privacy, quelling the nagging feeling that he was becoming too dependent on her field. "You've changed, Jonmair. It took courage to stand up to my father that way."

"You supported me," she replied, letting her field caress him. He leaned into it, unable to resist the way it eased his Need anxiety. "Simes and Gens support each other now. If the fear gas attack had come right after the Last Kill instead of last night, how many Simes would have struggled to save Gen lives?"

"Few," he agreed, finding it hard to concentrate on the conversation with Jonmair's field enticing him.

They went over to the window seat. Jonmair knelt on the banquette, looking out over the tiny garden in the courtyard below. Baird leaned back against the cushions, not having to touch her to bathe in her nager. This close to hard Need he could not help zlinning, but Jonmair's presence helped him maintain duoconsciousness. Thus he could also see Jonmair, the brilliant Gulf sunlight framing her silhouette, putting highlights of fire in her wine-dark hair, mirroring the way her nager sparkled with confidence, warmth, and life.

She was not looking at him or touching him, and yet she maintained a comfort zone that allowed him to know Need without anxiety. It was almost...pleasure.

Jonmair slid down onto the banquette, one leg tucked under her, facing him. She made no move to touch him, but her field grew ripe with selyur nager—the Need to Give. "Let me pull the drapes," she said softly.

It was the time they had been scheduled to attempt transfer, if the fear gas attack hadn't happened.

But they were supposed to do it under a channel's supervision.

Baird could not imagine anyone else sharing the moment.

Jonmair moved, shutting out the bright sunlight, her replete field welcoming. She sat facing him again, brimming with life, yearning to pour it into the void of his aching nerves. Only with Jonmair had he ever felt like a real Sime—she had allowed him to take his single guiltless Kill, that time in Old Chance's Pen—

Her fingers touched his, gently, a tingling caress as selyn sparkled along her nerves, dancing as if eager to escape her Genness and penetrate the depths of his Simeness. His laterals yearned toward the source of life.

But before his laterals touched her skin, he realized what was so enticing in Jonmair's field: courage.

Less than twenty-four hours ago she had suffered pure panic. Behind her intense desire—unquestionably genuine desire— faintly echoed that same nervous anticipation he had zlinned when he had taken her virginity, and again a few moments ago when she had stood up to his father.

Baird was so attuned to her at this moment that he felt even the feelings she hid from herself. The least fear during transfer, though, and she would resist.

The least resistance, and he would kill.

"No!" Baird gasped, retracting his laterals so hard they ached.

"It's all right," Jonmair coaxed. "I'm not afraid."

"Yes, you are!" he told her, his mind's eye clouded with images of that Pen Gen he had killed so thoughtlessly in her presence. He dared not give in while her anxiety hovered in the background.

"Stop!" Baird begged. "Jonmair, I refuse to kill you!" With every scrap of willpower, Baird forced himself to stop zlinning. It hurt.

Teeth clenched, he staggered to his feet and fled from the single point of light in the dark, quiet room.

Downstairs, he almost ran into Tonyo, just emerging from his interview with the police. "Baird! What's wrong?" Zhag's Companion asked. Then, "Why aren't you zlinning? What happened? Where's Jonmair?"

Zhag came running down the hallway, his channel's sensitivity enabling him to sense Baird's distress. "He's broken out of trautholo, Tonyo. Help me with him."

At the Gen's questioning look, Zhag explained as he and his Companion supported Baird out of the public corridor and into the room the police had just vacated. "Trautholo is...the commitment to transfer. It hurts like shen to break out of it." Leaving Baird leaning on Tonyo's neutral field, he brought him a glass of water, asking, "What happened?"

"Jonmair," Baird managed.

"Were you going to attempt transfer despite Thea's warning?"

"She...wanted to," Baird explained, "but I could sense bravado behind her selyur nager."

"That's dangerous," said Zhag.

"I didn't mean to let it go that far. It felt so good. By the time I realized...."

Zhag said, "You did the right thing. Jonmair has to have time to recover from last night. But Tonyo," he added to his Companion, "Baird is not a channel. He can't bounce back from a Gen's pummeling him. Be careful what you do to him."

"He's just supporting me," Baird defended Tonyo, who was indeed as professional as any Householding Companion at that moment, his field easing Baird's shock without engaging.

Zhag rummaged behind the bar and came up with a vial of fosebine. Baird accepted a dose, Need for once useful in masking the foul taste as he forced it down.

"When is your appointment?" Zhag asked. When Baird told him, he shook his head. "You're in hard Need. Let us escort you to the dispensary."

"No," Baird choked out, refusing to give in to yet another weakness. "I'll wait for my appointment."

"Then stay with us," said Tonyo. "I have to have a nap before our performance, or I'll fall asleep on stage!"

Zhag said, "It's soothing to be in the room where Tonyo is sleeping."

So Baird went with them to their dressing room, where Tonyo sprawled on the divan and dropped off to sleep like the healthy young animal he so often resembled. Zhag dozed in a comfortable armchair. Baird looked through a stack of books piled on the dressing table, and chose one on the founding of Carre, from the Householding library. He knew the general story, but this volume contained excerpts from the letters and journals of those who had dared to try in Gulf what they had learned from travels into other Sime Territories.

Eventually the fosebine soothed his nerves, and the peaceful nageric interaction between Zhag and Tonyo eased his mood. When Zhag stirred and said, "It's time for us to get ready for the show," Baird got up and stretched.

"Time for me to make my rounds before my appointment. Thank you—both of you," he added, as Tonyo sat up, yawning.

"Stay with us till it's time to go," offered the Gen.

"I have duties just as you do," Baird told him. "I'm fine now, thanks to you. I can hold out for another hour."

Although he didn't want to. When he left the bubble of quiet created by Zhag and Tonyo, the ambient nager of The Post hit like an ocean wave. The familiar mix of humor, lust, and greed was overlaid this evening with bittersweet memories of what had occurred last night.

The house was small, probably a third of the patrons they had had last night, but the inveterate gamblers were in their usual positions. Others had come seeking excitement, entertainment... anything to escape thinking.

The main salon was already filling—no one let tickets to one of Zhag and Tonyo's performances go to waste. Baird supervised the new security measures, but stayed out of the salon itself. Jonmair was in there, serving drinks. He could zlin that she had not donated. Could he manage to be in her company to walk over to the dispensary? If they were finally to succeed at transfer next month, they had to remain on the same schedule.

* * * * * * *

JONMAIR HAD TO COVER MORE TABLES THAN USUAL

that evening because Baird had stationed Sime staff members at all entrances to make certain no one brought in anything the size and shape of a fear gas cylinder.

No one minded the security. They probably would have rioted if anyone had tried to take away their knives or whips, but those had never been a problem at The Post before, so there was no reason to ban them now.

During her first shift in the gambling salon, more people than ever talked to Jonmair, asking her about last night. She didn't mind telling how Baird had saved her life, although it hurt to remember how he had used his new-found control to refuse her just an hour ago. *He's the one who's afraid,* she told herself, feeling perfectly safe, high-field in a room full of Simes.

Her tips were bigger than ever before, and she smiled and controlled her field, not wanting to entice anyone but Baird. She could go to the dispensary alone, but always before she had gone with him. She glimpsed Baird once on the other side of the large room, but he was obviously avoiding her.

It was a relief to go to the Main Salon for Zhag and Tonyo's performance, for there everyone's attention was on the musicians. The performance was sold out, as all their shows were, and despite last night's attack there were few no-shows.

Zhag and Tonyo were in top form for the day after turnover: musically perfect, but not able to put the emotion into their performance that they did when they were post. They adapted their setlist to their cycle, and both were exceptional nageric actors. Jonmair suspected that the Simes in the audience were less likely than the Gens to notice that Tonyo didn't bounce as much as usual, or that Zhag was more absorbed in the music and less in the audience reaction.

When it came to the point at which the attack had come last night, Zhag said, "This is where we showcase Tonyo's song, 'My Brother, He Turned Out Wrong.' Last night the performance was stopped before we could play it. But those thugs only succeeded in interrupting one performance."

Tonyo added, "Under the influence of fear gas, none of the

Gens here could protect themselves. Not just Zhag, but many Simes here helped get us to safety."

"A few people," said Zhag, "tried to take Gulf Territory back to the days before Unity. Their efforts were thwarted, not by police, not by soldiers, but by good people just like you. In the aftermath, this song takes on even greater importance: no matter how hard life is under Unity, when we remember what it was like before, we know it's worth the effort."

As always, they had to perform the song twice before they could take their break. Then Jonmair began dispensing drinks again.

Just before the lights dimmed, though, she told Lukis, the bartender, "Time for my appointment to donate," just as if she were a Sime with a transfer appointment. He nodded, and Jonmair slipped out, looking for Baird. Had he gone without her?

She could hear voices from Treavor Axton's office. Thinking Baird was with his father, she started in that direction, but realized as she came closer that neither voice was Baird's. Treavor Axton was arguing with a woman, the walls muffling their words.

Jonmair retraced her steps to see if Baird was in the gambling salon, when a man emerged from the winecellar. She had seen him somewhere before—but he was not staff. What was a customer doing in the cellar?

She would tell Baird, she decided. Holding her field neutral, she walked on toward the gambling hall, her focus on finding Baird. Behind her, the man exclaimed, "It's young Axton's Gen bitch!"

"Let it go!" said another familiar voice, and Jonmair realized the only chance she had to reach Baird was if they thought that because she was Gen she was also deaf and stupid. Fiercely controlling her field, she wished she could control her wildly beating heart. She knew that man—last night he had thrown fear gas canisters from the back of the salon!

Just then Baird came out of the gambling hall. The other

Simes retreated into Treavor Axton's office.

"Baird!" Jonmair whispered, trying to shield both of them with her field, "something's going on!"

"I don't care," he answered. "We have to get to the dispensary. Don't touch me!" he added as she tried to drag him into the small saloon that was not in use tonight.

She had to use her field to make him come with her and shut the door. "Jonmair—no! I won't risk your life!" he protested, obviously thinking she was going to try to seduce him into transfer.

"No!" she insisted. "It's that man—one of the ones who threw fear gas last night. He came out of your cellar! We have to get the police!"

Baird was both staring at her and zlinning her. "The police searched the cellar last night."

"Not then," she tried to explain. "Now!"

Just then Treavor Axton's voice, in a harsh whisper, came clearly through the door they were leaning against. "I told you to get out of town! I won't have The Post mixed up in your scheme!"

Then another voice Jonmair recognized: Old Chance, the Penkeeper. "You shedoni-doomed morons! Why'd you come back here? Git the shen out afore someone zlins you!"

"No," Baird breathed, hardly loud enough for even Jonmair to hear. But it wasn't his voice she was concerned about—it was his field. Those Simes out there were both killers and murderers. "Dad," Baird murmured, and Jonmair realized why he remained rooted here, instead of going out the other door to alert the police.

The thugs had come to Treavor Axton for protection. Had he known before last night what they were plotting? Had he had a tentacle in it?

"Come on," Jonmair whispered, tugging at Baird's hand. "We have to get help!"

"But...Dad," he protested.

"They tricked him," she said desperately. "He didn't know

what they planned to do. Come on, Baird, before—"

Too late.

"Go out this way," Treavor Axton was saying. "Take the back streets down to the docks," and he opened the door to the small saloon just as Baird and Jonmair made a dash for the opposite door.

In a flash Baird was pulled back and there were Simes on either side of Jonmair, one of them backhanding her. Though her ears rang, she now had a clear view of the curly-haired man she had described for Inspector Kerrk. The other thug held her other arm. Behind them were the woman from the bar, Old Chance, and Treavor Axton.

Baird shoved the man on Jonmair's left. Wainscoating cracked where he hit the wall, and Jonmair gasped, realizing how much selyn that augmented move had cost Baird.

She sensed his increasing Need as he rounded on the man holding her right arm, knocked the whip out of his hand, and kicked him in the solar plexus.

The second man fell unconscious, but pulled Jonmair down with him.

* * * * * * *

BAIRD BENT OVER JONMAIR, FIGHTING DIZZINESS as the last of his selyn reserves whirlpooled away in the highest level of augmentation he was capable of. There was no time to think, only to act on instinct to protect his Gen.

When he touched her, he zlinned only the selyn brimming within her, carrying a warning—?

He zlinned two Simes converging at his back, while behind them his father projected a strong negative.

Baird kicked Old Chance's feet out from under him, but the Sime woman who followed was young and strong and armed with a knife. The first man he had dispatched climbed to his feet, grasping Baird's upper arms and turning him so that the woman's knife—

"Nooo!"

Baird was thrown hypoconscious, his Sime senses deserting him as two voices howled the word in concert. His father leaped at the Sime woman, trying to wrench the knife from her hand, as Jonmair's grip on Baird tightened as if under augmentation.

Depleted, struggling to remain conscious, Baird prepared to kick the man trying to pull Jonmair from his grasp. Why couldn't he zlin? Was this attrition?

The fighting Simes dropped like sacks of meal.

Baird found himself staring into Jonmair's eyes. "Genslam," she explained—and suddenly he could zlin again.

For all the good it did him. On the edges of his awareness, he sensed other people arriving, too late to help him...but Jonmair was safe. From somewhere, he found his voice. "Live, Jonmair," he told her, and fell into cold darkness.

CHAPTER TWELVE
PARTNERS

JONMAIR GASPED AS BAIRD DROPPED, a dead weight. She fell to her knees beside him, hardly aware of the other Simes sprawled around them.

Had Baird used the last of his selyn augmenting to protect her, and died of attrition?

No—she could still feel his Need!

She had to press his lateral extensor nodes to force the delicate tentacles out of their sheaths, but once they emerged they instinctively sought her arms as she bent forward and pressed her lips to Baird's.

A whirlpool of Need dragged her toward a bottomless abyss. Survival instinct told her to resist—but if she could not fill him, Baird would die! Determinedly, she pursued the last spark of life in the man she loved.

When Jonmair charged forward to meet the void, everything changed. If Baird was cold and darkness, she was warmth and light, spilling joyfully into the space so perfectly made to hold her. It was welcome, exultant, homecoming as she had only felt in her sweetest dreams—everything she could ever have desired.

Too soon, it ended. Reluctantly, she lifted her lips from Baird's, but thrilled as she watched the strained lines of Need disappear from his face.

* * * * * * *

BAIRD WOKE TO THE MOST INCREDIBLE SENSATION.

Sweet, warm selyn poured into his depleted nerves, not only giving him back his life, but making it worth living. No transfer, no Kill, had ever been like this.

He recognized Jonmair's field enveloping and supporting him, confident, secure.

The luscious feeling ended too soon, but he was replete, strong, ready to face—

Memory returned with a sick shock. Baird looked up into Jonmair's face, seeing the bruise on her cheekbone where one of the thugs had hit her, her hair disheveled, but her smile beatific.

His awareness moved slowly outward, encompassing the small room they were in—the little saloon, furniture overturned and broken. They were alone on the floor.

Out in the corridor, though, was a whole crowd of people. He wanted to stay there, reveling in what they had just shared...but memory took him back to what had thrown him into attrition, and he had to open that door. Zhag and Tonyo stood blocking his view of—

"Where is my father?" Baird asked, the last of his joy and relief dissolving as—

The crowd parted, to reveal corpses. Sime corpses.

Old Chance had not survived Jonmair's Genslam, and neither had the man Baird had kicked in the chest. The other two thugs, still groggy, were held tightly by Post staff members.

But Baird's attention went to the third body lying in the corridor, a knife sticking out of its chest. Treavor Axton.

"We saw it," said Zhag. "Your father was trying to protect you, Baird."

Oh, how he wanted to believe that!

"That woman was going to knife you," said Jonmair.

The police accepted Baird and Jonmair's story, even though the two remaining thugs claimed that Old Chance and Treavor Axton, now safely dead, had plotted the entire attack on Norlea.

Baird's post reaction took the form of grief as he came to understand not only that his father was dead, but that at best he had known about the fear gas plot and done nothing to stop it. He clung to Jonmair's hand as he told Inspector Kerrk, "Dad's last transfer—I thought the channels matched him with a Gen, because he was so much better. But—he must have taken an illegal Kill. If anyone had connections to Genfarmers, it was Old Chance."

Kerrk eyed Baird and Jonmair's clasped hands. "I'll check the dispensary rolls. But I won't find you two on them, either, will I?"

"It was an emergency," said Jonmair. "Baird used up the last of his selyn saving my life. There was no way to get him to a channel."

The police officer nodded. "You're the reason I can believe Baird was not in on the plot."

"I think," Baird managed to get out, "I think I know where they hid the fear gas before the attack. When Dad came home with Old Chance yesterday morning, he brought a wine barrel. He said we'd tap it after it had settled, but...now I think it wasn't wine."

He took the police officers down into the cellar, where he himself had put that insulated barrel yesterday morning. It was still there, but when Baird lifted it he found it far lighter than the day before.

The top, he now discovered, came off with a twist. It was definitely not a normal wine cask. Inside, beneath heavy insulation and packed in cotton batting at the very bottom, were a few leftover fear gas canisters.

He knew, Baird realized, guts wrenching. *My father was a part of the plot.*

But Jonmair was saying, "Mr. Axton was a hard man, but he would never commit treason. If Old Chance told him that was a barrel of wine, he'd accept it as a barrel of wine. They were old friends."

Jonmair zlinned truthful because, Baird realized, she believed what she was saying.

"If he broke the law to take a Kill, though...," Kerrk suggested.

"We don't really know he did," Jonmair said staunchly.

Kerrk zlinned her, then Baird, and nodded to Gabi. His partner closed her notebook. "Well, Treavor Axton and Old Chance are both dead," said Kerrk. "They're beyond our law now. I'm convinced that you were not involved, Baird, but there will be more questions before it's all over."

* * * * * * *

IT WOULD BE A LONG TIME BEFORE EVERYTHING WAS OVER. First there were funerals. Norlea rang with dirges. People joined funeral processions whether they knew the dead or not, mourning the injury to their fragile, tentative Unity. Funerals for Gens, something rare and private in the past, drew crowds of respectful Simes.

Nearly everyone was post, so emotions ran high. Conta's Robert was buried with full military honors, side by side with the man who had killed him, in the Norlea Army Post's cemetery. A hastily erected marker named them martyrs to Unity.

Conta herself was exonerated by a military tribune, as were all the other Sime soldiers who had murdered attackers on what had been labeled the Night of Fear. No Gens were even arrested, although a handful had managed to fight back.

It didn't appear that Jonmair would be charged with or even interrogated concerning the deaths of Old Chance and the thug who had died from her Genslam, even though it had not happened on the night when Gens could be forgiven anything done under the influence of fear gas. Either Inspector Kerrk discounted the effects of Genslam, or chose to ignore its implications. The official report was that the thug died of nerve and heart damage when Baird kicked him in self-defense, and Old Chance, already suffering from age and abuse of his system, died of selyn system failure from the dual deathshock of that man and Treavor Axton.

The Post remained open and crowded, although now people came to share feelings instead of to forget their troubles. Zhag and Tonyo, having had their performances cut short two nights in a row, refused to cancel any of their sold-out shows. They changed their setlist, adding emotionally-charged pieces in place of some trivial bar songs, and restored the Unity Hymn as final encore.

If anything, the fear gas attacks had united Gulf Territory in determination to end the Kill. Even in Lanta, word was, perpetrators were hunted down and made examples. Before the Night of Fear Lanta's juncts might have resented being forced to disjunct, but they resented even more being used as weapons against their will.

Baird had to deal with the swarm of auditors who descended even before his father's funeral, assessing inheritance taxes, property taxes, licensing fees, and conversion fees. Treavor Axton had kept meticulous records, so although it took up a great deal of Baird's time, he assured Jonmair he would not have to close down even temporarily.

But with Baird handling Treavor Axton's work and more, there was no one to do Baird's job. Jonmair happened to see Chef, Lukis, and Cord coming down the hall toward the office in which Baird was ensconced with another accountant and, without thinking, merely wanting to save Baird an interruption, asked if there was anything she could do.

Chef had the day's menus. Jonmair knew he would have estimated correctly the amount of food they would require, and told him, "Just go ahead. I know Mr. Baird trusts you to handle the kitchen."

She told Lukis the same about stocking the bars, and went upstairs with Cord to "help him sort the linens," which turned out to be simply agreeing with decisions he had already made about what was too worn to be used again.

When she came back downstairs, it was time for lunch with Zhag and Tonyo—but as they were eating Miz Delancy came in. "Ah, there you are, Jonmair! I've been hoping you would come to see me."

"I was going to," Jonmair said, "but I've been too busy here since Mr. Axton died."

"She's doing the work Baird used to do," said Tonyo.

"Really," she said. "So the son recognizes your abilities as the father refused to. Still, I would like to see some sketches from you when you have time. My staff can do the sewing."

While Jonmair arranged an appointment for later in the week, one of the other customers came over to their table, a young woman wearing a dress of fine silk, even though she was obviously only out shopping. She wore green enamel citizenship tags on a perfectly-fitted gold collar even more elegant than the ones Zhag and Tonyo had had made.

"Hello, Tonyo," she said in a way that subtly indicated that she was one of his conquests—or considered him one of hers.

"Hi, there," the Gen performer replied. "Nice to see you again."

Ever the gentleman, Zhag supplied the name Tonyo had forgotten—if he had ever bothered to find it out. "Hello, Merita. I don't know if you've met Jonmair, our costume designer. I think you know Miz Delancy."

As the women exchanged "how do you do's," Zhag continued, "I hope your family got through the Night of Fear without any problems."

"We were fortunate," Merita replied, but her attention was fixed on Jonmair, studying the dress she wore.

Jonmair had not dressed in her Post livery this morning, because her status had changed. However, she had little else in her wardrobe, and had chosen the blue cotton dress she had made in her first days here, saving her two better dresses for upcoming formalities. The scrutiny from this well-dressed woman made her all too aware that her outfit was made from a bedsheet rescued from the rag bin—but she held her head high, pretending that it was as good as the other woman's silk.

"Jonmair," said Merita, "I love your costumes for Zhag and Tonyo. Do you design women's clothes as well? Did you make the dress you're wearing?"

"Yes," Jonmair replied warily.

"Jonmair is going to create some designs for me, Merita," said Miz Delancy.

"Too late," Merita sighed. "I was hoping to commission a wardrobe by Jonmair before her prices went through the roof." She turned to Jonmair. "May I?" she asked, lifting the collar of Jonmair's dress, and then investigated the tucks in the puffed sleeve. "Exquisite!" she said. "Such workmanship in plain cotton—what could you do with fine fabric?"

Realizing where the conversation was headed, Jonmair offered, "I have two other dresses I've made upstairs, if you would like to see them. One is a formal gown—"

"The one you wore to the opening!" Merita exclaimed. "I remember. Now I'm sure I want your designs even if I have to pay Delancy prices."

"And you will show them off perfectly," said Miz Delancy. "If you buy a whole wardrobe, we can arrange a discount."

Jonmair watched in disbelief as her dream came true before her eyes.

Merita grinned. "Good. You're going to be all the rage, Jonmair."

When Merita and Miz Delancy had gone, not without first making an appointment to choose materials and discuss designs, Zhag said, "Congratulations, Jonmair. Merita's right: you are going to be all the rage. I don't think you'll be serving drinks much longer."

* * * * * * *

BAIRD EMERGED FROM THE OFFICE THAT EVENING to find The Post running as smoothly as if he had supervised it himself. In every quarter, he was told, "Don't worry—Jonmair's already taken care of it."

Just as she had taken care of him last night.

He found Jonmair, back in her Post livery, serving drinks in the gambling hall until it was time to go to the main salon.

Baird frowned. Why did it feel wrong for Jonmair to go about business as usual?

Nothing, he realized, would ever be "as usual" again. He had changed, and Jonmair had changed. She looked wrong, now, as just another Post staff member. He remembered her last night, strong and in charge, the way everyone had described her today. He wanted that woman, not a barmaid.

Wanted?

True, his post reaction was not sexual, mixed as it was with grief—but he now had no doubt that it would be normal in the future. It was actually a good thing that his head was clear on the subject. He didn't want a sex partner so much as...a life partner. A partner in everything—transfer, business, and love.

But why should Jonmair want him? He had used her from the moment they met, treated her as he would one of his prized horses. Even when he had encouraged her to face up to his father, he had known that after he had invested so much in her, Treavor Axton would never let her leave The Post.

For the first time in his life, Baird thought about what a Gen thought of him—this Gen, this perfect complement to his Simeness. What if Jonmair had no special interest in him except as a friend—the way she was friends with Zhag and Tonyo? She had slept in his bed last night, but only slept. Did she care about him, Baird, or had she risked her life to save his only because she cared about saving a life?

She could go anywhere she pleased now. He would never use the debt she had owed his father to keep her here. What could he offer her that would allow her to use her talents in a way that could not be seen as demeaning?

You fool, he told himself. *Weren't you just thinking about what you want your relationship to be?*

* * * * * * *

BY THE TIME BAIRD APPROACHED HER, Jonmair had gone into the main salon, where he found her listening to Lukis explain how he determined which drinks to stock each evening.

"Chef tells me you approved the menus," Baird said. "Cord tells me you approved his inventory, and now I find you busy learning how to stock our saloons. Are you planning to take over my job, Jonmair?"

"I didn't mean—" she stuttered, fearing that he might feel she had overstepped her bounds. "You were so busy—"

"We asked her," Lukis came to Jonmair's defense. "We didn't think you wanted to be interrupted when you were doing all that legal stuff today."

"It's fine," Baird said. "Everything's running smoothly. Jonmair, please come with me."

They went to the office, where Baird asked her to sit down, and went to sit behind the desk. "Jonmair, I want to thank you," he said. "I hadn't even thought about training someone to take over my duties, because I didn't want to think about having to take over Dad's."

"I understand," she said.

"No," he replied, "I don't think you do. There isn't anyone else now. Dad's gone. Elendra's gone. The Post requires two people, one to run the business end—which will be more work than ever until everything is transferred to my name—and one to supervise the personnel. I'd like you to take over my old job of supervising personnel."

"But I don't know anything about that!" Jonmair exclaimed in amazement.

Baird smiled wearily. "You've been doing it all day. You know all about handling Simes, and all the staff except you and Penta are Sime. As for the details, Lukis was teaching you. Chef and Cord will do the same. Emlou takes care of her girls—all you have to do is make sure the staff keeps the rooms up."

"I...don't know what to say," Jonmair whispered.

"Say yes," said Baird. "We're transfer partners. Why shouldn't we be business partners as well?"

Because I want to be your partner in life, not business! Jonmair thought, her heart sinking. But she didn't say that.

Instead, she said, "I got another offer today. I'm designing a wardrobe for Merita Hardin."

"Oh." He seemed taken aback. "I know you want to design clothes. But perhaps you can do both? At least for now? Frankly, Jonmair, I need your help, at least for a time. If you don't like the job, I'll help you train someone else to take it over."

She understood his use of the word "need." The Post, after all, was Baird's life—it was all he had ever known, and he loved it. She had grown to love it, too.

The immensity of what he offered slowly dawned on her: a Gen in charge of the staff of the largest entertainment establishment in Norlea? How far she had come from that holding cell in which she had waited to die!

She remembered the day in the square when she had first seen Baird. She had been so eager to grow up then, to be independent, out from under her parents' authority. She had dreamed of running her own life, designing clothes, becoming famous.

And now, half a year later, despite turning out to be the wrong larity, she had it all! Every single thing she had dreamed of then was now hers: she was free, she was a designer on the brink of fame, and she had the choice of what she would do with her life.

"Yes," she said. "I'll do it, Baird. Thank you for the opportunity."

And she viciously pushed down the ache in her heart, telling herself that when she had everything she had asked for and even more, it was childish and selfish to want something more. If Baird couldn't love her, he certainly liked and respected her.

It would just have to be enough.

* * * * * * *

TREAVOR AXTON'S FUNERAL COULD NOT BE HELD FOR THREE DAYS, for there had been so many deaths ahead of his that the cemeteries were overwhelmed. The arrangements fell to Jonmair, in her new capacity as personnel supervisor. She consulted Baird about his father's wishes, then enlisted Zhag and Tonyo's help, and closed the gaming hall for the day. The staff covered the tables with flowers and Chef and Penta laid out a feast.

The mourners were legion. Customers, old friends, and the merely curious, they overcrowded the gaming hall and spilled into the corridors. Baird, who had never intended to leave Jonmair to cope with the inevitable crises alone, could not escape yet another auditor until almost the announced time— and emerged to find a procession of mourners moving quietly past the office.

"Put out more cheese buns and fruit," he heard Jonmair's voice, "and tap another keg of porstan."

"Yes, ma'am," replied one of Chef's helpers, and scurried off to the kitchen, while another staff member headed for the cellar. Baird watched and zlinned in satisfaction. Surely if his father could see how well The Post was functioning, even he would have to agree that Jonmair was doing a fine job.

Wearing her wine-colored dress, her hair twined at the back of her head, Jonmair moved as if she had been running The Post all her life. She went from table to table, making certain that trays and glasses were replaced as quickly as they were emptied. The room had been made dignified, gambling equipment hidden beneath flower arrangements and tablecloths. His father's coffin was at the front of the room, on the platform near the bar.

Baird in no way grudged the cost of providing food and drink to all these people—but he nevertheless noticed how Jonmair had arranged the lines so that people were encouraged to take something and continue on. There was no easy way to return for seconds.

Zhag and Tonyo, in conservative plain clothes, managed the ambient around the bier, allowing people their feelings but ready to shield if necessary. Baird knew he should join them, to accept people's condolences, but he wondered if he would ever get over not knowing how deeply involved his father had been in the fear gas conspiracy.

But propriety ruled, and he began moving through the crowd toward where his father's coffin stood heaped with flowers. Jonmair reached the other side of the room, turned, and started making her way back past another tier of tables. Baird was about to try to get her attention when she suddenly stopped, staring and turning pale.

Baird was too far away, and Jonmair too low-field, for him to zlin her through the crowd between them, but he saw that something had upset her. People near her zlinned it, turning to look at her, one woman putting a hand on Jonmair's arm, obviously asking what was wrong.

Jonmair shook her head and said something to the woman with a forced smile, then returned to stare at what to Baird appeared nothing more than a middle-aged Sime couple greedily sampling the delicacies laid out on one of the tables. He could not recall seeing them before, but there were many curiosity seekers in The Post today.

Baird worked his way through the lines, holding his field in a pattern that kept people from accosting him, and reached Jonmair's side just as the two Simes that had startled her looked up from the food—and shocked the ambient with their own reaction.

"Jonmair!" the woman gasped.

"We thought you were dead!" said the man.

Jonmair's field had disappeared, so Baird could not tell what she was feeling except from her outward appearance. That was calm as she said, "I'm alive, no thanks to you."

Who were these people? Working class, Baird judged from the conservative but cheap clothing they wore. What could they have to do with Jonmair?

"Is there anything wrong?" Baird asked as he stopped beside Jonmair, ready to defend her.

She gave him a faint smile and replied, "No. I just...never thought I would see my parents again."

These were her parents? The people who had sold her as a Choice Kill? Baird had to grasp control of himself as other people turned to stare and zlin.

"It's all right," said Jonmair, gently touching his upper arm. "They've only come to pay their respects to your father. They didn't know I was here."

"How could they not—?"

Even as he said it, Baird realized how foolish his question was. Of course they would never have attempted to find out what had happened to their daughter. That was what it was to be junct. Whether you gave up your Gen child willingly, or whether that child was taken from you by force of law, the only way to survive was never to think of him or her again.

That was the moment Baird truly felt it—not when he had resisted touching Jonmair on the Night of Fear, not when she had given him transfer, but now, finding it unimaginable to think and feel as juncts throughout history had thought and felt.

He was no longer junct.

I will never kill again because I could not stand to do so.

"You work here?" Jonmair's father asked.

"Yes," she replied, but did not elaborate.

"You got lucky," said her mother, eyeing the fine cloth of Jonmair's dress, the gold collar with her citizenship tags.

Baird felt ashamed that both the dress and the very expensive collar were gifts from Zhag and Tonyo, not from him. But he could give her something that would mean more to her. "Jonmair is a fine designer. You've heard of Zhag and Tonyo?"

"Yeah. They gonna play at the funeral?" asked the Sime woman eagerly.

"They are," Jonmair replied flatly.

"Jonmair is their costume designer," said Baird. "She's very talented." He stopped himself from telling them they should be proud of her. They had no right to be proud: they had had no tentacle in Jonmair's success.

Nor did Jonmair accord them any special attention, except to say, "If either Faleese or Wawkeen should establish as a Gen, I want you to send them to me. Don't bother to contact me for anything else."

As Baird and Jonmair moved away, preparing for the ceremony to begin, Baird asked, "Faleese and Wawkeen?"

"My younger brother and sister. I wouldn't put it past our parents to try to keep them as wards and sell their selyn. Not that they're likely to establish. I was the one in three in our family."

He didn't bother to remind her that it was only a statistical average that one in three children of Simes became Gen, and each case was individual. The important thing was that Jonmair would not allow the junctness of her parents to prevent her helping her younger siblings if they required it.

Once Baird took his place, the remembrance service for his father began. Nearly a hundred people answered the invitation to say something in memory of Treavor Axton, but most of them said only a few words: "He built this place into the best entertainment value in Norlea," or "He provided the best fun to be had after the Last Kill."

But some revealed things Baird hadn't known. At least half a dozen people told variants of "He hired me when no one else would, and got me back on my feet." One man told how Treavor Axton had lent him the money to build a saloon that was now one of The Post's major rivals. A woman said, "He banned me from the gambling tables when he saw I was addicted—and made me so mad I overcame it to prove him wrong."

Zhag spoke briefly about being hired as a down and out musician, to which Tonyo added, "Mr. Axton didn't even care about larity when it came to talent. He gave us both the chance to succeed."

Then they returned to their positions, Zhag softly playing his shiltpron, Tonyo providing only nageric accompaniment today, no singing. Many of the staff spoke, and finally Jonmair walked forward. A shock went through Baird when she began, "Treavor Axton bought me as a Last Kill for his son Baird. When Baird didn't kill me, though, I became Mr. Axton's ward. He wasn't easy to work for, but once I learned to stand up to him—that's when I learned that he would treat everyone fairly who asked for it. I think he would have adapted to the new world we're making here, and thrived in it. But he gave his life to save his son's."

Just as you gave yours, Baird thought.

Then it was his turn to speak. He looked out over the crowded hall and said, "My father built The Post as a refuge from life's hardships. I vow to keep it going in the tradition in which he started it. If I can ever be as wise and strong as my father was, then his legacy will continue." He didn't know what else to say, feeling lost when he remembered that Treavor Axton was no longer there to advise him.

Fortunately, no one expected Baird to be eloquent on the day of his father's funeral. But just as he was about to sit down, feeling his father would have been disappointed, Baird looked around at the elegant room, the flowers and tablecloths unable to hide that it was intended to be a place of revelry, not reverence.

"My father was not about sorrow and grief," Baird added. "He was about good business, yes—but that business was entertainment. It was music, it was dancing, it was fun. Remember him when you laugh. Remember him when you sing. Remember him when you come to The Post because you're post and looking for a good time. That's the legacy my father built!"

He could zlin the crowd supporting him, the ambient warm and welcoming as he gratefully retreated from the spotlight. Jonmair smiled at him, and friends came near to offer private words and feelings.

A good portion of the crowd followed along to the cemetery, Zhag and Tonyo joined by other musicians who had played at The Post over the years. After the coffin was placed in the family crypt, they followed what had become instant tradition for the many funerals of the past three days: everyone joined in singing the Unity Hymn before they turned and left the caretakers to close the mausoleum.

On the way back, the music changed. By the time they returned to The Post, everyone was in a party mood. The gambling hall reopened, the crowds returned, porstan flowed, music played, and Baird…suddenly had nothing to do. No more lawyers or auditors would show up this late in the day, and Jonmair was efficiently doing his old job.

Treavor Axton would have been at the card table with his cronies. But Baird wasn't interested in cards. He was interested in Jonmair.

His post reaction was finally asserting itself as desire, but three days into his cycle it was not an overpowering urge. Yes, he wanted to take her up to his bed, but that could easily wait until…he knew for certain that she wanted to be there.

* * * * * * *

JONMAIR WAS JUST LEAVING THE GAMBLING HALL to go to the main salon when Baird stopped her in the corridor. "Jonmair, please come into the office."

She followed him, both curious and concerned, for she could see that he was tense. What had gone wrong now?

"Jonmair…are you enjoying your new responsibilities?" Baird asked when they were in the office with the door closed. They both remained standing near the door.

"Yes," she said. "Did I neglect something?"

"Not at all. I want to thank you for the wonderful job you did today. And what you said about my father."

"I meant it," she said. "I think he would have come around, Baird. We're young, and it's not easy for us to adjust to a new way of life. It's much harder for older Simes."

"Have I spoiled your plans for the future?" he asked. "I know you want to design clothes and costumes. Have your own business."

"Perhaps I will someday," she replied honestly.

His eyes revealed that her answer had somehow disappointed him. "Then you plan on leaving The Post."

"Well," she hedged, "you know I will always be here for your transfers. Baird, I know now what Tonyo means. I need it as much as you do." Again she saw that her answer wasn't what he was looking for. "I'll certainly stay till I've paid off my debt."

"No," Baird said, "I don't want you working here for that reason." Jonmair's heart contracted until she could hardly breathe. "You don't owe me any debt—you saved my life."

Because I love you, she thought, but dared not say it.

"I had hoped," Baird continued, "that you would stay...with me. We...work so very well together."

Work. So that was how he defined their relationship. If he expected her to stay and help run The Post, nightward him when he was in Need, and be someone convenient to share post reaction until he found a suitable Sime woman to marry—no. She swallowed hard, gritted her teeth, and prepared to do the hardest thing she had ever done: walk away from Baird Axton.

But Baird's next words stopped her thoughts entirely.

"Marry me."

Jonmair stared, not believing he had said it.

"We met under terrible circumstances," he said. "But you're free now, Jonmair. I can't force or coerce you. I owe you my very life, so you don't owe me anything."

He came closer, eyes pleading. "I shouldn't have tried to keep you here with a job, even though you are doing it superbly. There's only one reason I will accept for you to say yes, and that is if you love me as much as I love you."

She saw his uncertainty change to a smile, and knew he had zlinned her answer before she could say it. "I do love you, Baird. And yes! I will marry you!"

And finally she was in his arms as she had always longed to be, loved instead of used, loved instead of post, loved instead of owned.

The fact that they were of opposite larities now meant that they fit together in every way. Softly, from the grand salon, came the notes of the Unity Hymn: "Peace to Sime and Gen together."

Together.

Forever.

ABOUT THE AUTHOR

JEAN LORRAH lives in Kentucky with her dog, Kadi Farris ambrov Keon, and two cats, Earl Gray Dudley and Splotch the Wanderer. The cats are licensed therapy animals who visit schools and nursing homes.

Jean has published more than twenty books through the years, several of them award winners and best-sellers. She teaches the occasional creative writing workshop in person, and with Jacqueline Lichtenberg runs a free workshop online on their domain, www.simegen.com. For information on Jean's latest publications, essays on writing, and anything else currently going on in her life, visit: www.jeanlorrah.com

Made in the USA
Monee, IL
07 January 2021

56502239R00173